PRAISE FOR THE STORM CROW

"*The Storm Crow* is a fantastic debut. Written with both power and charm, it showcases some of my favorite worldbuilding ever in a YA fantasy and has nuanced, wonderful characters and relationships. Dragon fans should get ready for their next favorite creature. I loved this."

—Jessica Cluess, author of
A Shadow Bright and Burning

"*The Storm Crow* is everything we love about YA fantasy, with an enchanting world and original magic that keeps the story fresh. Clashing kingdoms, thrilling action, and an imperfect heroine make this book a must-read. This soaring debut was a delight."

—Adrienne Young, *New York Times* bestselling
author of *Sky in the Deep* and *The Girl the Sea Gave Back*

"Josephson's debut displays ambitious worldbuilding and an engaging premise involving the magical crows, which affect everything from storms to healing; Anthia's battle with depression is portrayed with frank authenticity and features well-developed LGBTQ characters."

—*Publishers Weekly*

THE
STORM
CROW

THE
STORM
CROW

KALYN JOSEPHSON

sourcebooks
fire

Published by Sourcebooks Fire, an imprint of Sourcebooks
P.O. Box 4410, Naperville, Illinois 60567-4410
(630) 961-3900
sourcebooks.com

The Library of Congress has cataloged the hardcover edition as follows:

Names: Josephson, Kalyn.
Title: The storm crow / Kalyn Josephson.
Description: Naperville, Illinois : Sourcebooks Fire, [2019] | Summary: After
   their mother's death when the Illucian empire invaded, Princess Anthia and
   her sister Princess Caliza start a rebellion to bring back the magical
   elemental crows that were taken from her people.
Identifiers: LCCN 2018052406
Subjects: | CYAC: Fantasy. | Princesses--Fiction. | Sisters--Fiction. |
   Crows--Fiction. | Magic--Fiction.
Classification: LCC PZ7.1.J786 St 2019 | DDC [Fic]--dc23
LC record available at https://lccn.loc.gov/2018052406

Printed and bound in the United States of America.
VP 10 9 8 7 6 5 4 3 2 1

To Mom and Dad,
with love.

The Kingdoms of

KYTHRA

THE

THE K

The Seamounts

Underwater
Volcanoes

The River Ren

Verian Hills

ILLUC

The Seamounts

PORT
MARANOCK

SORDELL

The Etris Forest

SEAHALLA

The
AMBRIELS

ELAIR

MYCAIR

The ARDRAH
SEA

The Kessel
Woods

ARIS

BHODAIRE

N
TH
The Cut
VASHKA
ROVI
The Andia River
A
ALRON
JINDAE
Bay
The EASTERN
WASTELANDS
Tyross Mountains
TRENDELL
ESELIN

PROLOGUE

I was a storm.

Adrenaline ripped through my veins like lightning as I leaned close to the body of my crow, preparing to execute a dive. Iyla's warm, steady heat kept me grounded, even hundreds of feet in the air. Cold wind whipped tendrils of hair free from my braid, nipping at the skin around my goggles and stealing my breath.

The thin, well-worn saddle beneath me was nothing more than a strip of leather to bind stirrups to, the reins trailing from my hands to Iyla's beak, an illusion of control—this ride depended on trust and mutual respect. Anything less, and no amount of leather would keep me seated on Iyla's back.

Years of Estrel's instructions raced through my mind: *Keep your body low and tight in a dive. Give the reins slack. Keep your knees back so you don't put pressure on the crow's wing joints.* I knew it all like my own heartbeat.

I tucked close to Iyla's body, and we dove.

Water misted my skin as Iyla's storm crow magic split apart a cloud a second before we shot through it and plummeted toward the earth. My heart screamed into my throat, pure, unadulterated joy erupting through me with every passing moment. I held my breath as we fell, counting the seconds—we could only gain so much speed before Iyla's wings wouldn't be able to handle the strain of opening.

Fifteen, sixteen, seventeen...

We burst through layers of clouds, Aris spread out below us. The city was a blur as we dove, a sea of light and color fast approaching.

Twenty. I squeezed my knees, and Iyla's wings snapped open like the slice of a blade, catching an updraft to send us sailing in a gentle arc. Lightning buzzed at the tips of Iyla's wings as she let out a piercing call.

I sucked in a lungful of cold air and let it out in a laugh, the thrill of the dive resounding through me like a thunderclap. I craved that feeling like starved lungs craved air, letting it fill me until I felt impossibly alive.

We circled wide and low, descending the rest of the way until Iyla's shadow blanketed the city streets.

Aris unfurled beneath us like a colorful map, dense with thick green foliage and spotted with wildflowers. People called up to us, waving from crowded streets as revelers prepared for the festival leading up to Negnoch, the city's yearly hatch night.

In a few hours, every single crow from across the kingdom of Rhodaire would put on a masterful display of riding and magic, and the year's crows would be hatched.

One of them would be mine. Tonight, I would choose my own crow and become a rider.

We dipped lower, children chasing Iyla's shadow in the hopes of catching a stray feather to wish upon. This was my favorite part of flying. Even more than the thrill of diving or the magic of soaring through endless skies, I loved gliding peacefully above Aris, the wind brushing along my skin as the city passed below.

Even on the back of a stolen crow. Well, not quite *stolen*. Iyla belonged to Estrel, my teacher and mother's best friend, and while Estrel had let me ride Iyla alone before, she technically hadn't given me permission to tonight.

Probably because I didn't ask.

A gentle tug on the reins sent Iyla a little higher, and we fell in line over the crystal waters of the canal in the Rynthene Wing. To my left, earth crows helped work the fields, tilling land in huge swaths with the pulse of their magic. To my right, the fading sunlight glinted off an armored battle crow.

All over Aris, the crows and riders integrated into the city's inner workings would be finishing up the day's tasks. Later, they'd join the military pouring in from Rhodaire's outer reaches in preparation for the Sky Dance.

We followed the canal to the castle at the city's heart. The giant gray stone structure stretched into the sky, delladon vines sprawling across its pale face like laugh lines. From each of the four sides of the central tower, a crescent-shaped landing platform jutted out, and I used the nearest one as a marker to veer Iyla right toward the royal rookery. It was a tall, circular tower with wide windows on the third floor for easy landing.

My nerves jittered. Landing was the hardest part, even with Estrel's lessons branded into my mind.

Let the crow do the work; it knows what it's doing. Keep your weight back. Never dismount while a crow's folding its wings, or you risk straining the joints.

We glided easily through one of the rookery's large, open windows, Iyla as practiced in this maneuver as breathing. Her wings flared back, sending straw swirling across the stone floor as her massive black claws reached out, taking hold of the nearest T-shaped perch. We fell to a standstill, her wings tucking in tight to her muscled form. She was almost reptilian with a lean, muscular body, the proportions a little longer, a little more limber than a normal bird.

I let out a whoop, grinning as I tugged down my goggles and swung off her back, throwing my arms around her. Her long neck straightened as she stiffened, but I'd learned long ago that she'd not only tolerate hugs but secretly liked them.

"Anthia!"

My excitement went cold at my mother's sharp voice. A flurry of black wings filled the opposite window as her battle crow, Tyros, landed effortlessly on the perch across from Iyla, sending a gust of straw-filled wind into my face.

My mother swung down, stalking toward me with the smooth litheness of a jungle cat. With the setting sun at her back, she looked every inch the queen she was, the light making her brown skin and polished flying leathers gleam with an inner fire.

"What in the Saints' name do you think you're doing?" she demanded.

"Um, talking to Iyla?" I offered. Lying had never been my strong suit. To her credit, the crow let out a low caw, as if she were indeed part of the conversation.

My mother didn't smile. I didn't expect her to.

"Relax, Alandra." Estrel emerged from the nearby staircase at my side, her long, dark curls bound in a thick braid like mine. "I gave her permission."

The only person who could tell my mother to relax without getting eviscerated was Estrel, my aunt in every way but blood. She and Estrel had grown up together. They even looked like sisters, though my mother was taller and leaner.

My mother frowned, and I straightened beneath the sharpness of her steel-colored gaze. Her eyes always reminded me of knives, forever sculpting me in an endless quest for perfection.

"I executed a perfect dive," I offered, as if my ability to perform riding techniques far more advanced than my seventeen years might soften her gaze.

It only made her eyes narrow. "Taking another rider's crow out for a joyride to perform dangerous maneuvers is not only foolish, it's insulting." I flinched. "If you want to prove yourself capable of being a leader among the riders, you can start by not disrespecting every rule and custom we live by."

I refused to wilt beneath the heat of her words. "Well,

maybe if you spent more than a waking second in my presence, I'd know the rules better."

Estrel drew a sharp breath, but my mother went stiller than a shadow crow concealed in darkness. For a fraction of a second, I swore something pained flashed through her iron gaze, but it vanished quickly.

The circlet of silver feathers on her brow gleamed like molten starlight. "I expect you back here before the hatching." She turned to Tyros, who leapt from his perch to the wide window ledge, a perfect tableau of strength against a backdrop of approaching night. With a grace I hadn't yet mastered, she swung up into the saddle. Wings tucked in tight, Tyros leapt. They plummeted from view, gone for barely a breath before they soared up past the window, climbing into the darkening sky.

"That went well," I muttered.

Estrel smacked the back of my head, and I winced, rubbing the spot though the blow hadn't hurt. "Stop stealing my crow!" Despite the snap in her voice, an easy grin filled her face, and she let out a low laugh when I smiled back.

There wasn't a single other rider or a single other crow I'd ever dream of doing what I did with Iyla. Any other crow would snatch me by the leg with its beak and toss me off, princess or not. That was, until I had my own.

My gaze dropped to the gold and black edges of Estrel's Corvé tattoo that reached up over her muscular shoulders, denoting her as one of Rhodaire's nine crow masters. While the heads of each house saw to their people, each wing's Corvé saw to its crows.

Tonight, I would choose my own crow. I would become a rider. And one day, I would earn the tattoo and become the royal Corvé after Estrel.

"The Sky Dance starts in an hour," Estrel said. "Then it's back here for the hatching. Are you and Kiva going into the city tonight?"

"To Rua's."

She smirked. "Take a breath. Enjoy the night. You'll have your crow soon enough."

Soon enough felt a lifetime away as I bolted down the winding rookery steps, dodging a rookhand balancing plates of meat, and out into a perfect Rhodairen winter evening. The air was cool but not cold and filled with the possibility of rain. Storm crows would keep it at bay, though I wished they'd let it fall. I'd always wanted to see a Sky Dance in the rain.

The wind buffeted my escaped curls into my face as I shot along the gardens, through the castle gates, and into streets filled with thick green trees and climbing vines trickling down buildings like rivulets of rainwater.

I veered onto the main road between the Caravel Wing and Thereal Wing, then cut right into the Thereal section of the city, slowing as a wave of music and laughter washed over me. I made for Rua's, a bright-blue building on the corner where a crow had been painted in sunset colors across one side, done by a street artist in the night.

Native brown-skinned Rhodairens walked alongside colorfully dressed, dark-skinned travelers from Trendell, a kingdom far east of Rhodaire. Both were dwarfed by the pale, long-limbed Korovi of the northern kingdom. People came to Rhodaire from all over the world for Negnoch. I even spotted a few revelers from Illucia, the border kingdom to our north, though they were probably only here for festival discounts on Rhodairen weapons. Or maybe they were guards for the visiting Illucian dignitaries.

That was probably what had my mother on edge: their presence, and their queen who threatened war. She'd already taken two kingdoms.

Someone seized my arm, spinning me around. Kiva grinned down at me, her moonlight-colored hair freed from its characteristic braid and down to her shoulders in waves. She still wore her castle guard uniform, making her look older—sometimes I doubted she owned anything else. She even had her sword at her hip.

"I was starting to think you weren't coming!" she shouted above the clamor.

"And let you eat all the orange cakes?"

"Typical. Here for the food."

I nodded at her uniform. "Hoping to impress someone?" She'd been flirting with a girl at Rua's for weeks now.

Kiva's cheeks burned, and she nudged me with her shoulder.

I grinned. "Race you."

We dove into the crowd, dodging flying elbows and swinging hips. Along the sides of the streets, baskets of the last fruits of the season sat waiting to be eaten, from bright-yellow mangoes to fresh-picked oranges. Overhead, thunder boomed in a near cloudless sky, a storm crow marking the time.

The night passed in patches. I drank talcé after talcé, sweet juice drinks filled with pieces of fruit, and ate as many orange cakes as I could stomach. We danced and sang, following the street past acrobats and fire-eaters, carts of pastries and fruit pies. Children ran laughing through the streets, kites in the shape of crows tied to their wrists by long, thin strings. Tradition said if your kite made it through the night undamaged, you were destined to become a rider.

Thunder boomed again. The Sky Dance was about to begin.

Crows glided in lazy circles above the castle with riders on their backs, looking like shadows set adrift in the sky. The sun set behind them, painting everything deep mauve and carmine, buttermilk and fuchsia.

The drums started, low and steady at first, matching the rhythm of the crows as they circled. Then the speed increased, and higher drums joined in. The circling crows broke in all directions, some diving straight down, others surging upward in a powerful burst of speed. They twirled and dove, weaving around each other in exact, graceful movements.

A fire crow opened its beak and let loose a stream of blue-tinged flames at a wind crow, which buffeted the fire upward toward a water crow, which doused it into steam with water from its beak. Sun crows lit the sky in ethereal gold, their glow fading into wisps like the light of falling stars. Shadow crows wove ribbons of night around them, creating intricate shimmering patterns.

Each action a crow took was mimicked by another one across from it, one formation molding seamlessly into the next, creating a symmetrical design of beasts, people, and magic, all interwoven in a dance among the clouds.

The drums grew faster. Lightning struck and thunder rolled, keeping time with the beat. Crows dipped and twirled in perfectly timed maneuvers I longed to try. My heart raced with them, imagining the feel of the wind in my hair and the heat of a crow beneath me.

As the music peaked, every crow shot upward, carried by drafts from wind and storm crows. Then they dove.

As the echo of the final drumbeat sounded, the crows shot out in all directions in perfectly executed dives. Their deep, echoing cries filled the sky as the sun finished setting, and the crows blanketed the night.

Still ecstatic from the dance, Kiva and I moved off the main road to find another talcé vendor. The skies had cleared, and the crows had all returned to the rookeries throughout the city's wings to be unsaddled and fed. The images remained seared into the back of my eyelids. Soon, I would be a part of that dance.

"You're going to be late," Kiva warned as we navigated the crowded street.

"It takes at least half an hour for the crows to be unsaddled and fed."

"Which means you'll leave in half an hour."

"I'm not late *that* often—"

"Yes, you are."

"Okay, but—"

A scream ripped through the air. I froze. Kiva's hand went to her sword, and she stepped toward me, shielding. Silence descended like a curtain, sucking the air from the crowded street. My heart rose and settled in my throat, and for a wing-beat, everything stood still.

Then the Thereal rookery went up in flames.

The screams became a chorus, the screech of crows rising like a wave. One by one, the rookeries in each wing erupted with fire.

I stood rooted to the spot, the acrid smoke scorching my lungs, the light of the flames almost too bright to look at. Yet I couldn't tear my gaze away, my mind refusing to process what I was seeing.

The city was burning.

The words dropped through my mind like jagged stones, too heavy and sharp to hold on to.

The crowd closed in, people slamming into carts and each other, all attempting to flee in different directions. Kiva pressed into my side, her sword half drawn. The familiar screech of metal snapped me from my trance, and I seized her wrist. "Too many people!"

Scowling, she grabbed my arm and barreled through the writhing mass. She was head taller than nearly everyone, and the crowd parted to avoid her elbows and snarled threats. We pushed until we broke through the edge, gulping down open air drowned in smoke.

"Come on!" Not stopping to rest, I raced along the street and back toward the castle, Kiva at my back.

Fire fell like rain.

It dripped from buildings, clinging to crumbling stone and smoldering wood, spreading from the Thereal rookery like a flood. The bushes lining the road blazed like torches, trees heavy with fruit turning to ash and filling the air with a sickly, burnt-sugar scent. It mixed with the smell of seared flesh.

A burst of fire cut across our path, forcing us to stop. As an earsplitting scream tore past me, I realized it wasn't a fireball: it was a man, engulfed in flames.

My stomach turned, and I choked on the poisoned air, desperate to get it out of my lungs. Kiva seized my arm, hauling me along. The image of the flaming man cut through my mind over and over, until it felt like I'd never see anything else again.

As we turned up the castle road, I stumbled to a halt. Black smoke billowed from the royal rookery, darker than the night. Fire writhed, reaching out the open windows with hungry claws. A crow leapt from one of the windows, feathers alight. It barely had time to open its wings before an arrow pierced its heart. Another struck its throat. It dropped four stories to the earth with a sickening crunch.

This didn't make any sense. The eggs were in there, and the crows… My thoughts ground to a halt, unable to venture any further. Unable to think, unable to breathe.

I only became aware Kiva was shaking me when she nearly knocked me to the ground. "Move!" she screamed.

Slowly, I looked at her. She'd drawn her sword, and the firelight cast strange shadows across her pale skin. For an impossibly long moment, my smoke-riddled brain could process only her bright, unbound hair. It was white as bone.

She pushed me again, and I stumbled. "Anthia, move!"

I blinked. Guards were sprinting in every direction, shouting orders. Some had their swords drawn, dueling pale-skinned soldiers in black leather. Still others simply stood and stared at the rising column of fire and smoke. Slowly, I understood. I recognized the golden horse head emblazoned on their uniforms.

Illucia was attacking Rhodaire.

Illucia was killing the crows.

Someone moved behind Kiva. My mother appeared, gray eyes wild and face splattered with blood. She held a dagger in each hand. "Get inside the castle!" she ordered, but I didn't move. She sheathed a blade, her hand falling on my shoulder. "Anthia, you have to go inside. Please."

I felt warm. Too warm, but oddly calm. Like something had reached inside me and wiped away all the fear, the confusion, and the horrible, horrible understanding. My skin hummed, the sound filling my ears, my chest, my bones.

My mother cursed, said something to Kiva, then hesitated a second longer, her fingers digging tight into my shoulder. Something shone behind her eyes, a forgotten emotion threatening to break free—then she bolted toward the rookery. I lurched after her, but Kiva's strong arms pulled me back. My mother disappeared into the column of flames. Then Kiva was gone, and I forgot to blink. My vision filled with fire.

Swords clashed, metal screaming against metal so close to my ear that I turned. Kiva dueled an Illucian soldier inches away. Had that attack been meant for me? The thought barely registered. All I could think about was the growing heat and dying air, the screams of crows and people indecipherable in the night.

A Rhodairen soldier intercepted Kiva's fight, and I turned back to the rookery in time to see a shape fall in the doorway.

My body reacted. I sprang forward, screaming for my mother. The shape rolled, crawling toward the exit, the flames moving like a serpent preparing to strike. It wasn't my mother.

"Estrel!" I seized her arm, not processing that her clothes were on fire, that she was on fire, and pulled with all my strength. The flames leapt onto my sleeve, but I pulled harder, her form toppling out after me onto the damp grass. I rolled her over and over again, then Kiva was there, smothering Estrel with her cloak.

Kiva yelled something at me, but I couldn't hear her through the blood pounding in my ears. Then she seized me and flung me into the grass, slapping my hand, beating at it with the edge of the cloak to extinguish the flames.

I stared at the ravaged skin, now a patchwork of scalded white and red flesh. Red. Red as the fire raining down around me as it consumed the royal rookery, consumed my mother, consumed everything.

I felt Kiva beside me like one felt their shadow at their heel, an intangible presence. She spoke, saying so many things. Things that didn't make any sense. Things like my mother was dead, the crows were gone, the Illucian soldiers were coming, there were many were already here.

It took me a moment to realize I was staring at something in the sky. Bright as a miniature sun, a crow blazing with fire from beak to tail soared across the night, wings spread as if the flames had become a part of it, a flickering coat of smoldering feathers. Then the fire seared through feather and muscle and bone, and it plummeted to the earth like a falling star.

It struck the ground before me, erupting like a funeral pyre. Only my raw throat told me I'd screamed the entire time it'd fallen.

"We have to move!" Kiva yelled.

I had just enough of myself left to look at her. To see the tears streaming down her ash-stained face and to feel my own sliding hot against my skin, before my burns flared with pain, and the world went white.

ONE

T he crows were gone.
    Every day, I said those words to myself, but they didn't
feel real. The world didn't feel real. Each breath felt like a lie, as
if I'd climbed out of a cocoon into another realm, one of ash and
shadowed memories that tore at me like talons.

Without the beat of a crow's wings, the air stood still.
Silence smothered the castle garden, the charred royal rookery standing like a headstone in the distance. Even the sunlight looked wrong, rebounding sharply off the castle as if
afraid to get too close.

I sat at the patio table, tracing a finger along where the red
and white splotches of months-old burn scars met my skin, and
tried desperately to ignore the man standing across from me.

The Illucian messenger wore rich, finely cut blues lined in

gold, the material too thick for the Rhodairen summer sun. He wasn't a soldier, but he carried a sword nonetheless and would know how to use it. He'd been allowed to keep it, since asking an Illucian to give up their weapon was akin to asking a wolf not to bite your hand while you pulled out its teeth. As a compromise, two castle guards stood within easy striking distance.

The Saints must hate me. It'd been nearly six months since the Illucian Empire destroyed my life. I'd barely left my room since. I'd hardly gotten out of bed. Even now, I wanted to burrow beneath my blankets and disappear into the darkness. Then the one day I managed to drag myself downstairs, convinced it could be a decent day, I got stuck watching an Illucian.

His gaze bore into me, and it took everything I had not to look at him. I was afraid of what I might do if I did.

A spark of fury rallied against the prison of grief and pain that had grown inside me layer by layer over the last few months. I hated that he'd been allowed into Rhodaire, allowed onto the castle grounds. Hated that we had to hear out his queen's demands, that I didn't have a crow to seize him by his perfectly manicured uniform and lift him high, high into the air...

"Will the queen be here soon?" he asked for the second time, his accent light.

It sounded like a crow's talons on stone, and the back of my neck prickled with a chill despite the sun. We'd been waiting for my sister for nearly ten minutes.

"If you ask again, maybe I'll suddenly know." Not the diplomatic response, but politics had never been my strength.

"Will the queen be here soon?"

My eyes snapped up, locking with his. He smiled, and I gritted my teeth at giving him that small victory. *Ignore him.* Forcing my gaze out across the castle gardens, I exhaled slowly. I'd *promised* myself today would be a good day. I needed a good day. But faced with an Illucian, all I could think about was what they'd taken from us. What they still took. Terrorizing our borders, attacking our trade routes, sinking our ships.

Looking at the garden didn't help. My eyes naturally found the spots where the flowers had started to droop, stains of brown spreading among the green. Without the earth crows' magic, plants like the bright flowering delladon vine that climbed the latticework along the castle were a breath away from dust.

Rhodaire was dying.

I looked away, blinking slowly. Without storm crows to manipulate it, the hot, humid summer weather persisted unrelentingly. The sweet scent of fruit trees hung heavy in the air, pressing in on me from all directions. Only the messenger kept me alert. What did he want?

Voices filtered out through the open door. I straightened as my sister stepped onto the patio, a striking figure with her immaculate posture and dark hair loose to her waist. Kiva followed, the sun reflecting off the metal buckles of her silver-and-green guard's uniform. The tension in my shoulders eased as she slipped to my side.

"Your Majesty." The messenger barely inclined his head.

Caliza's steel-colored eyes evaluated him quickly, her face an impassive mask. "We can speak inside."

I frowned as the messenger followed her into the sunroom at the back of the patio. What didn't Caliza want me to hear?

Kiva dropped into the seat beside me, her hand falling to its natural position on the crow-shaped pommel of her sword. "Sorry it took me so long. She was in a meeting."

"Not your fault. Besides, we were having such a wonderful time." I slumped in my chair, leaning my head back.

Not a day passed where I didn't think about the crows. I couldn't shut out the memories. Scenes of visiting the royal rookery to tickle storm crow chicks until they buzzed with lightning or walking under the glow of a sun crow in the dusky moonlight played over and over in my mind. Seeing the messenger just made it all worse.

A flash of red made me flinch, but it was only a pair of summer tanagers flying by, their feathers the rich ruby of a ripe pomegranate. *You're fine. Don't think about it.* I rubbed my scarred arm in an absent motion.

Kiva eyed me intently. I sighed, straightening and readjusting the silver bracelet on my right wrist. "I'm not going to climb back into bed, all right?"

"Good. I don't have time to fetch a bucket of water to dump on you." She smirked, and I glared flatly back. She was joking—mostly.

"You would enjoy that entirely too much," I said.

Kiva's smile faltered. "I don't enjoy any part of seeing you like this."

I clenched my jaw but didn't respond. *I'm just sad. I'll get over it soon.* I repeated the mantra in my head, ignoring the quiet voice that whispered it had been nearly six months. While I hid, the world went on without me.

Guilt prickled low and hot in my stomach. I hated knowing Kiva worried about me. Hated knowing I was the cause of her pain. It'd taken me months to confide in her, convinced the moment I told someone how I felt, as if the world had split apart and swallowed me whole, they'd call me ridiculous. Dramatic. Weak. Instead, she'd listened, and then she'd held me while I cried until my throat turned raw.

Kiva leaned back, flipping her braid of white-gold hair over her shoulder and lifting a hand to shield her face from the sun. She'd been born in Rhodaire, but her pale Korovi skin burned easily. "What do you think he wants?" She nodded in the direction the messenger and Caliza had gone.

"Nothing good."

I hadn't seen an Illucian since Negnoch. Since Rhodairen traitors helped Illucian soldiers set fire to the rookeries, their elite archers shooting any crows that escaped the flames.

Ronoch, people called it now. Red Night.

If the Illucian army hadn't been spread so thin the night they attacked, they might have conquered Rhodaire then and there.

At first, I'd wanted revenge. Deep inside, the part of me that hated the defeated person I'd become still did. Now, I recognized we didn't stand a chance. Illucia had conquered nearly half the continent for a reason—their army was unstoppable. Soon, they would have Rhodaire too.

The messenger's voice suddenly rose from the sunroom. Kiva and I fell silent, leaning closer to listen.

"My queen has given her answer, Your Majesty," he practically purred.

My head snapped up at the mention of the Illucian queen, and I locked eyes with Kiva. Something flickered in my chest, a spark of anger springing to life. Then Caliza stepped onto the patio. The messenger loomed behind her with a smug look of satisfaction that made my stomach turn.

"We need to talk," Caliza said to me, then looked at Kiva. "Privately."

Kiva stood. "I have recruit training. Come see me after." She bowed to Caliza before sweeping past her. The messenger made to remain, but Kiva looked at him expectantly. Her imposing figure made it clear staying wasn't an option. Wisely, he went with her.

Caliza took Kiva's seat, removing the silver circlet shaped like a garland of feathers from her head and setting it on the table. I eyed the circlet. She took every opportunity not to wear it, claiming the edges got tangled in her hair.

It makes her think too much about Mother.

I understood. Its matching piece—the bracelet of silver feathers on my wrist—had belonged to Estrel. They were both dead now. My mother, they'd ambushed in the rookery, but Estrel... Her death hadn't been swift.

Caliza's voice interrupted my thoughts. "Do you have anything productive planned for today?" My eyes cut to her, narrowing. She sighed. "It's a fair question, Thia. You hardly talk to anyone, and you spend so much time in your room. If you'd try a little—"

"If this is what you wanted to talk about, I'm leaving." I didn't need this lecture again. Feeling this way—it wasn't my choice. I couldn't make it stop. I'd tried.

A vein in Caliza's forehead twitched. She looked so much like our mother when that happened, an impression aided by the thin oval face and high cheekbones they'd once shared.

I looked like her too, except my black hair was curly where Caliza's was wavy. The brown freckles speckling my face were absent from hers, and where she was tall and willowy, my body was hardened by years of rider training. Or at least it had been. Now my figure was a little less muscle, a little more curve.

We had the same eyes though, our mother's eyes. Not the typical dark Rhodairen umber, but bright gray like storm clouds lit by lightning.

"You're seventeen; you're an adult," she said. "You have to pull yourself together. You can't spend the rest of your life in your room."

"Pull myself together?" My voice broke. How could three simple words make me feel so small?

Her hand fell atop my unscarred one. I stared at it, feeling as though mine were someone else's hand. "You're alive, Anthia. Be thankful. Move forward."

I flinched, jerking my hand away. "You don't understand. I can't—I don't—" My throat tightened, locking the words inside. How did I explain something I didn't even understand myself? This was just like Caliza, to think a problem could be solved with only logic.

This was why I'd hidden in my room, why I wanted to run

there now. Alone, no one could make me feel like an ungrateful little girl, rejected and inferior. No one could look at me like Caliza was now: disappointed, impatient, accusatory. As if this were all in my head and it'd go away if only I tried hard enough.

Didn't she understand that I would if I could?

I swallowed hard. "What do you want from me, Caliza? To marry some foreign prince and pretend to like him so our countries can get along?" She stiffened, and I regretted the words instantly.

"I'm sorry. That wasn't fair," I said. Caliza had married Kuren because Trendell's support was helping keep Rhodaire alive without the crows. He was the second oldest prince of the eastern kingdom, a good man. Even now, he was in Trendell coordinating aid on Rhodaire's behalf. "Have you heard from him?"

"This morning."

I waited, but she said nothing more. The silence stretched. A familiar weight settled on my shoulders, the urge to crawl into bed and spend the day under the covers slowly growing stronger.

No. My hand found Estrel's bracelet. I pictured the weight as a snake like Kiva had once suggested, imagining it slithering off my shoulders until it was gone. Except it never truly left.

Caliza worried at a few strands of hair with her fingers. She even had our mother's nervous habits. They'd become more pronounced lately, though she still kept her emotions in an iron grip in front of other people. A skill I'd never mastered. Around me, she'd been snappier and more finicky than ever.

"What is this really about, Caliza?" I asked.

Her fingers stilled, and she met my gaze. Her eyes were silent and strong, but I saw the storm prepared to break behind them. It'd been growing for days.

"Armies aren't easy to build," she said. "They take time to grow, to train, to supply. After we lost the crows, what we taught our soldiers had to change. Trendell has been very supportive, and we've made progress in the last few months, but not enough. And with the food shortages and loss of jobs, with everything, if Illucia—"

"Are they threatening to attack?"

Caliza's mouth tightened into a thin line. "Queen Razel doesn't threaten. She subtly implies until you're not sure if she said it or if you thought it all up yourself. But whether she'll say it or not, she's made herself clear. Our scouts confirmed: half her army is now sitting on our border."

My breath caught, hands closing into fists. "What does she want?"

"I've tried to find another option, Thia. Please believe I would never willingly choose this. But we can't sustain a war with Illucia. We have no choice."

"What are you talking about?" My heart stilled. What had she done?

"I've agreed to a marriage between you and Prince Ericen."

The words pierced me like talons, hooking deep. I waited for the pain. Nothing came. Because this wasn't real. This wasn't happening.

My throat burned—I wasn't breathing. Caliza said

something, but her words sounded like they were swimming through honey to reach me.

Something touched my arm, and I sprang to my feet, knocking over my chair. Caliza had stood up, her hand outstretched as I stepped back.

"Please, Thia."

Something like a laugh bubbled out of my throat, except wilder, more dangerous. She hadn't even given me a choice. She'd engaged me to the son of the woman who'd ordered the destruction of everything I cared about, who'd killed our mother, caused Estrel's death, and left me permanently scarred.

A slow, insidious heat spread through my veins. "No." The word trembled.

"We have no choice."

"*We?* Are you marrying the son of a psychopath too? Have you heard the rumors about him?"

Caliza straightened. The storm broke in her eyes. "This isn't just about you. I have to think about Rhodaire too. This kingdom is on the edge of a cliff. We cannot go to war. I know this isn't ideal—"

"Not ideal?" I slammed my hand on the table. "Are you serious? Don't try to manage me, Caliza. I'm not some disgruntled house lord you can manipulate."

"Thia—"

"They set fire to our rookeries. They killed every single crow, nearly all the riders, and our mother!" I didn't care that I was yelling now. "Our *mother*, and you want me to forget everything and marry that bastard?" I thrust my burned hand in front of her face. "How am I supposed to forget?"

Caliza's face flushed a deep red. For an endless moment, she stared at my scarred hand. Then she met my gaze and let out a slow breath. "We are the leaders of Rhodaire. Our duty is to our kingdom, not ourselves."

The adrenaline drained from my body, leaving me hollow. "You're my sister. Your duty should be to me."

She looked away, and something inside me threatened to crack. I didn't know there were still pieces of me left to break.

"This is the only way to keep our people safe. It will give us time to strengthen ourselves, to prepare." Her words tumbled out in a torrent, her composure fracturing. "*Ardrahan's Theory of War and—*"

"Your history books don't know anything about our situation! Queen Razel will use this marriage to take control of Rhodaire. That's all Illucia wants. You're not buying us time; you're sealing our fate!"

Caliza's chin lifted, an all too familiar expression etched on her face. She knew what was best, not me. "The wedding will take place in Illucia at a date of Razel's choosing. Prince Ericen will be here tomorrow on his way back from Jindae to take you with him." She paused. "I'm sorry."

I seized the table edge for support. Caliza never apologized. The lump in my throat threatened to choke me, and I swallowed hard. She wasn't going to change her mind.

The urge to flee struck so powerfully, I nearly knocked over a chair bolting down the patio stairs. Caliza called after me, but I didn't stop. The wind roared in my ears as I raced along the dying castle gardens, choosing direction at random, blind to where my legs were taking me.

Suddenly, I was standing before the remains of the royal rookery, my stomach threatening to return my breakfast, my throat closing when all I needed was air.

The rookery entrance had been blocked off, but there was a hole big enough for me to crawl through on the side. I struggled through the opening, scraping my forearms and tearing the hem of my dress on the scattered debris, but I didn't stop as I charged up the soot-covered steps to the second level.

The tower went up several more floors, but the circular room had caved in, blocking the stairwell and creating a dark alcove. I huddled underneath it with my arms wrapped around my knees, not caring that my dress was covered in ash or that I'd scraped my elbow hard enough to bleed.

I felt like I had the night the crows died—like everything was out of my control.

Caliza had promised me to Prince Ericen. She'd bartered me away, and now I would lose everything. My friendship with Kiva, my home, what little normalcy I'd regained—for what? A few more months to prepare for a war we couldn't win even if we had years to recover? The Illucian Empire's soldiers were utterly elite. Nothing less could have destroyed the crows.

Surely, this was all a ploy by Razel. She was like a jungle cat toying with her food. This was probably some sick joke to her. Why else ask for this marriage?

The familiar weight slithered up my shoulders. I didn't even try to make it leave. I was floating in limbo, my future gone, my past all too present. Now, more than ever, I wished for a crow to carry me far, far away. We'd fly straight past Korovi and Jindae to the unexplored wilderness in the east. We'd never stop.

But the crows were gone.

TWO

G olden sunlight filtered in from what remained of the rookery windows. Heat and the scent of smoke permeated the
early afternoon air, but my bones had turned to ice. I hadn't
moved from my spot on the ground, though I'd drawn several
pictures in the ash and dust that a warm breeze gently erased.

Memories swirled around me like leaves caught in the wind:
meeting Estrel in the rookery for my rider training, teasing
Caliza when the crows ignored her commands, sneaking out in
the middle of a thunderstorm to sit with a candle among the
birds, warm, quiet, content.

I spun Estrel's bracelet around my wrist. My mother had
died not five feet from where I sat, killed by Illucian soldiers. I'd
have bet on her over a hundred Illucians, but that night…

I hugged my knees to my chest, trying and failing to imagine what she would do in my situation. Caliza had stuck to her like feathers on a crow, preparing to become queen. I'd spent more time with Estrel, studying as a rider. People said Caliza and I were our mother split in half: me, stubborn and independent, and Caliza, steadfast with a knack for handling people and politics.

Our mother may have swallowed her pride and married Ericen, like Caliza would. Or maybe she'd have thrown the proposal back in Queen Razel's face. You never knew which side of her you were going to get, if you had her attention at all. Sometimes, I'd struggled to get even that.

For half a second, I considered praying to the Saints, the eight original riders. Legend had it they established Aris with the help of the Sellas, the ancient creatures said to have created the crows. But the Saints hadn't come on Ronoch. Either they didn't exist, or they didn't care.

My thoughts pinned me to the ground. It'd been a mistake coming to the rookery. Too many memories slept inside.

It'd been at least two hours; Caliza would be worried. Some petty part of me found satisfaction in that and wanted to leave her wondering where I was. Controlling my emotions had never been my strength, but it'd been weeks since I'd reacted to anything as strongly as the engagement. Maybe it meant I was getting better, though I'd thought that before. Why couldn't I just be okay?

Sighing, I used the wall to stand. Soot clung to my dress, blood staining my elbow where I'd scraped it. I needed a bath. Besides, sitting here wouldn't stop Ericen from arriving tomorrow.

Today was supposed to be a good day. The words reverberated in the hollow space inside my chest.

As I dusted off what I could of the ash, my gaze snagged on a bit of scorched leather near the edge of the tower. I crouched beside it, running my fingers over the familiar pleats that formed the shoulders of a rider's flying leathers. Had whomever they belonged to made it out of the tower alive?

I stood, letting my fingertips brush along a blackened windowsill, trying to conjure the feeling the rookery used to instill in me. But it was like fighting against the wind; the feeling refused to come. I pushed deeper into the rubble, suddenly desperate for something, anything that might spark that familiar lightness inside me.

The anticipation of flight, the wonder at the power and strength around me, the safety I'd felt, enclosed in these circular walls—it was all gone. All that remained was ash and rubble.

Something sparkled in the corner of my eye. I stopped my search a half a step past it, and it vanished. Sunlight poured in from the window at my back, illuminating a patch of blackened stone. I stepped back, and it glinted again.

I had to duck under a fallen beam to reach the spot, but once on the other side, I could see the sparkle clearly. Something lay buried beneath the stones and months-old straw from the crows' nests. My mind whispered this was foolish, to stop before I was disappointed, but I ignored it.

As I carefully moved aside stones, filling the air with dust and ash, the glint turned to a soft, blue-black glow. Something hummed, vibrating against my skin like lightning-charged wind in a storm. Calming, like a familiar comfort I'd forgotten. It slipped beneath my skin, into my muscles and blood, my very bones, chasing away the ice settled there.

I moved the last stone and stilled.

I knew what I was looking at. Even as I touched the ethereal shell, glittering like the night sky trapped in glass, even as my brain rejected the hulking size, the silklike feel, and the undeniable hum of magic, I knew.

It was a storm crow egg.

Careful not to touch the remaining unstable stone pile, I reached in and pulled the egg toward me. It was nearly as large as my torso, and the more I touched it, the stronger the humming became. Bending deep with my knees for leverage, I hoisted the egg into my arms.

Something cracked, and everything happened very fast. The stone shifted, and I tugged the egg back just as something seized my dress and flung me away from the crumbling stone. The ground shuddered as the stone collapsed, crushing wood and broken glass. Dust and ash erupted into the air as debris swallowed the hole, burying the spot I'd been standing in.

I lay blinking at the floating specks in the sunlight, the crow egg clasped to my chest. My heart drummed against it. Kiva stood next to me, her hands on her knees as she caught her breath. Her pale eyes stared down at me accusingly.

Then she saw the egg. "Is that what I think it is?"

"Oh, don't worry. I'm fine. Thanks for asking."

"I know you're fine. I just saved your life." She helped me to my feet.

I started to dust myself off and gave up. My dress would need a proper cleaning. Sighing, I held out the egg. The sunlight rippled around it, as if being drawn in and absorbed by the celestial shell. The thrumming had quieted but still resonated along my hands like the hum of a plucked string.

"Do you hear that?" I asked.

"That's the sound of your stupidity ringing in your head."

"Quieter than that—the egg."

"I don't hear anything." She pressed her ear to the shell and drew back with a shrug. "Maybe you hit your head. What were you even doing up here?"

All at once, I slammed back to reality. "Illucia's threatening to attack, and Caliza's idea of solving the problem is agreeing to their demands for a marriage between me and Prince Ericen."

Kiva's lips parted and closed several times. She swallowed hard, set her jaw. "I'm going to kill her."

"That's treason."

"Seriously injure her."

"Still treason."

She threw up her hands. "Hasn't she heard the rumors about him? He's as vicious and cruel as Illucians come. Has she lost her mind?"

"Yes." Even as I said it, guilt swept through me. "No. She did this to protect Rhodaire." She'd probably fretted about it for days, poring over books looking for another way until her vision blurred, but in the end, she'd chosen the most logical solution to an impossible problem, like she always did.

Meanwhile, I'd done nothing.

Six months ago, no one would have dared threaten our kingdom. The riders were fierce, and the crows fiercer. A battle crow could take on six cavalrymen at once, and an earth crow could open a sinkhole beneath an army. Now, Razel threatened to conquer us like she had Jindae and the Ambriel Islands. She would destroy our culture, level our cities, and funnel our children into her army until everything we were had been forgotten.

"All this because those soldiers chose power over their kingdom." I clutched the egg closer, seeking its warmth. It still seemed impossible that some of our soldiers had betrayed us. They had sold their loyalty to Razel, providing vital information and allowing Illucian soldiers to slip through their ranks. They'd helped butcher the crows that trusted them.

Illucia had planned everything perfectly.

They'd known that at the end of the Sky Dance, every single crow from across Rhodaire would return to their rookeries. They'd known all the eggs would be gathered in the royal rookery. Instead of facing an army, all they'd had to do was destroy nine towers.

And they'd had help from our own people.

"Those soldiers deserved what they got." The derision in Kiva's tone was sharper than a blade.

Executed.

Razel had used the soldiers, making promises she would never keep, and then had them killed.

Scowling, I shifted the egg in my arms and kicked away a chunk of rubble, relishing the solid contact even as my foot ached. "What I want to know is why Razel offered this. Why promise us peace in exchange for this marriage? We're not in a position to deny them anything. What do they gain?"

"It gives Illucia a foothold in Rhodaire. She can't take it by force easily. Nearly a quarter of her army is running Jindae, another chunk is in the Ambriels, and now I hear she's threatening Korovi. Why squander men attacking Rhodaire if she can take it some other way?"

"Marrying me to Ericen won't give her control of the kingdom. There has to be another step to her plan."

Or another motive altogether. But what?

I ran my fingers over the egg, and it hummed against my skin. The feeling was both exhilarating and comforting at once. "I have to hatch this egg. If we had even one crow, Illucia would think twice about what they're doing. It's the only chance we have of protecting Rhodaire and my only chance of not marrying that bastard."

Kiva stared at me like I'd sprouted wings. "Be careful. You're dangerously close to sounding like this girl I used to know. Tongue as sharp as a crow's talons, menace to authorities everywhere, about this tall." She held a hand to her chest, a good few inches shorter than my actual height.

I glowered but couldn't suppress my smile. Kiva had a way of pulling me out of myself, perfected over a lifetime of friendship. I couldn't remember a time without her at my side. She filled my memories: sneaking into the riding school to watch the riders train, stealing orange cakes from the kitchens before dinner, hiding Caliza's books whenever she left her study table unguarded in the library.

Kiva had been there every minute to say what a bad idea it was, but she had always stayed. She was always there for me, like she had been for every day of the exhausting cycle of despair that had imprisoned me since Ronoch. I didn't have the energy to get out of bed, and lying there made me lethargic until my limbs became weights holding me down. My head would hurt, turning my thoughts slow and difficult, each one taking more effort than it was worth, until all I wanted was to fall asleep again. But sleep made it worse.

Without her, I'd never have started getting out of bed. I never would have left my room today, and I might not have ended up in the rookery.

Kiva grinned at my feigned annoyance. "Anyway, it got buried under rubble and nearly incinerated. Whatever's inside is probably dead."

"Crow eggs are filled with magic. It could have survived." The egg hummed in my arms as if agreeing.

Kiva looked doubtful but held out a hand. "All right. Let's crack it open and find out."

I hugged the egg against my body. "You can't just crack it open! It has to hatch naturally."

"How?"

I opened my mouth, then closed it, brow furrowing. How *did* the eggs hatch? They weren't like normal bird eggs. Something else happened to them, because every year on the winter solstice, they all hatched at once. For some reason, this one hadn't, despite surviving Ronoch when no other eggs had.

Maybe it couldn't. Maybe Kiva was right, and the egg was

nothing but an empty shell. I shook the thought away. However small the chance was the egg could hatch, I had to try.

Problem was, I'd never seen it done.

We climbed out of the rookery together and returned to the castle. Kiva gave me her cloak to wrap the egg in, and I hugged it against my chest, still not fully believing what I'd found. The egg's humming settled deep into my bones, resonating like the echo of a thunderclap. It felt so familiar, so alive. Like a piece of me had returned.

Something fluttered in my stomach, a feeling I'd almost forgotten. Something I hesitated to name, lest it disappoint me. Still, I clung to the rising hope, feeling as if I balanced on a glass precipice, waiting for it to shatter and send me careening into the nothingness like so many times before.

After Ronoch, we'd searched the rookery for surviving eggs and found nothing. When the third floor collapsed, nearly killing two riders, the search was put off until we could stabilize the rookery. But in the face of starvation and mass destruction, it had been forgotten.

We'd decided to ask Caliza about the egg. She'd shunned the crows most of her life and probably wouldn't know a thing, but we had no one else. Most of the Corvé were gone; they'd been targeted on Ronoch, just like the crows. Those that remained had never helped my mother with the hatching.

I looked at my feather bracelet. Only Estrel had.

We stopped by my room, where I hid the egg in a drawer of rarely worn sweaters in my closet armoire and changed into a clean dress. My elbow had stopped bleeding, so I wiped away the dirt and left it be. Then we sought out Caliza.

What would she say to me? Would she apologize again? I snorted at the thought, then crushed the tiny voice that hoped maybe she'd changed her mind. That never happened.

We found her in her office talking with a tall, broad-shouldered woman with pale hair. Larisa Mirkova, Kiva's mother and captain of the royal guard. They paused as we entered, but I still caught the tail end of their conversation. They were talking about the failing crops again.

Kiva saluted her mother, only relaxing when the captain nodded. Caliza met my gaze. Her expression remained impassive, but I knew what she was thinking: had I accepted my fate?

I held her gaze without blinking: not even close.

"Sakiva," Captain Mirkova said, her Korovi accent heavy. Unlike her daughter, Captain Mirkova had lived half her life in Korovi. "You should be helping with afternoon training. This is irresponsible of you."

Kiva stiffened beside me, but she didn't rise to her mother's bait. She'd always had more discipline than me.

I faced Caliza, getting straight to the point. "What do you know about hatching crows?"

She frowned a very specific frown, the one she'd used since we were children whenever I talked about the crows. "Why do you want to know?"

"Humor me."

Caliza's eyes narrowed. "I don't know anything more than you. They're all born on Hatch Night, on the winter solstice, but Mother said that was ceremonial."

"But what makes them all hatch at the same time? And why did they never hatch where we could see them?"

"I don't know, Anthia. And it doesn't matter. I'm very busy right now. I don't have time for this."

There it was. *It doesn't matter.* She rarely said anything else to me about the crows. *They're gone. It doesn't matter. Move on.* I could tell her about the egg, but she wouldn't care. She wouldn't believe one crow could save us. She'd never believed.

"The least you can do is answer a question or two," I said. "You owe me that."

Something flashed behind her eyes that had her turning her face away. "I really don't know more. Let it go."

Disappointment filled me, weighing me to the spot. Caliza had been a long shot, and now even that hope had been crushed.

What if the secret to hatching was lost forever?

Swallowing against the tightness in my throat, I stormed out of Caliza's office, Kiva on my heel. With the need I had to *do* something suddenly left without an objective, I felt untethered, my motivation leaking from me like blood from a wound.

I slowed to a halt in the middle of the entrance hall, my energy all but gone.

"Thia?" Kiva asked cautiously.

"I don't know what to do." I buried my face in my hands.

Kiva laid a hand on my shoulder. "Let's go for a ride. Some fresh air might help."

THREE

It felt strange being outside the castle grounds. I'd barely left my room since Ronoch, and I'd never once stepped into the city. I hadn't yet found the energy, the strength, to see what had become of Aris.

I already wanted to leave.

The Brynth Wing, once home to the earth crows, looked nothing like its former self. Managing the huge fields had become too big a task without the crows, who had been responsible for most of Rhodaire's farming. We had no system for the water, once delivered by water crows, and many of the crops weren't native to Rhodaire's humid climate, only surviving thanks to the storm crows. Nearly half of the wing's crops had failed. Without as much to tend and harvest, the farmers had to let workers go.

The broad streets built for massive crows seemed lined with

beggars, hidden in the dark spaces between shops or else pressed against buildings with cloths laid out before them. Signs advertised crow talons and singed feathers recovered from the flames. A dog dug through trash in the shadows of an alley, more skeleton than animal.

Gone were the deep cries of earth crows and the shouts of children as the earth rumbled at the whim of the crows' power. Gone were the feathers that would drift from the sky like fallen leaves, snatched from the air by young couples to wish upon.

Gone was the world I knew, and I'd let it be taken.

Shame burned my cheeks, and I slowed my horse outside the charred remains of a row of shops. They stood like ancient tombs, forgotten in the face of war and starvation. The streets, once bustling with people and lined with tables of glass figurines and brightly colored pottery, now echoed with the sound of our horses' hooves as they kicked up dust.

A cloud hung over the kingdom, like the one that haunted me. The void inside me slowly filled with the black emotions that shone in every pair of eyes around us: despair, anger, apathy.

Kiva moved her horse closer to mine. "Put your hood up. I don't like the looks we're getting."

"No one's going to hurt—" I stopped at the look on her face, nausea turning in my stomach. I lifted the hood of my cloak, swallowing against the tightness in my throat. I'd never felt unsafe in the city before, but I'd be a fool not to recognize that a portion of the wing's growing resentment was aimed at the crown.

At me, for abandoning them.

I met the eyes of a little girl half my age and watched as first recognition, then anger took turns in their brown depths.

Illucia had done this, and Caliza wanted me to marry Ericen.

My hands tightened on my reins as Kiva and I neared the Kessel Woods on the outer edge of the wing. The summer afternoon was mild, warm in the sun and comfortable in the shade. A perfect afternoon for a ride—except I hated riding horses, whose rocking gait was nothing like the smooth flight of a crow, and the images from the wing clung to me like burrs.

I had to hatch the egg, before Rhodaire passed the point of saving.

Yet even as I had the thought, it felt distant and detached, as if it'd come from another person. Trying to hold on to it was like trying to hold smoke with my bare hands. I knew what I needed to do, but working up the will to do it felt like trying to fight my way above water in a depthless ocean.

It was so hard not to drown.

Kiva and I stopped outside a small tavern in the Brynth Wing to get a late lunch, leaving our horses tied out front. It was small and cozy, with rosewood tables built into alcoves along the walls and carved figurines atop a mantel that encircled the room's edge. The low murmur of voices filled the air, and I leaned back against the bar with my hood up while we waited for our food. I didn't feel like eating, but I wouldn't hear the end of it from Kiva if I didn't.

People talked, even laughed, huddled over tables of cheese and bread, fruit and cakes. Glasses of fruit juice and jugs of beer sat interspersed among the food, and in one corner, a group of girls played a game of dice.

This was the Aris I remembered, the one Illucia had nearly destroyed.

As the barmaid set two large goblets of mango talcé on the counter, the sharp whinny of a horse cut through the genteel atmosphere. I stiffened, and Kiva's hand went to her sword hilt. Through the front window, I saw a man pulling my horse out of view.

I shot for the door, Kiva on my heel. We stepped out in time to see him disappear down the alley beside the tavern.

"Stop!" I shouted, bolting for the alley.

He did.

I froze a few steps into the alley. The man released the horse, slapping it on the rear to send it trotting to the next street over. Then he faced me, a slim knife in hand. My mind tumbled, expecting pale Illucian skin and black fighting leathers. But the man was Jin, from the eastern kingdom of Jindae.

Kiva stepped between us. "Go back inside. I'll cover your back."

I started to argue, but she shot me a sharp glare, and I fell silent, nodding. The shrill ring of Kiva drawing her sword followed me as I bounded for the mouth of the alley. Metal clanged, and I glanced back as Kiva swung her sword at the man. Snapping my head forward, I ground to a halt.

Another Jin man blocked the exit.

My mind raced to remember my rider training. I was a good fighter, but it'd been months since I'd practiced.

"What do you want?" I demanded, backing away slowly.

The man stepped into the alley, and the sound of the fight at my back kept me from retreating any farther. I never should have stopped carrying the bow that used to be constantly strapped to my chest. The man didn't respond, his expression set in a grim mask as he pulled a dagger from his belt. He lunged.

I dodged, twisting so I slammed sideways into the alley wall. He recovered quickly and blocked my escape, knife raised. I stepped forward, catching his forearm with mine. But I was rusty and remembered too late my block should be followed by a counterattack. The man drove his fist into my exposed stomach, and I stumbled back, wheezing. He brought his knife down, and I flung myself aside, hitting the ground hard and rolling to my feet.

Calm down calm down calm down. I forced a sharp breath in and flexed my fingers as the man squared up with me. I had to get that knife away from him.

He lunged. I sidestepped his strike, driving my elbow into his sternum, then slammed my arm into his. His hand and the butt of the knife struck the alley wall, knocking the weapon from his grasp.

Footsteps sounded, and I barely had time to step back before the hilt of Kiva's sword struck the man in the temple. He crumpled against the wall.

I panted, heavy breathing mixing with Kiva's. Blood stained her arm scarlet to the shoulder.

"It's not mine," she said in response to my horrified expression. "Get inside. I'll send someone for the guards."

I stumbled out of the alley and into the tavern, collapsing into the first booth I reached. Sounds and colors blurred, and I blinked rapidly. Movement at my side made me flinch, but it was only the barmaid setting a glass of water on the table. She muttered a quiet, "Your Highness," with a swift curtsy.

I felt my head with numb fingers, distantly registering my hood had fallen. Then I gulped down the water.

As the adrenaline faded and understanding struggled to settle, an aching in my stomach and shoulder took its place. Two men at the table beside me subtly shifted their chairs, placing themselves between me and anyone who might come through the tavern door. Some deep, raw part of me glowed at the gesture.

The tavern door swung open, and Kiva entered, pale skin flushed and glistening with sweat. The men let her pass, and she dropped into the seat across from me, her eyes dark.

"The man I fought escaped." Her voice quavered. "The other one is in custody."

"Who were they?"

"I don't know, but I don't think they were thieves." When I only stared, she hesitated, then paused as the barmaid brought her a glass of water. She pulled it toward her but didn't drink. "I think they were trying to kill you, Thia."

A chill jolted through me, and I wrapped my arms around my middle. "Why?" My voice barely crested a whisper.

Kiva shook her head. She hadn't touched her water, though

she was squeezing the glass hard enough to crush it. "The guards I met are sending men for us. We're to wait until they show."

I nodded numbly. Her words felt distant, like a story someone told about a friend. Only the chill clinging to my skin despite the room's warmth hinted it had even happened.

The guards brought fresh horses when they arrived, and we rode back surrounded by people. My mind churned with every step. Could this have something to do with my engagement to Ericen? The news wasn't public yet, but that didn't mean no one knew, and there were likely to be a lot of people who disagreed with Caliza's decision. But to kill me to prevent it?

Sighing, I slowed my horse and dropped back to ride beside Kiva. Her hands gripped the reins so tightly, she looked like she was trying to strangle them. When I spoke, she jumped in a very un-Kiva-like way.

"What is it?" I asked.

Her head snapped up, eyes focusing on me with such intensity that I drew back. When something was wrong, the last thing Kiva wanted was to be asked what it was. Especially not when it could make her look weak in front of someone. But the guards were far enough away that they couldn't hear us, and I couldn't stay quiet when something so clearly weighed on her.

Her gaze softened, and she let out a quiet breath. "Sorry. I'm fine."

It was what I'd expected her to say. I didn't push her. Rather, I laid a hand on her arm, feeling the tension in her body break. It lasted all of a second before she sucked her emotions back inside, straightening. She wouldn't let someone report back to her mother that she'd broken down.

We rode in silence the rest of the way back, but I stayed beside her the whole time. She'd talk to me when she was ready.

The chair I sat in was rigid and uncomfortable. My stomach was already a little sore from the punch I'd taken, and the sudden absence of all the adrenaline had left me hollow.

A dark oak desk stood before floor-to-ceiling windows across from me, two glass doors flung open behind it to let in the evening breeze. A guard stood on either side of the entrance, and Caliza paced behind the desk, the circlet glinting on her head. The vein in her temple was on full display.

Behind her stood Captain Mirkova, her arms folded. I sat in one of the chairs on the other side of the desk. Kiva hadn't been allowed in.

I wished Caliza would yell already, but she seemed to have forgotten I was there. When another minute passed and she still hadn't spoken, I stood. "Well, this was a wonderful talk. I'll just—"

"Sit down." Her voice was like a thunderclap.

I sat.

When I'd first gotten back to the castle, she'd hugged me like she hadn't seen me in years. But her joy had given way to a stone-cold fury I knew too well.

"What were you thinking?" she demanded at last. "You were nearly killed."

I crossed my arms. "I've gone into the city a thousand times and no one's ever bothered me. How was I supposed to know today was the day someone would attack me?"

"You're not. That's why you should have taken sufficient protection."

"I had sufficient protection. I had Kiva."

Captain Mirkova snorted. "My daughter, while skilled, cannot defend you against an entire city."

I leveled the captain with a sour glare. When we'd returned, instead of asking how her daughter was, Captain Mirkova had started demanding answers, criticizing, and yelling.

"Do you understand what you almost cost us?" Caliza asked. "You jeopardized more than your own life; you jeopardized our chance at peace with Illucia, at securing this kingdom's safety."

"At least I wouldn't have had to marry Ericen."

"This isn't funny, Anthia!"

I surged to my feet. "I am *not* laughing. Has it occurred to you that maybe whoever tried to kill me wanted to stop me from marrying Ericen? That your decision to ship me off to another kingdom is what nearly cost me my life?"

Caliza stiffened, drawing upright, but it was Captain Mirkova who answered. "You've been much removed from Aris lately, Your Highness. Your city has changed. There are people in it who would not find delight in seeing your face."

I swallowed hard, collapsing back into the chair. "You think they did this because they're angry?"

"It's very possible," Caliza said. She sat down across from me, her shoulders rounded. The sight of her with anything less than immaculate posture made my throat tighten. She looked so small.

I thought back to the cold, hard faces of the men. No one had ever looked at me like that. I'd walked freely through Aris's streets, visiting the canal market in the Rynthene Wing or the weapons masters of the Turren Wing. People had smiled and waved. But that was before Ronoch, before Illucia took everything from us.

"They have to know we're trying our best." The words stuck in my throat. Because I knew they were a lie. By their silence, Caliza and Captain Mirkova did too.

Caliza was doing her best. I was hiding.

Caliza straightened. "I'm forbidding you from leaving the castle without my permission."

I started. "You're joking."

"We can't risk this not being an isolated incident. I mean it, Anthia. I'll post guards if I need to."

I almost laughed. For months, I'd hidden in these walls, and now that I wanted to leave, I wasn't allowed?

I stood. "What a time for you to take an interest in my well-being."

Her lips parted, but I didn't wait for a response before stalking from the room. Kiva fell into step beside me. The blood had dried on her shirt and skin, turning a muddy brown. She looked as exhausted as I felt.

We climbed the stairs to the second floor. "What did your mother say?" I asked.

Kiva's expression turned grim as it always did when we

discussed Captain Mirkova. "The usual." Her voice changed as she mimicked her mother's Korovi accent. *"Here I thought you were good enough to work alone, Sakiva. You need to train more. Perhaps I shouldn't have you teaching my new recruits, Sakiva, if you're going to make mistakes like that. You should know better than to go alone."*

"You nearly sounded like her that time," I said with a small smile.

I returned to my room, where my bed sat warm and inviting with the promise that if I climbed under the covers, everything would be okay again when I came out. My people wouldn't hate me, Ericen wouldn't be arriving tomorrow, and the crow would hatch and protect us from Illucia.

I didn't try to fight it.

FOUR

The next morning, I lay beneath the darkness and warmth of the covers and tried not to think about what was coming. I'd never met Prince Ericen, but everything about Illucia made my stomach turn. Their vain focus on appearances, their militaristic lifestyle, their cold, rainy weather; I hated it all.

Groaning, I rolled over to face the massive floor-to-ceiling windows on one side of my room. Windows meant to open for crows. The sight made me feel even worse. I'd been trying to convince myself to get up for hours.

On the nightstand beside my bed, papers had been tossed in a haphazard pile. Letters. Some were from riders and house lords and ladies, others from soldiers I'd sparred with during training. Some were even from Caliza, written in invisible ink made from shadow crow feathers, like we'd done as children. All failed attempts to cheer me up. All asking if I was okay, if they could help. I didn't deserve it.

Useless. The word echoed in my head, and images from my ride through the city yesterday joined it. People selling fake mementos on the dusty ground, Brynth masons with ice in their eyes, that little girl silently asking me why.

A fire kindled in my chest, but it wasn't the first time I had lain there and let it die.

Someone knocked, and Kiva entered. The dullness in her normally bright eyes was stark, and her characteristically perfect braid was loose and frayed.

I frowned. "Don't you have morning training?"

"My mother decided she wanted to take over for now." She sat on the edge of my bed.

"Are you all right?" The question came out before I could stop it, and her reaction was what I expected.

Her jaw set, eyes narrowing. "I'm fine."

I sighed, forcing the questions back down with the utmost restraint.

"You're still in bed," she noted.

I looked away, and something squirmed in my stomach. This was the worst part. The moment when I knew I needed to act, but my body refused to comply. With only days to hatch the egg, I needed a plan. But the need felt like it'd been swallowed by quicksand, there but buried.

You're running out of time. Move.

Nothing.

"I could go get the bucket of water"—Kiva stopped with a smile as I shot her a glare—"or you can at least sit up."

Grudgingly, I pushed myself up against the headboard and pulled the covers above my chest. This was ridiculous. Ericen would be here soon, and as much as I wanted to stay hidden in my room, I had to accept what was happening and handle it like a princess of Rhodaire should.

Problem was, the feeling inside me didn't care about what I had to do. It didn't care that I wanted to help Rhodaire, that I wanted to restore normalcy and peace and happiness. All it did was remind me that if I couldn't even do those things for myself, I sure as Saints couldn't do anything for Rhodaire.

"Take a few deep breaths," Kiva said.

I forced air deep into my lungs, then back out. Already, my head felt a little clearer.

"Sit beside me."

I moved to the edge of the bed. She stood. Slowly, I did too.

"Now get dressed. I'll be back to get you soon."

I marched into my closet, still feeling tired but better. That was always Kiva's point—I had to take everything one step at a time. I just wished she'd let *me* help *her.*

Kneeling before my armoire, I pulled open the bottom drawer, shifting aside sweaters to reveal the egg. I ran my fingers along the smooth shell, and the quiet humming danced up my arm, settling my stomach and chasing away the snake coiled about my neck.

Bonds weren't formed between crow and rider until after the hatching, and yet something about the connection between the egg and me felt intensely personal. It made me feel *seen*. Like the crow inside already knew me and I, it.

If I couldn't hatch it, I couldn't stop my engagement, couldn't protect Rhodaire or begin to rebuild it.

But first, I had to survive the next few hours.

I stood beside Caliza among a small crowd gathered outside the entrance hall, Kiva at my back. The massive wooden doors were pinned open, revealing the circular courtyard beyond leading to the north gates and the main road between the Thereal and Caravel Wings.

Caliza's handmaid had helped me dress, as I didn't have my own. A lifetime spent wearing pants and shirts made it unnecessary, especially when I often rose earlier than the castle staff to train, and most Rhodairen dresses were simple enough that it wasn't needed.

While I couldn't care less about impressing the prince, there was no denying the dress Caliza had commissioned was beautiful. It was made in simple Rhodairen fashion, with several silvery tiers of sheer cloth layered like the petals of a rose over a gray base.

I'd almost worn gloves. After the fire, I'd worn them constantly to hide the bandages, and later, the scars. Most people refrained from asking me exactly what'd happened, but almost everyone stared. Kiva had talked me into going without them once, and I'd left them behind since.

The late afternoon sky mirrored the gray of my dress, turning the air humid and threatening thunder.

Caliza wore a swirling steely dress lined in white that complemented my own. I imagined us from Ericen's perspective, two storm clouds drifted down from the sky, and my confidence surged.

This was my territory, my home. Whoever Ericen was, I could handle him.

Horses rounded the bend ahead, followed by a navy-blue carriage and several more mounted soldiers. The carriage was elegant, bedecked in gold that sparkled even in the filtered sunlight. The horses were beautiful, massive creatures, larger than any I'd ever seen, with glistening coats of pure black. The soldiers made for imposing figures on their broad backs, clothed in dark armor and armed to the teeth.

Caliza slipped her hand into mine. Before I could pull away, she squeezed it gently and let go. I released a breath and forced my face to go blank. I refused to be impressed or intimidated.

The procession pulled around the courtyard, the carriage stopping directly before us. My chest constricted, my fingers drumming on my leg. Two soldiers dismounted and approached the carriage door. I curled my fingers into my dress. The carriage door glided open.

Prince Ericen was one of the most attractive men I'd ever seen. With a short crop of black hair and eyes brighter than a bluebird's feathers, he was all crisp, clean edges and rich, manicured Illucian style. Near my age, he had broad shoulders and a lean build, and although tall, he was still shorter than Kiva.

The prince approached, flanked by two guards. His cold eyes scanned the crowd, the castle, the grounds—evaluating, judging, and duly unimpressed. His lip curled, a sneer spreading across his face.

A man standing beside Caliza bowed and said, "May I present Prince Ericen Rulcet."

The prince stopped a few feet away and bowed to Caliza— barely. "Your Majesty." His low voice had a slight rasp to it.

Caliza inclined her head. "Welcome to Rhodaire, Prince Ericen. May I introduce my sister, Anthia Cerralté."

I dipped into a small curtsy that he met with a half bow, his gaze sweeping over me until we were eye to eye. He smiled, but it didn't reach his eyes. They peered unrelentingly into mine, cold and sharp as daggers carved from ice. I held his gaze without blinking, straightening my back and tilting my chin up.

Caliza's voice broke our silent battle. "Please come inside, Prince Ericen. We've prepared dinner."

Ericen's gaze held mine a moment longer before finding Caliza. "Thank you, Your Majesty."

The crowd slowly dispersed as people returned to their work, and we led Ericen through the castle to the back patio. Two of his guards stayed with him, as large on foot as they'd looked on horseback. Their presence felt tangible behind me, but I kept my eyes forward until we arrived at the patio table.

Caliza and I sat at one end with Kiva and her guards behind us. Ericen took the other end with his. The table laden with fruit, cheese, and bread made my stomach churn. It looked like a simple dinner, but it felt like a war negotiation.

"How was your trip, Prince Ericen?" Caliza asked while filling her plate.

Ericen did the same. He kept shifting his shoulders, like trying to adjust for a new weight. Or a missing one. He was Illucian; where was his weapon?

"Smooth as a trip across kingdoms can be," he said. "Though I wasn't prepared for the weather. Is it always this horribly hot and humid?"

Caliza gave a tight smile, inclining her head. "The climate here is very different from yours. If you haven't brought anything that suits it, I can have my seamstress provide you with new clothes."

The prince bowed his head in thanks, and suddenly, I realized I was glaring at him. I looked quickly at my empty plate but could only think about chucking it at him.

Ericen was the embodiment of everything I hated. Even the way he blinked set me on edge, slow and self-satisfied like a lion cleaning its claws after a kill. He might not have been dressed like a soldier, but I could see his training in his movements and rigid posture, in the way he sat with his back toward the castle so he could see everyone and how his eyes flitted from spot to spot.

A servant stepped onto the patio, whispering something in Caliza's ear before returning inside. Caliza stood. "My apologies, but I have a quick matter to attend to. I'll return shortly." She gave me a short look before following the servant, her guards at her back.

My heart sank. For once, I didn't want to do the talking.

Ericen's gaze settled on me, and I held it out of spite. "If our relationship is going to consist of staring contests, I'll go mad," I said.

His lips twisted into a one-sided smile. "At least mine's a pleasant sight." His eyes slid along my body. Slowly.

My skin prickled. "I can't say the same."

His smile widened, becoming wolflike. "I've heard a lot about you, you know. The princess who won't leave her room."

I stiffened, my cheeks threatening to flush. "And yet here I am. Congratulations. Your arrival warranted my presence."

Ericen continued as if he hadn't heard me. "I've also heard you're not good at doing what you're told."

"I like to think of myself as a free spirit."

"And that someone tried to kill you."

The air turned thick as mud, sticking in my throat. Ericen sat back, folding his arms and looking infuriatingly self-satisfied. "Now why would someone want you dead? What have you done, Princess?"

Nothing. I'd done nothing. Which was why it didn't make any sense. How did he even know about the attack?

Forcing myself to relax, I schooled my face into a look of feigned disinterest Caliza would be proud of. "My theory? They heard about the engagement and wanted to spare me the misery."

Ericen's smugness evaporated.

I took the opportunity to pounce, leaning forward. "I, on the other hand, haven't heard a single thing about you." Rumors didn't seem worth mentioning. "Strange. You'd think in a kingdom of soldiers, the prince would have made a name for himself. I didn't even know yours before now."

A muscle feathered in Ericen's jaw, but Caliza reappeared before he could respond. I leaned back from the table, flashing him a quick sneer.

We spent the rest of dinner talking, each minute of conversation dragging longer than the last. I barely noticed Ericen's veiled insults or Caliza's deft handling of them, only joining the conversation when he said something particularly infuriating. By the end, my fingers had nearly drummed holes into my leg.

"Well, with the loss of your pets, I imagine things have changed drastically," Ericen said.

My spine snapped straight, and before Caliza could respond, I snarled, "They weren't pets!"

He raised a single black eyebrow. "Oh? Now that I think about it, I suppose I did hear that they were integral to nearly every one of your industries. Adjusting must be difficult."

I didn't realize I'd leaned forward until Caliza cut across me, interceding. "I'm sure you've had a long trip and would like time to rest. I'll call someone to show you to your room."

She stood, but Ericen didn't acknowledge her. His eyes were locked with mine, one corner of his lips twisted into a knowing smile I longed to pummel from his face. Riders and their crows had been servants of the crown, servants of Rhodaire. They'd been partners, the bond between them stronger than blood. Stronger than steel. It had been more than love and understanding; it'd been magic, a physical connection between two beings that transcended any other.

They were not *pets*.

The servants Caliza had called arrived. Only then did Ericen break his gaze from mine and stand. "I'd like a tour of the city tomorrow morning, Your Majesty."

"I'll arrange for someone to escort you."

His eyes shifted to me. "The princess, perhaps?"

I stiffened, but Caliza didn't so much as blink. "Unfortunately, Anthia is otherwise engaged." A lie. Caliza just didn't want me out of the castle.

"I'm sure she can find the time." His tone dripped with implication. He knew he had power here, and he wanted to be sure we did too.

Caliza's lips pressed into a line. "Very well."

The prince inclined his head in the shallowest of bows before following the servants inside.

"Bastard," I hissed.

Caliza's head snapped toward me. "Maybe he wouldn't have felt it necessary to prove his control if you weren't so intent on making him angry. I thought you were going to give him a chance."

"I did. He blew it quickly. Pretty sure he insulted everything from our food to our architecture."

"Posturing and Illucian snobbery. Did you expect anything less?"

"No. That doesn't mean I have to accept it. He likes getting a rise out of us."

"Out of you," Caliza corrected. "You make it easy for him."

I scowled but bit back my retort. "Look, I'm not any happier about this than I was yesterday. Give me a chance to adjust before I sell my soul."

Caliza's stern expression relented. Barely. She rose without a word and strode into the castle. I stood too, Kiva moving to my side.

Grinding my teeth, I stepped toward the castle. Ericen's smug smile lingered in my mind. He'd been here all of a couple of hours and was already throwing his weight around. No doubt he'd asked for the tour to scope out the state of the city. By this time tomorrow, he'd know exactly how little we'd recovered from Ronoch, and we had no choice but to let him.

Yet another thing I could do nothing about.

Scowling, I changed direction abruptly, heading toward the downstairs library. "Come on. Maybe we can find answers in the library."

Kiva eyed me as if seeing something she hadn't expected to find. "I hate to say it, but Ericen might actually be good for you." I must've looked absurd, because a grin split across Kiva's face, and she hastened to explain. "Don't get me wrong. He's worse than an ice bear in heat, but I haven't seen you that engaged with something in months."

I stared at her. "An ice bear in heat?"

She shrugged. "They're notoriously foul and vicious. And strangely fond of chocolate." I rolled my eyes, and she laughed. "I'm serious, Thia. You've always needed an opponent. Your mother, Caliza, other riders; you're the most competitive person I know, and Ericen's nothing if not a challenge."

I snorted, but as per usual, Kiva knew me better than I knew myself. I crossed my arms. "A challenge I'll win."

She grinned.

FIVE

I groaned, slamming shut *Proper Crow Care* with a puff of dust on the table before me. A couple of off-duty guards looked up from their reading, averting their eyes when Kiva gazed coolly back at them. Night had crept in, the large, windowless library lit by sona lamps, inventions from the Ambriels that burned longer than normal lights.

"Anything?" I asked.

Kiva shook her head, tossing the book onto the table with the sort of reckless abandon that would make Caliza pale. "To be honest, I haven't been paying attention," Kiva said. "I can't stop thinking about the Jin prisoner." I raised an eyebrow, and she leaned across the table, lowering her voice. "Who else would a citizen of Jindae serve if not Razel? The Jin monarchy was torn to ruins when Illucia conquered the kingdom, the entire royal family murdered. But Razel gains nothing if you're dead."

"Great, so my people hate me and want me dead."

"No." She gave me a flat look. "I heard a rumor among the guards this morning. Some of them have family in Jindae. They're saying the Jin princess survived. They think she sent the assassins."

I sat up, leaning close. "Have they seen her?"

She shook her head. "It's secondhand information, but I think the attack only proves it. If the princess is trying to organize a rebellion to take back Jindae, the last thing she'd want is for Rhodaire to ally with Illucia in any way. That makes more sense than a random attack by angry Rhodairen citizens."

I shoved a book across the table. "Even our allies are enemies then." I pressed my face into my hands. It was all too much. Too many questions, too many things to do, too much effort. I'd just started getting out of bed every day; how was I supposed to handle all this?

"We'll figure it all out, Thia," Kiva said. "One step at a time."

One step at a time. She'd said that to me every day for weeks. I struggled to latch on to the words. We'd possibly discovered who had ordered the attack on me. Now, I needed to hatch the egg. But how in the Saints' name was I supposed to do that?

I attempted a smile. "One step at a time."

I woke paralyzed.

As I'd slept, each of my worries had climbed into bed and

settled on my chest like crows to roost. Late morning sunlight poured through the windows, teasing me with its light and warmth, but crawling out from under the covers seemed too big a task.

Move.

Nothing.

This was how it was. One moment, I was moving forward, and the next, I couldn't move at all. No matter how important the day or what I needed to do, the feeling came and refused to leave.

I hated it.

Why was I so weak? I'd been worthless the last few months. I still was. I couldn't hatch the egg. Couldn't help Rhodaire or myself.

Useless.

Illucia had taken everything from me, and I'd given up. They'd taken everything from the Jin princess too, and if the rumors were true, she'd organized a rebellion in response. Not to mention to have known about the engagement, she either had spies in our castle or Illucia's.

She'd lost everything, and she'd moved forward. Why couldn't I?

Someone knocked. I burrowed deeper into the blankets, blocking out the golden sunlight. Staying in bed was so much easier than getting up and facing everything waiting for me.

The knocking came again, more fervent, which narrowed it to Kiva or Caliza. The door banged open. Caliza then.

Loud footsteps preceded a flood of light as she tore back my blankets.

I glared up at her. "Don't you have more important things to do besides force me out of bed?"

"You're late for the tour."

Damn it. Pushing my pillow behind me, I slid up to sit against the headboard. "I forgot."

"You can't keep fighting me every—"

"I forgot!"

She drew a sharp breath, nostrils flaring. Her words came out taut as a bowstring. "I understand you're in pain, Anthia, but you're not the only one, and you can't keep wasting away your life wallowing in self-pity when—"

"It isn't self-pity!" I screamed. "I'm depressed!"

My words echoed through the room, my chest rising and falling in quick bursts. The anger ebbed out of me, leaving behind a feeling I didn't recognize. A beast inside me slowly uncoiled, releasing a tension so deeply ingrained, it had become a part of me.

I'd never said those words before.

I'd thought them. Kiva had hinted at them. But *I'd* never actually *said* them. Even now, repeating them in my head, they sounded ridiculous. I was sad and severely hurt, even angry, but depressed? I'd always told myself that it would pass. There had been good days.

Good days, but never easy ones. Even now, some days were more manageable than others. Some hours, some seconds, I could handle, and the next, I wanted to let the world swallow me up. There were days where I couldn't breathe, couldn't move, couldn't *think.*

I'd been depressed. I still was.

The hard edge in Caliza's eyes softened. How long had I yearned for that sympathy? Now that I had it, I wanted it to go away. It made me feel pathetic.

I threw back the covers and sprang out of bed, stalking to the far side of the room and back again. The air felt thick and charged, biting at my skin with implications. My defeat had burrowed under my skin and into my bones. It had carved out a space inside me and hooked in so deep that it smothered everything else I had been.

I couldn't remember feeling anything other than pain and misery and fear, all of it overlaid by a layer of guilt thick and suffocating as smoke. I'd shown more emotion in the last two days than I had in the months before.

Illucia had destroyed my world, and now they'd come to take what I had left, and what had I really done? Snarl a few times at Ericen?

This wasn't me. I was a ghost living in my own skin.

Caliza stood, and I faced her, jaw clenched as I waited for the inevitable lecture. The one where she told me to get over it and control myself. Her chest swelled, then suddenly, she deflated. "I'm sorry."

I blinked. "What?"

"I know what you must think of me, but I don't want this for you, Thia. I'd marry him myself if I could."

The river of anxiety rushing through me slowed. Caliza had apologized twice now, and this wasn't even her fault. Not really. It was an impossible situation. "I don't want that either."

She collapsed onto the edge of my bed, burying her face in her hands. "I know. And I know I've been horrible, and I know I've been—"

"Colder than a water crow's ice?" I offered. She choked out a laugh. I reached out, then hesitated. I was used to seeing Caliza like steel, like our mother. Now she looked small and a little broken. I didn't know how to comfort her.

I sat beside her and laid my hand on her shoulder. She leaned into it, the tension in her body melting. "My life changed too, you know," she said. "When we lost the crows. I had to learn to be queen, to take care of the kingdom and of you. I forgot to be your sister."

"I didn't exactly make it easy."

She shook her head. "No. This isn't your fault. The way you feel isn't your fault." Her words pulled loose something inside me, like a coil of yarn unspooling. "I'm so sorry for the things I said, Thia. I thought, if I was like Mother, if I pushed you..." Her lips pressed firm, her throat bobbing. "It was wrong. *I* was wrong."

A shudder racked my body, and I swallowed down a sob. I'd known she hadn't meant to hurt me with the things she'd said, but it hadn't stopped the pain.

She met my gaze. "I don't want you to go, but I can't see what other choice we have. Everything I've read, everything I've been told says this is the right decision. We can't stand against Illucia. They have the Ambriels and Jindae. If they declared war, they would destroy us."

"What about Trendell? Is Kuren trying to persuade them to fight?" My voice came out hoarse.

Caliza smiled faintly at the mention of her husband. "He's trying, yes. But the Trendellans are a peaceful people; they want no part in this. I'm sure they don't want to send their few soldiers to slaughter either."

"So you'd surrender without a fight instead?"

"This kingdom has already lost so much. It couldn't survive another war."

I pulled my knees to my chest. "It won't survive my marriage either. Illucia won't settle for a lawful connection to Rhodaire. I don't know whether they're forming this bond until they're ready to attack or what, but this can't be all they're planning."

"I know. But for now, it's our only option. We both know I couldn't refuse Razel. If anything, it'll buy us time to think of something else."

I bit my lip. "What if we had a crow?"

Caliza went rigid, and I knew I'd said the wrong thing. She stood. "The crows can't help us, Anthia. They're the reason we're in this mess. We were too dependent on them, and now they're gone."

"Except they're not." I stood too. "I found a storm crow egg."

Something in her expression flickered, as if considering my words, before her resolve hardened. "Even if you could hatch it, it won't be enough. You don't understand what we're up against. You never have. You shirked your duties as princess even before Ronoch!"

"And you've never understood the crows! You've always hated them, and they knew it. It's why none of them would ever let you ride them."

Caliza's face flushed, and my anger broke as understanding settled. "That's it, isn't it?" I asked. "Why you're so against them?"

She dropped back onto the bed. "I wasn't meant to be a rider. Mother always said so."

"What?"

"She told me to give up on the crows. I tried anyway, but she was right. The crows rejected me."

I sat beside her. "I had no idea."

Caliza smiled tightly. The circlet on her head sat askew, her usually immaculate hair tangled around it. Tension rippled across her skin like an earthquake. Then she straightened, letting out a single shuddering breath. "We cannot win this war with a single crow."

"Maybe. But we could win with a crow and Trendell's support. And they might help us if they thought we had a chance."

She didn't respond at first, fingers worrying at a few strands of hair. Her fingers were so thin, delicate, not made to grip a sword or hold fast to a saddle hundreds of feet in the air.

"Please, Caliza. You have to trust me." Reaching out, I took her hand in mine. Her fingers stilled. I leaned forward to meet her gaze, and swore for a fleeting second that tears threatened her eyes. Then she blinked, and the look was gone.

"I'm so sorry." Her words tumbled out in a torrent. "I've been so overwhelmed. I didn't think there was another way—I still don't. I mean, I don't know if hatching the egg is possible, and I don't know if it will help, but you're right. If there's even a chance, we have to take it." Her hand tightened around mine.

I squeezed it back. "I'll do whatever I can."

She smiled. "You always were the fighter. I think that's why you were Mother's favorite."

A bark of laughter escaped my lips. "If by favorite you mean least disliked, maybe, but I still think you were imagining things."

Her smile faded. "I miss her."

"I know." I swallowed hard. "So do I." Even if our mother hadn't been as warmhearted and open as I would have liked, I'd still loved her. Still wanted to make her happy, to earn her respect and praise despite the distance that stretched between us.

"In the meantime," I said, "I'll play nice with Ericen."

She eyed me. "I know it's difficult, but we have to placate him. Particularly if we're going to break our agreement. He can't suspect us."

I nodded. "I'll try."

"I'll send a bird to Kuren about Trendell. If we had their support, a storm crow could be enough to inspire them to stand against Illucia. But without the crow, I don't think Trendell will listen."

I nodded and reached for the circlet on her head, centering it.

She gave my hand another squeeze. "We'll get through this. I promise."

I believed her, even as I withheld the truth: I had no idea how to hatch the egg. But I would find a way. I just needed time.

SIX

With Caliza's and my plan in place, I felt more confident facing Ericen. The engagement seemed less like a storm on the horizon than a single rain cloud. We would hatch the egg, gain Trendell's support, and stand against Illucia.

In the meantime, I'd try not to insult Ericen with every breath.

A small army accompanied us into the city for our tour. Apparently, Ericen's arrival had stirred several protests. A few abandoned shops had been broken into, one even burned. What would people think once the news of why he was here spread?

With every step, my mare shifted nervously next to Ericen's. I didn't blame her. His horse looked like it might eat us both. The prince rode like he'd been born to it, the *thwomp* of his stallion's steps drowning the soft clatter of my mount's hooves.

People stared as we passed, faces infused with hate. I understood. Looking at Ericen, all I could think of were burning rookery towers and the screams of crows and people, indistinguishable from one another in the night. But bitterness lurked beneath the hatred of some, and it wasn't for him.

I gestured to our right. "We'll go into the Thereal Wing first."

"The wings are named after each of your Saints, aren't they? And they correspond with a type of crow?" Ericen asked. "So this would be the wind crows?"

Fire hurtled through my veins, but when I shot Ericen a sharp glare, the anger vanished abruptly. He wasn't looking at me, and his normally cool expression had warmed into a look of curiosity, until he caught my gaze. The look of interest disappeared, replaced by a slight sneer.

I scowled. "Yes."

We followed a broad street that circled the castle and cut through each wing, forming a circle around the inner city. In the fading chill of morning, street performers gathered in the shade of side streets. Shops set in bright, colorful buildings propped open doors, and the soft hum of a violin resonated through the air as a musician tested the strings.

The Thereal Wing was known for entertainment. That hadn't changed, but a subdued atmosphere hung over the usually lively wing. The street no longer teemed with visitors, and the echoes of distant music sounded like a melody of pain and sadness.

Ericen scanned everything with an imperious look, his back

straight, head held high, exuding a confidence and strength I longed for. As he slowed to behold a gymnast warming up, I caught sight of a familiar blue building at the street corner.

I urged my horse toward it subconsciously, staring but not seeing. Memories flashed: sneaking out with Kiva to go dancing, music as quick as a heartbeat after a flight, a crow painted in sunset colors across the building's side...columns of fire, smoke choking the air, the screech of crows and screams of people.

I slowed my horse outside Rua's. The door to the pub was chained shut, the windows boarded. Thick vines obscured the crow painting, its vibrant colors muted.

Already, the hope I'd felt setting out dwindled away. Each boarded-up window and crumbling building I saw leeched more of my strength. I braced my hands on the back of my saddle, shoulders curving, head bowed.

Aris had been a city of wonders. A place people came to from all over the world to trade, to learn, to live. Now it was slowly fading, drifting into nothing like an abandoned ship into the night.

In the distance, what remained of the Thereal rookery loomed like a pillar of shadows.

"Why don't you knock that down? It's useless now."

My spine went rigid, and I turned to look at Ericen. He stared at the remains of the rookery with a critical frown. When I didn't respond, he glanced at me.

Every muscle turned to stone. "Say something like that again and I'll—"

"What?" he asked. "What will you do, Princess? Yell? Curse?

Hurt me?" He laughed, and the sound ripped into my chest like talons. "If you so much as touch me, if you push me too far, I'll end this engagement and Rhodaire's future along with it." His eyes glinted like sunlight against the tundra. "Give me a reason."

My words turned to ash in my throat, smothering my breath. Fire and frost danced along my skin like the waves of a fever as I fought to move, to think, to breathe. But all I could picture was the army on our border, the rows and rows of cavalry and archers who would kill without thought or mercy.

Ericen shook his head pityingly. "What am I saying? This is the girl who's been hiding in her room for months. You're not going to do anything, are you? Cowards never do." His gaze flicked over me again before he kicked his horse into a trot down the street.

A heartbeat. Two. Still, I couldn't follow.

Coward.

I'd leave him lost in the streets, spook his horse into throwing him off, lead him down a dark alley and—No. He was right. I couldn't do so much as scratch him, or he might end everything. Somehow, I had to stay calm, had to keep from letting him push me off the edge.

Drawing a deep, shuddering breath, I urged my horse onward.

We passed through the Kerova Wing, once home to the shadow crows. The clatter of our horse's hooves echoed like an unanswered call, the hot air still and thick with humidity, making me long for the mist water crows used to trail in their wakes as they soared overhead.

"There's not much to see here," Ericen said. His rough voice stuck out like a dove among crows.

"Then let's move on." While Ericen saw nothing, my eyes found only shuttered windows and smoke-stained walls, all blurring with memories of a night filled with fire and blood.

We went through the Turren Wing next, once home to the battle crows. Smiths called prices above the din of hammers and conversation, standing behind tables laden with weapons or in open doorways to larger storerooms. Thick heat wafted from outdoor forges, now small and hand-fed. There'd been a time when the Turren smiths shared the heat and power of the central forge, a massive structure at the heart of the wing that had fed countless other forges. Without fire crows to keep it blazing, it now lay cold and dormant.

Ash smudged the stone and brick buildings, sparks crackling like snapping bone. I stuck to the center of the broad streets, well away from any flames, and focused on my breathing. We still had over half the tour to go; I couldn't lose it now.

Ericen cast a disdainful look down at the beggars lining the streets. Half the shops were closed, many sellers ousted to small tables along the main road without enough money for rent. He had no idea what these people had once done, the magic they'd once created.

The first time I saw a battle crow armor up, its feathers turning sleek and metallic, I'd screamed. At four years old, I'd thought the crow was dying. Then it'd released one of its gold-veined black feathers like an arrow, and a Turren smith had dropped it into a melting pot over a simmering fire. When

Estrel had explained it was how we made black gold, a rare metal stronger than the finest steel, I'd prayed to the Saints for a black gold weapon of my own.

Estrel remembered. She gave me my bow for my tenth birthday.

Ericen slowed his horse to walk alongside mine. "Does it unsettle you, knowing your people could betray you again at any moment?"

My head snapped toward him. "You don't know what you're talking about."

"Oh? I know before either of us was born, a group of your Turren riders attacked my mother's family on an unsanctioned mission to avenge your father's death. I know they were relieved of their crows and Lord Turren was banished." He moved his horse closer, the hot flesh of the beast's muscular body pressing against my leg. I couldn't move away without threatening to step on the items laid out for sale or the people tending them.

Ericen continued, his voice soft and slow, savoring each word. "I know when my mother came to Lord Turren, offering him the power and prestige he once had, he sold his loyalty to her, and his men's loyalty, and helped us destroy every single crow."

I squeezed my eyes shut and turned away, trying to block him out, to block the memories out. After the fires had burned to cinders and only the smoke remained, people had wanted blood. Caliza had to show them she was taking action, but nearly half our army came from the Turren Wing. The people she needed to enforce the hunt for traitors had been suspects themselves.

And I'd done nothing but hide in my bed.

Coward.

Slowly, I became aware of something digging into my skin and looked down. I'd twisted the reins around and around my wrists and hands, tethering myself to the spot.

Ericen let out a low, rumbling laugh and dismounted with two of his guards to look at the weapons set out for sale. I stared at my hands, adrenaline leaking from my muscles like water from a punctured jug.

Today was only the second day of my time with Ericen. I couldn't face an eternity with him.

Loosing a quiet breath, I unwound the reins to reveal angry red and white flesh and stiff fingers. I massaged my hands and scanned the crowd, spotting Ericen at a nearby table and his men at the one across from it.

Even without black gold, Turren weapons were still highly sought after, but the glowering eyes of several smiths made it clear Ericen and his men weren't welcome. Others, desperate for any coin, called them to their tables, forming a line of tension that turned the air thick.

Ericen's guards didn't pay him any attention. The prince ignored them equally, investigating a pair of slim daggers with tiny sapphires set into the hilt. I eyed the weapons. What would happen if I plunged one into Ericen? Nowhere fatal, just somewhere very painful.

If you so much as touch me, if you push me too far...

The words echoed in the hollow space inside me, and I longed to run from them, to hide. The sensation of angry, questioning eyes pressed in on me from all directions. I tried to meet them, but every black stare that gazed back replaced my emptiness with a white-hot weight.

My horse shifted nervously underneath me, whinnying. Smiths and sellers glared at the Illucians with open hostility, more than one with a hand on the hilt of a weapon. A Rhodairen man to Ericen's left leaned to a woman beside him, muttering. His expression looked wrong.

A sharp clatter rang out. My gaze snapped to a nearby stand, where one of Ericen's guards had carelessly tossed a dagger onto the table, causing it to topple off. "Worthless," the guard said.

A scowl broke across the smith's face. "Pick it up," she said.

The guard snorted and turned away. The smith's hand shot out fast as lightning, seizing his arm. A dagger shone in her other hand.

The action rippled through the crowd, everyone from sellers to patrons to the faces watching from the shadows going still. A space cleared around the two. Hands went to weapons. The air evaporated. In the heat and dust, my guards moved closer as a hush descended.

A flicker of blue, and Ericen shattered the stillness. He shot forward, breaking the woman's hold and shoving his guard back a step all before I even considered intervening. The smith switched her hold on the dagger, and Ericen seized the hilt of his guard's sword from behind, unsheathing it halfway.

"Stop!" My voice erupted, and I regretted the word instantly. The last thing I wanted to do was tell my people not to hurt an Illucian, but a showdown between elite Illucian soldiers and the weapons masters of Rhodaire would end bloodily.

For a breath, no one moved. Then slowly, the smith lowered

her dagger and set it on the table. Her brown eyes never left mine. "Your Highness." She bowed.

Only once her hand returned to her side did Ericen sheathe his guard's sword.

"We should go," I croaked, no longer looking at the smith, at anyone.

Ericen didn't argue, the thick silence and dark looks probably enough to convince him. He swung back onto his horse in one fluid motion. "We're leaving," he said to his guards.

They didn't acknowledge him, already at the next table as if nothing had happened.

Ericen's face flushed. "Now."

One of them looked back, frowning. He muttered something to the other guard, then they both mounted, and we set off. The feeling of eyes on my back dug in like claws, and I kicked my horse into a trot. I wanted to tell myself their anger and resentment was for the Illucians, but not all of it was. It was for me, for my abandonment, for my uselessness.

My throat tightened, and I urged my horse on. The smith's dark eyes seared in my mind, burning with accusation.

Coward.

I kicked my horse into a canter, breaking away from the group as the road opened onto a broad street packed with merchant carts and people. My guards yelled, but I didn't slow. The crowd parted, and I reined in my horse. Nearly leaping from my saddle, I wove through the vendors and shoppers and ducked into the privacy of a nearby alley, collapsing against the wall.

Anxiety writhed in my stomach. Pain, fear, anger—they

infected every wing. Infected me. Where did we even begin to fix things? One crow might protect us from war, but what about the decay spreading from within?

Something prickled at the back of my neck. I pushed off the wall, turning, and nearly slammed straight into someone. I stepped back, hands raised, and found Ericen staring back at me with a smirk.

"You ran off," he mused. "Your poor guards are frantic." His gaze lifted over my shoulder. "Something interesting about this particular alley?"

"Anything's more interesting than talking to you." Before he could respond, I marched back into the crowd. The cool air wafting off the canal chilled my hot skin, and I made straight for a nearby House Cyro cart, where I paid for an orange cake in an attempt to pretend I'd simply been in a hurry to get dessert. Except my fingers fumbled the coins, and I gave the vendor a silver talon instead of copper, and I nearly dropped the cloth-wrapped bundle in my attempt to pocket it.

I forced in breath after breath, trying and failing to fight away my anxiety, and moved to the edge of the canal. Except the murky water, once kept pure and glistening by water crows, reminded me of why I'd bolted into the alley to begin with.

Ericen appeared like a specter beside me. I stiffened. He moved so soundlessly.

"You're shaking. Is something the matter, Princess?"

Before I could respond, footsteps echoed from behind, and I faced my guards as they emerged from the crowd panting and flushed. I winced.

"I'm sorry," I said quickly, withdrawing the orange cake from my pocket. "I saw the vendor, and there wasn't a line, and that never happens, so..." I trailed off when I caught Ericen's smile. As if to say I could lie, but only because he let me.

The guards straightened, the one in the lead bowing his head. "Of course, Your Highness. Please just give us warning next time."

I nodded, swallowing hard and addressing the prince. "If you're not going to explore the market, let's go." I didn't wait for an answer before cutting back through the crowd to where a guard held my horse. Thankfully, Ericen followed.

We mounted and set off along the next wing, riding in tangible silence. I glanced down at the orange cake in my hand, and my stomach roiled in response. I let it drop to the ground.

The delicately crafted statues and intricate carvings of the Brynth buildings passed in a blur, my horse following the ones ahead on its own. In my mind, the scene in the Turren Wing replayed over and over again. The Illucian soldier's mocking words, the Turren smith's disappointment as she looked at me.

A shadow fell over me, and I blinked rapidly, clearing fuzzy vision I hadn't noticed. My horse had stopped, as had the others, and Ericen sat merely a foot away, looking down at me from his massive stallion.

"I said, what are these?" He gestured to the rows of pure white statues on either side of us, carved into figures twice the size of a normal person. Each stood beside the black marble sculpture of a crow, or what was left of them. Several had chunks missing from their wings and bodies, and one of the figure's hands was missing.

More damage from Ronoch shoved to the wayside in the face of bigger problems.

"Saints' Row," I responded. We'd reached the other end of the Brynth Wing already?

"The riders you worship." He said the words with derision.

"Some people do." The stories said the Saints were the first riders, gifted the crows by the Sellas. Together, they'd built Rhodaire, and when the Saints passed, they ascended into godhood. Before Ronoch, I'd believed that as wholeheartedly as anyone. Now I wanted to know why they hadn't helped us. Why they hadn't protected us.

At the end of Saints' Row stood a building nearly as large as the castle. The citadel, a place of learning and research, where academics studied architecture and chemistry, crow flight patterns and the origins of magic. Before Ronoch, it'd been the earth crows' unending project, slowly expanding upward and outward like a living thing. Now the unfinished upper level sat exposed like fractured bones, scaffolding slowly rusting in the humid air and tarps flapping in the wind like white flags of surrender.

"They certainly didn't do much for the people that did," Ericen said.

I scowled. "If you want to find your own way back to the castle, that can be arranged."

He raised a single black eyebrow, the unspoken reminder echoing in the hot air. *If you push me too far...* I looked away, and in that moment, I felt the eyes of the Turren smith on me again, dark with disappointment and shame.

I'd begun this tour with renewed confidence, then let Ericen take it from me without so much as a fight. My whole life, I had fought: for my mother's approval, for my place as a rider, for my skills and strength and knowledge. I'd pushed unwaveringly, and when I had met a wall, I'd shattered it.

When had I stopped fighting?

No more. I was done.

Forcing a sharp smile, I met his gaze. "You know everything, don't you? Who I am, what to say to make me react, how to use my people's history against me. But if you truly knew everything, you would know better than to piss me off."

"Are you threatening me, Princess?" His eyes flashed.

I kept my voice low enough that only we could hear. "Do you feel threatened? You're practically alone in an enemy kingdom filled with people who would line up for the chance to personally disembowel you."

"If a single person here touched me—"

"Your mother would rain down upon us with the full strength of the Illucian army. Yes, I heard you the first time."

His jaw clenched, but I kept talking. "Don't worry. No one's going to touch a single hair on your pretty little head. But Saints damn me if I keep my mouth shut again. Your mother didn't demand this engagement just so you could end it because your skin isn't thick enough."

He stared at me, eyes narrowed. I waited, my heart thundering in my chest, filling my ears with a roaring. What if I'd been wrong? What if this marriage really was simply a way for Razel to torment us further, and she would happily let it dissolve at her son's whim?

Finally, the prince smirked. "Not as useless as I thought, it seems." Tension washed from my shoulders, and he continued, "But I would advise you to remember that I have an army on your border, and your kingdom needs this. We don't."

I straightened, keeping a neutral mask. A small victory. He still held the power, but at least I knew, to some extent, Illucia wanted this marriage to happen. "Let's go."

I didn't wait for his approval before urging the group on to the Garien Wing, once home of the storm crows.

As we passed quickly along the light stone buildings, their windows shining with stained glass of amethyst and saffron, cerulean and gold, each color flowing into the next like a sunset, I felt endlessly lighter. Better yet, Ericen remained quiet throughout the ride, even as we crossed into the Cyro Wing, where the memory of fire crows lingered in the scorch marks on buildings and in the street.

I glanced at my burned arm before I could stop myself, and when I lifted my head, Ericen was staring too. My face flushed, but I didn't look away, waiting for the snide remark. Nothing came.

As we passed beneath a row of pale pink orchid trees, a hummingbird flitted out from behind the tree and zipped over to him, hovering excitedly at eye level. He watched it curiously, trying to track its movements as it jumped around his head, then sped off.

I blinked. He was *smiling*. Not the wolf grin that made my skin crawl. An actual, *human* smile. He saw me staring and quickly turned away, making a show of adjusting his grip on his reins.

He could smile at a bird, but me he had to drive wild?

"Princess! Princess!"

A trio of small boys came running toward us, their harried mother calling after them a step behind. The smallest of the three broke ahead, a broad grin across his face. One of my guards shifted, but I waved him away, and he allowed the boy to approach.

The boy raised his hand in offering. A single daffodil rested between his small fingers, the petals stark white as snow. Behind him, a trail of them led back to his mother and brothers, having slipped from his hand in his race to reach me.

I took the flower, the beginnings of a smile tugging at my lips. "Thank you."

His mother called for him then, and the boy flashed me another grin before rejoining her. She bowed her head, and I nodded, watching them disappear down the road.

"When you're done entertaining the riffraff," Ericen intoned, "I'd like to get out of this miserable heat."

We moved on to the Caravel Wing, once home to the city's sun crows. After Ronoch, their absence had been felt the strongest. The crows' healing abilities had been sorely needed. Nearly half the wing was educated in the healing arts, but they hadn't been nearly enough to help all the injured.

I ran a finger along my scars, the daffodil still clutched

against my palm. A sun crow could have healed the wounds before they scarred. They could have saved Estrel. For a selfish second, I wished the egg I'd found had been a sun crow. But that wasn't what Rhodaire needed to survive.

Aris was crumbling bit by bit, more than I had realized. Seeing it had been painful. Seeing Ericen witness it had been worse. Though that pain lingered, this time, it didn't overwhelm me. I couldn't stop myself from snapping at Ericen, but as I watched his proud form, head held high, riding like a conqueror surveying his prize, I found I didn't care.

I wanted him to know that I was angry, that as close as I'd come, I had not been defeated. Rhodaire had not been defeated.

I wanted him to know I would still fight.

SEVEN

O nce home, I washed and changed for dinner, which Caliza had condemned me to eat with Ericen. We had to keep up appearances, but I would have rather stayed hungry, even though my appetite had started to return.

As I dropped into the seat across from Ericen on the patio, the door opened, and several servants stepped out carrying plates of food. They set the dishes on the table before bowing and returning inside. I didn't so much as look at the prince as I filled my plate.

"I can tell this is going to be a very productive meal," he mused.

"Here's an idea. You sit there and eat your meal, silently, and I'll sit here and eat mine, while pretending you're not there."

"Is that your plan for the rest of our lives or just today?"

My face broke into a scowl. "That depends. Are you always this much of a pain in the ass?"

"Are you?"

"Only to people who deserve it." I stabbed a piece of meat with my fork.

Ericen smiled, and a glorious silence descended. Thick enough to cut with a knife, but quiet.

Then, "Your Turren Wing reminds me of the streets around Darkward Academy in Illucia. Everyone carries a weapon, and over half the shops sell them. I graduated from there a month ago."

I leveled a flat gaze on him. Despite all our bickering, he couldn't seem to let the conversation die. Like we could talk as if there weren't a dark and bloody history between our people. "What in the Saints' name makes you think I would want to talk about anything to do with the Illucian military? Or about you for that matter?"

Ericen didn't respond, his gaze resting briefly on my scarred arm before he turned his eyes to the garden beyond. I wanted my gloves.

Finally, he let the conversation die. I moved the steak around my plate with my fork. Once, Iyla would have nudged me with gusts of wind from where she perched on the patio railing until I tossed her a snack. Without her, without Estrel and my mother, the patio felt empty, the table too big.

The patio door opened, and servants cleared away dinner before bringing us each a slice of chocolate cake. Ericen eyed his as if it might bite him.

"What? Is our dessert not good enough for you either?"

"We didn't have sweets at Darkward."

"That explains a lot."

He barely seemed to notice the insult, instead taking a bite of the cake. His expression didn't change as he ate it, and he didn't say a thing, but he finished his slice before I did mine and watched me eat every last bite.

Then, as if he'd simply been waiting for me to finish, he reached into his pocket, withdrawing a folded letter with Illucia's royal seal. He slid it across the table to me, but I didn't take it.

"This," he said, "is a letter to General Castel. She leads the army currently sitting on your border."

A chill dripped slowly down the back of my neck, turning every muscle to ice. He continued, "In it are instructions to destroy your outposts for ten miles in every direction and to leave no survivors but one, who will be sent back here as proof that my order has been carried out."

My breath slipped in and out quick as a wingbeat, my jaw aching from clenching it so tight.

"Say whatever you'd like to me, Princess. Snap and curse and insult until your throat is raw. But remember why I'm here. Remember there's an army sitting on your border full of soldiers who have been trained to do one thing their entire life: kill."

The word echoed with promise. He was playing with me, trying to make me feel powerless. It worked. The situation felt slippery, out of my control.

He left the letter on the table and stood. "We leave for Illucia the day after tomorrow," he said and stalked back inside. His presence lingered, the space he'd occupied as solid as if he were still there.

I sent a servant to Caliza to convey the news of my imminent departure and Ericen's threat. Then I ordered the letter burned. Only once every fragment had turned to ash did I go upstairs.

I couldn't sleep. Ericen's threat had followed me upstairs and draped itself across my shoulders, whispering promises of burning towers and bloodstained earth.

Tomorrow. I had tomorrow, and then we left for Illucia.

I knelt before my armoire, the egg cradled in my lap, my fingers skimming along the shell. Its soft humming gave me little comfort in the face of everything that stood before me.

Tomorrow.

Tomorrow was my mother's birthday. Or would have been. Now it was my last chance. There was no guarantee I could hatch the egg, so we couldn't risk denying Razel. But if I could figure out a way to hatch it before I left, I wouldn't be forced to leave tomorrow for Illucia, the spoils of a phantom war.

There had to be a way.

Tucking the egg away, I dressed in boots and a cloak before slipping out of my room. The hallways were quiet, the sona lamps burning low against the darkness. I plucked one carefully off the wall, holding it at arm's length as I traced my way to the nearest stairway leading to the upper levels. Moonlight poured in through massive windows, illuminating the stairwell and revealing dust and cobwebs thick as my hair.

I stepped out two floors up. The stone walls were bare, the hallways empty. Any art and furniture had been relocated to the bottom floors or sold. My footsteps echoed in the unfilled space, trailing me like ghosts. A shiver trickled down my spine, and I held the sona lamp higher.

It felt strange being in the upper levels again, and I made a point of walking more softly. Making noise felt wrong, like any sound might shake more than dust free from the walls. So many memories slept in these halls. I half expected to see shimmer-ences, the spirits that dwell in forgotten places, floating in the air in wisps of silvery smoke.

The upstairs library was at the end of the corridor. Perhaps the downstairs one hadn't had the books I'd needed because they wouldn't have been moved down there. They'd have been left to gather dust in the hopes they could be forgotten.

I pushed open one tall oak door, the image of a crow carved into the wood. The sound echoed in the high-ceilinged library, and I paused in the doorway. Rows of half-empty shelves spread out before me like a sea of tombstones. Several long tables sat near the back of the room, only visible by the beams of moon-light trickling in from the tall, narrow windows.

I stepped forward, turning up the gas on my lamp, and began to search.

Nearly half an hour later, I had a sizeable stack of books set on one of the back tables, my sona lamp casting a warm orange glow across the page of a tome spread open before me. I'd searched for anything to do with the crows, focusing mainly on instructional texts. I'd even found several with chapters about hatching, but each of them skipped over the details of the actual process, and nothing hinted at why they hatched simultaneously.

Hours later, my eyes strained in the darkness, and a throbbing pain gathered behind one temple. Each useless book was like a nail in my coffin.

Sliding another failed book to the side, I reached for the last of my pile. It was thin, with a cover so worn that most of the title was illegible, only the word *Magic* decipherable on the faded leather. I'd expected it to be on the different types of crow abilities, but as I scanned the first page, I realized it wasn't a book at all but a journal written in a large, looping scrawl.

"Little is understood about how magic truly worked for the Sellas before their disappearance," I read quietly to myself. "But one aspect scholars agree on is the existence of magic lines, or hereditary magic. After thorough research, I believe these magic lines create a connection across generations, perhaps similar to the way a crow and a rider are linked. And like other traits vary among family, growing stronger or weaker along the line, so too can the magic line manifest differently, even among siblings."

I read faster, skimming through the journal beneath the fading glow of my lamp. It was short and half-finished, consisting mostly of Sella lore and history the author used to support their claims. If they were right, this might explain why riders typically came from the same families over the course of generations. Maybe whatever it was the crow latched on to was passed down from parent to child.

Could the way to hatch the crows be related to these lines somehow?

Footsteps echoed outside the library. Frowning, I doused my lamp and moved behind a nearby bookcase. The footsteps grew louder, and a light appeared down the center hall between the shelves. I peered around the edge.

Ericen stood in the doorway, glancing from bookcase to bookcase as if trying to decide where to start. I cursed silently. He was everywhere; I couldn't escape him. Surely, it would only be worse in Illucia. He was in my head, in my thoughts and my emotions. He'd burrowed underneath my skin with his vicious smiles and barbed, caustic words, and everywhere I went, there he was.

I stepped into the glow of his lamp. "Need help finding something?"

To his credit, he didn't jump. Only drew a sharp breath, the line of his jaw tightening. "Anthia. What are you doing up here?"

"That should be my question."

His eyes narrowed, and he turned back the way he'd come without a word. I hurried after him, pulling the library door shut in our wake.

"No witty comeback?" I asked. "No clever explanation?"

He kept walking. "I wanted something to read."

"There's a library downstairs."

"A small one."

I snorted. "I can't imagine what you'd be looking for that you'd just assume it wouldn't be there."

He didn't respond, and a chill trickled down my spine. I actually could imagine something. Information from a bygone time. The sort of thing left in a forgotten place.

I cut him off, forcing him to an abrupt halt. His blue eyes looked silver in the moonlight, the shadow of his broad frame stretching into infinity.

"How did you even know there was another library up here?" I asked.

"I suggest you move."

"I suggest you talk." I held his gaze unflinchingly. He stared back, his eyes searching mine. "What are you looking for?"

After a moment's pause, he said quietly, "I feel bad for you." I bristled reflexively, but he wasn't mocking me. His eyes had softened, his shoulders lowering. "You have no idea what's happening."

He didn't wait for a response before brushing past me. I let him go, unsettled and confused by the feeling writhing in my chest.

EIGHT

The next morning, I lingered in bed for several minutes,
a familiar heaviness weighing me down. I left for Illucia
tomorrow, and my books had yielded nothing definite. I left for
Illucia tomorrow, and I couldn't hatch the egg. I left for Illucia
tomorrow, and today was my mother's birthday.

Missing her was a dull ache, like a bruise in my chest that
throbbed anytime I remembered her.

Kiva had told me a thousand times it wasn't my fault, but
some days, I couldn't keep the regret at bay, couldn't stop the
heavy snake from slithering up my shoulders. I knew better than
to think I could have convinced my mother not to go after the
eggs, but I still wished I'd tried. Maybe she would have listened.
Maybe she'd still be alive.

I felt myself sinking. Felt the familiar weight pressing me

so deep inside myself, my body hardly felt like my own, until drawing air felt like breathing water, and I wondered what might happen if I simply stopped.

The door clicked open. I expected Kiva, so when I saw Caliza, her eyes red from tears and her cheeks flushed, I stared. She'd barely closed the door when I started crying. Fumbling with my sheets, I tumbled out of bed, meeting her halfway. Warm arms encircled me, and I buried my face in Caliza's chest as she pulled me close, each of us seeking the others strength. My knees wobbled, but she held me up until I was able to find the will to stand on my own. Several minutes passed before I drew back.

"I don't know how to hatch the egg. I leave for Illucia tomorrow, and Mother is—" I squeezed my eyes shut, unable to finish the sentence.

Caliza released a quiet breath before leading me to my reading chair by the window. I collapsed into it, drawing my knees to my chest and wrapping my arms around them. She sat down across from me on the ottoman, a hand on my arm, squeezing tight. We stayed there for what felt like hours, and the familiar snake curled around my shoulders.

"Get that look off your face."

I almost jumped at the sharpness in Caliza's voice. "What?"

"I know that look. You've had it almost every day since Ronoch. It's the look you get when you've given up."

I turned away. Guilt gnawed at my insides, even as the quiet voice in my head promised this was for the best. Giving up was easier. It was better not to try, not to care.

"Thia." The forcefulness of Caliza's voice pulled my gaze.

"What else am I supposed to do? There's nothing in the library, no one else to ask. There's nothing left!"

"There's you."

My jaw clenched. "Like I said. Nothing."

"If Ericen said that to you, you'd punch him in the face, and rightfully so. It's a lie."

"Maybe it's not. If I can't hatch the egg, then what use am I?"

Caliza shifted in her seat, facing me. "Do you know why I wanted the crows to accept me so badly?" I shook my head, and she continued, "Because I was jealous of you."

I laughed, but her face remained impassive. "I'm serious, Thia. I was jealous of the future you had waiting for you. A life of magic and flight, respect and strength. While you prepared to harness an ancient power, I prepared to shackle myself to a life of politics and planning. Don't get me wrong," she said quickly when I started to protest. "This is what I wanted. But it's not quite so impressive as soaring hundreds of feet in the air on the back of a legendary beast."

"It's pretty damn impressive to me," I muttered.

She smiled softly. "Those reasons could have made me jealous of any rider, but I wasn't. It was only you. Because I, like everyone, knew what you were."

"A delinquent?"

"A storm." She locked gazes with me. "A tempest of lightning and thunder with the kind of heart found only in legends. A heart full of kindness and courage and strength. And when I looked at you, I saw only the woman you would become. The leader you would become."

She took my hand, holding tight. "Don't let Razel win. Don't let her silence the storm inside you. I might be queen, but you were meant to be so much more. Crow or no crow, one way or another, you will fly. You were always meant to rule the sky."

I stared at her, my hand holding so tightly to hers, it had gone numb. When she spoke, it was so easy to see what she saw. To see the future I could have had, the leader I could have been, and how I'd let it slip away, day by day, sinking deeper and deeper into oblivion.

Don't let Razel win. Don't let her silence the storm inside you.

I swallowed hard, closing my eyes until the burning behind them stopped. Then I drew a long, slow breath and let it out. When I opened my eyes, fire burned through every inch of me, and yet I felt strangely calm.

"You're right." A smile tugged at my lips.

She smiled back. "I usually am."

My hunt for Kiva ended in the hall outside Caliza's office. She had stopped abruptly, hand clapping against her hip where her sword should have been. She'd forgotten it.

Kiva never forgot her sword.

That's enough. Before she could fully turn around, I tackled her through the open door of a nearby empty sitting room. She stumbled but kept her feet.

"I can usually hear you coming," she said with a frown.

I took in her sloppy braid, her rumpled uniform, and the

spot where her sword should hang, its absence so notable, the emptiness felt like a void. This wasn't Kiva; it was an imposter hiding in her skin, like the creatures from Sella stories that were no longer told.

Catching on to my intentions, Kiva tried to slip away. I blocked the door, arms folded. I'd waited long enough.

"Talk," I ordered.

"I have nothing to say."

"And crows can't fly. Come on, Kiva. Something's eating away at you." Literally, judging by the growing shadows beneath her eyes. I unfolded my arms, stepping toward her. She recoiled, and the space between us stretched. Every inch felt like a talon in my chest. I never should have waited.

"What happened that day?" I asked softly. "Please, Kiva. Let me help you."

She held my gaze, unblinking, her silence trapping my breath in my throat. Then finally, she blurted out, "The man I fought is dead."

"What?"

"He didn't escape." Her voice broke. "I killed him."

I stared at her. Repeating the words in my head, I tried to force them into making sense. Though Kiva had been a member of the guard for several years before Ronoch, she'd never seriously hurt someone before. Never killed. Until now.

For me.

"You saved my life." My voice came out hoarse. "Those men tried to kill me, and you saved me."

Her hands curled into fists. "It's not—I don't feel—" She turned, toppling a nearby chair with a swift kick. "How in the Saints' name am I supposed to protect you, to become captain, if I can't handle killing *one man?*" She sent another chair skidding across the floor. "I felt sick for hours afterward! I still do. I feel like a mess."

"You look like one too." I tucked the escaped hairs from her braid behind her ear. If only I could fix the damage inside as easily. Kiva always knew what to say to me; all I wanted was to do the same for her.

I tried to smile. "There's nothing wrong with that though."

"Nothing wrong? I can't implode every time I kill someone!"

"I didn't realize you planned on doing it often."

"I'm not! But if I need to..." She trailed off, shaking her head.

I set the chairs back on their feet and settled into one, patting the seat of the other. Kiva dropped into it, pressing her head into her hand, messy blond hair tumbling into her fingers.

When I was upset, I needed Kiva to shake me out of it, to break my pattern. On the much rarer occasion that she needed me, I had to take a different approach.

"If we'd had this conversation a few days ago, I'd have said you were worrying about something you shouldn't," I began slowly. "But now, there's a real possibility our lives will be in danger again, and maybe it'll come down to you or someone else. And that's not your fault."

Kiva had probably thought these things herself, but words could be so much more powerful coming from someone else. I'd told myself a thousand times to get out of bed after Ronoch, but without Kiva's help, I might never have.

"Your guilt is a good thing," I said. "If you ever don't feel it, that's when you should worry. But you can't let it destroy you. You've worked too hard to get where you are, and I need you there too much. That day proved it. I needed you to protect me, and I'll need you more than ever in the next few weeks."

The truth of my words settled in my chest like leaves fluttering to the earth. I couldn't do this without Kiva. "You're more than my friend, Kiva. You're my family. And whenever you need me, I'll be there, and, if worst comes to worst, you can repeat all this nonsense back to me, and maybe we'll be okay."

She held my gaze like a lifeline, the pain behind her eyes fading. Then slowly, she leaned forward. I caught her in my arms, holding tight. We were like children again, Kiva seeking refuge from her mother's critical gaze. She didn't cry; she never did. She just stayed in my arms until she didn't need to anymore, then I helped her fix her braid and smooth out her clothes, and we left the room together.

I paused a step away, the implication of my own words catching up to me. I'd said I would need her in the next few weeks, but... Drawing a deep breath, I said, "I leave for Illucia tomorrow."

"You mean we leave tomorrow." She didn't even blink.

"We?"

She smirked. "Yes, we."

Something loosened in my chest, and I let out a breath. I hadn't asked Kiva to come, afraid if I did, she'd say no. She had a life here, a career, a dream—I knew what it was to lose those things.

Still, I should have known better than to think she'd choose them over me.

"Do you know where your mother is?" I asked. "I've been thinking, and I have an idea."

It was time I stopped living in the past and started preparing for the future.

A few minutes later, everyone I'd asked for was gathered in Caliza's office. Kiva leaned against the wall beside the desk, Caliza behind it with Captain Mirkova a rigid force at her side. In one of the chairs across from them, Lady Kerova, head of House Kerova, sat poised like a swift bird, her hands folded in her lap. Tama, delicate tattoos of the Jin guilds, curled up her neck and along her jaw in red and gold ink that shifted when she smiled.

I hadn't stood face-to-face with one of the house leaders in weeks. Seeing her, memories flashed: her gentle smile whenever I tried and failed to sneak up on her, she and Estrel playing games of dice at the patio table late into the night, her shadow crow materializing suddenly from the darkness to startle me in an endless game, Caliza peering at her around corners, her childhood crush obvious to everyone except her.

Next to Estrel, she'd been my mother's most trusted friend, as well as her war advisor.

I didn't sit. The last few days had awoken something inside me once smothered by ash and grief, and a wild energy coursed through me.

"I have an idea," I began. "And it's a little absurd."

Four pairs of eyes rested on me, and for the first time in a long time, I felt what Caliza had been talking about that morning. I felt the storm in my veins.

"I want to ally with the other kingdoms against Illucia." I looked at each of them in turn.

Caliza and Captain Mirkova exchanged looks. Lady Kerova's expression remained serene as ever.

Kiva grinned. "I like it, but there's no chance Korovi will help. They've got their heads too far up their—"

"Sakiva!" Captain Mirkova hissed.

Kiva scowled. "What? Am I wrong?" she asked.

The captain looked as if someone had carved her from stone. Arms crossed, jaw set, every muscle honed by years of training drawn taut.

"They won't give a damn about another kingdom," Kiva spat. "They don't even care about their own people."

Captain Mirkova said something low and furious to Kiva in Korovi, and Kiva shot something twice as hot back, leaving both women red-faced and white-knuckled.

"It's worth a try," I pressed, my tone turning desperate. "Snow and mountains won't keep them safe from Razel forever."

Captain Mirkova quickly regained her composure, leaving her daughter fuming silently. She regarded me with pale eyes, considering.

"It's an interesting idea," Lady Kerova said in her silken voice. "Something I once considered. But Jindae and the Ambriels have been beaten down and torn apart. What remains of them likely resents Rhodaire for not aiding them when they needed us most. Their faith in us is broken."

I hadn't thought of that. Jindae had been our allies for years, stretching back to the war with Illucia that killed my father before I was born. It seemed like the natural conclusion for us to work together.

"So we restore it," I said, meeting Caliza's gaze. She nodded, and I looked from Captain Mirkova to Lady Kerova. "I found a storm crow egg."

Lady Kerova drew a sharp breath, and Captain Mirkova's eyes widened.

"Do you know how to hatch it?" Lady Kerova asked.

"Not yet, but I'll figure it out," I said.

"And you think this will be enough to mend these broken relationships?" Captain Mirkova asked.

I lifted my head. "Even our own people practically worshipped the crows as gods. They believed in their power the same way they believed in the Saints. To the other kingdoms, they're legends."

"Legends that left them to die," Lady Kerova said softly. There was something tight in her voice, like an old memory lodged in her throat. Her mother was Jin. Had she wanted to send aid when they were attacked?

"But they still believe in their power," I said. "I believe in their power. A storm crow can rain lightning down on an army or hail bigger than my fists. It can change a field to mud, turning soldiers into archery practice. But more than magic, a crow could be a symbol. A symbol that Rhodaire has not given up, and neither should they. A symbol we can rally around."

A soft smile turned Lady Kerova's lips. "You remind me very much of your mother when she was young."

I straightened beneath her gaze, her words weaving a complex web of emotions inside me I couldn't begin to decipher. "Kiva and I think the Jin princess survived Razel's massacre and is leading her people. Can you find out?"

Lady Kerova nodded. "I will reach out to my family in Jindae. Some are involved with the rebels."

"Trendell may be willing," Caliza said. "I wrote Kuren about the egg yesterday."

I looked to Captain Mirkova, Kiva staring at her as if trying to pierce a snowstorm.

"I will go to Korovi," the captain said, her words hewn of ice. They left me wondering what I'd just asked of her.

"What about the Ambriels?" Kiva asked.

"They are not worth it," Captain Mirkova replied.

Caliza nodded. "Even before Illucia attacked, they were highly dependent on the empire and already had a strong relationship. What remains of their high council is corrupt and loyal to Razel."

"My shadows have heard whispers of Ambriellan rebels," Lady Kerova said. "Masked riders in the Verian Hills on Illucia's coast who have been disrupting shipments of goods from the islands."

"Could you send someone to get in contact with them?" I asked.

She nodded.

"Then do it. Tell them I want to set up a meeting."

Caliza straightened. "That's not safe. Forget whether these people are trustworthy or not; if Razel caught you…" She trailed off.

The back of my neck prickled, but I didn't give the fear purchase. "I won't waste any more time, Caliza, and I won't hide while other people fight for my kingdom. I'm doing this, no matter the risk."

She didn't argue. Out of the corner of my eye, Kiva grinned at me.

"You should release the Jin prisoner in your dungeons to my custody," Lady Kerova said. "I will take him with me to Jindae as a show of good faith."

"What about the prince?" Captain Mirkova asked. "If he discovers the prisoner is gone or who he left with, it will raise suspicions."

"Then we convince him the prisoner is dead," Caliza suggested.

"He won't believe we executed him without a trial," I said.

"Then we convince him he took his own life to protect his people's secrets," Lady Kerova said. "Leave it to me. I've had a shadow on him since he arrived who can feed him false information." As leader of the Kerova Wing, she commanded the division of our army responsible for spies. Even without their crows, her shadows were still unsurpassed.

"Has your shadow learned anything about the prince?" I asked. "I caught him snooping about the castle halls last night."

Lady Kerova's face darkened, a disquieting look on her normally serene features. "The prince has proven himself difficult to follow. My shadow has lost him twice already."

Kiva frowned. "Shadows don't lose their marks."

"It would appear the prince is skilled in disappearing," Lady Kerova replied. "His shadow is still unsure how he managed it."

Another thing about Ericen that didn't make sense. It was about time I learned a little more about him, and our weeklong journey to Illucia would be the perfect chance.

We finished discussing some of the specifics of our plan, including the passwords Lady Kerova's shadows would use to identify themselves. The swift messenger birds they raised and trained would be our main source of communication, our letters containing benign conversation on one side and true messages hidden in invisible ink on the back, only to be revealed by firelight once the ink was coated in a special black powder.

There was one topic I'd selfishly avoided addressing so far. Taking a breath, I asked, "What do we do with the egg?"

Caliza frowned. "I'd assumed you were taking it."

"Into Illucia?" Captain Mirkova asked, saying exactly what I'd feared someone would. It didn't make sense for me to take the egg, not when I didn't have any idea how to hatch it.

"We may not have a choice," Lady Kerova said. "I may not have been privy to the secrets of crow hatching, but I believe it is something only the royal family can do. Why else would we bring all the eggs to the royal rookery, where often the current king or queen is the only one present when they hatch?"

Jittery anticipation filled my veins. This sounded like what I'd read about magic lines in that dusty journal. If only the royal family could hatch the crows, then it had to be me or Caliza.

My hope dwindled. "So then the egg stays with Caliza."

Caliza snorted. "I wouldn't know the first thing to do with it, let alone if I actually managed to hatch it. It's a risk sending the egg with you, but if only one of us can hatch it, we have a much better chance if the one trying is you."

The others nodded, and relief swept through me. "And what if I figure it out? I'll need a way out of Illucia."

"Part of this plan relies on you finding a way to obtain some level of autonomy," Caliza replied. "If you can't, there will be no meeting with Ambriellan rebels or even much room for working on the egg. But if you can get it, we can get a ship into Port Maranock just outside Sordell to bring you home."

And if I couldn't, then I might be stuck in Illucia permanently. For a moment, I let the implication settle. Drawing a deep breath, I said, "If the other kingdoms ally with us and I can't escape, Razel will use me against you."

Kiva stiffened, her hand going to her sword as if to battle the words. She would fight with me if that happened, and the thought eased the twinge of uncertainty in my chest. We would fight together, as we always did.

I locked eyes with Caliza, steel meeting steel. "If that happens, I want you to do it anyway."

My words settled across the room like feathers drifting down from the sky. What had started as my selfish desire not to marry Ericen had turned into a volcano waiting to explode into all-out war.

Caliza nodded. "I understand."

Either the remaining kingdoms banded together against the empire, or we all crumbled beneath it.

NINE

I waited on the patio for dinner that night, my mind so packed with the day's revelations, I almost missed the harsh whispers coming from the hall. Recognizing Ericen's voice, I rose and slipped to the door, pressing against the wall to listen.

"I don't really give a damn what you think," Ericen growled.

A shiver prickled at the back of my neck at the low, primal danger lurking in his voice.

"You have orders," replied a voice laced with disgust. "Even you wouldn't disobey your queen and Valix."

"Watch yourself, soldier."

The other man snorted harshly. "Engaged to a Rhodairen, rejected by your own mother, distraught over the death of a worthless Jin. I'll speak as I wish, Princeling."

There was a sharp crash and a grunt of pain. Before I could

move, Ericen rounded the corner. I froze. His broad shoulders filled the doorway, blocking the firelight from behind and casting him in shadow. He stared down at me, the sharp cut of his icy eyes softening with surprise. I'd barely registered any of it before he regained himself and swept past me to the table.

Inside, his guard clambered to his feet, holding a bloody and likely broken nose. He glared furiously before retreating into the castle.

I sat down at the table. Ericen still didn't speak. Even as the food arrived and we filled our plates with roast chicken and vegetables, he remained subdued. I kept catching him staring into the distance or sometimes at me. Every time, he made a point of smirking before focusing on his food, which he pushed around his plate.

Engaged to a Rhodairen, rejected by your mother, distraught over a Jin...

It seemed Ericen had taken Lady Kerova's bait. But to be bothered by it?

"Find anything interesting in the library last night?" he asked suddenly. "Or were you just reading for nostalgia?"

I eyed the prince, trying to fake indifference even as my heart raced. I'd forgotten to put the books back. Did he suspect what I'd been looking for? "This again?" I asked. "You're awfully interested in my life."

"Shouldn't I be interested in my future wife?"

I snorted. "I give you full permission to ignore me. Besides, this game is getting old. So why don't we skip the part where you try to use my past to hurt me?"

Ericen started to respond, then stopped, eyes narrowing. He went back to pushing his food around, hand tight around the fork as if it were a weapon. The silence stretched. He looked like he was trying to work himself up to something, to make a decision.

To follow orders? I frowned. Illucians didn't disobey orders.

Ericen set his fork down. "It's too bad the man who attacked you died before revealing who sent him." His voice was low, his words tight. The emotion had drained from his face, leaving him eerily calm. It looked wrong. "Apparently, your people are just inept at keeping things alive. It's lucky for you my mother's been gracious enough to offer this alliance. You should be more grateful."

My hand tightened around my knife.

He shrugged nonchalantly. "Oh well. One less rebel in the world."

"You're a bastard," I said.

Ericen stared at me, lips parted, before they slowly formed a smile. "You Rhodairens are very blunt."

"No. You Illucians are just conniving monsters."

His smile widened. "True."

I blinked. Surely, I hadn't heard what I thought.

The prince leaned back, an arm over the back of his chair, and met my gaze without wavering. "Maybe I'm not half as bad as you think, Princess."

Was this another part of his game? He looked and sounded so genuine. No cruel smile, no frost to his gaze. He said it simply, matter-of-factly, and yet I still couldn't believe him.

This was the man who'd threatened to have his army attack to prove a point.

"You're not what I expected," he added quietly. In the dim light, he looked haunted, his muscles tight and eyes soft and full of exhaustion. For half a breath, I saw someone else entirely.

Then, as if suddenly remembering himself, his eyes glazed over, and his smirk returned, that other person vanishing like a phantom in the night. "But I suppose you're not half of what you once were," he mused.

I shook away the image I'd had of him, focusing instead on the sharp lines and lupine features of the warrior before me. How could I ever have seen anything else? "At least my soldiers treat me with more respect than a pile of feathers, *Princeling*," I said.

He stiffened. "Do they? What about your people? I imagine they'd take issue with a princess who turned her back on them."

I scowled, but his words settled deep. I stood, picking up my plate. "You can eat alone."

I finished dinner in my room with Kiva, where I relayed my conversation with Ericen. We'd cracked open the windows, letting in fresh evening air sweetened by the scent of fruit trees, and I'd piled my pillows at the end of the bed and plopped down. She sat on the floor, her sword in her lap.

"I think you're imagining things," she said when I mentioned how difficult it had seemed for him to talk tonight. As if he hadn't wanted to say those things.

"Maybe." I rolled onto my stomach to face her, releasing a breath. "I can't believe this is happening."

"It was inevitable. The world is reaching a breaking point." She pulled her sword from its sheath, the black gold rippling like molten night. The tension that had seemed permanently ingrained in her face earlier that day had subsided. The dark circles under her eyes remained, but she looked better.

She met my gaze, her pale eyes soft. She knew what I was thinking; she always did. "In Korovi," she said quietly, "my first kill would have been celebrated. In Miska warrior tradition, I would have a ceremony, and the sword that spilled my enemy's blood would be named."

I stayed perfectly still. Kiva rarely talked about Korovi. All I knew was her mother had been forced to leave while pregnant with her, shamed by scandal for breaking their most sacred laws. Which was probably why the captain had looked like she'd rather walk barefoot on glass than return to Korovi for aid.

Kiva ran a cloth along the length of black gold. "A Miska warrior of my age without a named sword would be a disgrace." Her lips twitched into a small smile. "Of course, I'm already a disgrace, and in Korovi, I'd never have been a Miska warrior."

The Mirkova line was an ancient one, a powerful one. Kiva's grandmother practically ruled the snow kingdom, and as a noble, Captain Mirkova was forbidden to marry. Believed to be daughters of the goddess, Lokane, noble women in Korovi had children by chosen suitors outside of marriage, then devoted their lives to the goddess as priestesses or leaders in the government.

The two roles were so intertwined, it was nearly impossible to tell where one began and the other ended.

As a noble, Kiva would never have been allowed to join the Miska, a unit of all-female warriors known for their unparalleled swordsmanship.

I sat up, asking carefully, "All this because your mother married?"

Kiva snorted. "All this because she married a Northman from beyond the Cut, and for barely a day."

"Before they forced her to leave?"

"Before they killed him."

I recoiled. "You've never told me this."

"It's not really mine to tell," she said softly. "But I think I needed to."

Sliding off the bed, I came to sit cross-legged before her. Her sword lay between us, a ripple of night against my bright carpet.

"We can name it?" I suggested. "Not for the reasons they would, but in spite of them. Maybe something from the old language. Don't the Northmen still speak it?"

She nodded, the shadows in her eyes receding. "My mother tried to teach me. I don't know much." Her brow furrowed before a grin spread across her lips.

"I'll name it Sinvarra." The old-language word was like a growl in her throat. "It means *spite*."

TEN

C aliza had organized most of my packing. She'd even super-
vised the removal of clothes from my closet, ensuring no
one so much as touched the armoire drawer hiding the egg. The
morning of my departure, all I had to do was wrap the egg in as
many blankets as I could find and settle it gently into a trunk.

The idea of taking it on such a long journey, deep into
enemy territory, made my stomach turn. But Caliza had been
right. I was our best bet.

I folded my flying leathers on top and added my black
gold bow, then used a couple of pillows to prevent the egg
from rolling around. Then I locked it and didn't let the servants carry it out until they'd sworn to do so with the utmost
care. I still ended up following them down to the courtyard to
watch them load it.

When they were done, I started back to my room to do a last check for belongings to take with me, my mind lost in daydreams of hatching the crow, of feeling the wind against my skin again and the endless strength of a crow beneath me.

I almost walked straight into Ericen. He caught me, and I reeled back from his touch. He grinned. "Where are you coming from in such a state? You're practically glowing."

I tried to step past him, but he wouldn't let me. Scowling, I stepped back. "What, Ericen?"

"You know, that's the first time you've addressed me by name."

"Is there a point to this? Because I have things to do."

His smile faded, as if my abruptness had bothered him. "We're going to be traveling together for nearly a week. And if you haven't forgotten, we're engaged." It took effort not to cringe at those words. "I thought you and I should...I don't know. Start over."

"Start over?" I laughed. "Is this a joke or just more of your games?"

"Neither. I mean it. I'm not what you think. What would I get out of lying to you?"

"The usual sick pleasure."

He sighed, moving out of my way. "Just think about it, please. It'd certainly make traveling a lot better."

I stalked past him, keeping my expression neutral though my mind was a maelstrom of thoughts. Flustered by the conversation, nervous about leaving, anxious about the egg, I felt like a storm readying to break. I needed air.

Diverting from the stairs, I walked quickly down the hall and out through a side door that opened onto the south grounds.

Crisp morning air cooled the fire in my veins, but it couldn't settle the turbulence gathering inside me.

One moment, Ericen dug so far under my skin I wanted to pummel him, and the next, he acted like he'd been misunderstood. I hated these games, the deception and confusion. I wanted straightforward. I wanted clear lines and paths that didn't split.

I followed a winding dirt path through the gardens to the royal graveyard. A black metal fence surrounded dark stone mausoleums spread across thick grass, and I had to navigate to their center to find the simple grave my mother had requested. A small crow statue perched on the tombstone with wings spread, fallen leaves scattered across the grave.

For several minutes, I simply stared at the grave, breathing in the crisp morning air. I never knew what to say to my mother. In my memories, she was always turning away from me, always sweeping into another room when I was nearby, quick to put a solid door between us. Even in death, anything I could say, anything I could do, felt inadequate. Always inadequate—it was practically my motto.

"I hope you know what a mess you've left us in." My hands curled into fists at my sides. "You should have told me. You should have trusted me. Now I have a chance to save Rhodaire, but I don't know how, all because you had to do everything yourself."

My throat tightened, but the words pushed through. "You never should have gone into that damn rookery!"

A nearby tree shook as a startled bird took flight. Leaves dislodged by its sudden movement fluttered through the air and resounding silence, settling on the grave. Something shifted inside me, like a rope given slack after an age of being pulled too tight.

"All this is because of you," I whispered to the silence, to the earth, to the gravestone. To the memory that slept underneath. "And now you're not even here to help us."

My mother and I may not have been close, but in a way, she'd held us all together, held our kingdom together. Her death had splintered mine and Caliza's relationship, sent me spiraling down inside myself, and set our kingdom unraveling.

Her legacy haunted us all, casting a shadow I couldn't outrun. Even in Illucia, people had known her name, affording her a grudging respect even as they cursed her. They'd called her Crow Queen.

My fists closed tighter. Caliza had tried to be our mother and failed. I had failed too. We would always fail, and maybe that was for the best. We didn't need to be her. *I* didn't need to be her.

I needed to be better.

"Goodbye, Mother." I set my hand on the tombstone.

A vibration like an earthquake shot up my arm. I tried to pull away, but my hand wouldn't move. Voices in a foreign language echoed in my head, flashes of trees and silver eyes swirling in my vision. Then everything shifted violently. I smelled the warmth and hay of a rookery, felt the heat of flames, saw Illucian soldiers dying all around me—then a man with eyes like golden fire.

In an instant, it was over. My hand came off the tombstone, and I stumbled to the side, breathing hard.

I bolted for the castle, trying and failing to process what

had happened. Had I hallucinated? The stress and nerves were finally getting to me. I was cracking.

I sprinted inside, up the stairs, and into my bedroom, slamming the door behind me and falling back against it. It took several minutes before my breathing and racing heart even began to calm.

"Nothing happened," I whispered to myself. "You're fine. Nothing happened."

Except my fingers still tingled from the touch. And the vibration… It had felt familiar, like a massive jolt of the feeling I got when I touched the egg. Magic?

The door shook, and I yelped, leaping off it and whirling around. It clicked open, revealing a bemused and uncertain Kiva. She raised an eyebrow, but I shook my head.

"It's time," she said.

Ericen's carriage looked overloaded with both our belongings, and we ended up hitching a wagon to a couple of horses to lighten the load. Then suddenly, everything was ready. Ericen had already climbed inside, a package tucked under one arm.

"Are you sure you don't want your own carriage?" Caliza asked, worrying at a few strands of hair with one hand.

I shook my head. "I have to learn to deal with him. Besides, the better I know him, the better off I'll be. Whether that means outsmarting him or having one Illucian in that damned kingdom who doesn't want to stab me in the back."

She didn't look convinced.

"I'll be fine," I assured her. "For all your worrying, you forget I'm a trained rider. Crow or not, I can still kick someone's ass."

She flashed a brief smile that turned into a grimace. "I just hope you don't have to."

I dropped my voice. "I won't stop trying to hatch the egg. We'll find a way to win the other kingdoms' support. This isn't over."

She flung her arms around me, hugging tighter than ever before. I returned the embrace, trying to memorize the way it felt. If things didn't go as planned, it may be a while before I hugged my sister again.

"Keep your head down," she whispered. "I know it'll be hard, but don't give Razel a reason to pay attention to you. Don't make her angry. She can be…unpredictable."

I nodded but didn't let go. Maybe if I never did, the world would just pause. I wouldn't have to go. Rhodaire would be okay.

Caliza squeezed tighter, and finally, we pulled apart. She smiled, and I returned it. "Here." I undid the clasp of Estrel's bracelet, then wrapped it around her thin wrist. Her breath caught as I secured it.

"Keep this safe for me," I said. "I'll be back for it."

Caliza's jaw set, and she nodded. I stepped reluctantly away.

Kiva made a mock grand gesture toward the open carriage door from where she sat on a dappled mare. "Your handsome prince awaits you." Though she smiled, I could see the tightness in it, the pain behind her eyes. This was difficult for her too. She was losing everything.

I pretended to gag, eliciting a laugh, but she wasn't wrong.

With a final wave to Caliza, I climbed inside, and a servant shut the door, silencing the outside noises.

The sudden quiet was deafening. It pressed in on me like a flood, and I imagined myself throwing open the carriage door and leaping out. I didn't want to do this. I didn't want to leave. I wanted to curl up in my bed under the covers and—*no. I'm doing this.* This was my opportunity to help my people, my friends, and my family. To help myself.

The carriage set off, passing through the castle gates. The hum of voices changed. Conversation turned to shouting. My jaw set—protests had been growing in the streets. The news of the engagement had spread, and people weren't happy. Caliza would be hearing from the house lords and ladies before morning.

People would think she'd cracked under pressure, that she'd forgotten the past too easily. Caliza would suffer the whispers, the mistrustful glares, because she could and because it kept our people safe from the knowledge of how close we'd come to war.

Swallowing hard, I faced Ericen and found him watching me intently.

"I have a present for you." He offered me the package that had been under his arm.

Eying him skeptically, I took it, removing the ribbon and pulling off the lid. The scent of orange flooded the carriage in a flurry of powdered sugar. He'd gotten me a box of orange cakes from the House Cyro cart at the canal.

I stared at the cakes, then at him, entirely caught off guard. "What game are you playing?"

"No game. Can't a man buy his fiancée a present?"

"A man, yes. A cold-blooded snake, not so much."

He laughed, the sound like needles of ice prickling my skin. "And here I was trying to be nice. I can do that on occasion, you know."

I closed the box and set it aside. "Are you saying you're not normally a prick?"

"Oh no, I am. Just usually a more charming one."

I snorted. "If by charming, you mean arrogant."

"If by arrogant, you mean extremely capable, then yes, we agree."

I stared flatly at him. "Is this your attempt at a truce? Because you're failing miserably."

He smiled back, draping himself along the bench like a sunning cat. "Do you hate me because I'm Illucian?"

"I hate you for a lot of reasons."

His lips twitched. "Fair enough, but perhaps I'm not so bad as you think."

"You're right," I replied. "You're worse."

"Come now, Princess. I was just having a little fun." He leaned forward, his pale gaze trapping me like a specimen for study in a glass case. "What better way to learn about my fiancée than to push you to the edge and see how you reacted?" His voice turned teasing. "People are their truest selves at their most desperate."

My face flushed with heat. "My truest self wants to throw you out of this carriage and let the horses trample you."

He laughed, sprawling back in his seat once more. "Part of

you likes this game as much as I do, or you wouldn't be so quick to play it with me."

"This isn't a game!" I snapped. It was so much more than that, not that he cared.

The amusement in Ericen's face faltered. If I didn't know better, I'd have thought he looked confused. As if he hadn't expected me to get genuinely angry.

He held up his hands in mock surrender. "This was meant to be a peace offering. Clearly, I've handled it miserably. The last thing I want is for you to hate me. We are, after all, engaged."

Engaged. The word settled around my shoulders like a scarf, one twist away from strangling me.

"What do you want?" I asked.

He shrugged nonchalantly. "To start over."

I didn't know how to respond. This had to be part of his game. Maybe he'd seen he couldn't break me, so now he wanted to manipulate me. I met his gaze, reading the sincerity behind it. It meant nothing. A day ago, he'd been equally as convincing in his malice.

He let the conversation drop after that, and I was grateful. I didn't know how to react to this strange attempt at civility. *Liar,* my instincts screamed. *Murderer. Illucian.* But my curiosity demanded I see everything. His smile, his wonder at the crows, his guard mocking him for being distraught over the Jin man's fake death.

It's all a game to him, I reminded myself. Those moments had been like everything else about him: carefully calculated to elicit a specific response. Whatever reason he had for playing nice—well, his approximation of nice—it was for his own gain and nothing more. Anyone who could shift through emotions like masks couldn't be trusted.

And soon, I'd be surrounded by an entire kingdom just like him.

The days passed quickly, during which Ericen and my conversations remained mostly limited to bouts of verbal sparring. He couldn't seem to resist the urge to dig his claws under my skin, but it was different than before. His words were playful and teasing, not the vicious cuts he'd inflicted in Rhodaire. Part of me reveled in the challenge.

In moments of silence, I planned. My first goal in Illucia would be to secure some measure of autonomy. I would need a hobby or a friend, something no one would question when I left the castle.

We camped rather than stop in towns for lodging, and I noticed that though Ericen sat with his men, he rarely spoke to them. In the free hours before and after dinner, Kiva and I would slip away to train. A short run followed by sparring and weapons training that made my body ache.

It'd been too long since I'd exercised, too long since I'd held my bow in my hands. Each maneuver and shot, technique and drill, threatened to make me think of Estrel. My wrist felt empty without her bracelet, but I sealed the memories away and pushed harder. In a kingdom of bloodthirsty soldiers, I had to be able to defend myself.

On the fourth day, we reached the border.

I heard the army before I saw it. Voices echoed across the camp, intermixing with the whinny of horses and the clatter of metal. My nails dug into my palms, and I forced my hands to relax. Ericen claimed we were only going to stop for fresh horses, but even a breath was too long a time spent surrounded by banners of blue and gold.

Don't look out the window.

Calls went up as the carriage broke through the first line of tents. I could feel Ericen's eyes on me. My own bore into the corner of the carriage, colors flashing at the edges of my vision as the camp flew by.

"We'll be quick," he said.

My gaze slid to meet his. "Why hasn't the army pulled back?"

"My mother has ordered it to remain until the marriage is official."

Heat pooled in my stomach. "If they touch a single Rhodairen—"

"I have no doubt you'd happily gut us all. Don't worry. Their orders are very clear, and they will obey them." He paused, then added softly, "So long as things continue as planned."

It wasn't a threat but a warning. Razel wouldn't hesitate to use this army to ensure her plans weren't disrupted.

The carriage slowed, and despite myself, I glanced out the window. The rows of blue-and-gold tents were endless, an ocean of vicious weeds.

My skin prickled. This was only half Razel's army?

When Ericen didn't move, I turned back to him. "Not going to visit with your soldiers?"

"Like I said. This will be quick." His voice was low and sharp.

Sure enough, the horses were exchanged without much fanfare, and with a few final hollers between soldiers, we set off again. I stared out the window, the army passing in a blur of horses and blue.

So close. They were so close to Rhodaire, and there was so little we could do against them. Without the crow, without the aid of the other kingdoms, these soldiers would destroy us.

The air grew colder as we journeyed farther north, the nights even more so, until I had to sleep in sweaters or inside the carriage to keep warm.

"Why don't you sleep by the fire?" Ericen asked me one day in the carriage.

"Why don't you talk to your soldiers every night?" I returned.

We both fell silent after that.

The next night, I retreated to the carriage after dinner. Kiva came with me, though the seats were too short for her to lie across comfortably. The days of travel made sleep come easily, and I'd nearly drifted off when I felt it. A prickle at the back of my neck. A warning. Did the carriage feel warmer? My half-asleep brain fought to process the sense of heat building near my head.

My eyes flashed open. Orange coated the inside of the carriage, flames dancing in the windows.

The carriage shook, and my heart quaked along with it as I scrambled to sit up, to understand.

The carriage was on fire.

Move! The word ripped through my mind, but my body refused. In the firelight, I saw embers falling from the sky like rain. I felt ash coating my skin, my nose, my throat. I heard myself screaming.

The memories clung to me like smoke, refusing to let me breathe.

Kiva rolled to a crouch on the floor, seizing Sinvarra. People shouted, one voice above the rest. A familiar voice.

The fire vanished.

I sucked in a ragged breath, the sudden darkness startling me. My gaze stayed fixed on the nearest window, the afterimage of flames a vicious sunset every time I blinked. How could the fire just disappear?

I felt myself trembling as Kiva threw open the door and leapt out. I hesitated, afraid for one senseless moment the fire would reappear to claim me. Then Ericen yelled. The carriage shook again. I sprang through the door, landing unsteadily on my feet. Kiva seized my arm, holding me upright, and I nearly collapsed against her, relishing the bite of the cold, fresh air.

Ericen had one of his guards up against the carriage, one of the man's hands pinned to the side, where it clutched an extinguished torch. Two other guards lay groaning on the ground, torches at their sides. Slowly, the scene came together.

The carriage had never been on fire. It'd been a trick. A cruel prank.

Fury twisted through my veins, disconnecting me from myself. It chased away the pain and the fear and the guilt that threatened to swallow me whole until my insides burned hotter than any fire. Distantly, I was aware of my shaking hands picking up one of the discarded torches. Without a sound, I stepped ghostlike toward the prince and the remaining guard and swung with the force of a hundred repressed screams.

Ericen barely had time to dodge before the torch connected with the guard's ribs. Something crunched, and he wheezed, dropping his torch and crumpling to the ground. I drew back to swing again, my arms burning with the need to strike and strike and strike until the fire inside consumed me.

"Anthia!" Ericen seized the torch and spun me around in one swift move, taking it from my grasp. My chest rose and fell in short bursts, my eyes finding his. Slowly, I became aware of the pressure of his hands on my arms, of Kiva appearing at my side, pushing him away. He barely stepped back, gaze still holding mine.

I didn't speak. I couldn't. Kiva tugged gently at my arm, and I allowed her to lead me back into the carriage. I felt like a kite someone had cut loose, left to the mercy of the slightest breeze that could tear me apart. Kiva shut the door behind us. Rather than return to our respective benches, she organized our blankets on the floor, and we settled down together.

I lay there for several hours, trying to remember what it felt like to be safe.

The next morning, I woke feeling hollow. Several of Ericen's guards were bruised and battered, and the one I'd struck glared murderously at me every time I looked at him. Was this what it would be like for me in Illucia?

We packed quickly and moved on, Kiva riding close to the carriage. Ericen lounged across his bench as he always did, but there was an edge to him now. The silence turned the air thick with tension, like the moment before a lightning strike, until I couldn't stand it anymore.

"Why did you stop me from attacking him?" I demanded. "You were doing the same."

He surveyed me coolly. "Because you're my responsibility, and I didn't give them permission."

"That's all?"

"Were you hoping for something more?" The ice in his gaze melted, and he smiled in a way that made me feel like a mouse in the claws of a cat.

I hated it. Hated the way it made me feel bared and the fact that I couldn't shake the voice in the back of my mind that whispered it was a lie. He was deflecting.

"You know," I said quietly, "you're not quite so perfect a liar as you think."

Something flickered across his face, his lips parting, but he said nothing. I allowed myself a small smile.

I'd told Caliza I wanted to ride with Ericen to get to know him, to be better able to handle him. Maybe it was time I learned to play his game and saw where it led me.

ELEVEN

The deeper into Illucia we got, the more the landscape changed. We were due to arrive in Sordell in the late afternoon, having just passed through the Etris Forest into countryside of rolling green hills and small villages of thatched cottages.

A few hours later, during which my stomach had tied itself into several knots, Ericen shifted closer to the window. "We're here."

I leaned over beside him, peering out. The city had been built on top of a cluster of hills, a ripple of stone and color. I couldn't see the end of it. Overhead, a blanket of storm clouds floated, dark with the promise of rain. At least those I could relate to.

Ericen sat back to give me more space, and I pressed closer to the window.

The stone buildings were tall and narrow, shoulder to

shoulder like soldiers. Clean cobblestone streets had walkways on the sides for people to keep out of the way of carts and horses. Everywhere I looked, there was green: moss growing on the sides of buildings, vines snaking along roofs or up lantern posts. Yet it all looked perfectly manicured and carefully designed, as if the city's inhabitants had recognized they couldn't make it disappear, but they could damn well organize it.

The Illucians were obvious, dressed in crisp clothes with sharp edges. Nearly all carried swords or other weapons, and they walked straight-backed with their heads held high, like soldiers prepared to salute a commander at any second. As the carriage passed, some of them did.

Then I started noticing the other people. The men and women with the dark hair and bronze skin of the Jin or the golden skin and fair hair of the Ambriellans that didn't match the bright gaze and pale complexion of the well-dressed Illucians they accompanied. The bent-backed, downcast-looking ones who trailed a few steps behind or else hurried along alone without lifting their heads.

With their economies decimated and their towns destroyed, many of them came to Illucia looking for employment, others to follow children conscripted into Razel's army. They were paid, though probably not enough. From the downtrodden looks they wore like cloaks, I doubted any amount ever would be.

I sat back from the window, barely noticing the lingering smile on Ericen's face slip away as he registered my disgust. Three years ago, Illucia had decimated Jindae, murdering its royal family and destroying the lives of its people. The children had been funneled into Illucia's army, raised as soldiers in a strange land that held no respect for them and their art. The adults worked tirelessly, both here and at home, trying to survive beneath Razel's suffocating taxes and the knowledge that everything they produced went straight to supporting the army that had broken them.

Two years before that, the Ambriels had fallen under Illucian control with little protest, and Razel had allowed the nobles to keep playing at having their own government. Still, a great many of their people suffered the same fate as the Jin.

I wanted to lean out and yell that something was being done, that we were fighting back, that they hadn't been forgotten, but I swallowed the words.

The carriage carried us through the city and up a sloping hill to the castle. I'd lost interest in looking out the window, and it all flew by in a flurry of gray. As we pulled to a halt, everything about Ericen changed. He sat taller, more rigid, his head held high. Even his eyes hardened. He leapt out of the carriage to hold the door for me, and I followed, then instantly wished I hadn't.

It was *cold*.

I wrapped my arms around myself for warmth, my loosely knit woolen sweater doing little against the rising evening chill. Caliza had had some warmer clothes made for me, but they were packed away in my bags, and they were supposed to be for winter. But if summer was this chilly, I had a feeling they wouldn't be sufficient for the colder months.

"Here." Ericen removed his cloak and dropped it over my shoulders.

I pulled it tighter, staring at him in confusion. "Thanks." I caught Kiva's disapproving look as I faced the castle but ignored it. It. Was. *Cold!*

The castle loomed like a great dark beast with spikes. Instead of towering high in the air like the castle in Rhodaire, it sprawled across low, sloping hills, some parts lifted higher than others by the uneven ground. Black stone towers and spires sprouted on either side like sharp talons and jagged teeth.

The guards we'd brought were shown away to the barracks. Only Kiva remained, regarding the castle with open disdain. I glanced back, my eyes finding the trunk with the egg in it as the bags and boxes in the wagons were unloaded. I silently prayed they treated everything with care.

Ericen strode past, gesturing for us to follow. He led the way through two stained-glass doors depicting massive black horses before a backdrop of golden sky.

Inside, the castle was beautiful, though dark and rigid. As we passed through the entrance hall and into a corridor with windows crowded by trees, the castle closed in on me. The hallways were narrow and the windows small, not built for crows to pass through. The deep, rich colors accenting everything grew even bolder in the filtered sunlight. It was a cave.

"Is it going to rain?" I glanced at the darkening sky.

Ericen shrugged. "Maybe. It always looks like that. Sometimes it rains, sometimes it doesn't."

Kiva and I exchanged looks. Clouds without rain? Days of dark and dreary weather?

Longing for the broad, open halls and warm weather of my

home swept through me, threatening to lock my knees and pin me to the spot. I forced my feet forward, but the hallway gaped like the dark mouth of some mythical beast, the wall torches flickering like fiery teeth. We passed Illucian soldiers in the hall, the look behind their eyes sharp as glass. Judging. Evaluating. Condemning.

These people were my enemies, and they surrounded me.

I forced a deep breath, then released it. The urge to run quieted but didn't leave. Would it ever? My life had changed so much since I'd discovered the crow egg. I'd moved forward, but the depression I'd been battling for months still sat like a coiled snake in the back of my mind, waiting for me to falter.

I won't.

We stopped outside a set of thick oak doors. The guards posted on either side saluted Ericen, though their movements were delayed, as if they'd thought half a second about not doing it.

"I'm going to introduce you both to my mother," he said. "Don't say anything stupid."

I snorted. Now that sounded more like the Ericen I knew. He faced the guards, and I swore he took a steadying breath before they pulled the doors open.

We stepped into a simple yet elegant throne room. A white marble floor stretched before us, meeting walls adorned with golden metalwork. Gilded curves rose and fell, swirled and twisted along the walls like dancing ribbons. Massive black hearths burned with crackling fires on either side of the room, filling the air with a rich, earthy smell I'd experienced once in the Ambriels: peat.

I stared at the flames. They were huge, filling the hearths like a blaze in the mouth of a fire crow. I'd stopped walking without realizing, my breathing quickening. Someone tugged on my arm, and my head whipped around. Kiva met my gaze, holding it unrelentingly, her hand tightening on my arm. I forced a deep breath in, then out, and nodded. We started walking again.

A dais sat in the center of the room, two gleaming black thrones perched upon it. One was empty, but in the other sat the most beautiful woman I'd ever seen.

Queen Razel had long, rose-gold hair that fell to her waist in loose ringlets, framing a thin face with delicate features and porcelain skin. She stood, revealing a slender, muscular frame, and smiled. It didn't reach her eyes.

She embodied everything wrong in my life, and I had to stand there and pretend to be pleased to meet her.

The prince led us forward as she descended the dais. As we stopped before each other, her eyes scanned us all in a quick evaluation, their color pale blue as frozen ponds. A chill prickled at the back of my neck. Her eyes were like glass, cutting through me to see what was inside.

Despite wearing a deep golden dress with long slits up the sides of her legs, the grips of two weapons strapped to her back stuck up over her shoulders. Like most everyone in Illucia, she was a soldier, and her graceful step and powerful bearing reinforced the image with every motion.

Razel swept Ericen into a hug. I was surprised to see him stiffen until she let go. "Welcome home, my son," she said. There was something about her voice that made me uneasy, a sweetness turned rancid.

Ericen stepped aside without looking at his mother, his shoulders back, hands clasped behind in a soldier's stance. Her eyes fell on me, and she smiled again. The sudden urge to wipe it off her face forced me to concentrate on not fisting my hands. "Welcome to Sordell, my dear."

The feeling came again when she spoke, as if each word carried a warning behind the pleasantries. A warning to remember I was very far from home.

"Thank you." I forced the words out and performed a small curtsy.

The queen didn't even spare Kiva a glance and continued, "I'm glad we were able to reach an agreement. It will be best for both of our kingdoms."

Afraid I wouldn't be able to control what came out if I opened my mouth, I simply forced a tight smile.

Razel laid a hand on Ericen's shoulder, and he stiffened again. As if recognizing the effect her touch had on him, she gripped him tighter. "We'll talk more at dinner. I'd like a moment alone with my son. Auma will show you to your rooms."

I'd traveled across kingdoms at her whim, and she had dismissed me already. I forced my hands to relax, refusing to let her make me feel like an unimportant pawn, and turned the way she'd indicated.

I nearly jumped. A thin Jin girl had appeared beside us. Even Kiva hadn't noticed her, judging by the uneasy look on her face. The girl wore a simple gray smock, the only color coming from a ragged red-and-gold scarf around her neck. She was pretty, with glossy black hair and dark eyes. She didn't speak and kept her head slightly bowed.

"Thank you," I said through gritted teeth.

As Auma led us out of the throne room, I glanced back. Razel spoke earnestly to Ericen, who still refused to look at her. Then the doors swung shut.

We retraced our steps, and Auma took us down a left-hand passage and up a flight of stairs. I eyed the girl as we went. Something was off about her.

Without Razel around, she walked taller, her shoulders back like a tree straightening after a strong wind, but it wasn't that. I blinked, realizing she was studying me as much as I was her. She turned away without a flicker of expression.

What life had she led before coming here to serve a foreign queen, and what desperation had driven her into the heart of enemy territory? Employment? A conscripted family member? She didn't have any tama, the marks Jin earned when they apprenticed themselves to a guild, which meant she'd likely been in Illucia since before her sixteenth birthday. Either way, she'd lost everything, something Kiva and I could relate to. Did the echoes of her past haunt her too?

Auma slowed outside an ornate wooden door where two Rhodairen guards had been posted. They bowed as we approached, and I nodded in return.

"His Highness sent word you would prefer a shared room." Auma's voice was quiet but not soft, like the gentle grumble of a jungle cat. She opened the door.

The chambers consisted of four rooms joined together. The entry opened to a sitting space with large, comfortable red couches set before an already roaring fire, which I eyed warily.

Massive rugs stretched across portions of the stone ground, and behind one of the couches sat a round dark wood table and chairs. At the back of the room, a door led in each direction.

Another overture of friendship from Ericen. I was thankful he'd thought of it; I didn't want to be far from Kiva.

Auma followed us inside, then moved to the center door at the back of the room and opened it to reveal a large bathing chamber. Then she pointed to the doors on either side of her in turn. "These lead to the bedrooms. Your things are inside." Quick. Blunt. She certainly didn't mince words.

"Thank you," I said as she retreated.

She paused at the door. "Her Majesty requests your presence for dinner in an hour. I will return to escort you." She bowed and left. I stared after her, finally realizing what was so strange: her footsteps didn't make any sound. Where had she learned to walk like that?

"She's an odd one." Kiva's gaze lingered at the doorway. "Cute though."

I smirked and, recognizing my luggage, dashed across the sitting area to the room on the left. Sona lamps lit a spacious room of dark wood draped in blue and gold. Two tall, narrow windows let in the fading sunlight, and a plush black carpet warmed the dark floor at the foot of a massive bed piled high with pillows.

Kiva filled the doorway as I dropped beside the trunk with the egg, fishing the key from my pocket and unlocking it. Carefully, I pulled away the blankets, my mind filled with images of cracks and scattered shell pieces. The last blanket fell away, revealing the egg, whole and in perfect condition.

A knot released in my chest as I pulled the egg into my lap. Going days without feeling the connection between us had felt like a form of withdrawal. Now, the warm, reassuring feeling that spread through me when I touched it made me feel safe, as if the crow had shrouded me in its wings.

"Now what?" Kiva asked.

I ran my fingers along the shell, the humming of the egg working away at my anxiety. "First we get through dinner. Then I see about getting out of this damn castle."

Unlike in Aris, where dinner was family and close friends, Razel held a full court. The banquet hall was wide with a high vaulted ceiling, a massive glass chandelier dangling from the center, and on a small platform built into the back, Razel sat with her distinguished guests. Tonight, that meant me.

Razel had stuck me between her and Ericen. On her other side sat a handsome nobleman in his late twenties, who Razel occasionally flattered with her attention.

We faced a room with four long tables, each filled with food and richly dressed lords and ladies. Or were they soldiers? I couldn't tell the difference. Some wore thick shirts and pants with matching jackets so rigid, they looked like uniforms, others uniforms so suave and finely cut, they looked like suits.

How many of them had family members sitting on Rhodaire's border, threatening my people?

From my place at Razel's table, I could see the sneers the rest of the room tossed in my direction. They stared with open disdain, their expressions made more hostile by the weapons they all carried. Mostly straight swords after Illucian custom, but some had baldrics of knives across their chests or simple daggers at their waists.

What I didn't expect was the way they looked at each other, as if each tablemate were an opponent to be outmaneuvered and destroyed. I'd learned from tutors that even among families, Illucians cared only about competition for rank and prestige, but the way they looked at each other made my skin crawl. They were like wolves looking for a weak spot, their postures rigid in preparation to strike and scramble up the ranks.

Kiva sat at one of those tables, her elbows spread to each side to create space. We locked gazes across the room, and she flashed me a sharp smile to show she was all right.

"I do hope she's not planning on skewering anyone tonight," Ericen remarked. He lounged in his chair in a lithe, imperious way, as if the chair should be grateful to hold him. His expression held an air of disinterest, and once again, I saw the arrogant, vicious prince who'd ridden into Rhodaire.

"You're a little far from her reach," I replied.

His lips quirked in that one-sided smirk.

At our backs, Auma and an Illucian servant rushed about, refilling goblets with wine or water and tending to whatever needs we might have. I made sure not to have any. The Jin girl had readopted her meek exterior, and it made me uneasy to see her bustling about so swiftly. Everyone else simply ignored them, as if they thought their glasses refilled themselves and their empty plates vanished into thin air.

I wore a simple pale-green gown I'd selected because it was my warmest, but my arms still prickled with cold despite the heat of the fires around the room, and it didn't escape Razel's notice.

"We'll get you some warmer gowns and a nice coat made," she said. Her sugary tone made me sick.

"Thank you." I forced a smile to crack across my face and went back to my food, but she kept talking.

"You'll have free rein of the castle, of course. I want you to be comfortable here." Her eyes scanned me, falling at last on my scarred arm. "And not to worry. It may be too warm for gloves where you're from, but you'll be perfectly comfortable with them here. We'll get you some fine ones made."

Where you're from. As if she couldn't even deign to speak my kingdom's name.

My scarred hand curled into a fist of its own accord. "I don't want to cover my scars, if that's what you mean."

Ericen went still.

Razel picked up a knife and cut a slice of butter. "Of course not, dear. Gloves are part of Illucian fashion. I know how important it is for girls your age to fit in. We'll make a proper Illucian princess of you yet."

Not before I strangle myself. Or you. The thought had barely crossed my mind when I met Kiva's gaze. She eyed my fist, and I opened it, but the tension in my shoulders felt permanent. I scanned the tables full of people—no one wore gloves.

I glanced at Ericen, who made a point of not catching my eye. This time, I saw the truth beneath his posture. The easy sprawl, the look of constant mild irritation mingling with disgust: it disguised the tension underneath. Why did he look as on edge as I felt? And what exactly was Razel's game? She was like a shark trying to trick a smaller fish into thinking it was safe.

Razel stood, and the crowd went instantly silent. Soldiers snapped to attention, and every set of eyes settled on the queen. No one so much as whispered. A chill prickled my neck—they looked at her with reverence fit for a goddess.

The queen stared back with a look I recognized. I'd seen it on my mother's face a thousand times. A delicate blend of strength and a faint protective edge, something almost maternal.

She could level kingdoms and massacre families, but she cared for her people. Either that or she was very good at pretending. Considering she was Illucian, I figured the latter.

"I give thanks to Rhett for this special evening," she began.

Every Illucian in the room clapped a fist to their heart simultaneously in recognition of their god's name.

"Not only has my son returned to us, but he's come with his wife-to-be, Princess Anthia Cerralté of Rhodaire. Please join me in welcoming her."

Applause sounded, and I tried my best to look bashful and appreciative instead of glaring murderously as everyone's eyes fell on me.

I felt like I was on display. Like Rhodaire had already been conquered and I was the prize.

"One week from now, we will have a ball in Rhett's name to commemorate the occasion."

A murmur spread through the room, and I nearly gagged, hiding it with a cough in my hand. A ball? Imagining the fake smiling Illucian faces and even faker compliments nearly had me sinking under the table.

Did she plan to announce the date of the wedding at the ball? Caliza had said it would occur when Razel wanted, and the idea that it could be sprung upon me at any time made it yet another thing out of my control.

Razel sat back down, and the hum of conversation picked up again. I scanned the faces in the crowd. How many of these people had been involved in Ronoch? How many of them would flaunt it in my face at the ball?

I spent the dinner angled toward Kiva's side of the room so Razel couldn't easily get my attention. More than once, lords or ladies came up to the table to pay respects to the queen and be introduced to me so they could offer their congratulations. Some greeted Ericen enthusiastically, others with an air of disinterest. He responded to them all with the same sharp smile and a dangerous gleam in his eye, exchanging stiff pleasantries that sounded like funeral rites.

Razel knew people's names and asked after their families. They glowed beneath her attentions, but their exchanges felt fake—stiff and formal, like soldiers to a commander. Not like when my mother or Caliza spoke to people, where a true camaraderie existed.

The nobles' smiles turned to half-concealed sneers when they addressed me.

"I'm sure you're happy to get out of that abhorrent heat."

"How gracious of our queen to extend a peaceful hand during your time of struggle."

"Nice scars."

My head snapped up, but the soldier who'd spoken was already bowing to Razel. I stared him down. He flashed me a haughty smile before stepping from the dais, his movements languid. My gaze followed him back to his table, where he sat beside the guard whose ribs I'd broken with the torch during our journey, slinging his arm across his shoulders.

Great.

"Making friends already, I see," Ericen mused. His gaze had followed the blond boy back to his seat, and it rested there as if he might freeze him in ice with sheer willpower.

I fell back into my chair. "Are all your noblemen so pleasant?"

"Only the ones who don't know their place." The bite in his tone hinted at a larger history, but he smoothed it over with another smile. The ease with which he melded one expression into another made my stomach turn.

Barely a day in, and I already wanted to leave. It took several deep breaths and a reminder of what I'd come for, of the alliances I intended to build, to help me through the rest of dinner.

By the time Kiva and I returned to the room, I was exhausted. Not only from the long trip and night of talking, but from keeping every thought that crossed my mind sealed inside. More than once, I'd been forced to lie through my teeth to different lords and ladies about how gracious Razel was for having me, how lucky I was to be marrying into such a prestigious family, and what a great alliance this was for our kingdoms. I wanted to scrub my mouth out.

The quiet voice of the coiled snake whispered for me to go to bed, to hide, to wait for someone else to act from under the safety of my bed sheets. Fear I might give in swirled in the pit of my stomach, but I ignored them both. I could handle this.

"I have to say, I'm impressed." Kiva threw herself onto one of the couches before the fire.

"With what?" I flopped onto the one farthest from the flames. Thankfully, the fire had already started to die.

"I've never seen you curb your tongue like that. Your face was so impassive, you almost looked like Caliza."

I snorted, but she was right. Normally, I would have told Razel exactly what I thought of her pretend show of playing nice. I'd even managed to smile at a few members of her court. "I guess spending time with Ericen had at least one benefit."

There was a knock at the door, and I called for them to enter. Auma stepped inside, and Kiva bolted upright, smiling. Auma blinked at her, head tilting a fraction in the first show of emotion I'd seen from her. During dinner, she'd kept a neutral mask, no matter how harried she'd been.

Even now, her face had already returned to an impassive wall. She stood a little straighter than she had at dinner and held my eyes in a way she never looked at Razel. "Prince Ericen has requested you join him tomorrow morning. I'll escort you after breakfast."

"Thank you, Auma," I said. "If I have a letter to send, could you help me with that?"

She nodded once, and I dashed into my bedroom to compose a quick letter to Caliza. Pulling out the invisible ink Lady Kerova had given me, I wrote a visible message saying I'd arrived safely and missed her and an invisible portion indicating the egg was safe.

When I returned, the silence in the room had the delicate tension of unspoken words. I looked from Kiva to Auma as I handed the latter the letter. "Thank you."

She nodded once, eyes flashing momentarily to Kiva, before she stepped from the room.

I eyed Kiva as I retook my seat. "That was smooth."

She dropped back onto the couch. "Let's talk about the fact that you and Ericen are spending time together instead. Snakes don't make good pets, Thia."

I chucked a pillow at her.

TWELVE

T he next morning, Auma woke us for breakfast. I'd slept
horribly, waking constantly from dreams of fire and blood.
Utter blackness greeted me each time, and I swore the darkness
twisted and moved, mocking my fear.

For several moments, I lay in bed, dreading the day to come.
Though I'd chipped away at the weight inside me, I'd only
begun to work my way through this.

After dragging myself out from beneath the covers, I
checked on the egg. Each time I saw it felt like reuniting with
a lost friend, and deep below the excitement and anticipation,
that scared me. Because what if it never hatched?

What if it *did*?

I would be dragging the crow inside into a war. If I was
this attached to the egg already, how would I be able to put the

creature inside in danger? The idea of losing it cut through me like a cold knife. I closed the trunk, banishing the thought with an expelled breath.

I couldn't think about things like that. Not when I didn't have a choice.

Auma had lit the fire by the time I emerged, filling the room with the earthy scent of peat. I stayed away from it, near the table in the sitting room, which had been laden with plates of eggs, fresh fruit, scones with cream and lemon curd, and pots filled with hot chamomile tea. I'd sampled tea once before in the Ambriels, but no one drank it in Rhodaire.

Kiva tried to get Auma to eat with us, but she excused herself and was gone in a wisp of air. Kiva eyed the spot she'd been standing. "She has a hunter's step."

"More than that. It's like her feet don't touch the ground." The Jin were known for being masterful trackers. The prestige of the hunter's guild came third only to the artist and gem guilds.

I sipped my tea and sighed. "This is so good."

Kiva smirked. "The way to your heart really is through your stomach. But I'm glad to see you eating again."

"Let's talk about the way to your heart instead." I glanced at the door Auma had left through, and Kiva's eyes widened the slightest bit.

"I think she's cute. That's all."

"And you respect her skill." I hadn't missed the admiration in Kiva's tone when she noted Auma's silent step. "All she needs now is talent with a blade and you'll be smitten."

"I will throw things at you."

"I'm thinking a spring wedding."

"Thia."

"You can't wear your guard's uniform though. I bet we can find a nice suit for you to borrow."

She seized a scone, and I leapt from my seat with a laugh, narrowly avoiding being pelted in the head.

An hour later, Auma led us down the corridor, my bow a familiar weight across my back. One of the guards posted outside my door had followed us, but my head stayed on a swivel nonetheless. I didn't trust anyone here besides Kiva and my own soldiers. Still, I already noticed something different in the eyes of the people we passed. Eyes that saw my weapon and didn't look quite as disgusted as last night's dinner guests.

Auma led us downstairs to the first floor and through to the back of the castle, where we entered a long, rectangular room. Light flooded the space, forcing me to blink several times to clear my vision. The entire back wall consisted of floor-to-ceiling windows, granting light to a room filled with chairs and couches, all organized in clusters around small hearths lit with roaring fires.

Thankfully, the fires were on the edges, and the room was fairly large. I could walk through the middle without getting close to any of them.

A quiet buzz of conversation filled the room as several nobles from last night's dinner lounged and drank together. A drizzle of rain tapped at the windows, a light haze of fog filling a massive courtyard beyond.

Tension crept into every muscle as my gaze jumped from

Illucian noble to soldier and back again. My guard remained stationed at my back, Kiva at my side, both as tense as I was, surrounded by so many potential opponents.

"Good morning." Ericen's voice drew me from my inspection as he approached. I stared.

He wore all black leather down to his boots. Black leather straps formed an X across his chest, the hilts of two swords sticking up over each shoulder on his back. Not an inch of pale skin was visible besides his neck and face. He'd become a shadow.

Only the golden head of Illucia's horse insignia emblazoned above his heart broke up the darkness.

Auma bowed to both of us, then moved deeper into the room, by which point I'd schooled my expression back into neutrality. "Taking down a small army today, are we?"

He smirked. "This is the uniform of the Illucian Vykryns. I didn't wear it when I was in Rhodaire because it's a little—"

"Ridiculous?" Kiva suggested.

"Pompous?" I added.

"I was going to say dark for a Rhodairen summer, but I appreciate the compliments," he said, looking bemused.

"What's a Vykryn?" I asked.

He straightened. "Illucia's most elite warriors. It's a title granted to only a few of the soldiers who graduate Darkward every year."

My eyes narrowed, my humor gone. Kiva and I exchanged looks. These sounded like the kind of people you sent to cripple an entire nation. The kind that excelled in archery and could kill a crow as it leapt from a burning rookery.

"Good for you," Kiva said drily. "Do you have a team chant too? Or just matching outfits?"

Ericen's smile sharpened. "Yes, I suppose they're not quite as glamorous as the Korovi Miska. Though I suppose you've never seen a Miska warrior, have you? *Okorn*."

Kiva's hand flew to Sinvarra, and I seized her wrist a second before she could draw. The room went deathly silent, until only the thunder of my own heart filled my ears. *Okorn* were what the Korovi called children of banished countrymen.

My voice dropped low enough that only we could hear. "Speak to Kiva that way again, and I'll put an arrow in you."

Ericen grinned, actually *grinned*, as though my threat enthralled him. "That's not quite what I brought you here for." And with that, he spun for a glass door in the windowed wall, as if the floor hadn't very nearly been coated in blood.

Releasing Kiva's wrist, I watched him go, trying to fit together the pieces of him I'd seen. He wasn't the boy I'd ridden with in the carriage, trying and failing at civility, nor was he the cruel prince I'd hated in Rhodaire. His flippant comments were like a reflex, as though he'd spent his entire life snapping back and didn't know how to stop.

Kiva's gaze drifted to where Auma was piling dishes at an empty table, some of her frustration ebbing. I hid a smile as I said, "I'll be fine if you want to wait here."

A very uncharacteristic blush turned her cheeks pink, and she nodded, likely all too happy to go anywhere Ericen wasn't.

I followed the prince, catching the gaze of one of the soldiers near the fireplace: the boy who'd commented on my scars at dinner. He smiled dangerously. I smiled back until he looked away with a scowl.

The door led out into the courtyard, immediately surrounding me in biting air. I folded my arms over my chest for warmth. Ericen didn't even seem to notice the chill as he led the way into a massive training area.

There were several distinct sections, from open arenas to archery targets, sword training to endurance courses. Soldiers trained in each one, shouts and the clangs of metal echoing in the courtyard.

On the far side, an open door revealed the empty healer's quarters. Estrel had once said that Illucian soldiers looked down on healers. Apparently, getting treatment for a wound was akin to throwing your honor into the dirt and stomping on it. It would take a severe injury for soldiers to willingly subject themselves to treatment.

"Saints," I breathed.

"These are the royal training grounds," Ericen said. "If you think this is a bit much, you should see the ones at Darkward."

I wasn't sure I wanted to. There was something about the swift efficiency of every soldier wherever I looked that made me uneasy. No matter their task, they completed it with the utmost power and skill, driving arrows into targets or pinning their opponents without mercy.

The ones who weren't training stared at us, some with open fascination, some with suspicion. It was the ones who looked disgusted that made me bristle though. Ericen noticed them too, though from the way his expression changed, it seemed he thought they were looking at him. He stared them down, his eyes like jagged ice, until they looked away. He didn't relax.

"Anyway, I wanted to show you in case you and Kiva wanted to train," he said, his voice a little tighter now. "It'll be pretty busy with people training for the upcoming Centerian."

I stiffened. "The sword tournament?"

He nodded, and the morning chill permeated my skin. The Centerian only occurred every five years. Illucia's most dangerous fighters would descend on Sordell to participate in the test of strength and skill. The renown for winning the tournament was unprecedented.

And here I'd thought Illucia couldn't get any more dangerous.

"Also, I was thinking we could skip dinner tonight and go into town." Ericen's voice drew me from thoughts of ice-cold eyes and glinting steel.

"Yes." My eagerness surprised me as much as Ericen, but I already needed a break from Razel. Kiva had said she was impressed at how I'd handled myself last night, but I still wasn't Caliza. I couldn't promise I wouldn't let a few choice words slip. Or a knife.

"I'll send someone for you this evening then."

I nodded, turning to go, and almost ran smack into a black wall. My hand went reflexively to my bow as I stepped back, finding two men in Vykryn uniforms blocking my path. The one in the front smiled—the boy from dinner. He was near my age, broad shouldered but lean with blond hair and royal-blue eyes.

My guard shifted, on edge. Then the soldiers parted, revealing Razel approaching.

I stiffened. The smell of burnt flesh, a flash of fire, Kiva yelling—*Stop*. I couldn't lose myself in bloody memories every time I saw her.

The training grounds quieted as soldiers saluted. Ericen stiffened, his attention jumping from the blond Vykryn to his mother. Razel drew to a halt before us, cold eyes focused on me. She wore a gilded version of a Vykryn's uniform, her rose-gold hair pulled back in a tight braid and weapons strapped to her back.

"Thia dear, I see you've found the training grounds. If you'd like, I could have one of our masters tutor you."

The blond Vykryn snorted amusedly.

My nails dug into my palms. "I've already been trained by the best."

A smile curled her lips. "In that case, perhaps we could spar? Illucian skill versus Rhodairen...determination." She said the last word slowly, the unsaid message clear: *At least you try.*

Logic told me to say no. Razel was the queen of Illucia, the leader of a warrior kingdom. Caliza'd said she had won the Centerian at barely a few years older than me. But at the same time, I longed for the chance to take out the anger and hatred boiling in the pit of my stomach. Even if I only got one blow in, it would be worth it.

I smiled. "I'd love to."

"No." Ericen stepped forward. The blond Vykryn's attention snapped to him, and Ericen stared him down. Something silent smoldered between them.

Razel raised an eyebrow. "What was that, Eri dear?"

"Yeah," I growled. "What was that?"

"I'll fight you in her place." Ericen didn't even acknowledge I'd spoken. He'd angled himself so his back was toward me.

Razel chuckled. "This isn't a duel. No one needs to fight in her place. We're just going to have a friendly spar."

"With weapons," Ericen said, and something dangerous glinted behind Razel's eyes. This was a different Ericen altogether. The hard, angry one, who had looked like an imposter in his mother's embrace.

"If you insist," Razel said. "Sorry, Thia dear. He's so demanding sometimes."

Ericen didn't spare me so much as a glance before stalking over to one of the fighting rings. I watched him go, scowling. Razel followed after the prince, the two Vykryn on her heels.

Someone stepped up beside me, and I flinched.

Kiva raised an eyebrow. "Jumpy. Guess that's to be expected when you challenge death to a duel."

I rolled my eyes. "She just wanted to spar."

Kiva gave me a long look. "Don't be naïve. Razel would have laid you out just so you knew she could."

I gritted my teeth as we followed the group over to the sparring ring Razel and Ericen had entered. He had his dual short swords in hand, she a pair of curved, dome-shaped blades with small spikes sticking out from the edges of the grip. Jin moonblades.

Anyone else, I'd have said she used the moonblades because she liked them. But this was Illucia. Using those blades sent a message: *I own these.*

The soldiers who'd stopped to watch stood at Razel's side of the ring, clearly staking their support.

"Shearen," Razel said, indicating the blond guard. "If you would."

"On one!" Shearen called. "Three, two—"

Razel lunged before he finished the second number. Ericen had anticipated it, catching the first strike of both her moon-blades on one sword. They executed swift and merciless attacks, metal ringing in a shrill call. Razel clearly had an edge in speed, Ericen in strength.

People started to gather around the training ring, forming a circle. There were calls of support and whistles for the queen, Shearen's voice rising above the rest. My guard pressed closer to my back, hand on the hilt of his sword.

The fighters struck and parried, twirled and dipped, each avoiding close calls from the other's blades. Ericen barreled through his attacks like a man dead set on proving himself, while Razel's every strike made it clear she aimed to injure. Her eyes gleamed with a strange dark fire, as if Ericen were a demon she fought for her very soul.

As she blocked one of Ericen's attacks, she ducked under his follow-up strike and sprang up, driving her elbow into Ericen's chin. He stumbled back, barely bringing a sword around to knock aside the thrust of her blade. The ferocity of her attack struck the sword from his hand, leaving him with one.

Off balance, it was all Ericen could do to keep up with her torrent of strikes. She struck high and low, forcing him to cover a wide range and expose new targets. Right as she sliced at his neck, she swept low with her foot, catching him in the knees. He struck the ground hard, and she leapt over him, driving her weapon down.

Ericen just managed to get his sword around to deflect the blade. It shot down and away, the metal screaming. The blade sliced across his cheek. He didn't make a sound. Razel straightened, hovering over him like a wolf over a fresh kill, blood dripping from the curve of one blade. They held each other's gazes, unmoving. Then she smiled, stepping off him.

Ericen rolled to the side as the crowd clapped. His eyes met mine for half a second, the cut stretching from his jaw to cheekbone leaking blood. The realization of what I'd nearly gotten myself into slammed into me, and I sucked in a ragged breath.

The prince shot to his feet and grabbed his other sword. He sheathed them both and slipped out of the ring. I started to go after him, but Kiva seized my arm before I could move an inch. Then she casually slipped in front of me. "Razel's watching."

"So what?" I hissed.

"Do you want her to challenge you again?"

The tension washed out of me. "No." Not after what I'd just seen. If she could take down Ericen like that, I wouldn't last a second, as rusty as I was.

Razel exited the ring, sliding her moonblades into their sheaths on her back with smooth precision. She hadn't even cleaned the blood. She caught my gaze, the challenge pulsating in the air between us. Then she smiled and turned back for the castle.

A chill trickled down my spine—this wasn't over. Razel had come to make a power play, and Ericen had intervened. She would find another way.

THIRTEEN

A couple of hours later, Ericen and I sat in a carriage heading down Sordell's main street. The rain had let up, and though the sky hadn't cleared, patches of stars shone overhead. Beneath them, Illucian citizens mixed almost indecipherably with soldiers in the streets.

Ericen wore his Vykryn uniform, and I'd changed into a dress along with a thin leather coat and boots. The prince didn't say a word. When he'd left the arena, he hadn't gone to the healer's quarters to get the wound bandaged. It had stopped bleeding, however, the cut much shallower than I'd thought.

I studied him as he studied the city outside. Why had he intervened with Razel? Had he been that eager for a fight with his mother, or had he known I wouldn't be prepared? Either way, I couldn't shake the feeling something had shifted between us.

As the door opened, Ericen met my gaze for the first time, and I raised an eyebrow. "I can tell this is going to be a very productive meal."

He smiled in the way that made me think he might not be as horrid as he seemed. "Stealing my lines is a cheap move."

"You're not worth more effort in this state."

"Fair point. I shall endeavor to be more infuriating." He stepped out of the carriage, offering me his hand. I climbed out on my own.

We stood at the opening of a massive bridge, easily the width of five normal roads. The river it spanned was nearly double that, with several arches along the bridge's length letting water through in a multipronged waterfall. Colorful lights reflected off even more colorful buildings, casting a rainbowlike glow across the water. The bridge was a part of the city itself, like the creators had met the river and continued building right across it.

"People call it the Colorfalls. A hundred years ago, the bridge was a gift from Rhodaire to cross the River Ren," Ericen said as we started toward the bridge. "It was made with the help of your earth crows. All the city's best food is here."

Though it seemed strange to imagine, it made sense that Rhodaire and Illucia might not have always hated each other. When had that changed?

The cobblestone street sidewalks were damp from the rain, but people were still out in full force. Giant potted trees lined the street, hung with shards of colored glass reflecting the lantern light. Shops sold everything from thick sheep wool sweaters and scarves to blocks of peat bundled together with dried herbs for different aromas. We passed the open doors of restaurants, the air filled with the scent of freshly baked bread and cooking stew. From a tavern to our right, the music of a string instrument filled the night.

Hanging overhead, strung from one side of the buildings to the next all along the street, dangled countless colored sona lamps. They had glass of deep crimson and purple, bright gold and sunset orange, all casting brightly colored glows on the stone buildings.

I stared at the colors. Sona lamps weren't cheap; we barely had enough to light the main castle halls in Aris.

This was what conquering kingdoms gave you: wealth and technology.

Without a reliance on magic, Illucia had found other ways to stay competitive. Maybe that was why everything here was so clean, so crisp, as if the city had been newly built. It was beautiful but cold, and I longed for the soul and authenticity of Aris. We may not have sona lamps at every corner or walkways of stone and manicured streets, but at least it felt real.

Ericen led the way to an empty hole-in-the-wall restaurant in the middle of the bridge. The man who greeted us bowed deeply before seating us at a table by the window. He returned a few moments later with cups of water and a bottle of Trendellan wine, pouring us each a glass.

I eyed the wine. "I thought Trendell didn't trade with Illucia."

Ericen hesitated a moment before responding. "They don't."

Which meant this wine had been stolen. Maybe even from shipments to Rhodaire.

I pushed the glass aside. "This city's so clean and organized. Does your army patrol the streets righting overturned flowerpots and straightening askew signs?"

"Only the particularly crooked ones," he replied, and a traitorous smile tugged at my lips. Ericen's eyes grew warm as he said, "People take a lot of pride in Sordell. My mother doesn't tolerate laziness. Everyone in the city has a job or supports the kingdom in some way."

"She sounds like a military commander."

"She is." He smirked at the surprise that flitted across my face. "Darkward is also Sordell's school. All children attend from five until sixteen, when they can either finish the final two years or pick another trade. Over half the city stays committed, but only the best are chosen as Vykryn."

My gaze dropped to the golden horse head symbol on his chest. *Like him.*

"No one's afforded more respect in Illucia than soldiers, except maybe the masters at Darkward. But my mother was trained like every queen and king before her, both to rule and to lead an army in battle. She's the Valix, leader of the Vykryn, and I will be after her." He straightened, as if bolstered by his own words.

It made sense. It wasn't difficult to imagine Razel astride one of those massive Illucian warhorses, prepared to destroy an entire kingdom.

"You're glowering again."

I straightened, blinking rapidly. "What?"

"Whenever we discuss my mother, you get that look on your face."

Heat flushed my cheeks, and I hurriedly took a sip of water to cover it. Clearly, I hadn't yet gained Caliza's level of controlling my emotions in front of people.

"Yeah, well. I have a lot to think about."

Ericen's smile faded. "I know this must be hard for you. Being here with us. Constantly."

I almost dropped my water glass. He looked so genuine, sounded so convincing, as if he might actually care how I felt. A laugh bubbled in my throat at the thought.

He *had* stepped in to fight Razel for me, and so far, he'd shown me every courtesy since arriving, but caring seemed more than a little unlikely.

"It doesn't help that I never know which prince I'm talking to," I replied. "You've been practically civil. You're about due for a flippant comment."

I expected sarcasm but instead found him weighing me with thoughtful eyes. "I don't want to be your enemy, Anthia."

I froze. Surely, I hadn't heard him right. "What?"

He drew a finger along the intricate design in the tablecloth. "I meant what I said in the carriage. I'm not quite so bad as you think. The things I said to you in Rhodaire—" He stopped, jaw clenching as if to hold back the words. In the end, he simply said, "I regret them."

I bit my lip. My instinct was to believe him. Kiva always said I was too quick to trust people. She was right, but sometimes I was too. Her mother had raised her to question everything and doubt everyone. I always told myself she was doing as she was trained, that she was being protective. But listening to myself talk with a boy who was supposed to be my enemy, feeling myself begin to trust him, I doubted myself.

"You don't believe me," Ericen said.

"I don't *understand* you. Your mother hates me. She hates Rhodaire. All Illucians do. How could you want to be friends?" Razel had organized Ronoch for revenge. The last war between our kingdoms before I was born had claimed my father's life, but it had also resulted in the death of part of Razel's family. Her father hadn't lasted long after, and she'd been crowned queen as young as Caliza had been. Didn't Ericen care about any of that?

As much as I hated Razel, hated Illucia, that much I understood. Her need for revenge was the same one that burned in my chest every time I looked at her.

Ericen held my gaze. "I'm a Vykryn, and I'll be Valix after my mother. I serve Illucia, and I serve her." He spoke slowly, as if choosing his words carefully. "But I don't condone what she did to Rhodaire, or Jindae, or the Ambriels. I don't believe the world is ours to take."

He's a loyal soldier. Ericen accepted his place and obeyed orders, and he cared about Illucia and its people, but I was starting to think he didn't fit. Perhaps he wasn't the man he'd been pretending to be when I first met him, at least not completely. Was that why his soldiers didn't respect him? Why the people on the streets barely inclined their heads, if they noticed him at all? Because he wasn't the Illucian prince they wanted.

My eyes flickered to his wound. "Is that why you don't get along with her?" I asked.

He stiffened. "What makes you say that?"

"Oh, I don't know. Everything."

"Ah, yes, the expert on people is the girl who's avoided them for half a year."

"See?" I threw up my hands, and his fingers curled into fists, as if trying to draw back the words.

He was saved from answering by the arrival of our food. A platter of short ribs, a bowl of mashed potatoes and garlic, and a salad with tomatoes and goat cheese, along with the plate of thick bread that seemed to accompany every meal in the kingdom.

I picked up my fork and knife but quickly found the knife to be unnecessary. The beef was so tender, it practically fell apart. I was so focused on it and intent on ignoring Ericen that his next words were like a shock of ice.

"Tell me about the crows," he said quietly.

I nearly dropped my fork, my answer leaping out reflexively. "No."

He didn't look surprised, but he did seem bothered by my answer, his brow furrowing. I didn't care. No matter who he was, kind or cruel, I would not talk to an Illucian about the crows. I couldn't.

We finished dinner, which Ericen paid for despite the cook's protests, and stepped back out onto the bridge. Rather than return to the carriage, Ericen directed me to a shop across the street nearly shrouded in trees.

"I didn't get dessert, because I figured you'd like this place."
He held the door open for me.

Bakery was too small a word for what surrounded me. Glass
case after glass case filled with pastries of every kind, the air
thick with the smell of sugar and freshly baked bread. Where a
moment ago, my stomach had been achingly full, I now wanted
to try everything I saw.

"We can get some to take back too." Ericen smiled at my
slack-jawed expression, and I faltered. That smile, that *real*
smile, was like a glimpse of gold veined in stone. It made me
want to trust him.

We spent the next ten minutes stuffing a box with pastries, the
woman behind the counter letting us taste whatever we wanted
along the way. We tried nearly everything in the shop: a lemon
tart with berries on top, a chocolate mousse with caramel chips,
an oatmeal cookie with swirls of butterscotch. By the time we left,
a box of pastries tucked under my arm, I could barely move.

Mist had begun to gather along the bridge, turning the sona
lamps into spots of blurred color that blended into each other
like paints on a canvas. People talked and laughed, walking arm
in arm along the pristine sidewalks.

Something was missing. I paused, scanning the length of the
street. There were no patrols, no soldiers on duty.

And not a single Jin or Ambriellan.

The mist prickled at my skin. Up here was a world of light
and color, while a few streets away, people slowly forgot what
those words meant as they toiled beneath a regime that cared
nothing for them.

Ericen slowed as we passed the tavern with the music. "Do you want to dance?" he asked.

"What?" My thoughts were still on the contrast between the city's areas. He didn't seem to hear me, instead taking my hand and pulling me into the tavern.

The tables had been cleared aside, leaving a space filled with people spinning and hopping to the music. I set my box of pastries on an empty table a second before Ericen drew me into the throng. I nearly resisted, but the music pried at the tension in my shoulders and demanded I let it out.

We couldn't have stood out any more: he dressed in his Vykryn uniform, dual swords across his back, and me with my brown Rhodairen skin, so much darker than the pale faces around us.

It wasn't difficult to pick up the moves. The pattern was repetitive, and I'd done a similar dance once when visiting the Ambriels. We hopped and spun, skipped and twirled. I couldn't help but laugh at the incongruous sight of Ericen armed to the teeth and dancing in time to the music.

Half his attention seemed to be somewhere else though. He kept scanning the crowd, his bright eyes narrowed. I missed a step while watching him, skipping to the side when I should have gone forward, and collided with a burly man beside me. I stumbled, and Ericen caught me before I could lose my balance entirely.

"Watch it!" Ericen snapped at the man, who scowled.

"Maybe your Rhodairen whore should keep an eye on her feet."

Ericen surged toward him, and despite the man being a head taller, pinned him easily against the wall. The music stopped. People stared, the dancers nearest us backing away to create space.

"Maybe you should learn a little respect for your future king," Ericen snarled. The violence in his voice startled me.

The man's eyes found the emblem on Ericen's chest and widened. "I'm sorry, Your Highness. Please forgive me."

I touched Ericen's shoulder; it was solid as marble. "Leave him. It's not worth it. Let's go."

Ericen didn't listen. "It's not me you need to apologize to."

The man's eyes shifted to me. My cheeks burned. "I'm sorry, my lady. Please forgive me."

"You're forgiven," I said hastily. "Ericen, let's go!"

He gave the man a final shove, then released him. I grabbed his arm, barely remembering to seize my box of pastries before tugging him out into the cool night. It had started to rain again, a thick mist obscuring the buildings and road. By the time we climbed inside the waiting carriage, we were drenched.

I set the box beside me and wiped my soaking curls out of my face. Ericen sat rigid with his arms crossed in the corner. This was the prince who'd faced Razel, the one who'd seemed determined to prove something.

"That was unnecessary, you know," I said. "I ran into him."

"He called you a whore."

"Welcome to the life of a woman. Men say stupid crap to us all the time. So don't try and tell me that was about defending my honor. It was about defending yours."

Ericen scowled. "What are you talking about?"

"I see the way people treat you. You're the prince of Illucia and a Vykryn, and people still don't respect you."

He bristled. "It's none of your business what my people think of me."

"It is if you're going to use me as an excuse to demand respect from people!"

"Just because you don't give a damn what your people think of you doesn't mean—"

I snarled, and he slammed his fist into the side of the coach. Without a word, I tore open the carriage door and leapt out. I moved blindly back the way we'd come, my skin hot with fury and shame at Ericen, at my own foolishness, at this whole damn situation.

I'd been so focused on considering the ways he had changed since Rhodaire that I'd missed the ways he'd stayed the same. He was still a product of his culture, utterly concerned with respect and pride. It hurt him that his people disregarded him, which made his anger nothing but loneliness and disappointment made manifest. I'd done the same thing—except where my pain became depression, his became anger.

"Stupid load of shi—ow!" I stumbled back, ready to curse whatever brick wall I'd just run into. Except it wasn't a wall—it was a young man. Or what one would look like after standing in a rookery during a thunderstorm.

Each strand of his hair looked as if it were trying to escape the one next to it, sticking up despite the rain, and he wore an ill-fitting tunic under an emerald-green vest with homemade pockets sewn haphazardly across the front. His brown pants were stained with more colors than a rainbow, and he clutched a bundle of papers against his chest. The rest had fallen to the ground when I'd struck him.

He blinked at me with wide green eyes. "Sorry, I wasn't—I mean, are you—"

I cut him off. "It was my fault. I wasn't looking." I bent down to pick up the now damp papers and caught a glimpse of the title written in large, shaky scrawl: *Lab Assistant Needed*.

"You're a scientist?" I stood, offering him the papers.

"Yes. Sort of." He took the stack, warm fingers brushing mine. "An inventor, really."

He looked more like a soldier or a street fighter. He was as tall as Kiva and twice as thick, with the distinctive golden tan skin of an Ambriellan.

"Anthia!"

I stiffened at Ericen's voice, immediately starting forward. Ericen's hand closed around my arm. I felt the heat of his touch, the strength of his hold, but before I could even move, the Ambriellan boy stepped forward. He seized Ericen's wrist, wrenching it free. In return, Ericen dislodged his hand from the boy's grasp and grasped a sword handle. All in barely more than a wingbeat.

No one moved. The air felt tight and packed between us like quicksand threatening to suck us in. Mist danced in wisps, curling and winding, obscuring and revealing. I moved ever so slightly between them.

"Ericen, let it go," I said, voice low.

The prince's eyes flashed. "He grabbed my arm—"

"And you grabbed mine."

His jaw tightened, eyes switching from me to the boy at my back. I could feel his body behind me, sense his tension, and hear the sharpness of his breathing.

Slowly, Ericen lowered his hand.

I faced the boy and almost faltered. The bright sea-green of his eyes had turned hard as jade. There was something in them. Something familiar that made my chest ache. He'd crushed the flyers into a roll in one hand, the fingers of the other quivering at his side. Both were peppered with thin white scars.

He saw me looking and tucked his free hand deep into a pocket. Guilt swept through me. I hated when people stared at my burns.

"Sorry." I met his gaze. The hardness had vanished.

"It's okay. I just—they always—I mean I can't—" He stopped. Let out a sharp breath. Shook his head. "Will you be all right?" His eyes flickered to Ericen.

"I'll be fine. Good night."

He nodded. I smiled, and he returned it before I followed Ericen back to the carriage with a glower.

FOURTEEN

E ricen and I didn't talk on the ride back, and I left him at the carriage the moment we arrived at the castle. I knew the way back to my rooms well enough to manage it on my own, but each Illucian soldier I passed in the halls, their bodies heavy with weapons, made me regret not having a guard with me.

Sealing my uncertainty inside, I kept my head high and met the gaze of everyone I passed. Their pale eyes burned with the same hatred that simmered inside me, but I refused to look away. Who knew what they'd been given permission to do or what rules they'd risk breaking.

With half my mind on my night with Ericen and the warmth of the Ambriellan boy's body beside mine, I almost didn't notice the voices drifting down the corridor. As I grew closer, they turned sharp and loud. I slowed. Someone cursed, a loud thud following, then the harsh ring of metal sliding against a sheath. My stomach dropped, and I dashed around the corner.

My door guards stood beside Kiva, Sinvarra drawn. Shearen and three other Vykryn faced them, hands on their weapons.

"The queen—" he began.

"Are you serious?" Kiva's voice cut across his. "If you think your queen's orders mean anything to me, you're stupider than you look."

"What in the Saints' name is going on?" I hurried forward.

Kiva's eyes didn't leave Shearen as she responded, "He says Razel ordered your guards sent home."

"That's Her Majesty to you, Korovi dog," one of the other Vykryn hissed.

Shearen smirked. "You don't have enough soldiers to resist us."

"We have enough to kill the three of you." Kiva lifted Sinvarra.

I laid a hand on her shoulder, my mind spinning. Razel wanted my guards sent home. Tendrils of ice crept down my spine, but I pushed back my fear. If this fight started, it wouldn't end until one side was dead or severely injured.

I couldn't refuse Razel's order. Shearen knew that. Razel knew that. I drew a deep breath and addressed my other guards. "Go with him. Tell everyone else to follow the orders they're given. I'll talk to the queen." The words were knives in my throat, but I forced them out steadily.

The guards bowed. Kiva stiffened beneath my touch but said nothing.

I faced Shearen. "Bring me to Razel."

He smirked and then nodded at one of the Vykryn at his back. She sneered as she pressed past me.

"Come on," I said to Kiva. She sheathed Sinvarra, her movements stiff with frustration, and we fell into step behind the Vykryn. My mind ripped through options for what to say. Was this in response to Ericen taking my place in that fight?

We stopped outside two ornate oak doors, the dark wood carved with a pair of rearing horses. A Vykryn soldier stood on either side.

One soldier inclined her head, saying tightly, "Your Highness."

"I need to speak with the queen," I said.

"The queen is in council. No one may disturb her prayers."

"Too bad." I surged forward, but the guards closed the space between them, blocking the door.

The other Vykryn's hand went to his sword, and Kiva's went to Sinvarra. "Give me a reason," the soldier growled.

Before I could respond, the door swung open. Auma appeared in the doorway, a fresh mark reddening her right eye. Kiva's lips parted with surprise, then curled into a snarl worthy of a Korovi ice bear.

Auma hesitated, meeting Kiva's gaze, before she bolted down the hall. One of the guards caught the door, holding it open as Razel stepped into view. Her lips twitched into a smile. "Thia dear, do come in."

The two Vykryn stepped aside to let me pass but blocked Kiva once I was through. The door slammed shut.

Razel's rooms dwarfed Kiva's and mine. The lounge consisted

of a single large square room of dark wood and golden metal. The left side of the floor had a shallow indentation in it, with two short, carpeted steps leading down to where a massive black desk stood before a hearth roaring with a fire taller than me.

Above the mantel hung a portrait of a young girl with golden hair and a beautiful black horse in an open field of long grass and wildflowers. The girl's arms hung about the horse's neck, a smile on her lips so warm, I almost didn't recognize the young Razel.

A life-sized black stone sculpture of a rearing horse occupied the left-hand corner of the room. Several golden dishes lined the base, a small prayer cushion sitting before it.

My eyes narrowed. Was that blood in the dishes?

The queen glided up to me, her icy eyes outlined in kohl. She wore a beautiful black dress with a golden bodice, the hilts of her moonblades resting like wings on her back. My gaze snagged on a series of thin slices on the backs of her forearms. They'd stopped bleeding but still shone red in the firelight like bloody smiles.

My stomach turned as I realized what they were: sacrificial cuts. Illucians believed praying to Rhett gave you strength. The more you prayed, the stronger and more skilled you would become. But first you had to offer that strength to Rhett. The strength of your blood.

"Did you need something?" Razel's tone twisted dangerously.

I forced my gaze away from her cuts. "Where did Auma get that mark?" It wasn't the question I'd come to ask, but it spilled out nonetheless.

Razel gave me a considering look. "How I punish my servants isn't your business. Tell your Korovi friend the same. I heard the two of them had dinner this evening, and I don't appreciate her distracting the girl from her work."

"You hit her, didn't you?"

A smile ripped across Razel's face like a jagged cut. "I won't repeat myself. Now, I assume that's not what you came for?"

I scowled. "You ordered my guards sent home. I want to know why, and then I want them returned."

"Whatever for? Do you feel unsafe?"

Something about her faltering smile, about the wild look to her gaze, made me pause. I'd felt unsafe from the moment I left Rhodaire, for the months before it since Ronoch—now? Now, I felt threatened.

"You have my guards to protect you, my servants to look after you, and your friend remains. I don't see any need for your people to stay." Razel swept toward the fire, and the light danced across the moonblades strapped to her back. She stopped before the flames, looking back at me.

The orange light played tricks across her pale skin, creating shadows that turned her face hollow and gaunt, like a skull lit by a candle. I gritted my teeth and stepped closer to her and the fire.

"I'm not afraid of you," I said. "And I won't let you control me either."

Razel's eyes flashed, and she grinned like a hungry jungle cat. "Let's be honest with each other, Thia dear. This is your home now, and it's my territory. If I wanted to hurt you, a few of your soldiers wouldn't be able to protect you."

A chill straightened my spine, and I took a step back.

She advanced. "I've been gracious with you, and I see no reason why that can't continue. I've given you free rein of the castle, promised warm clothes for you, and allowed you to keep you dearest friend at your side. But make no mistake." She seized my scarred wrist, dragging me toward her with surprising strength. "I'm not my son, who I hear has been more than tolerant of you, the spineless fool. Continue testing me, and I'll happily treat you like the crow-loving dog you are."

She stepped back, hauling me a step closer toward the hearth and wrenching my hand toward the flames. The warmth of the fire taunted my skin. I gasped, pulling back, but her hold only tightened. Something feral and distant gleamed in her eyes, as if she stared into a different world.

"I offered your sister peace, but I'd love nothing more than to send the army sitting on your border to crush what remains of your family and friends for Rhett and my people, for the lives of my family." She pulled my arm closer to the fire until the flames snapped at my fingers.

My heart threatened to burst as I clawed frantically at her hand with my free one and threw my body weight into leaning away.

"Maybe I still will." She let go.

I tumbled to the floor and crashed into the desk, clutching my arm to my chest. Razel stood over me, the fire leaping and roaring at her back, the shadows of her moonblades reaching up like two great claws above her shoulders.

"But as I said, I see no reason why we can't be civil with each other." She smiled another serrated smile, then stepped over me and disappeared into a connecting room.

Out of breath and desperate to escape the flames, I scrambled to my feet and bolted for the door, dashing down the hall before Kiva could even get a word out.

It took time for the fear to fade. When it finally did, it left a hollow pit in my stomach. Shame burned my cheeks, and I buried my head farther beneath my pillow as if it might spare me from my emotions. At first, Kiva had banged on my door, begging me to let her in. It'd made everything inside me twist and writhe. When she stopped, the stillness was worse.

That night with the carriage, now this. Razel hadn't even burned me. She hadn't needed to.

I hadn't hesitated to clamber into bed and hide. The warmth and darkness of the sheets pulled me under, locking me in place. A new fear took root. What if I could never truly escape this?

The hollow pit in my stomach simmered. Razel must have noticed the way I'd reacted to the fire in the throne room, must have seen my burned hand and connected the two. She knew I was afraid of fire, and she'd used it against me at the first sign of defiance. And I'd let her.

The simmering turned hot and vicious. All I wanted was to hide beneath my covers and let the world fade away. Someone else would come. Someone capable. Someone unbroken. I could just lie here and wait until…until what? Until Razel conquered

Korovi and Trendell and burned Rhodaire to the ground? Until she fulfilled her religion's promise for ownership of the world?

I'd told Razel she couldn't control me, and I'd meant it. I wouldn't let her condemn me to a life weighed down to my bed. Not again.

Throwing back the covers, I changed from my still-damp dress into a clean one. As I tossed the old dress to the floor, a crumpled paper tumbled from one of the pockets. I scooped it up, unfurling it to reveal one of the Ambriellan boy's flyers. Had he slipped it into my pocket?

Something had been scrawled across the top of the paper. I stared openmouthed at the word, then bolted from the room.

"Kiva!"

She catapulted off the couch, but before she could ask, I thrust the flyer in her face. Her eyes locked on the word at the top. *Catternon.* "That's the password," she said. "The one for communicating about the Ambriellan rebels in the Verian Hills. Where did you get this?"

I grinned, quickly filling her in on my run-in with the boy in the Colorfalls. Whoever he'd been, he hadn't run into me by accident.

"We have to go see him tomorrow," I said.

"Will Razel let you out of the castle?" Kiva asked. "And what in the Saints' name happened earlier?"

I gritted my teeth at the mention of the queen but told Kiva everything.

"*Zyuka!*" she snarled, throwing her hands down onto the table before her. From my spot where I'd dropped onto the couch facing her, I let out a low whistle. Kiva rarely spoke Korovi.

"Agreed," I replied, though I didn't know what the word meant. "I should have expected it. Besides, I'm supposed to be keeping my head down, and challenging her wasn't the best way to do that."

"She sent your guards home! She's trying to isolate you and make you easier to control."

Was this why she hadn't set the wedding date? She wanted to break me first? Caliza had said Razel didn't make threats, but clearly, something had changed. She'd looked unhinged. "She'll come after you next. It's probably why she let you stay."

Kiva snorted. "I'd like to see her try."

Her confidence ate away at the anxiety inside me. "I won't sit here like a pawn for her use. I'll convince her to let me go." I spread the paper out between us, pointing at the title. "I think this advertisement is real. It could be a good cover for coming and going from the castle."

Kiva leaned closer. "A lab assistant?"

I nodded. "More than that, he might be able to help us hatch the egg." She looked up at me, her lips already parting to tell me it was a foolish idea. I hurried on. "No one knows how, and the information's not in any book I could find. So I need someone who can figure it out on their own."

"You want to experiment on it?"

"It's either that or do nothing."

She frowned. "And what? Hope he doesn't ask what this egg-shaped thing is doing with this very Rhodairen-looking girl? You can't trust him."

I spun the paper so the writing faced me. "First, he's

Ambriellan, so I don't think he'll be looking to turn me over first chance, particularly if he's a rebel. And second, I'm not planning on bringing him the egg. But a few theoretical questions won't hurt."

Kiva leaned back, folding her arms. "I don't like it, but I don't have another idea."

I smirked, scanning through the flyer again. At the bottom, written in almost illegible handwriting, was the address and his name: Caylus Zander.

FIFTEEN

I t felt good to have a plan again, as difficult as it would be to enact. It relied on me playing a part I wasn't sure I could. Razel wanted to control me, to break me, and like a desert snake with its prey, the more I riled against her, the more she'd constrict. So I had to stop reacting, stop challenging her, and instead play the demure, compliant little princess she wanted.

It started with asking for permission to leave the castle.

After my morning check on the egg, I sent a note to Razel asking to take a trip into the city, then left with Kiva for the training grounds, where we found a small space far away from Illucian soldiers to train. It felt like walking into a den of wolves. The force of their glares was palpable, as if each one of them were imagining the feel of their blade piercing my flesh.

Their treatment of one another wasn't much better. All

around us, they bested one another viciously in the sparring rings or at swordplay, leaving their opponents bleeding in the dust. There was no camaraderie here, no love or respect. Just sharp blades and the smack of bone against flesh.

My focus waned as Kiva and I stretched. I kept catching groups of soldiers looking at us, then quickly away, their laughter echoing across the foggy grounds. News of my encounter with Razel last night must have spread.

"Ignore them," Kiva said.

I tried. I really did. But when one soldier imitated me cowering in fear to the snickers of her cohorts, I snatched up my bow, seized a dulled practice arrow, and nocked it. In one smooth movement, I turned, drew, and loosed. The arrow struck the practice dummy they were standing around between the eyes.

They stopped laughing.

Kiva grinned. "I forgot how good you were with that thing."

Satisfaction warmed my blood, but as I turned the gold-veined black bow over in my hand, thoughts of Estrel crept in, and the feeling faded. How many hours had she spent teaching me to shoot with this bow?

The smile vanished from Kiva's face, and I spun about to find Razel striding toward us, Shearen and another Vykryn her ever-present shadows. My skin instantly grew hot, my heart beating erratically.

Breathe. I drew a deep breath, holding it until my lungs burned, then let it out silently as the queen halted before us.

"I received your request, Thia dear." She held up my note between two fingers, her head tilted like a predator considering its prey. "After last night, I have to say I'm concerned for the safety of my citizens. You clearly possess an unhealthy amount of rage." Her eyes slid from me to the arrow I'd driven between the dummy's eyes. "What if you were to lose your temper and hurt someone?"

My eyes widened. *I* possessed an unhealthy amount of rage? *I* was a threat to her people? She'd practically tried to kill Ericen yesterday! I started to reply when something jabbed into my side. My gaze snapped down to the pommel of Kiva's sword as she shifted it out of view.

Right. Demure. Compliant.

"I apologize for last night." Each word scraped against my throat like hot coals, but I forced them out. "I panicked, and I reacted poorly. It won't happen again."

Razel's kohl-lined gaze didn't waver. A heartbeat later, I realized I hadn't blinked either and quickly bowed my head.

"Very well," the queen said.

I didn't dare look up. I didn't think I could control myself if I saw the satisfaction dripping from her voice reflected in her face.

Footsteps sounded and then faded, and I raised my head to watch her leave. Around us, the training Vykryn smirked and muttered to each other.

I forced myself to breathe against the sickening feeling twisting inside me.

Kiva stepped up beside me. "It's worth it. Remember why you're doing this."

"I remember."

We stepped out of the castle to a dry but clouded day, where a blue-and-gold carriage sat waiting with two Vykryn on horseback beside it. I exchanged looks with Kiva as she gave our driver the address and we climbed inside.

"We need a way to get rid of them," I whispered.

Kiva peered out the window at one of the massive black horses as the carriage rumbled into motion. "They only care you don't escape. Maybe they'll stay outside."

Several minutes later, we rounded a bend of houses, and the Colorfalls sprang into view. They were far more muted during the day, the colors turned pastel from the pale sunlight filtering through the parting clouds.

I asked our driver for directions, and he pointed at the bakery Ericen had taken me to. The warm smell of bread drifted out as we approached, the quiet music of a wooden wind chime jingling. A massive willow tree obscured nearly half the building, and thick green vines curled around the edges and along the roof.

Our Vykryn escorts dismounted and handed their horses off to the driver. Their presence made me uneasy, and I didn't miss the casual placement of Kiva's hand near Sinvarra. Like all Illucian soldiers, they moved like hunters. Lithe. Powerful. Dangerous.

Thankfully, they stayed outside when we entered the bakery. The inside was warm from the ovens, chasing the morning chill from my skin. Fresh bread and pastries filled baskets and glass cases, samples of cherry tarts set atop a stand by the door. I popped one in my mouth, the sweetness of the fruit coating my tongue, and barely avoided stepping on a snow-white kitten lapping milk from a tin.

A woman with a kind, round face stood behind the counter, shaping dough on a bed of flour. She smiled as we approached. "Can I help you?"

I pulled the flyer out of my pocket, swallowing my sample. "I'm looking for Caylus Zander."

She dusted her hands on her apron, moving toward a door in the back. "Caylus!"

He appeared a moment later, his massive frame taking up most of the doorway. Something fluttered in my stomach. His bright-green eyes widened, and I smirked. He had flour in his hair.

I lifted the flyer. "I wanted to talk to you about this position."

He looked at the paper, then over my shoulder. I turned, but the Vykryn weren't visible through the window. Was he looking for Ericen?

"I… We can go upstairs." He started to turn, stopped, and spun back, nearly knocking a mixing bowl off the counter with his elbow as he faced the woman. He seized the bowl, steadying it as he asked, "If you don't need me?" She waved him off, and he stepped out from behind the counter, starting toward a staircase in the corner.

Kiva cast me a doubtful look, somehow managing to infuse her raised eyebrow with an ocean of sarcasm. Her hand hadn't left Sinvarra.

We followed Caylus upstairs, the rickety wood creaking. The stairwell emptied onto a too-small landing, so Kiva stood on the stairs while Caylus undid the lock. And the next lock. And the next lock. I counted five, and his quivering hands prolonged the process before the door swung open.

I glanced at him, but he wouldn't meet my gaze, and even in the dim light, I could see the scarlet creeping up the back of his neck.

The entryway led into a kitchen, which contained only a square island in the center, dusted with leftover flour. The wall behind consisted of a built-in brick oven, a loaf of bread cooling inside, and beside that a stove with a kettle set on top. A mix of morning buns and muffins sat on the island, filling the room with the smell of warm bread and sugar.

"Scientist, inventor, and baker?" I asked as Caylus removed his apron, setting it on the island. He wore a rumpled and patched tunic underneath. It hung loose and off kilter on his broad shoulders, revealing a swath of tanned, muscular chest. I stared until Kiva elbowed me in the ribs.

Caylus didn't seem to notice. "I work in exchange for the rooms." He dusted his hands off on his pants, coating them with flour. I waited, but he didn't say anything more. He wouldn't look directly at either of us, and he shifted his weight in a constant fidget.

"Right," I said at last. "I'm assuming you know why I'm here?"

"Catternon," he said, speaking the old language password from the flyer. It was an ancient name for the yearly festival the Ambriels held in honor of their sea god, Duren.

Kiva slowly canvassed the room. Besides the kitchen, there was a closed door to our right and a set of stairs that led to another closed door. She peered up the stairs, then pushed open the downstairs door to reveal an empty bedroom.

Caylus watched her silently, not interfering. Once Kiva seemed satisfied, I said, "You're a rebel."

He shook his head, then stopped as if reconsidering. "Sort of. Not really." I raised an eyebrow, and he explained, "I know the leader, the one organizing the raids in the Verian Hills. She asked me to get a message to her contact in the castle, but when I saw you..."

"She has a contact in the castle?" Kiva asked. "Who?"

"And how did you know who I was?" I added.

Caylus shifted his weight again. "There aren't many Rhodairens around here. Not any, I don't think. And you were with the prince."

So he had recognized Ericen. Yet he'd still intervened last night, knowing full well who he risked angering. An image of his scarred, shaking hands surfaced. Where had those scars come from?

He glanced at Kiva, then away again. "I think you should talk to her about this, not me. I owed her a favor."

"Can you set up a meeting?" I asked. "Here, preferably. And soon."

"Tomorrow evening? At sunset?"

I nodded, my heart rate rising. This was happening. "What about the assistant position? Is that real?"

He bit his lip. "It, um, doesn't pay..."

Kiva snorted, but I said quickly, "That's fine. I need a reason to come here, or the queen may be suspicious."

At first, I thought he didn't hear me, but then I realized his eyes were focused through the window over my shoulder, where the two Vykryn who'd accompanied us stood across the street.

"Something wrong?" Kiva asked, her tone low. "You look worried."

"I—No. I'm fine. Anthia, right?" His eyes fell on me. His lilted Ambriellan accent turned my name into a song, and I half considered letting him call me by my full name just to hear it.

"Just Thia." I jerked my head to the side. "This is Kiva. Don't mind her. She wouldn't trust a chair to stay still long enough to sit in it."

Caylus blinked, his head tilting, the puzzled look on his face suggesting he hadn't noticed Kiva's insinuations at all.

"Do you know who I am, Caylus?" I asked. "What it is you're involved in?"

"Unfortunately."

I glanced at Kiva, but a small smile tugged at Caylus's lips. He was joking.

Kiva hooked her arm through mine. "Right. See you tomorrow," she said.

I waved as she jerked me toward the exit, closing the door behind us. As we descended the stairs, I heard the locks click.

We waved to the woman behind the counter and left the shop, the two Vykryn mounting as we climbed into the carriage.

The moment the door shut, Kiva said, "He's weird."

"I think he's cute."

"I don't trust him."

I rolled my eyes. "You don't trust anyone."

"There's something not right about him. He gets this look in his eye like he's planning something. I've seen it in criminals."

"He's an inventor. He probably thinks a lot."

She leveled me with a flat stare, and I sighed, leaning forward. "He's in a difficult spot, Kiva. He's in enemy territory, helping to facilitate an alliance against them. Give him a break."

"I'll give him more than a break if he screws us over," she muttered.

SIXTEEN

Our carriage pulled along the circular drive of the castle, but when the door opened, it wasn't the driver standing alongside it. It was Ericen. He stepped aside as we climbed out.

"Did you enjoy your trip to the city?" he asked. The wound on his face had scabbed over, the bruising on the edges starting to fade.

"It would have been a lot better if I didn't feel like a prisoner," I replied, glancing at the two Vykryn.

"More like an honored guest."

"Who can't leave."

He smirked. "Right. Could I borrow you?"

Kiva interjected before I could reply. "I think the words you're looking for are 'I'm sorry I'm such an ass.'"

A muscle feathered in his jaw. "Yes. I was getting to that."

She raised an expectant eyebrow, and Ericen sighed. "I'm sorry for the way I acted last night."

"Close enough." Kiva stepped toward the castle. "I'll meet you inside."

I nodded, trying to hide the smile threatening my lips. "I'm assuming you didn't come down here just for that?"

"To be scolded like a child? Surprisingly, no." He smiled. "Come with me. I want to show you something."

He led me along a dirt path that curled around the castle. It sloped upward toward a large barn lined with wide square doors that split across the middle. Several were open, revealing the black heads of massive warhorses. At the main entrance, two wooden doors had been pinned open.

Horses stood secured to metal loops in the barn walls as stable hands brushed them or else swept the main walkway clear of hay and horsehair. Ericen traced a path through the horses, taking us much closer to their back hooves than I'd have liked, but he seemed as comfortable around them as I'd been with the crows.

We stopped outside one of the stalls, where a horse had her head poking out toward us. Beside her, a tiny foal trembled on uncertain legs, its coat black as night.

"My stallion's the sire." He nodded at another stall, the name *Callo* carved into the wood.

I grinned. "It's adorable."

Ericen leaned against the stall door. "Wonderful, I'll tell the stable master. I'm sure he'll appreciate knowing his newest warhorse is *adorable*." He ran his hand along the mother's neck in an almost reverent touch.

I snorted. "Did you think a cute animal would make me forgive you?"

"Depends. Is it working?"

"A little bit."

The foal wobbled toward us, and I reached out, but Ericen seized my hand. I started to snap at him but caught sight of the mare's dark eyes watching me keenly.

"The mothers can be very...protective." He released my hand.

I stepped back, then again as a stable hand with a bucket of feed moved toward us.

"Pardon me, Your Highnesses," she said.

Ericen moved aside as the girl lifted the bucket over the edge of the stall and onto a hook on the other side.

My mouth fell open. "Is that *meat*?"

"They have a big appetite." He grinned, but it quickly faded, the lines of his face hardening. Something molten gleamed in his eyes, and I followed his gaze as Shearen entered the barn and disappeared into a stall.

"Not that I wouldn't like to pummel the guy myself, but is there something between you two?" I asked.

Ericen blinked. He'd been staring hard enough to bore holes. "We just don't get along."

"The truest hate is born from the truest love," I said softly. A Trendellan proverb Caliza's husband had taught me. The relationship between Shearen and Ericen, the emotion I saw in each of their faces, it didn't just manifest overnight.

Ericen's expression hardened. "We were like brothers

at Darkward. Almost through our fifteenth year, we were inseparable."

"What happened?" I asked.

"He was under a lot of pressure. His family and mine have always been close, so he had the eye of his superiors, as well as generations of expectations. Then my mother came to visit." Ericen toyed with a lead line dangling from a wall hitch, as if he'd told this story a thousand times and grown tired of it. "All anyone cared about was catching her attention and earning her favor. Shearen fell in with a new group. At first, I think he was trying to earn her approval, but the person he became to do it, the things he did..." He trailed off, jaw clenching.

I stared. Was the Illucian prince reproaching a fellow soldier for being *too* horrible?

The stall door Shearen had stepped through opened, and he reappeared leading a pure black stallion. His eyes found us, and he went rigid, then jerked his horse's lead to direct it outside.

Ericen watched him leave, face impassive. "He became obsessed. We disagreed on everything until, eventually, it drove a wedge between us. Now I think he wants my mother's approval as much as I do. It's all he has left. It's practically become a competition."

The high expectations of a mother were something I understood. The thought made me pause. Was I *empathizing* with him?

Shaking away the thought, I turned back to the stall, watching as the mare nudged her foal with her nose. "Did you mean what you said at dinner the other night?" I asked. "About not wanting to be my enemy?"

"Every word."

"Prove it. Convince your mother to let me go into the city alone. I went to escape the castle. I may even have found a hobby. Something to make me forget where I am and who I'm trapped with. But having those soldiers on my back makes me feel like a prisoner."

Ericen regarded me in silence, his bright eyes quiet. Then, "I'll talk to her."

I let out a breath. "Thank you." Strangely, some small part of me felt guilty lying to him. But I didn't have a choice. I needed to be able to visit Caylus alone tomorrow. The future of my kingdom depended on it.

Kiva and I trained again the next morning, then returned to our room to bathe and change. Feathers fluttered in my stomach the entire time, the anticipation of meeting the Ambriellan rebel leader nearly overwhelming. I'd been planning what to say to her all morning, to the point that my distraction had made it easy for Kiva to best me in sparring. Even sitting with the egg for a few minutes did little to calm my nerves.

When I emerged from my room, I found Kiva talking to Auma in the doorway. Kiva leaned against the door frame, arms folded, posture softer than she ever allowed it to be. Around her side, I could just see Auma, so much smaller yet somehow equally as strong a presence.

Lunch had been delivered and now sat on the table, an

assortment of sandwiches and tea. When Auma spotted me, she bowed and excused herself.

"What do you two talk about?" I asked, settling down to eat.

"We don't, really." Kiva joined me at the table. "She listens a lot."

"You always did like the quiet ones."

She rolled her eyes before her expression hardened. "She told me how she ended up here. Serving Razel."

I paused halfway through a sandwich bite and swallowed hard. "I have a feeling it's not a nice story."

Kiva swirled her teacup in a slow circle. "She was fourteen when Illucia attacked the capital. Her mother died in battle, and her father was a guild leader. He refused to step down, so the Illucians killed him too."

I set the sandwich down, the sight of it making my stomach squirm. When I'd learned about Illucia's victory over Jindae in my lessons, it'd seemed so far away. Since the guild leaders handled most of the day-to-day politics in Jindae, the first thing Razel did was demand their allegiance. Those who didn't relinquish their authority lost their lives instead.

Hearing it again now, knowing Auma—my hands curled into fists.

"They conscripted her older brother too." With each word, Kiva's expression darkened, her hand straying to Sinvarra as if the blade could fight away these truths. "She used the last of her money to pay a merchant traveling to Sordell for travel so she could follow her brother here. She earned a position as a servant at the castle and has been trying to find him since."

Her words settled like hot coals in the pit of my stomach. "I can't believe my mother never did anything to help. Rhodaire let this happen."

Kiva's hand tightened around Sinvarra's hilt. "That's why we're going to help undo it. Starting with tonight."

By the time we ordered the carriage, my nerves were bolts of lightning zipping through my veins. What if the rebel leader didn't come? What if they refused to help? With no news from Jindae, Trendell, or Korovi and no progress on hatching the egg, this meeting was the real first step toward stopping Illucia.

It had to go perfectly, and that started with Ericen convincing Razel to remove our escort.

As Kiva and I reached the front courtyard where the carriage waited, I slowed, scanning the sodden grounds. No Vykryn.

"I guess Ericen kept his word," Kiva said.

I started to nod, then halted in the main doorway as someone appeared around the side of the carriage. Razel. The same stinging warmth that flushed my skin every time I saw her surged to life.

Her eyes fell on me, and she smiled. Had she been suspicious of Ericen's request to remove our escort? Was she going to stop me from leaving?

"Thia," Kiva muttered.

My nails dug into my palms, Razel's expression turning bemused. She didn't believe my faked subservience. How could she when I couldn't stop my emotions from playing across my face? But she probably enjoyed seeing me struggle to try, probably knew that even though I was pretending, it still made me feel weak, still kept me controlled and powerless, exactly like she wanted.

To get what I wanted, I had to give her what she wanted: obedience.

I propelled myself forward with sheer willpower, straight down the gravel path to the waiting queen. Kiva stayed close at my back as I stopped before Razel.

"My son has informed me you wish to remove your protection," she said.

Protection. My jaw clenched. "I do."

"And why is that?"

"I've taken a position as an assistant for a man in the Colorfalls as a hobby to occupy my time. He's very…private. He doesn't like the guards being there."

Razel smiled. "A servant? How fitting. Perhaps it will teach you the humility you lack or at the very least how to dedicate yourself to something. I've heard such stories about the princess who abandoned her duties."

Fury prickled like a shiver down my spine, but I kept my mouth shut. Beside me, I could feel Kiva's tension, but she didn't betray a thing. Somehow, I had to learn to do the same.

Razel continued, "If you want to visit this man unprotected, I expect to see some proof of your progress."

I forced myself to nod.

"For example," she said, voice dripping with rancid honey, "you should say 'Yes, Your Majesty,' when I give you an order."

"Yes, Your Majesty." The words came out tight, but they came.

"And you should bow."

Slowly, I lowered my head.

"Lower."

I bowed lower, forcing myself to breathe slowly. To remember why I had to obey.

"Very good, Thia dear. You may go, but your friend stays."

Kiva tensed as I snapped upright, but my protest died in my throat at the look on Razel's face. One that dared me to contradict her, lest she take more from me than that. It was smart, really. She'd removed the guards, but she knew I wouldn't leave Illucia without Kiva.

"Yes, Your Majesty," I said through gritted teeth.

Razel strode past me. "Be back before dinner each day. If ever you two leave together, there will be consequences."

"I don't like you going without me," Kiva grumbled once she'd gone.

"I'll be okay," I promised. "Write to Caliza. Let her know I'm fine and what's happening."

Kiva nodded as I climbed into the carriage. "Good luck."

At the bakery, a girl behind the counter made me wait while she found the woman from the day before. My fingers drummed heavily on my hip, and I kept glancing at the stairs to Caylus's room. Was the Ambriellan leader already there?

"It's my first day," she apologized, noting my frustration.

The woman appeared from the back room. "He's upstairs," she said and waved me up.

At the top of the stairs, I waited for the locks to be undone. The door opened slowly, revealing one green eye and a band of tan skin, before Caylus opened the door entirely. He moved aside to let me in, then closed the door and redid the locks.

Caylus retreated toward the center island. He wore an apron over his tunic and pants, a strange lump in one of the pockets centered over his stomach. No one else was here.

"I made tea if you want some while we wait," Caylus said quietly. Always quietly. Like he hoped no one would notice. Yet somehow, his voice still seemed strong, like the quiet rush of a stream that could easily become a river.

"Sure." I slid onto one of the stools alongside the island. Caylus poured me a cup with unsteady hands, then set it on a saucer alongside a blueberry muffin, still warm from the oven. The lump over his stomach wriggled as he moved.

The tea had an earthy scent tinged with orange, and I breathed it in deep. "So what kinds of things are you expecting me to do as your assistant?" I asked.

Caylus leaned on the island but didn't meet my gaze. His eyes kept flickering to my face, then away, and once again, I saw something achingly familiar in their green depths. "Cook, clean, kill spiders," he said.

I stared at him.

"Joking," he said. A smile split across my lips, and he added, "Small stuff. Measuring, writing, things you need...well, steady hands for." His fingers curled around his cup of tea.

I thought of the scars along his fingers but didn't ask. He hadn't so much as looked at mine.

The lump over his stomach squirmed again, and a tiny white head poked out. The little kitten I'd seen downstairs crawled from the pocket and scaled Caylus's chest to perch on his shoulder. He didn't even seem to notice as he pushed away from the island, tea in hand. "I can show you the workshop?"

"What about the meeting?" I asked.

"She'll be here soon."

I followed him upstairs, the kitten balancing on his broad shoulders with ease. The stairs emptied onto a small landing with a door to the only room upstairs. Caylus pushed it open, and we stepped in.

Every wall had a long wooden workbench pushed against it, strewn with sheets of metal and rows of glass vials, bottles, and jars. Half-dismantled pieces of machinery sat beside stacks of paper, all organized around books propped open to marked pages and annotated diagrams. The room had a strange haphazard continuity to it, as if each scattered item had grown organically from the one beside it.

My gaze caught on a sketchbook in the center of a cleared space, the bottom corner and spine worn as if frequently opened. I lifted the cover, but the page underneath was blank, and none of the pages looked to have been torn out. Beside it sat several glass vials of what looked like bird poop and a book pinned open to a page with colorful drawings. One vial was labeled *Magpie* and lay beside another vial titled *Raven*.

"What are you working on?" I asked.

Caylus looked up from readjusting his perpetually askew shirt. He'd removed his apron and even ran his scarred hands through his hair in an attempt to fix it, but it didn't help. He gave up, looking as defeated as a puppy thwarted by a door handle. The kitten batted at a stray curl, and I resisted the urge to pat the lock into place.

"I'm looking at the properties of bird feces from species that look related to the crows." He approached the desk with the vials.

I went rigid. "Why are you doing that?"

"I'm looking for signs of magic." Caylus tapped the open book. "The crows weren't the only source, with the Sellas and all. I want to find another. There are a number of ways I think it could work with technology."

The way he spoke about the crows threw me off, so casual and normal. Like he didn't fully recognize who he was talking to. Though I was starting to realize that Caylus wasn't very good at noticing things. He was also talking about the Sellas as if they hadn't been gone for hundreds of years.

I, on the other hand, was having a hard time not noticing the hard lines of his body beneath the tunic or the specks of white scarring along the golden skin of his arms. Or the way his size made me feel small in a strange, safe sort of way, like the crows always had.

"...considering the crows showed a lot of elemental applications of magic, you know?" Caylus finished.

I blinked. Saints. He'd been talking that whole time. He didn't miss my bewildered look, a blush rising in his cheeks. "I was rambling, wasn't I?"

"Not really," I lied. I peered at the title of the book. "*Saints and Sellas?* You're reading a book of myths for information? You must be desperate."

I hadn't read the stories in years, but I'd heard them all. Some of the best memories I had of my mother came from when she'd tell me stories about the Saints and the ancient Sellas whose magic gave birth to the crows, according to legend.

"Myths are rooted in history and culture," Caylus said. "They may be distorted retellings of fact."

"Or entirely made up," I said.

"Or entirely made up," he agreed, dropping into his desk chair and pulling the kitten from his shoulder. He set it in his lap, where it curled up. "I'm desperate. People here don't have much on record about crows or the Sellas."

The stories said Sella magic had once blanketed the land, but humans did something to anger the Sellas. So they left, taking their magic with them. The religion around them was nearly extinct now, to the point that most people thought they'd never existed, that the stories were just that. Hardly anyone spoke the old language anymore, and there weren't many copies of the book left.

I opened to a page with a drawing of the Wandering Wood, a beautiful forest of massive, colorful trees that looked like someone had spilled a bundle of dyes across their leaves. Pale spring green melded into buttery yellows and robin's egg blues. There were even trees the bright pink of sunrise and the deep mauve of dusk.

The story said the Wandering Wood was an ancient well of

magic that only appeared on the full moon. During that time, it allowed the chosen to come and go as they pleased, but you had to be out of the wood by sunrise, or else you'd be trapped until the next full moon.

Right now, that didn't sound half bad.

Caylus set his cup on the desk. "You would have known the crows well, right?"

His question plucked at a heartstring, sending a quiver through my chest. "Yes."

His eyes lit up, and for the first time, he met my gaze fully and unwaveringly. "Can you tell me about them?"

For half a second, I remembered Ericen asking me the very same question and the way my entire being had revolted against the idea. But with Caylus, the curiosity in his eyes, the light—it made my heart beat faster and my stomach turn in anticipation, an echo of the feeling that engulfed me moments before a flight. To my surprise, I *wanted* to tell him.

I leaned against the workbench. "What do you want to know?"

"Everything."

So I told him. I told him about the types of crows, from how a shadow crow could deceive your perception of space, camouflaging itself in night, to the way a sun crow's golden touch could heal a wound in minutes. I told him how a battle crow could turn its feathers to metal and release them on command and about the black-gold weapons the Turren masters made from it.

He asked questions, more than I'd ever been asked. He

was quick, easily picking up on the patterns of their magic and remembering the smallest details.

"So a water crow could turn water to ice?" he asked, and I nodded. "Could they create mist then too?"

"Yep. On especially hot days, riders would drop mist from the sky to cool workers in the fields."

"And your students at the riding school. Not all of them became riders?"

"Only about half."

Becoming a rider took a lifetime of dedication. Even before contenders entered Kalestel, the riding school, crows would have been their lives. They'd have been raised working with them, learning their strengths and weaknesses, the extent of their abilities, the history of their wings. And after all that, less than half of them would become riders.

Typically, it was a mantle passed down from parent to child, uncle to niece, staying firmly rooted in familial lines. Anyone could apply to Kalestel, and they frequently took students outside of established rider families, but it was rare for a crow to form a connection with one.

In the end, they became involved in other ways. Working at Kalestel, turning to wing-specific trades focused around the crows, like the Garien leatherworkers who crafted the finest saddles.

Caylus tapped his fingers on his leg, absently moving them about for the kitten to pounce on. "It's strange that it stays mostly in families. I wonder…" He trailed off, his brows furrowing and his head tilting in a way I'd come to understand meant he was faced with a problem he couldn't solve.

"Wonder what?" I asked.

He blinked. "Sorry. I wonder if forming a bond with a crow has an impact on a person's physiology somehow. Something passed down generation to generation."

I grinned. "You're good. Some Rhodairen scholars thought the same thing. They called it magic lines."

He leaned forward, eyes bright. "But then the question is what exactly is passed down."

"Crows form bonds with their riders," I said, excitement prickling my skin. "Unbreakable bonds, as strong as a real cord strung between them. This journal I read thought it might be related to them."

He nodded enthusiastically, not even noticing as the kitten pounced, digging his tiny claws into the back of Caylus's hand. "But the question is, do the chosen riders already have magic, or do the crows grant it to them when the bond forms?"

He leaned back, one finger stroking the kitten's head as he retreated into another silence. It wasn't until the room was quiet that I realized what I'd just done. I'd talked about the crows, and I'd done it without spiraling into a pit of dark emotions.

Something about Caylus had made me feel comfortable enough to share, and from there, our shared natural curiosity had driven away any lingering doubts. I wanted to know, and so did he.

A three-beat knock sounded on the workroom door. Caylus rose quietly, crossing the room to open it. My heart thudded with each step, the distance between the threshold and me stretching. Suddenly, I couldn't remember all the things I'd wanted to say.

A figure slipped in, a hood obscuring her face, as Caylus closed the door behind her. I stood facing her. She wore a simple half-white, half-black mask split down the middle, like the ones worn in the Ambriels during Catternon, meant to symbolize the split between the sea god, Duren, and his dark sister, the Night Captain.

"Princess Anthia," came a hard voice from beneath the mask. She wore all black, her clothes thick and concealing. Leather gloves and heavy boots adorned her hands and feet, every inch of her obscured. Even her eyes were dark as obsidian.

This was it. This was happening.

"Who are you?" I asked.

"You may call me Diah." She had the easy bearing that came with knowing your place at the top, and I longed to project the same.

"After the Night Captain?"

Diah nodded. "I represent the Ambriellan rebels. We were contacted by one of your people. I was told you wished to negotiate an alliance."

"We do." Despite the confidence I projected, inwardly, I analyzed everything. My posture, my expression, my tone. This was the beginning of Rhodaire's salvation—or its end. I needed her to hear me, to trust me.

Diah chuckled. "The mighty Rhodaire seeks our help. Now that Illucia threatens your borders, your people. Where were your armies when the Ambriels fell? When Jindae fell? Where were your crows?"

"I—" I stopped. What explanation could I possibly give?

My mother had sent minimal support to both kingdoms, and it hadn't been enough. We'd opened our borders to Jin and Ambriellans fleeing Illucia, gave them food and shelter, but nothing more.

"You abandoned us," Diah said. "Why should we not do the same to you?"

The nervous tension strung through me snapped, pooling sharp and cold in my chest. It struck me that I didn't know how to do this. Talking to people, negotiating—this was Caliza's world, not mine. What could I possibly say that would sway her?

I looked from Diah to Caylus, who had leaned back against the door, his hands tucked behind the small of his back. He looked up, meeting my gaze through curls of messy hair, and I saw that familiar something in them. Something that had led me to tell him about the crows.

Something painful. Something broken.

So many broken people.

This had begun because I didn't want to marry Ericen. Then it became about protecting Rhodaire. But it was bigger than both of those things. Illucia had to be stopped before they were all that was left.

I drew a breath. "You can't defeat Illucia by raiding transports in the Verian Hills. Jindae can't defeat them with their court scattered to the wind. We can't defeat them with the remnants of our army. Alone, none of us will win."

I straightened. "I don't know why my mother refused to send aid to the Ambriels or Jindae, but it was wrong. We had the power to help, and we didn't. I won't make her same mistake. Either we work together, or Illucia will destroy us all."

Diah was quiet for a moment, her depthless eyes betraying nothing. She held my gaze, as if searching for the truth inside me. At last, she inclined her head in the smallest nod. "I require time to consider what you're offering. I will notify Caylus when I have an answer."

I nodded, and in a flutter of dark cloth, Diah turned for the door. Caylus moved out of her way, closing the door once she'd passed.

I released a heavy breath. "I can't tell if that went well."

Caylus smiled slightly. "Diah is...very critical. She didn't refuse you outright. It's a good sign."

"I hope you're right."

One kingdom down; three to go.

SEVENTEEN

A letter came from Caliza during breakfast the next morning. Lighting a candle and setting it on the dining table, I read quickly through the visible text describing how much she missed me before sprinkling black dust over the back of the letter. I held it as near to the flame as I dared, and the invisible ink materialized.

Thia,

The king and queen of Trendell have agreed to host an alliance meeting. They'll hear us out, but they want to see the crow. They've set a meeting date for near a month from now, on the Trendellan holiday of Belin's Day. We have to hatch the crow by then.

*Things here are growing more precarious.
Skirmishes have broken out on the border, and the
Illucian army has raided as far south as Mycair.
We can hold them off for now, but they're choking
our supply lines, and the latest report on crops isn't
good.*

We're running out of time.
Please stay safe.

Love,
Caliza

The letter crumpled in my fist. We'd acquiesced to all Razel's demands, and yet she was still terrorizing my people.

Kiva plucked the letter from my hand, read it, and then crossed the room to toss it into the fire.

"Well, at least Trendell has agreed to host the meeting," she said. I'd updated her on the meeting with Diah. Things were finally moving. "The only question is how do we get there."

"And with a hatched crow," I said. *We're running out of time.*

Standing, I left my breakfast untouched and went to my room to pen a return letter for Caliza, writing in invisible ink that I had a lead on the egg and would update her soon. Then I wrapped the egg in a blanket, set it gently in a bag with a book and sweater to disfigure the shape, and returned to the common room.

Kiva nearly dropped the teapot she'd been pouring from. "What in the Saints' name are you doing?"

"Taking the egg to Caylus."

She set the teapot down with a thump. "Did I hit you too hard sparring this morning?"

I rolled my eyes. "You read Caliza's letter. We're running out of time. Caylus is with the rebels. If we can't trust them, this is all for nothing anyways. And right now, he's my only chance of hatching this egg."

Kiva looked like she wanted to argue, but in the end, she let out a grumbling sigh.

"Send this out for me?" I handed her the letter.

She took it. "I hate that I'm stuck here."

"At least you can spend more time with Auma." I shot for the door before she could throw something at me.

Caylus had just finished up a shift when I arrived at the bakery, his hair and skin dusted in flour like powdered snow. He smiled when I entered, and we went upstairs to his workshop. He sat down at one of the workbenches beside the kitten, who lay curled on a blanket near the sona lamp. "Is something wrong?"

"I need your help." I pulled the bag at my hip onto the workbench, then paused. Despite what I'd said to Kiva, trusting Caylus was a risk. But he already knew about our plans with the rebels. If he was going to betray us, he would have already.

I unwrapped the blanket, revealing the egg.

Caylus's eyes widened, and he ran quivering fingers along the smooth shell. I gave him a moment. When he finally looked back at me, I said, "We need to figure out how to make it hatch."

He blinked. "You think it's still alive?"

"I'm hoping." *Praying.* "Can you do it?"

Caylus regarded the egg, head tilted. "I have no idea. This is uncharted territory. Though maybe if I..." He shook his head. "What makes you think it's still alive?"

"I can feel it. It hums when I touch it." He felt the shell, and when he didn't react, I added, "Kiva couldn't feel it either, but I swear it's there."

"I believe you." Caylus sat back, rubbing the side of his face with one massive hand. "Well, what do we have to go on? Don't they have to hatch on the winter solstice?"

"That's just tradition." The words came quickly. I felt jittery and unsteady. Was he actually agreeing to help? "They can hatch anytime. But something makes them hatch, and I don't know what."

"Are you...asking me to experiment on it?" he asked.

I nodded. "Chemicals. Herbs. Anything that's not likely to damage it. Maybe the egg will react somehow."

He hesitated, and my heart seized. "Will you help me?" I asked.

He ran his fingers over the egg. "I don't know if I can do much, but I'll try."

Relief swept through me in a cool wave. "Where do we start?"

An hour later, I sat beside Caylus with a paper and pen in hand. He alternated between laying out ideas and allowing the kitten to attack his fingers while I translated everything into an actual plan, taking quick notes.

With every new idea one of us suggested, the mountain we had to climb grew taller. By the end of our discussion, the idea of hatching the egg felt impossible. *One step at a time.* The familiar phrase calmed me. Right now, we planned. Then we tested.

We started with herbs. Murkwood root and dried delladon vine, lavender and monkshood. We crushed them before laying them on the shell, Caylus watching for physical indicators while I focused on the humming. Then we cleaned the spot and tried the next one, moving on through powdered metals and basic liquids.

I'd told him that it seemed to have something to do with the royal family, but simply willing the egg to hatch didn't have an impact. So either it was something else about me or there was another factor. With each new thing we tried, I focused on willing the egg to hatch, but nothing changed.

As we worked, we talked. Or rather, I talked. Well, asked questions that Caylus answered in as few words as possible. He didn't seem to mind them; he just didn't have much to say. He was nineteen, his mother taught him to bake, the kitten's name was Gio, and yes, he made his own vests. Even getting that out of him was like prying open a crow's beak.

I also learned he was from Seahalla, the capital of the Ambriels, where the corrupt remnants of the high council still pretended to rule under Razel's control. The real power there was the Drexel family. They called themselves rebels, but they were just a vicious gang profiting off the slowly crumbling nation.

"How long have you been doing this sort of thing?" I asked from my seat in one of the workbench chairs as Caylus sifted through a pile of papers.

"All my life," he said.

"Ever sold anything?"

He paused, his scarred fingers curling around the edge of the stack of papers he held. "Some."

"Ever answer a question in more than three words?"

"Only during high tides."

I blinked, and he smiled over his shoulder at me. I really had to get used to his deadpan delivery. "Funny. You're funny."

He found the paper he was looking for and returned to the chair beside me. "You ask a lot of questions."

"I like to know stuff."

"So do I, though I usually ask books." He patted a nearby stack. "They're more reliable."

"But not as fun."

"Less liable to get annoyed."

"More liable to get chucked at you when someone does get annoyed."

"You sound like you speak from experience," he said.

"Books are very underrated weapons."

He laughed, the sound rich as molten chocolate. It pulled a grin across my lips and brought a flush to my cheeks that felt strange and unfamiliar but pleasant.

He smiled faintly, his eyes bright as spring leaves. "You'd have gotten along with my little sister."

"Does she live in Seahalla?"

His smile faded, his expression clouding. When he didn't answer, I started to ask but clamped my mouth shut when I caught the look in Caylus's eyes. The same look that always seemed to be there, only ten times darker: pain.

"You support the rebels," I said quietly, "but you aren't one. Why?"

His hands closed into massive fists in his lap. "I'm...tired of fighting."

My eyes flickered to his scarred hands as I remembered the way he'd dislodged Ericen's grip on me with ease. I'd thought he was a street fighter or a soldier. Maybe he had been, once. I didn't ask, smothering the urge to run my fingers along the lines of his scars like I had so often done my own, as if it might help me understand them.

We spent the next hour waiting for a mixture to brew, during which Caylus made tea. A light rain tapped against the window as he delivered a cup of steaming bergamot tea to the only clear space on a workbench beside me, a fresh scone beside it.

Hours later, the only thing we'd learned was the shell seemed to have an affinity for iron. It stuck to the slippery surface like tree sap, and I couldn't be sure, but the humming seemed slightly stronger.

"This isn't working," I said at last. My eyes were tired, and my hand cramped from writing.

Caylus sat back. "It isn't working *yet*. We'll try again tomorrow."

Caylus locked the egg away in a padded trunk. Though the

idea of leaving the egg anywhere I wasn't made me uneasy, transporting it in and out of the castle was too risky. Still, as I climbed into the carriage to return to the castle, I felt like I'd left a piece of myself behind.

EIGHTEEN

T he next couple of days followed a similar pattern. Caylus worked at the bakery in the morning, so Kiva and I used that time to train. That morning, I found her already at the training grounds, Auma a nearby shadow, watching her dance with Sinvarra. They'd continued to have lunch together despite Razel's warning.

At first, I'd worried she might get the girl into trouble, but when I mentioned it to Kiva, she said she'd already tried talking Auma out of it for that very reason. Auma had made it very clear that she could take care of herself and would make her own decisions.

In the afternoon, I returned to Caylus's to run through experiments. While we waited for things to brew, I helped him with other little projects for his newest inventions, but our results yielded nothing.

Ericen was nowhere to be seen. When I asked Razel at dinner where he went, she simply smiled her knifelike smile and turned back to conversation with her newest male guest at the table.

My unease never settled. The eyes of the Illucian servants held mine with quiet dislike, and I never turned my back on a soldier. Each time I saw the blue-and-gold Illucian banners, my skin flared hot, my hands itching for my bow with each sneer of an Illucian guard. The added appearance of decorations for the upcoming ball only made me sick.

With every failed experiment, the warmth of my bed called out to me, free of scowling faces, but I didn't listen. Each morning, it was a struggle, but I dragged myself from beneath the comfort of the covers, pushing against that pull to sit, to wait, to spiral deeper and deeper inside myself, and each day, it got a little easier.

On the evening of the promised ball, I left Caylus's a bundle of nerves. Earlier that week, Razel's seamstress had offered to make me a dress, but I'd declined. I had one. I'd never gotten to wear it, as it had been made in anticipation of the day I would become a rider. Another thing I'd thrown in my closet and planned never to look at again yet couldn't leave behind.

Servants helped me dress, one even spending a good half hour bundling my curls atop my head, despite the fact that they would escape within the hour. Several long pieces twirled down my back and around my face.

The dress fit wonderfully. I stood before the floor-length mirror in my room, admiring the misty gray and silver material.

It clung to my upper body, a single gossamer strap curving over one shoulder and around my neck in a tight circlet lined with silver to keep it rigid. The skirt stopped just below my knees, overlaid by bands of sheer cloth reaching the floor, enveloping me in a shroud of mist. A maelstrom of black feathers had been done in delicate needlework from below my waist to my shoulders, and small hematite stones glittered along the bodice in the fading sunlight filtering in from the high windows.

My heart ached. I looked like my mother.

A knock at the door preceded Kiva entering. Her pale hair had been braided back, her typical guard uniform replaced with an all-black version. Sinvarra was strapped to her hip, polished and gleaming in the light of the sona lamps.

"Wow." She blinked. "You look great."

"Thanks." I managed a smile. The crow design of my dress wouldn't go unnoticed, but I didn't care.

We left together, the castle corridors darkening as storm clouds gathered over the setting sun. The frosty chill of the night had crept inside, but it grew warmer as we descended the stairs toward the ballroom filled with people. Voices echoed through the halls, the great doors of the entrance hall pinned open to reveal a line of carriages in the circular courtyard.

Gold-and-blue cloth hung from the banisters, matching flowers lining every surface. Rich savory smells floated down the halls from the kitchen, mixing with the sweet mouthwatering scent drifting out of the bake house.

Someone fell into step beside us, and I stiffened until I saw who it was.

Ericen strode beside me, his Vykryn uniform gone and replaced by a beautiful navy-blue jacket lined in gold and a pair of dark pants. His black hair had been styled to the side, and he had a slight flush in his cheeks, as if he'd just arrived in a hurry from somewhere. He smiled, but it felt off. It didn't reach his eyes.

"I see we're going for tactfully rebellious," he said, gaze switching from my dress to Kiva's military-esque outfit.

"What were you going for?" Kiva asked. "Arrogant prick?"

Ericen's jaw flexed, and I had a feeling he'd just resisted saying something extremely rude.

That's a first. Maybe he'd finally realized insulting Kiva wasn't the quickest way to get on my good side. The idea that he even *wanted* on my good side still felt foreign.

"I wasn't sure you were coming," I told him. "I haven't seen you in days."

"I just returned from an assignment," he said as we approached the tall doors of the ballroom. The crowd had thickened around us, filling with Illucian nobles and soldiers dressed in dark suits and blue and gold dresses. Every one of them was probably armed.

"What kind of assignment?" I asked.

Before he could respond, a frantic servant blocked our path. "Your Highnesses, please come with me. Her Majesty requests your presence on the dais for the introductions."

"I'll see you inside," Kiva said before slipping into the crowd.

"I think I'm growing on her," Ericen said, offering me his arm. "She glowered mildly less."

I snorted but slipped my arm through his, squeezing a little tighter than I meant. My eyes stayed trained on the back of the servant as he led us through a side corridor. At the end of a long hall, we turned right into an open sitting room lit by sona lamps. A couch sat along one wall, along with several chairs separated by small tables.

Razel sat on the arm of the couch, a glass of wine hanging between two fingers. She wore a dress of ice blue, the tight-fitting strapless bodice lined in citrine gems that glimmered like trapped sunlight. Sleeveless, it bared the crisscrossing scars and fresh cuts along the back of her forearms like trophies.

"There you are." Her eyes alighted on Ericen. "I hear your trip was successful."

He nodded but wouldn't meet my questioning gaze.

"And how lovely you look, Thia dear," she added with a smile that didn't match the long, pointed look she gave my dress.

"And you, Your Majesty," I said as genuinely as I could.

Razel stood. "I will announce you both, and you will dance to begin the ball. Do it without the grimace you both wear so often, and we might end the night without any trouble."

Ericen shifted, and Razel smiled again. "Come along," she said, turning for a door in the far wall.

Ericen offered me his arm again, and I took it, if only for something to force me forward. My muscles had turned stiff, my breath becoming shallow. I didn't want to be paraded in front of these people, to see their hungry eyes devour me like the helpless prize they believed I was.

Razel pushed open the door, and we stepped out onto the

dais. The conversation slowly quieted as a loud male voice announced her. A raucous chorus of applause followed. Then Razel announced Ericen and me, and only the sheer force of his body moving forward convinced mine to do the same.

The sound of clapping roared in my ears, and suddenly, we were standing beside Razel, a room of pale faces staring back.

The crowd quieted again. I took a deep breath, centering myself in the moment. I needed my wits about me. I forced myself to focus on the blue and gold decorations and the tables of food and drinks on the outskirts of the room. In the center stood a hollowed-out wooden sculpture of a rearing horse.

Razel spoke. "Welcome. I'm sure everyone is eager for the party to begin, so I won't waste your time. Let the first dance in honor of Prince Ericen and Princess Anthia's engagement begin beneath Rhett's watchful eye." She stepped aside.

I was still inspecting the room when Ericen held out his hand to me. For a moment, I simply stared at it. Then I lifted my gaze to his, surprised to find a smile on his lips. It was encouraging and terrifying all at once. Something about him still looked wrong.

I took his hand. It was warm and calloused and so much larger than mine. A soldier's hand. Would he one day stand across from me on a battlefield?

He led me down the stairs, and the crowd cleared a space for us. The prince faced me, and my eyes found his. "Do you even know what you're doing?" I asked.

He smiled. "Just keep up."

The music began, a quick, harsh sound. A wingbeat later, we were moving across the floor, the music quickening. Ericen kept me in a rigid hold, as the dance demanded, one hand on the back of my shoulder, the other clasped in my own. I'd done the dance before, but it was his sure-footedness that kept me steady throughout.

I matched his every step, my dress furling around my hips, my movements sure and swift. Two weeks of training had paid off. Though my muscles protested at first, the movement eased the stiffness of days of vigorous exercise, and it took some time for my breathing to quicken. It satisfied me to note Ericen's had as well.

The music accelerated and so did our pace, until the faces and colors around us blurred. My breath rattled in my chest. Ericen's grip on my hand tightened to keep from slipping. Then the music erupted and fell silent, and the dance ended.

I didn't even notice if people were clapping. Ericen's bright-blue eyes stared down at me with a look of slight perplexity, as if he didn't understand what he saw. Then they cleared, and he leaned close. I nearly pulled away, thinking he meant to kiss me, but he only lowered his lips to my ear.

"You look beautiful tonight." His breath was warm on my neck, his voice a low rasp. Before I could respond, he'd drawn back and was already clasping hands with several Illucian nobles.

People swarmed me, pelting me with questions and comments. What did I think about the marriage? What an *interesting* dress I'd chosen. Did I love Ericen? I must be so grateful. What did this mean for Rhodairen and Illucian relations? I muttered quick responses or pretended not to hear them. I needed air.

The barrage of people didn't slow. The responsibility of

who I was demanded to be faced. I didn't know what to say or how to say it. I might not be hiding under my covers anymore, but I still wasn't Caliza.

A woman stepped in front of me, her skin the color of wet desert sand flecked with gold. She regarded me with keen eyes, a scar across one that had turned it a milky white.

"So Rhodaire has sided with Illucia?" she asked in a light Ambriellan accent.

"No." I responded without thinking. Who knew who this woman was? She could work for Razel for all I knew. "We've entered into negotiations," I clarified.

Her sharp eyes narrowed. "The type fit only for the Night Captain. The type done in the shadows and that slowly takes your soul."

I frowned. "I don't know what you mean. It was this or war. Who are you?"

She looked me up and down, and I felt myself straighten reflexively beneath her critical gaze. When she met my eyes again, there was no warmth in her face. "An ally. An enemy. Who is to say?"

"Wait!"

But she was already moving, slipping between bodies like smoke. I moved after her, but the crowd closed, carrying her away from me. My heart shuddered, and I stumbled back, suddenly unsteady.

I saw Kiva fighting her way through the crowd toward me, then Ericen was at my side, his hand pressing into the small of my back. "Are you all right?"

"I'm fine." I let out a breath. He nodded, then made to turn away again, but I grabbed his arm. "Where have you been the last few days, Ericen?"

His jaw tightened. "I told you. I had a mission."

Someone shifted behind him, and Shearen faced us just as Kiva reached my side. Shearen slid an arm over Ericen's shoulders in what would have been a show of camaraderie if Ericen didn't stiffen at his touch.

"Don't be modest, Eri," Shearen said, though his eyes were on me. "Thanks to you, we escorted the first successful shipment of new additions to Her Majesty's army through the Verian Hills in months. And killed a few rebels while we were at it."

I stared, unblinking, at Ericen. He held my gaze like a rabbit in a hunter's trap, and I realized what was different about him. His eyes, normally bright as the sun on the ocean, looked dull. Like something was missing.

"Thia—"

The rest of what he said was lost to me as I turned into the crowd, Kiva at my back. The sharp sound of Shearen's laughter followed us as I pushed for the far wall, the thud of my heart against my chest leading me onward.

The room was too tight, too full. The mix of perfume and food made the air too thick to breathe. I barely avoided slamming into someone as I pushed through the front doors, through the main hall, and out onto the front steps.

The air was so cold, it burned, but it was fresh, and I gulped lungful after lungful of it until my racing heart slowed. Something tapped my cheek, then again, and I turned my face skyward as rain fell, every drop a shocking touch. I spread my arms and let my head fall back.

Kiva, mercifully, said nothing. She simply stood beside me, her arms folded, shoulders squared in a way that dared anyone to come near us.

I couldn't explain the betrayal I felt. Over the course of the carriage ride, through our dinner and our talk in the stables, I'd come to understand Ericen a little. But the position he was in wasn't easy, and it wasn't like he'd made me any promises. He was an Illucian soldier, and he'd never pretended to be anything else.

But he did make you think he was more.

The rain fell harder. I drew in the night air. What would my mother do right now? She certainly wouldn't have run away from her own engagement party. She'd have put on a strong face and played her part. Always the diplomat.

Estrel wouldn't have stood for any of this. She'd have laughed in their faces and walked out without looking back.

"What are we doing here, Kiva?" I asked. "Caylus and I haven't learned anything, and even Trendell hasn't fully committed. Now some of the people we needed are dead. Who knows how many."

She faced me, arms unfolding. "What else can you do?"

"Stop wasting time at stupid balls," I replied. In the distance, the Colorfalls shone in a hazy glow. Was the egg all right? Had Caylus made any progress?

"Then go," Kiva said. "I'll cover for you."

My heart leapt at the idea, surprising me. It wasn't just the need to *do* something or to escape this ball that coursed through me. I wanted to see Caylus.

Kiva smirked like she knew exactly that. "Good luck." She disappeared inside.

Not wanting to give anyone time to notice I was gone, I didn't bother returning to my room to change. Flying down the stairs into the courtyard, I commandeered one of the waiting carriages. The driver's expression bemoaned my soaking dress and hair, but he complied, making quickly for the Colorfalls.

ℕINETEEN

R ain pelted my face and chest as I stepped out of the carriage, wind whipping my hair in a violent flurry. I could
barely see, the streets lit by dying sona lamps and patches of
moonlight through the dark clouds. Torch flames danced dangerously in the wind.

It was near midnight, and the windows to the bakery were
dim, but I knocked heavily on the door until light flared to life
inside. The light grew stronger until it peeked around the edges
of the curtain-blocked windows, and I stared expectantly at the
glass until the face of the new girl appeared.

She pulled open the door, looking annoyed. "We're closed,
miss."

I brushed past without an explanation and hurried up the
stairs. At the top, I pounded on the door, calling Caylus's name

until he answered. It took a moment for him to undo the locks and open the door. I stepped inside, and he closed it, redoing the locks. Then he simply stared at me.

I grimaced. "I know. I'm a mess. I promise to clean the floor."

He blinked rapidly, as if suddenly remembering that was something his eyes required of him. "Uh, no. No. That's not what—no. You look nice."

I smiled, and he returned it, eyes lingering in a way that chased the chill of the rain from my skin.

"I just put the kettle on," he said. "If you want tea. And I'll..." He trailed off, already moving. "Stay here." He sprinted up the stairs two at a time and returned a moment later with a bundle of clothes. "They'll be too big. But they're dry."

"Thanks." I took the clothes and crossed the hall to the only other room downstairs: Caylus's bedroom. I moved toward a small washroom in the back, cringing at the trail of water left in my wake. I stepped inside, then paused. I'd never seen Caylus's room before. I stuck my head back out.

It was nearly empty. Besides a bed pushed into one corner, there was a small nightstand and nothing more. He spent most of his time in the workshop, often including nights, but still. Not even a book? A forgotten teacup? The table and bed had a fine layer of dust, as if no one ever used them. And while most of the downstairs smelled of herbs and fresh bread, the empty room smelled musty.

Frowning, I retreated into the bathroom. A towel hung from a rack it seemed Caylus had installed himself, judging by the places where his hammer had hit the wall instead of the nail.

I dried off, setting my dress inside the tub before pulling on the clothes. The tunic fell almost to my knees, and I had to hold the pants with one hand, but they were both made of soft cotton smelling faintly of tea leaves and petrichor. Like Caylus.

After rolling up the pant legs and with one hand clasped on the waistband, I returned to the kitchen to find two cups of tea waiting. We carried them upstairs, Caylus bringing a plate of scones and muffins. I swiped one as I dropped into my customary chair beside his workbench. Gio lay curled in a ball on a sweater Caylus had abandoned to the cat, and I ran my fingers along his soft fur.

Caylus retrieved the egg from the locked trunk, setting it in its stand. The familiar humming that came from it worked its way through my veins, and I drew a breath that felt like the first one I'd taken all night. Being in that ballroom, surrounded by those people—I'd felt like I couldn't spin fast enough to protect my back.

Here, I could fall asleep to the hum of the egg and Gio's quiet purring, while Caylus worked by lamplight late into the night.

"Why don't you sleep in your bedroom?" I asked.

He stopped flipping through a book to look at me, green eyes slightly wide. In the yellow-orange light of the lamp, they looked hazel. He went to respond, then stopped. Looked away, then back. Finally, he said, "There're no windows."

When these words didn't erase my confusion, he added, "I don't like rooms without windows. They…" He trailed off. My gaze dropped to his hands; they'd started shaking. He clenched them into fists, and when the shaking didn't stop, he pressed them flat on the workbench. The lamplight illuminated the jagged look of his scarred fingers.

I smoothed my right hand down my left, the skin bumpy from old burns. "When the crows were killed, I was outside the rookery. My mother came running. She told me to stay, and I did while she ran inside."

Caylus's eyes found mine, emboldening me. I kept talking. "The rookery was on fire. It was the middle of the night, but it was as bright as midday. I saw someone fall. I thought it was her, but it was my mother's friend, Estrel. I didn't think before I grabbed her. She was on fire, and the flames burned me too."

I lifted my hand for him to see. He knew the scars were there, but I wanted him to really look at them. Under his gaze, they didn't feel wrong. They felt like something else, like a symbol of my survival.

"For the longest time, I let these represent everything I lost, but I'm done. I won't let my scars define me. Not anymore. From now on, they're a symbol of what I have left to fight for. Of what I won't let Illucia take from me."

Caylus closed his eyes, his hands pressing harder into the wood. Slowly, as if afraid of spooking a wild animal, I stood and placed my hand over his. Gradually, his shaking stopped, and he collapsed into his chair. I pushed myself onto a clear space of the workbench and waited.

"My family's in Seahalla," he began softly. "My mother was a baker, and my father…" He clenched his jaw. "My parents were poor, so my siblings and I learned trades. I apprenticed with a blacksmith. That's where I learned…" He trailed off again, gesturing at the workshop.

"When I was thirteen, my dad lost his job. He started drinking. Picked up gambling." He pulled his hands into his lap, wrung them. "The Drexels run the gambling houses. He took me with him one day, and I figured out pretty fast if you kept track of the cards, you could cheat the game. I didn't know that's what I was doing, but my dad did. He pulled me out of my apprenticeship and started bringing me to the gambling house whenever he went."

My stomach churned. I'd heard stories of what the Drexels did to people they caught cheating.

"They found us out a few weeks later. Didn't know how we were cheating, just that we were. We ran for it, and my dad… He said they'd go easier on me since I was a kid. He left me to be caught, but they asked who I'd been with. At first, I didn't answer, but they…forced me to." His left hand curled around his right. "Then they broke my hand for stealing."

I swallowed hard, a quiet heat gathering in my stomach. I wanted to hurt whoever had hurt him.

Caylus seemed to have forgotten I was there, as if the only way he could tell this story was to pretend he was alone. "They went to my dad demanding he pay back his winnings. He said he couldn't pay the debt, but he'd give them me instead. That I was good with numbers and fixing things. They agreed."

"He sold you?" I asked weakly.

"He called it a job. I would be paid, and once I'd earned back my father's debt, I'd be free to go," he said. "I served Malkin

Drexel. He started training me to fight. I didn't want to, but... I kept thinking, especially with the fights I was winning, that I'd pay off my dad's debt soon. But Malkin kept finding other things for me to owe him for. Food, clothes, lodging, lost fights. Years passed. My room, it didn't have any windows. That's why..." He trailed off again, flexing his hands in front of him.

"The punching nearly destroyed my hands. I broke my knuckles more times than I can count. Then just over two months ago, I got the news my mother had died. When Malkin told me—" He paused. "He told me my father had paid off his debt months ago, but Malkin said I still owed him. That I had my own debts now, and my father hadn't used a bit of the money he'd made to help." His fisted hands tightened. "It finally sunk in that no one was coming for me, and Malkin was never going to let me go.

"I'd been saving portions of my winnings without him knowing for some time. I had enough to convince a smuggler to get me out of the city to Sordell."

My lips parted, and I stared at him, the words biting like acid eating through my skin. No wonder he jumped at every sound and flinched at every touch. Caylus had left the Drexels' service without paying his debt; they'd be looking for him. It certainly explained the locks on his doors, not that they would do him any good against the Drexels.

I'm tired of fighting, he'd said the day I asked why he hadn't joined the rebels. Tired, because he'd done so much of it. And yet when I'd asked for his help, he'd given it willingly, knowing each moment he spent with me embroiled him deeper and deeper in this conflict.

"Yet you're still helping me," I whispered.

He bowed his head. "A few weeks ago, a contact of mine said Malkin killed my younger sister. Because I left." His breath came out in a shudder. "She was the only one who ever visited me. The only one who tried to help. And now—" His voice died.

My throat tightened. I didn't know what to say.

"Malkin's only in power because of what Illucia's done to the Ambriels," he said, voice low. "If they were free from Illucia, free from him…"

Then maybe no one else would have to go through what he did. Was that why he aided the rebels despite his hatred of fighting? To stop Malkin?

He lifted his gaze to mine, and I drew a sharp breath. That was it. The look I'd seen in Caylus's eyes from the beginning. The look of someone who'd had a pit gouged so deep inside them, filling it again seemed impossible. Someone like me.

He wasn't looking at me, but I could still see the pain in his eyes. I wanted to take it away.

Slowly, I reached out. My fingers brushed his cheek, then cupped it, and I let my thumb smooth along his warm skin. His eyes closed, and he leaned into my touch. My skin tingled where it met his, the feeling dancing up my arm like the hum of the egg's magic. He was tall enough that even sitting, he wasn't far, but the space between us was still too much. I wanted it gone.

I leaned forward and kissed him.

It was like being in a Rhodairen storm, thunder and rain all around, equal parts soothing and shocking. Heat flushed my face, my neck, my chest. He brought a hand to my head, entangling it in my still-damp hair. Then he stood, and I was looking up at him, our lips a breath apart. He leaned in, kissing me this time, and I slid my hands back onto the table to catch myself.

"Saints!" I jerked back and ripped my hand from the table to find my palm bleeding from a shallow cut. I looked around for the offending object, ready to condemn it to a vicious death, and found a piece of bloody glass.

"Are you all right?" It wasn't until Caylus spoke that I realized he'd stepped closer. The concern on his face made me catch my breath. His first reaction had been to protect me.

All too aware of his closeness, I inspected my throbbing cut. "I need water." He looked reluctant to put space between us, and I was reluctant to let him, but he nodded and crossed to another workbench.

I shook out my hand to ease the stinging, droplets of blood flying onto the workbench and—

"Saints!" I shouted again, leaping to my feet. Caylus whirled around, but my eyes were locked on my hand.

Lady Kerova had said only my family could hatch the crows, and there was only one thing we shared.

Our blood.

TWENTY

C aylus and I stood side by side. He'd brought me a cup of water and a cloth to wash and wrap my hand, and for the last few minutes, we'd both stared silently at the egg where we'd bundled it in blankets on the floor.

"Try it," Caylus said at last.

I'd thought the same thing a hundred times in the last couple of minutes but hadn't said it. What if it didn't work?

What if it *did*?

My entire body seized at the idea, at the possibility of what was about to happen. It seemed so simple. Could my blood really be the key? Did that mean my family had some sort of magic line?

Slowly, I unwrapped my hand. Taking a deep breath, I pressed my wound against the egg.

It glowed.

My breath caught, my muscles going rigid as the humming doubled, the vibrations dancing up my hand and arm all the way to my chest until they became one with my heartbeat. My doubts vanished; the crow inside was still alive. Gio let out a low hiss and clambered up Caylus's shoulder.

The iridescent colors in the shell lit up, the entire thing encased in a golden sheen as the humming became a vibration.

Then the shell cracked.

"Saints!" My hand flew to my mouth. I stumbled back, a hand seizing Caylus's arm. It was *working*.

The crack lengthened, traveling along the side of the shell. A piece broke off, revealing the sharp black beak of a crow chick. Then it vanished, replaced by a length of feathers.

I laughed. Once and sharp. My heart felt as if it might leap from my chest, like something huge and growing inside me was trying to get out. Joy, I realized. It was joy, as wild and powerful as a storm, and it was hope, as tentative and newborn as the hatching crow.

I flung my arms around Caylus's neck with a scream of delight, his own coming around to encircle me. He lifted me off my feet, a deep, breathy laugh rumbling in his broad chest. I laughed again and kept laughing until the laughter turned to tears, and even then, I couldn't stop.

Caylus set me back on my feet, but he didn't let me go. He held me close as we watched the crow struggle. It took all the strength I had not to help it. But it needed this. It needed to fight, to grow stronger. And it did. With each movement, it cleared away more shell, minutes longer than any I'd ever experienced stretching out one after the other as it fought to free itself.

I crouched beside it, my fingers itching to pull the shell away. My legs burned, but I didn't move, barely breathing.

After what felt like hours, the egg finally broke apart, and the crow pushed its way out in a bundle of black feathers. It tumbled onto the blanket, wet, chirping, and looking nothing at all like a creature meant to save us all.

I laughed again, the sound bubbling over me in a wash of relief and happiness that made me feel as if I could float away.

We'd done it.

I threw my arms around Caylus, and he held me tight. At his back, the sun broke over the horizon, flooding us with warmth. Still chirping, the crow swayed unsteadily, its silver eyes falling on me as Caylus released me.

A storm crow.

The hum of the magic had vanished, replaced by a small, comforting feeling in the pit of my stomach I could describe as nothing but a connection, like a rope strung between us.

"It worked." I barely dared to speak the words. They didn't seem real. I repeated myself, dazed. "It worked."

I crouched down, tracing a streak of pale yellow on the cracked shell. This was why the ceremony was always done in secret. If people knew our family's blood was the key to hatching the eggs, our enemies may have tried to use us or even kill us.

But how did we have this power? It wasn't the elemental magic of the crows. It was something different.

I let out a whoosh of breath, then sucked it back in greedily.

But no amount of air seemed like enough. I felt empty and full all at once, like an hourglass of shifting sands.

"I've never seen you smile like that," Caylus said softly.

I blinked; I hadn't realized I was still smiling.

He blushed before saying, "It looks nice."

My smile widened, and I stood, leaning into him, content never to move again.

"I can't believe this is happening," I whispered, and he held me tighter. When at last I pulled away, I settled down beside the crow. The floor was hard and uncomfortable, the wool blankets itchy, but I didn't care. I lay my head down beside his, taking in every detail of his small form, from the curve of his beak to the ridges of his feathers.

The connection between us emitted a faint humming, a quiet song I could listen to forever. I ran one finger over the curve of a talon, carefully, reverently. The sounds of Caylus returning to his work faded into the background until my world became enveloped by the gentle breathing of the creature before me.

I didn't realize I'd fallen asleep until I woke with a blanket over me. Panic rippled in my chest—I hadn't meant to sleep, and I'd be missed at the castle. I nearly bolted upright until I realized the crow had shifted in his sleep, tucking his head into the crook of my arm.

As carefully as I could, I extricated myself from him, wrapping the blanket Caylus must have laid on me around him instead. The door opened, and Caylus entered, a cup of tea in hand.

"How is he?" he asked.

"Perfect," I replied.

I needed to go. Kiva needed to know what had happened.

Then I had to send a letter to Caliza, develop a training plan for the crow, and figure out how Kiva and I were going to escape. We'd have to wait at least a week for the crow to be strong enough to move, maybe longer.

But he was here. He was alive. And I couldn't quite tear myself away just yet.

I knelt beside the crow, listening as he chirped gently. With every sound, the feeling in the pit of my stomach gave a little tug, as if someone were pulling from the other end of a long cord. I imagined myself tugging back, and he chirped again.

An indescribable happiness welled in my chest. This was what I'd waited for my entire life. This connection, this bond.

"What are you going to name it?" Caylus asked from beside me.

I smiled. "Resyries. It means *stormbringer*."

Leaving the egg at Caylus's had been difficult. Leaving a newborn crow had been practically impossible. I'd left him detailed written instructions on how to take care of it, including clearing a very wide space for it on the floor far away from any of the many things in his workshop that could hurt it.

With each second of growing space between Resyries and me, the cord strung between us grew thinner and weaker, until I could barely sense him as we pulled into the castle courtyard. The link was nothing more than a gentle pulling feeling now, but it would get stronger and more nuanced the more we trained together. Yet it still felt like I'd left a piece of myself behind that kept tugging me back.

Kiva was sitting at the breakfast table when I burst in wearing my dirt-stained gown from the previous night. Slamming the door behind me, I whirled to face her.

"We figured it out," I said in a barely controlled whisper. "Caylus and I! We figured it out!"

Understanding dawned on her face. Her eyes flared wide, her hands flying back to brace herself. "Did it—?"

"Yes!"

Kiva shot to her feet, enveloping me in a hug as I flew to her. She let out a yell, and I laughed wildly. She laughed with me, her entire body shaking.

We pulled apart, Kiva's face flushed with excitement and her eyes brighter than I'd seen them in months. I explained everything that had happened after I left the ball, leaving out only the things about Caylus's past.

"You kissed him!" she half shouted.

"Did you miss the part where I told you my blood is the long-lost secret of crow hatching?"

She rolled her eyes. "How was it?"

I laughed, tried and failed to explain how right it'd been, how happy I was, even now, when I hadn't slept all night.

"I need to write Caliza," I said, bolting to my room.

"And take a bath!" Kiva shouted. "You smell horrible."

With the letter sent, I took a bath before climbing into bed. Despite the giddy energy sparking through me, my eyelids felt heavy, my body slow. When at last I fell asleep, I slept dreamlessly.

When I woke, the first thing I thought of was Res, and I scrambled to locate the connection between us. It hummed quietly, tugging gently in my chest. I let out an uneasy breath.

It would be days before he was strong enough to move, and he'd likely sleep all of today and that night. Come morning, he'd be all hunger and caws. Keeping up with his appetite would be a challenge; crows grew incredibly fast.

I'd slept most of the morning and afternoon away, and though I longed to see Res, I wouldn't have enough time to get to Caylus's and back again before dinner.

Needing something to occupy the nervous energy inside me, I dressed to train. I pulled my flying leathers out of my trunk, simply staring at them at first. They hadn't left my drawer in months. When I'd shoved them in there so long ago, stained with soot and smelling of smoke, I'd thought I'd never wear them again. Now, it felt right. People would notice; they'd recognize the armor. But I wanted them to. I wanted them to know that the legacy they'd tried to stamp out still smoldered in the ashes.

I slipped on the upper piece of my leathers, which combined the pauldron, vambraces, and chest plate of normal armor into a single lightweight, flexible piece. The leather was a multitude of small pleats shaped like feathers, creating the illusion of two great wings draped protectively around my shoulders.

The belt fit securely around my waist, lined with two pouches, and the light leather pants were still flexible and strong. As I stared at myself in the mirror, I could almost imagine being a rider again.

The thought made my chest ache. Not because it hurt but because that dream was possible again.

I braided my hair back and went to meet Kiva in the training arena, checking the connection with Res along the way. I couldn't dismiss the fear the link would disappear. His sleepy contentment floated back to me like drifting clouds across a summer sky.

In the courtyard, rain fell gently, sliding off my leathers in droplets. I'd just joined Kiva at the edge of the archery section, my black-gold bow in hand, when a familiar drawling voice said, "Cute outfit."

I spun to face Shearen, two Vykryn at his back, including the one whose ribs I'd broken. The boy looked like a jungle cat about to tear apart his dinner.

"Those went out of style in Rhodaire a while ago." Shearen grinned, and the soldiers with him laughed.

My free hand tightened into a fist, the wound from the night before twinging. Kiva touched my shoulder, but it wasn't necessary. Being around Razel had helped me learn how to keep my mouth shut when necessary, like when we were faced with three highly trained Illucian warriors clearly trying to cause trouble.

Trouble was the last thing I could afford now.

I turned around and pulled an arrow from my quiver. Kiva stayed angled toward the men, watching my back.

"I guess we really did beat you all into submission," Shearen said. "Not that it took much effort. Rhodairens are weak. You hid behind the crows, and without them, you're nothing." Derision dripped from every word. He truly did hate us. The feeling was mutual.

"Your people deserve what happened to them," he pressed, his voice scraping against my skin. "If it were up to me, I'd have seen you all burn. Maybe I'll still get to." He laughed, but it cut short abruptly, followed by a sharp yell and a loud crash. I whirled, arrow nocked and drawn, then relaxed.

Ericen had slammed Shearen into the ground, his boot on the back of his neck, one arm wrenched painfully behind him. "I'd appreciate if you didn't talk to your future queen that way."

"You bastard—Ah!" Shearen's face twisted in pain as Ericen tugged harder on his arm. His friends stepped forward. I leveled the arrow at them. They stopped.

"All right!" Shearen yelled. Ericen released him, and he scrambled to his feet, massaging his injured shoulder. He glared murderously at Ericen, but behind the anger, something else seethed.

"Watch your back," he hissed, but for some reason, I didn't believe the threat for a second. He was like a cat puffing out his hair to look bigger, only he lacked the teeth and claws to back it up.

Without another word, Shearen pushed past his friends for the exit, and they followed.

I only lowered the arrow once they were gone. "We could have handled that ourselves."

Ericen opened his mouth to respond, then shut it and stalked away, his shoulders hunched in frustration.

I turned back to Kiva, whose face was frozen in a wide-eyed stare. "Did you see him take that guy down?" she asked.

I shook my head.

"I've never seen someone move like that. Be careful around him, Thia."

A chill trickled along my spine, and I turned grudgingly back to the targets. "Come on. I need to shoot something."

I went looking for Ericen when Kiva and I finished. A servant showed me to his rooms, though I had a feeling he wouldn't be there. Finding them empty, I traced my way back to the main hall, then out into the rapidly chilling evening.

Rocks crunched underfoot as I followed the curving path to the stables. Whenever I'd been angry or sad, I would spirit myself away to the rookery, where the quiet presence of the birds made me feel safe. When Ericen had shown me the stables and I'd seen the way he looked at the horses, I knew they were a similar refuge for him.

In some ways, we weren't so different, and I didn't know what to make of that.

The grounds were quiet, the horses stabled for the night and the workers and servants reduced to a skeleton crew. But the large front door was cracked open, and a sliver of firelight spilled out.

I slipped in, spotting a figure halfway down the walkway. Bathed in a pool of moonlight from the open windows above,

Ericen leaned his elbows on the edge of a stall door, his face pressed against the massive black head of his stallion, Callo. His eyes were closed, his shoulders rounded, as if he'd gone to sleep. He looked peaceful.

The horse's ears flicked, and he snorted, lifting his head. Ericen went rigid, spinning on the spot with one hand on a sword hilt. I froze.

"I'm sorry. I didn't mean..." What didn't I mean? I'd meant to come looking for him, but I hadn't expected to find him so vulnerable. It felt like an intrusion.

He relaxed, letting his hand drop to his side. "It's all right. What are you doing here?"

I approached slowly. "I came looking for you."

"Funny. I could have sworn you've been avoiding me since last night."

I paused at the edge of the barn door. "Is that why you threw Shearen on his back? Old-fashioned jealousy?"

Ericen smirked, crossing his arms. The moonlight caught the edge of his black jacket, illuminating the definition of his arms. Kiva's warning echoed. "First, Shearen has a boyfriend. Second, he deserved it."

"No doubt. But that's what I have Kiva for." One overprotective friend was enough. "But I haven't been avoiding you. I left the ball early last night, and I was in town this morning." Neither of those were lies exactly.

"Right. Your new hobby." He sounded skeptical. "Maybe I could go with you—"

"No." The word came too quickly, and I cursed silently as his mouth pressed into a thin line. "What I mean is, being here—it's not easy for me. Visiting the Colorfalls is a break from it all. It's still Illucia, but it's…I don't know. Easier."

He regarded me with a sidelong look, and for an instant, I saw Caylus, his curls falling over bright, curious green eyes, head tilted in question. I blinked the image away to find Ericen regarding me strangely.

"I understand. Though I have to say I thought we'd moved past that."

A warning prickled in my chest. "Moved past what?"

He looked at Callo as he said, "What my mother did."

"You mean ripping everything and everyone I ever loved away from me?" My voice surprised even me with its cool edge.

He stiffened, fingers curling and uncurling into fists. But he didn't respond. For some reason, his silence was worse. It broke something inside me, and what came rushing out was hot and sharp.

"You destroyed our way of life!" My voice erupted. It seemed strange it'd taken this long for this conversation to happen. But as I stood glaring at him, my hands clenched, I understood why. Because until now, until this moment, it wouldn't have mattered.

My hatred for him when we'd first met had softened. At the beginning, I'd thought accusing him of taking everything from me would have just given him satisfaction. Now, some absurd part of me actually expected him to apologize, to explain, to say it wasn't his fault.

I wanted him to give me a reason not to hate him.

Ericen was quiet for a long moment, focused on Callo

as the horse ate. Finally, he found my gaze, his blue eyes nearly silver in the moonlight. "Do you know why my mother attacked Rhodaire?"

"Because Illucians are power-hungry mongrels who want to own the world?"

He smirked, and the familiar one-sided twitch of his lips made me want to punch him. "Yes, that's part of it. But with Rhodaire, it was personal."

"Some rogue soldiers from the Turren Wing killed part of your mother's family," I said quietly. "But they were punished by us and her." She had used their anger at Rhodaire for stripping them of their ranks and crows to sway them to her side and carry out Ronoch. Then she'd executed them.

"Do you know exactly what they did?" When I shook my head, he continued. "They cornered her husband, mother, and older sister, and she was forced to watch as they ordered their crows to tear her family apart."

I felt behind me for the barn wall and leaned against it, my throat tightening.

"My mother didn't even want to be queen." A despondent smile crossed his lips. "She wanted to breed horses. But with her sister dead and her father soon after, she had no choice."

She had had her family and future taken from her in one bloody night. I understood what that was like. And Ericen—he hadn't called Razel's husband his father.

"Your father…" I began.

He shook his head. "They didn't touch her, not like that. I never even met him though. Calling him 'Father' seems…strange."

I understood. I'd never known my father either. He felt so far away, like a figment of my imagination or a memory faded over time.

"I wasn't part of the raid that killed your crows," he added quietly. "I was still at Darkward. If that means anything."

It did, and I hated that it did, because Ericen was supposed to be my enemy. I was supposed to come here and pretend to be the good little fiancée while I organized a rebellion against his kingdom and hatched a crow.

I wasn't supposed to care about him.

"Why do you help her, Ericen? Why are you going along with any of this? You must know it's wrong. The conscription, the conquering, all of it."

"Of course I know! But Illucian soldiers serve for life. If I left, I'd be hunted down and executed without mercy." His eyes narrowed. "Don't look at me like that."

I drew back. "Like what?"

"Like you feel sorry for me. I'm not telling you this to earn your pity. This is just the way it is." He shrugged, as if that simple action could dismiss the severity of his words. "I will earn the respect my mother denied me. I will take her place as Valix and king and do something better with this kingdom than she has."

"By killing rebels and conscripting children?" I asked.

A muscle flexed in his jaw. "I didn't volunteer for that raid. My mother ordered me to go in exchange for your trips into the city without guards."

My anger seized, as if it'd struck a wall. He'd made a deal

with his mother. If he hadn't, who knew what trouble those Vykryn could have caused. They might have been tailing me the night of the ball and followed me to Caylus's. And Res... I shuddered and prayed Ericen thought it was the cold.

"Thank you," I said. A wind gusted through the stables, taking the tension with it.

"I meant what I said, Thia," he said softly. "I don't want to be your enemy."

I felt as though I'd reached the edge of a cliff, and tipping over, letting myself fall, could mean redemption...or destruction. Could I really trust this boy, who was at once everything I had learned to hate and yet none of it at all?

"If not enemies," I began, "then what?"

"Friends?" he suggested, stepping toward me. "I'm in rather short supply."

"Have you tried being nice to people? I've heard that works wonders."

He smirked. "Sounds boring."

I laughed, and his eyes gleamed as though the sound delighted him. He leaned against the stall door, his lips curving in something dangerously close to a smile.

"Come spar with me tomorrow," he said.

"What?"

He pushed off the stall. "In addition to the raid, my mother made me agree to another deal. If I want to be Valix after her, I have to win the Centerian."

I drew a sharp breath. "You're entering that bloodbath?"

He pressed on as if he hadn't heard me, stepping closer.

"And since it's your fault I had to make that deal in the first place, the least you could do is help me prepare for it."

"*My* fault?" I repeated.

He stood directly before me now, his broad frame blotting out the moonlight trickling in behind him. "Unless you're afraid, of course."

The thrill of danger alighted across my skin like an icy breeze. "Oh, this is going to be fun."

TWENTY-ONE

I sat with Kiva on the couches that evening, having just relayed what had transpired in the stables over slices of whiskey cake, an Ambriellan dessert I'd fallen in love with the time I'd visited. I felt like I always had the night before Negnoch; not ready to sleep but desperate to go to bed and for tomorrow to come so I could see Res.

"There's something broken in him, Kiva," I said quietly, the image of Ericen with his head pressed against his stallion's still fresh in my mind.

"I'm sure there is, but it's not for you to fix. Have you forgotten who he is?"

I cast her a halfhearted glower. "No. But I don't think he has to be our enemy." She laughed, and I pressed on. "I'm serious. He doesn't want to be his mother. He wants to be better."

Ericen hadn't told me those things from a place of self-pity;

he'd told me because he intended to do something about it. He wanted to fix his broken pieces. I understood that, just like I understood his desire to be better than his mother. My mother had made mistakes, ones whose echoes now haunted me and Caliza both. We'd inherited the consequences of her decisions, and I would do better.

She set her half-eaten cake on the table. "You could never trust him."

"I think I could, in time. I think even you could, if you let yourself try."

"No thanks."

I sighed, setting my empty plate beside hers. "Have you ever heard the story about how the crows were created? The one from *Saints and Sellas.*"

"I never read those fairy tales. They're a waste of time."

I smiled. "It's my favorite out of all of them. My mother told it to me one night with only a candle burning in my room. After that, I memorized it."

Kiva shifted in her seat, leaning back against the armrest so she faced me, and I began to talk.

"When the Sellas made the crows, the night lasted for a year. They drew their power from the night and from it formed the crows. Its darkness became their feathers, its vastness their power, its tranquil silence their quiet wisdom. The night grew angry with the Sellas and refused to give way to the day. Time passed. Crops and people alike started to sicken from the lack of sunlight, withering as the night grew lush and full. The Sellas begged the night to end, but it refused."

I remembered each moment of the night my mother had told me the story with stark clarity. I'd snuggled deep into my covers, my mother's rich voice enveloping me. Outside, the night had been thick as velvet, as if waiting to be formed into something greater than itself.

"The Sellas went to the crows, born of night, and asked for their help as repayment for creating them. The crows agreed. The sun crow gave them light in ribbons of gold, the fire crow and storm crow, warmth in crackling fires and pleasant winds. The water crow and earth crow revived their crops, and the battle crow kept them safe from the creatures that haunted the night. The shadow crow challenged the night to a battle, and the night agreed. They dueled, battling at the speed of darkness, too fast and shadowed for the Sellas to see. The fight went on and on in silence, the only indication it raged wisps of black that escaped from the night like ink dispersing in water, until finally, the crow emerged from the dark, victorious.

"The night kept its word and ended, returning to its natural cycle with day. The Sellas thanked the crows and welcomed them into their homes. And so began the relationship between them."

The firelight flickered, throwing shadows across the room. "When I asked what the speed of darkness was, my mother said, 'Snuff out the only candle in a room. Watch how quickly the darkness comes.' And she blew out the candle at my bedside, dousing us in night."

"I'm guessing there's a moral here?" Kiva asked.

"Darkness spreads quickly," I replied. "Quicker than light. If we keep doing what we're doing, if Rhodaire and Illucia keep retaliating against each other, it's never going to end. The darkness will spread and spread until everything is consumed."

She regarded me with heavy eyes. "Pain begets pain," she whispered. "That's what my mother said to me when she told me what happened to my father. I asked her why she didn't destroy the people who did it, and that's what she said."

I nodded. "The only way to end the cycle, the only way to truly defeat Illucia, is to help them change. They need a better ruler. A better leader. And I think Ericen could be him."

Kiva pulled a couch pillow over her face, groaning. "You want to ally with him too, don't you?"

"I figured our job wasn't hard enough already if you have time to flirt with Auma every day."

She chucked the pillow at me, and I laughed, snatching her remaining cake and scurrying to the other side of the couch before she could stop me from eating it.

"What about you?" she demanded. "Falling for those green eyes of Caylus's, are you?"

I scoffed, but she wasn't wrong. They were pretty. I dropped onto the couch across from her, cake still in hand. "Talking to him is so easy. I love how curious he is about everything."

"You just like having someone as nosy as you are."

I smirked. "I just don't understand how someone can be so observant and so oblivious at the same time. He doesn't notice anything!"

She gave me a coy smile. "He notices you."

My face heated, but she was right. Caylus didn't notice a liquid boiling over above the fire, but he noticed which tea I liked, which muffin was my favorite, and had both ready and waiting when I arrived.

"You notice him too," she added. "I think you'd live in that workshop if he'd let you."

My blush deepened. "He's easy to be around," I muttered.

"Easy to look at too."

I laughed. An image surfaced in my mind: him standing face-to-face with Ericen, his eyes hard as jade. At the same time, I thought of him in his workshop, his long limbs twisted into awkward positions in a too-small chair in an attempt to get comfortable, the sunlight illuminating streaks of red in his messy auburn hair, Gio snuggled on one shoulder.

He made me feel safe, comfortable, even happy, and that was all in the middle of Illucia, with the fate of my kingdom at stake.

Kiva fetched Sinvarra and her cleaning materials, then laid the sword out on the table to begin her meticulous polishing process. Someone knocked, and I rose to open the door, revealing Auma. She handed me a letter, though her dark eyes found only Kiva. I thanked her, and she bowed, slipping away.

Beside my name on the envelope, someone had written *Lokane*, the password we'd decided Captain Mirkova would use for news from Korovi. Had she convinced them to help us? I tore it open, then nearly dropped it when I beheld the simple message:

No.

Upon seeing my face, Kiva rose and snatched the letter from me, then cursed so violently in Korovi, I considered asking the

Saints to forgive her. Except wasn't this just another sign there was no one there? No one listening.

"Saints-damned isolationist snobs!" she finished, chucking the letter into the fire. The flames gobbled it up with the tenacity of Kiva's curses.

I forced a deep breath. "It's okay. We still have Jindae, Trendell, and the Ambriels. That's more than enough."

"If they all agree."

All through morning training and the carriage ride to Caylus's, I couldn't stop checking the connection between Res and me. Every time, the cord hummed contentedly, and I would breathe a little slower until the fear compelled me to check again.

A day old, Res's appetite would be kicking in, so I'd visited the castle kitchens with the intent of pilfering some meat. The castle cook was already preparing meals for that evening's dinner when I slipped into the warm, cobblestone room.

After learning his name was Tarel and asking for some cooked chicken, a man shaping dough beside the oven had grinned at me in a way that made his dimples show. "So you're the one who's been ordering all the desserts," he said.

My cheeks flushed. "I hope it's not too much trouble."

"Are you kidding?" replied Tarel as he folded chicken in a cloth for me with nimble fingers. "He's just happy to make something other than sugarless tarts."

It'd taken me several more minutes to escape and only after

learning the dimpled man was Lyren, Tarel's husband and the castle baker, along with how many years they'd worked there, how long they'd been married, and their opinions on who'd win the Centerian that year. By the time I'd slipped away with promises to return, I had an additional cloth wrap with scones, hard cheese, and dried fruit.

The carriage slowed outside the bakery, and I leapt out, darting inside with a quick hello to the woman behind the counter on my way up to Caylus's. He answered the door after the first knock, as if he'd been waiting on the other side.

"How is he?" I asked the moment the door shut.

"Asleep," Caylus replied. He had purple shadows under his eyes, and his hair had reached a new level of disheveled.

I frowned. "Did you sleep?"

He shook his head. "I didn't want to leave him alone."

Something warm and pleasant welled in my chest, and I smiled, taking Caylus's hand to guide him upstairs. His fingers curled about mine, their trembling still. We hadn't talked about our kiss, and some part of me didn't want to. Caylus knew about my engagement with Ericen and my plans to stop it, and if he didn't want to make a big deal of it, neither would I.

Getting caught didn't worry me—kissing another boy was the least of my subversion.

Res lay cocooned in soft blankets of Ambriellan wool. There were more than when I'd left, as if Caylus had gotten concerned the crow might be cold. A small water bowl sat beside him.

This close, the cord between Res and me felt stronger, the connection a comfort. I knelt beside him, and his silver eyes opened. On his stomach, with his little head tucked in, he was no more than a pouf of feathers with a beak.

He cawed softly, the cord thrumming with something like recognition. One day old, and he was nearly as large as my torso. In less than a week, he would be a fledging, his wings a flurry of feathers as he fought to build strength, to learn the feel of the wind.

And then we would escape Illucia.

"We're going to have to stock up on a lot of meat," I whispered to him, stroking the soft feathers at the top of his head. He nipped affectionately at my fingers, and I tapped his beak, earning a quiet squawk of protest.

"What now?" Caylus sat down beside me as I unwrapped the chicken in my lap and fed Res a small piece.

"He should start showing signs of magic any day now," I replied. "Is someone going to come knocking if he makes noise?"

Caylus looked around his haphazard workshop. "They haven't yet."

I rose to join Caylus at the workbench, and Res let out a low screech. His feathers fluttered as he tried to follow me.

"I'm not going anywhere," I reassured him, but when I tried to step away again, the cord between us tugged. Sighing, I returned to his side and wrapped the blankets carefully about him, then scooped him into my arms.

"Only until you fall back asleep," I said as he snuggled into my embrace.

We spent the rest of the day working on some of Caylus's

projects, though I wasn't much help with Res in my arms. Despite what I'd said, I held him long after he'd fallen asleep.

I'd nearly started to doze myself, lulled by the sound of Res breathing and the warmth of his body, when something struck the workbench and Gio yowled.

I sprang to my feet, whirling to find Caylus staring mournfully at an overturned beaker of yellow liquid, Gio having narrowly escaped atop a pile of books. Blood trickled from Caylus's temple, a sharp-edged hanging basket still swaying from where his head had struck it, causing him to overturn the beaker.

"Are you okay?" I gently set the still-sleeping Res back down in his pile of blankets, then grabbed Caylus a clean towel as he dropped into a chair. He touched two fingers to his head, then pulled them back, staring at the blood.

"I think so." He stiffened as I pressed the cloth against his wound.

"I thought measuring was my job," I teased.

"Yes. I... You were with Res. I didn't want to bother you."

"Well, next time, bother away." I poked his arm.

A blush rose in his cheeks, and he averted his gaze, studying Gio as if he'd never seen a cat before.

"Maybe you ought to reorganize your workshop," I suggested, dabbing gently at the scrape. It wasn't deep; it'd barely required a bandage.

Caylus looked from me to the hanging basket and back again. "But then how would I ever find anything?"

"Are you saying you know where everything in this mess is?"

"Except my book on early Illucian technology. I haven't seen that for weeks."

I paused, staring at him. "That's a joke." He smiled, and I shook my head. "We really need to work on your sense of humor."

He laughed, and the silence that followed felt comfortable and full, like a cozy room lit by a crackling fire. Suddenly, I became aware of our closeness, of my palm brushing his face, my fingertips touching the soft hairs at his temple. Caylus swayed, as if unsure whether to lean away from my touch or into it. The memory of our kiss hung between us.

I cleared my throat, turning away as a flush crept into my cheeks. Instantly, I felt the absence of his warm skin against mine. "You'll be fine. It's already stopped bleeding."

I grabbed a few more towels and tossed them to Caylus, then fetched a jug of water from across the room, cursing myself as I went. I'd kissed him, and now I couldn't manage to stand a foot away from him?

When I returned, Caylus had started mopping up the mess, remnants of scarlet lighting his golden skin. He grabbed the water jug without a word and dampened a cloth with it, cleaning quickly.

As he carried the used cloths away, I picked up some papers where the liquid had caught the edges and spread them out in the light of the wide front window to dry. The edge of his sketchbook had also gotten wet, and as I moved it into the sun, two papers fluttered out. I picked them up, careful of the damp edges.

Night incarnate stared back. A crow hovered, its wings drawn up and flared out as it landed. They curved forward, creating a cocoon around a proud figure in flying leathers. My lips parted.

Caylus had drawn my hair in a braid down my back, several curls left loose and caught in an invisible wind. The leathers he'd drawn to the tiniest pleat, and they clung to me like armor. With a bow strapped across my chest and a quiver of arrows at my hip, I looked formidable.

A rush of heat filled me from my brow to the tips of my toes. How had he done this with his shaking hands that could barely form letters? It must have taken him hours. Days.

The wooden floor creaked behind me, and I turned.

Caylus shifted nervously in the doorway. "I, um, hope I got the flying leathers right. The only drawings I could find weren't very detailed. Makes sense. I guess the people making them wouldn't want anyone else knowing the design, and no one in Illucia cares. But I didn't know how accurate they were and—"

"It's amazing," I breathed. "Thank you." Looking up, I found his soft eyes gazing back at me, head tilted, his lips slightly parted. Lips I wanted to run my fingers along, to feel if they were as soft as they'd felt last night. Then he seemed to realize what he was doing, gave his head a little shake, and stepped over to a workbench like he was looking for something.

I swallowed hard and lifted the page to look at the second drawing underneath, revealing a very different image. This too was of me, but I sat sideways in one of the workshop chairs, my legs dangling over one arm and my back against the other. My elbow rested on the back of the chair, propping my head up, my eyes staring unfocused at some spot out a rain-sprinkled window. I looked...sad.

I held the papers up. "So which am I? Proud warrior or despondent thinker?"

He tapped the one of me in the chair. "I was actually going for excessive tea drinker in that one. I think I'm actually out of bergamot." Sure enough, a pile of empty teacups sat in the background of the drawing.

I gave him a flat look, and he smiled, leaning back against the workbench. "Why can't you be both?"

I tucked the second drawing underneath the first and set them on the workbench. "I've wasted enough time being sad."

"There's nothing wrong with being sad. Everyone feels that way one time or another."

"Some people for longer than others," I muttered.

Caylus stepped up beside me, sliding the top drawing over so they lay side by side. He pointed at the one of me curled in on myself. "What do you see?"

"Weakness."

He smiled, sending a rush of warmth into my cheeks. "I see someone who cares about something enough to worry about it so strongly, she loses herself in it."

My flush deepened. "I think you've inhaled too many fumes."

He continued as if he hadn't heard me. "You think about the crows, don't you? When you go quiet," he said.

I folded my arms. "Maybe I just don't feel like talking in those moments."

He raised an eyebrow, giving me a doubtful look as if to ask, *You? Not talk?*

I deflated. "Yes. I think about the crows."

He moved closer, the heat from his body dancing along my skin. I became all too aware of his closeness, of the bright green of his eyes. The kind of green that pushes up out of the ashen earth to remind you that life struggles on.

His fingers grazed mine, surprisingly steady. Sharp heat prickled behind my eyes, and I bit the inside of my cheek to keep the growing tears at bay. He must have seen them anyways, as his fingers brushed my cheek gently.

I leaned against his chest. To my relief, his arms encircled me, wrapping me in a warm strength that chased the tears from my eyes and the tightness from my throat. I might have Res, but he was the last of his kind, and he wouldn't live forever. One day, the crows would disappear for good.

Something shattered, and we both leapt. Behind Caylus, Gio sat on the workbench edge, his paw outstretched, disinterested yellow eyes staring at the broken remains of the beaker he'd knocked to the floor.

Caylus grabbed a towel from the workbench to deal with the glass. The moment he stepped away, I felt his heat leave with him, and I almost reached out to pull him back. Instead, I touched the drawing of me as a rider, the paper rough beneath my fingertips, and felt a spark of something come to life deep inside me. I breathed deeply, and it grew with my breath, smoldering, steady, strong.

"You can keep that if you want." He didn't look at me, but the back of his neck was red as he scooped up the glass.

I folded the paper and tucked it in a pocket, the image imprinted on the back of my eyelids. Was that how he saw me? A warrior cloaked in shadows, the night itself standing sentry at my back?

Was that who I could be?

I resolved to pay more attention the rest of the day. Caylus had apparently been preparing to mix a powerful acid, and while the idea of making liquid fire made my skin crawl, I slid on a pair of thick, elbow-length gloves and set to helping.

After dinner, I changed into my flying leathers and met Ericen down at the training grounds, leaving Kiva sitting at the dining room table with Auma, playing a game I'd never seen before involving painted cards.

The training grounds were empty, the first wisps of evening mist coiling over the castle corridors and down along the grass. Ericen was already running through drills with a practice sword in one of the rings. I blinked. He was shirtless.

Lean, corded muscle pulled taut with every motion, his movements tight and controlled. I felt my eyes widen reflexively before wiping the expression off my face a second before he spotted me.

"No uniform tonight?" I asked, trying to sound casual.

He smirked, as if knowing he'd unsettled me. "Centerian fights are shirtless. Makes it easier to see the blood."

"Of course. That's very important."

He offered me a hand, and I grasped it, letting him haul me into the ring with an ease that made my heart stumble. This was not going to be an easy fight.

Up close, the torchlight illuminated countless tiny scars flecking his pale skin from years of training, including those along his biceps and forearms, layered in even, clean lines. Like Razel's.

He followed my gaze. "I don't practice." His voice was cool. "Not since it became my choice."

Frost prickled my skin. Razel had forced him. Had soldiers held him down while his mother sliced his skin, offering his blood to her brutal god in exchange for his favor?

"She seemed to think she was saving my soul." The emptiness in Ericen's tone only made me feel sicker. He turned his arm to hide the scars, clenching his fist. The muscles in his arm flexed as he said, "It felt more like I was losing it." He snorted derisively. "Oh well. What's another disappointment in a sea of failures?"

"I wouldn't call that a failure," I replied.

His silver-blue gaze lifted to meet mine, and the intensity behind it pinned me.

"It's difficult to walk against the wind." Another Trendellan proverb from Caliza's husband. "It takes strength."

"Funny, my mother called it weakness. I don't suppose you'd consider having this talk with her?" Despite his flippancy, some of the tightness ebbed from his face.

I gave him a flat look, and he chuckled as he approached a corner of the ring where a sheath hung on the post. He slid the sword in, then returned to face me in the center of the ring.

"First one to concede loses?" he asked.

"I don't concede."

He grinned. "So I'm learning."

I shifted my stance, and he did the same. "On one," he said. "Three, two, one."

Ericen shot forward, releasing a volley of strikes. I dodged with room to spare, then slipped around him and backed toward the other side of the ring. Those had been test shots; he was feeling me out.

He came at me again, faster this time, his movements stronger and quicker. I dodged and blocked, turned and swirled, and with each blow of his that missed or I knocked askew, his expression grew tighter, and I nearly grinned. He couldn't hit me.

The problem was my strength had always been in my speed and reflexes. I could avoid an opponent all day, but I hesitated to end a fight. Estrel always told me to tire them out, but two weeks of training wasn't enough to compete with the stamina of a fully trained Vykryn.

Ericen had clearly realized the same thing, as he seemed content to continue until I couldn't any longer. Already, my breathing started to labor, my movements to lag. He nearly clipped me twice in a row.

Then, in what I mistook for another punch, he tackled me to the ground.

The ring floor gave only slightly, compressing just enough to spare my back, the air gushing out of my lungs in a loud gasp. Ericen was easily twice my size, his heavy body pinning me with little effort. My chest heaved. He felt like a miniature sun, his skin burning with expended energy and slick with sweat.

He grinned, then clearly thinking he'd settled the matter, peeled his hand off my arm to wipe the sweat from his brow. I punched him in the jaw.

His head whipped to the side, but his body remained planted over mine. My knuckles sang, but all I cared about was the red mark they'd left on his face. He blinked, and then he smiled. A real smile, not the stupid one-sided smirk or the grin that made me want to gut him.

"You're better than I gave you credit for," he said.

I'd just about regained my breath enough to talk. "You're not."

He laughed, the sound strangely rich and menacing at the same time, and rose, offering me a hand. I let him lift me to my feet, my back protesting.

"You need to work on your counterstrikes," he said. "You fight like a poorly trained Jin."

"You fight like a brick wall," I growled back, fully aware that didn't make much sense. But it was the only way I could describe his curt, solid movements and sturdy stance.

He laughed again, and I simmered, hating that he was right. The Jin fighting style used an opponent's weight and movements against them, making them skilled dodgers, like me. But they also knew how to end a fight.

I sought the connection with Res, knowing it would calm me. It flooded into my veins in a quiet rush, stronger than it had been yesterday from this far away.

"Next time," I said, "I'm bringing my bow, and we're doing this with weapons."

Ericen grinned. "Deal. In the meantime, let me show you a few moves."

By the time I returned to my room, I was so exhausted and sore, I nearly missed Kiva at the dining table. She'd fallen asleep there, her head resting on her forearms. Someone had tucked a blanket over her shoulders.

TWENTY-TWO

Kiva and I trained together and ate breakfast, and then I ordered the carriage to take me to Caylus's. I took a detour through the kitchens, where Tarel and Lyren already had a bundle of chicken waiting, along with a parcel that smelled of sugar and orange.

When I unwrapped it, I found a batch of freshly baked orange cakes dusted in powdered sugar.

"The prince said you liked those," Lyren said. "I had an old recipe from a Rhodairen friend."

I smiled. "You have a Rhodairen friend?"

Tarel snorted at the word *friend*, and Lyren ran a hair through his silver-specked hair with a laugh. "There was a time our people traded in more than blood and steel, you know."

I knew, and I hoped one day we would again.

Caylus and I sat shoulder to shoulder before Res, taking turns tossing him pieces of chicken. Caylus had made bergamot tea, and we'd devoured the entire parcel of orange cakes in a matter of minutes.

"Do these have whiskey in them?" Caylus had asked, already covered in powdered sugar.

"They're soaked in it," I replied. "But most of the alcohol burns off when they're set on fire."

He blinked. "Set on fire?"

I smirked, remembering something Estrel had once said. *It's like you in a dessert. Zesty, sweet, with a dash of flames.* My heart panged at the memory. "It caramelizes them," I replied.

I tossed Res another piece of chicken, which he snapped up eagerly. He'd grown overnight and was already starting to flex his wings and shift rather than just lay about.

"Has he shown any signs of magic?" I asked Caylus. When he shook his head, concern flickered through me. Storm crow chicks often sparked weak lightning or coalesced patches of mist sporadically.

He's only two days old, I reminded myself. It wasn't unheard of not to have seen magic at this point. Still, the sense of unease I'd woken with simmered in my gut. A crow without any magic wouldn't inspire much confidence, and securing the other kingdoms' aid was Rhodaire's only hope.

Res struggled to stand, revealing legs lined in glossy black scales. He almost made it before collapsing back into the blankets with an indignant squawk. The cord between us tugged with an indistinct sensation.

I grinned. "We're going to have to start working on strength exercises," I told him.

Caylus perked up, eyes bright. "What kind of exercises?"

"Mostly for his wings," I replied. "We'll start with basic movements to stretch and strengthen them and then move on to drills that simulate flight." Had Res been born before Ronoch, his mother would have taught him most of this, though he wasn't the first orphan crow to be raised by a rider. Hopefully, I wouldn't make a poor substitute.

Caylus's curiosity dimmed, his gaze switching from Res to me. "Once he's strong enough, you're going to leave," he said softly.

"Come with me." The words came out on reflex, and only as the idea settled in my chest like the piece of a puzzle did I realize how much I wanted him to say yes. But I was asking for more than his company. I was asking him to involve himself in something so much larger than us. Something where he'd have to fight again.

One of the things I liked most about Caylus was the open honesty in his face. He never hid his true feelings. That knowledge was little comfort as his expression turned hesitant and uncertain.

Before he could answer, someone knocked. Cursing, I pulled the edge of the blanket over Res, willing him into silence. Frowning, Caylus rose and padded downstairs. Several lock clicks later, I heard the door open, a rushed exchange of whispers, and then two sets of footsteps climbing the stairs.

Diah entered after Caylus, her mask in place. She slipped

into the room on steps light as air, then put her back to a wall, facing us both. On her leather belt hung three identical tiny knots of black rope.

She traced my line of sight, and for the first time, I noticed something strange about the eye on the black half of the mask. It looked dull.

She touched a hand to the ropes. "Ambriellan death knots," she explained. "One for each soul that was lost."

Ambriellan knots were a superstition, the various colors and knot work designs representing different things, from good luck to safe travels. These looked like wisps of shadow, curled in on themselves like someone protecting their heart.

"I was sorry to hear about your friends," I said. Had their loss driven her here? Maybe she was starting to realize she couldn't do this alone.

Diah straightened. "Such is the cost of war, as you will soon come to know."

Her words settled inside me like stones sinking to the ocean floor. "If we help each other, that cost might not be so high. Trendell has agreed to host a meeting and hear our proposal for an alliance. Join us there. Make your choice then."

Slowly, Diah nodded. A knot in my chest released like a line snapping. We were moving forward.

After giving Diah the date and location, I returned to a letter from Caliza at the castle. This time, I skipped the fake visible conversation and flipped the letter over to sprinkle powder on the invisible ink on the back. Kiva hovered beside me as I read quietly aloud by sona lamp:

Thia,

I am so proud of you, and I know if she were here, our mother would be too. Thanks to you, we have a real chance to protect Rhodaire.

A letter arrived from Captain Mirkova. She said she sent you one too. I know it's not the answer we wanted, but we can still do this. She's staying in Korovi to proposition them for supplies.

I've convened the council.

I paused, exchanging looks with Kiva. Rhodairen rulers only convened the council during wartime, when the heads of all the houses gathered in the castle. They would eat and sleep there instead of their own homes, working together to prepare Rhodaire for battle.

I kept reading.

Illucia now occupies five towns on our outer border. My letters to their general and Queen Razel have gone ignored. Lady Turren has suggested we poison the towns' water supply, as well as those of any neighboring villages (I'm starting to suspect she may be just as merciless as her father was). She says our greatest advantage is the heat, as he believes the Illucians are unprepared for a Rhodairen summer. But I'm not sure I can do that. It would mean evacuating the towns and quite possibly making them unlivable. I don't want to destroy people's homes.

Lord Rynthene has stripped one of his ships of identifying marks to send for you. It's currently docked near the border in a fishing village on the coast. Elair. Do you remember it? Mother took us there once on our way to the Ambriels. You ate so much fried fish, it made you sick.

I miss you. Stay safe, and send word the moment you're prepared to leave.

Love,
Caliza

Kiva tossed the letter into the fireplace, nudging it with the metal poker until it turned to ash. "Things are getting worse," she said. "How much longer until we can move?"

"A few more days," I told her. "Res is still too fragile."

Kiva stabbed the hot coals with the poker. "Let's pray Rhodaire has that long."

My mind strayed as Ericen and I ran through drills in the misty courtyard. Even as I focused on the correct steps and forms of the new moves he'd taught me, I held tight to the cord with

Res. It'd grown even stronger, and the more I focused on it, the more I felt him there.

The link between us thrummed, filling me with a sense of annoyance. Not my own but his.

It wasn't the first hint of emotion I'd felt from the crow. It'd taken me a while to realize the wisps of feelings weren't my own, and even now, I couldn't always tell the difference. But with each passing minute, the connection between us grew stronger, like a rope pulling taut, and more and more of his emotions flared to life along it.

His magic had to be close to manifesting. I could feel it.

I only prayed it was enough to seal this alliance. Enough to stop Illucia.

My gaze flickered to Ericen, who was moving through a series of sword poses. The Centerian was in two weeks. If everything went according to plan, I'd be long gone by then. Would he be strong enough to win? And if he did, would he serve at his mother's side in this war?

Would he fight against me?

As though he felt my eyes on him, the prince paused in his drills to face me, his bare chest rising and falling with heavy breaths. "Taking notes?" he asked with a catlike grin.

I didn't smile. "What if you lose?"

"I won't," he replied without hesitation.

"I'm serious, Ericen." I folded my arms, the chill of the thickening mist sending a shiver down my spine.

His grin faded, and he drove the tip of his sword into the soft earth at his side. "So am I. Losing isn't an option. Why do you care?"

Why *did* I care? Ericen might not be as horrible as he'd led me to first believe, but if war broke out this instant, he would still be my enemy. I'd told Kiva I thought I could trust him in time. But how much time did we really have?

I don't want to be your enemy. That was what he'd said to me that night in the stables.

Maybe he didn't have to be.

TWENTY-THREE

With each passing day, the weather grew colder as Res grew stronger, but he never showed the slightest hint of magic. Even as his fluffy down molted into feathers of iridescent black streaked with midnight blues and purples and he struggled about his blanket, his thin wings opening and closing and pressing against the ground like a pair of arms to steady himself, no gust of wind came to his aid, no spark of lightning erupting in his frustration.

I sent a letter back to Caliza expressing my fears, then threw myself into my training with Ericen. We met each evening, trading blows alongside stories about past teachers and lessons. The ease with which we talked made the ground feel unsteady beneath my feet, as if it were constantly changing its tilt, uncertain of which way to send me, and leaving me unsure where I stood with the prince.

My afternoons I spent training with Res. Caylus and I had created a miniature obstacle course for him, using chicken as bait to encourage him from one point to the other. When he was strong enough, I carried him to the bottom of the stairs, then sat a few steps up with a handful of chicken.

Frustration ebbed along the link alongside a distinct feeling I'd identified as hunger. "Up the stairs then," I told him, waving the chicken.

In response, he let his wings droop and hung his head.

I stared at him. "Are you *begging?*"

Caylus stuck his head out from the workshop. "Oh, um. That might be my fault."

I gave him an exasperated look, and he smiled sheepishly. "I mean, he just...well, look at him. He looks so sweet and adorable when he does that and I—" He bit his lip as my expression hardened. "Well, the point is I think he expects it to work now."

I groaned, covering my face with my hand. "Fantastic. Now he thinks being adorable will get him whatever he wants."

"He's not entirely wrong."

"Caylus!"

Caylus's face flushed, and he muttered something about boiling liquids before fleeing back into the workshop. I glowered at Res, who'd given up on his show of *poor little me* while we'd been talking but resumed drooping the moment I looked at him.

"Up the stairs or no chicken," I said, folding my arms. It took a few minutes, but Res finally gave in. The first stair presented a struggle, but once he figured out he could hop up each one, he reached me quickly. I gave him chicken, then climbed farther up the stairs, and we repeated the process until we reached the top.

"Great," I said. "Now let's do it again."

Something like a groan ground down the cord between us, and I laughed. Was this what Estrel had felt like, pushing me through drills?

We repeated the exercise until Res was breathing heavily and his wings drooped from exhaustion instead of dramatics. He'd figured out that if he fluttered his wings as he leapt, it gave him an extra boost, which meant he got to the chicken faster.

It would be a couple more weeks before he could fly, but each new tiny indication that he was growing closer made me shiver in anticipation.

A week and endless training sessions later, I sat with Caylus in his workshop, marveling at how much Res had grown. He stood taller than my waist and could eat more than his weight in chicken and did so happily. In fact, he was obsessed, flopping to the floor whenever I refused to give him more and lifting his wings like a sheet to protect his food as he ate. We'd had to start getting chicken from other sources than just Tarel, lest he start wondering why I needed so much.

Res hopped over to where I sat, sending Gio hissing and scurrying away. The kitten clambered up Caylus's leg, scurrying along his side until he'd reached the safety of his shoulder.

Res nudged my hand with his beak. His movements were

already smooth and lithe, the strength and grace of the crow he would become evident in the growing cords of muscle along his lean form. Unlike normal birds, crows had almost reptilian bodies, making them thicker and sturdier than their featherlight counterparts.

I pulled a piece of chicken out of the pouch in my pocket and tossed it to him. He swallowed it one gulp and nudged me for more, making a low throaty noise reminiscent of Gio's purring.

By the time we escaped and reached Trendell nearly three weeks from now, Res would be almost full-grown.

Caylus looked up from the drawing he'd been working on, the slightest tremor in his large hands. "I've been thinking about what you asked the other day."

It took me a moment to realize what he meant: the day Diah had come. The day I'd asked him to leave with us.

I rose, joining him at the workbench. My arm brushed his, and this close, I remembered the thrill of the night Res had hatched. The night Caylus and I had kissed.

He slid his hand over, and I met it with mine, our fingers interlacing. His skin was rough, lined with so many scars. Tilting his head forward, his deep green eyes met mine, the stray auburn curls dipping above them turning nearly red in the sunlight.

"If you...you know...if you still—" He bit his lip, and my fingers twitched. I longed to touch his lips, to trail my fingers along the line of his jaw. "I know about your engagement, and I know it's not what you want, and I'm okay with this if you are, and—" He stopped again.

"If you still want me to go with you, I will," he said unwaveringly.

Without hesitation, I replied, "I do." And kissed him.

For one perfect moment, it was just my lips against his. It was sweet, safe silence, and a promise of something better.

Then Gio yowled as my shoulder pressed into Caylus's, catching the cat's tail, and Res let out a demanding caw, the cord between us tugging.

I laughed against Caylus's lips and felt him smile back. I pulled away, but he captured my face in his hands, their broad expanse forming a gentle cocoon. Heat fluttered through me, my body waking up bit by bit like a fire sparking to life. By the time we pulled apart, my throat was raw and my lungs burned for air.

Caylus's hands slid away, and I captured one in my own, smiling as Res nudged me again. I tossed him a piece of chicken from the pouch, and he snatched it out of the air with the dexterity of a hunter.

Physically, he looked perfect. He was bigger than I'd expected him to be, even for a male crow of his age. Full-grown, he'd be massive.

But his size wouldn't be enough.

"I don't understand," I said, watching as he hopped over to his water bowl to drink. "He should be showing signs of magic by now. I've never heard of a crow taking this long before. What if something's wrong with him? What if Ronoch damaged him somehow?"

"Whatever it is, I'm sure there's a reasonable explanation," Caylus replied.

I snorted. "You would say that. But this is magic, not science. Who knows what the rules are?"

"We'll figure it out." Caylus squeezed my hand.

"I hope so. For all our sakes."

TWENTY-FOUR

When I returned to the castle that evening, I had a letter for Caliza telling her Res was strong enough to move. The letter would take two days to arrive in Rhodaire, then a day for her to contact the ship in Elair, and two days for them to sail here. We only had to make it five more days.

I fell asleep to the knowledge that it was time to find a way out of Sordell.

A soft touch at my shoulder woke me. I opened my eyes, expecting sunlight and Kiva's face. Instead, I found night and the shadowed form of Auma a foot away, nearly enveloped in darkness.

I bolted upright. "What is it? Is something wrong?"

"I have something for you," she said, holding out a small envelope.

I took it, expecting more of an explanation, but she only waited. Pushing myself back against the headboard, I opened the envelope and withdrew a letter, finding a fake message from Caliza.

"Where did you get this?" I asked.

"It was intercepted by the queen." Auma's eyes were pools of shadows in the faint moonlight.

"And you...stole it?" My half-awake mind struggled to parse what was happening. "Why?"

"It did not belong to her," Auma stated simply, as if that were the only reason that could possibly matter.

I wasn't going to argue with her. "Razel's going to notice this is gone."

"I will take the blame if she does."

I studied her. "I don't understand you. You'd risk your safety to bring me this, but when you're around Razel, you pretend to be weak. Why? I know you're not afraid of her."

"Strength comes in many forms," she said. "The lion fears only the fox."

A Trendellan proverb. There was no greater advantage than being underestimated for what you lacked in physical strength. It was the quick, quiet predators you never saw coming.

"Thank you," I said.

Auma inclined her head. "I have another message as well: *Myzae.*"

I went stiff. *Myzae.* The Jin used the same word for both art and magic, and it was the password we'd decided on for news related to Jindae.

"The Jin princess will hear out your proposition in Trendell."

"What? How? Auma!" I hissed, but she was already gliding from the room on silent feet. By the time I untangled myself from my covers and dashed across the room, the common room door was swinging shut.

My heart fluttered, my breath thinning as my mind raced to catch up. Somehow, Auma was connected to the Jin rebels. She knew what we were doing. I looked to Kiva's closed door. Was that why she'd stayed close to Kiva? Was she a spy?

Whoever she was, it seemed she was on our side. As were the Jin, for now. They would listen, like Diah would listen, but would they truly pledge their people's lives to this alliance?

The unanswered questions stretched out before me like a dark, endless hall. Most importantly of all, why had Razel confiscated my letter? Did she suspect me, or was this just another method of control?

I retreated to my room for some powder, then approached the dying embers of the fire with care. Coating the paper in the powder, I unfolded the letter and held it as far away from the fire as I could while still illuminating the invisible ink.

Thia,

I talked to Lady Kerova about Res's magic. She says this is very common with orphan crows. Without his mother or eggmates around to learn from, you're his only source of guidance. She also said without his eggmates to challenge him for dominance, he might feel like he doesn't need his magic. Apparently, some crows just need a little push. I have no idea what that means, but she said to focus on the bond between you and you'll figure it out.

Good luck,
Caliza

A push? I closed my eyes, reaching along the cord to Res and receiving soft thrums of sleep in response. The feeling flowed through me in a soothing rhythm, like the ebb and flow of the tide.

I prayed Lady Kerova was right.

TWENTY-FIVE

I skipped training that morning, eager to get to Caylus's and put Lady Kerova's advice into action. Leaping from the carriage, I burst into the bakery to the scent of sugar and lemon and raced up the stairs, a wrapped parcel of chicken from Tarel in hand. The door was already opening when I reached the top.

"Res was going wild like he does when you're close," Caylus explained with a smile.

I grinned, slipping past him and nearly barreling straight into Res, who cawed happily, lifting and lowering his wings in a flutter of excitement and nudging my empty hand with his beak.

"I don't suppose there was any inexplicable lightning last night?" I asked.

Caylus closed the door and glanced out at the clouded sky. It was a clear, sunny day by Illucian standards, patches of blue among the gray. "Sorry," he replied. He retreated to the kitchen island where he picked up a chocolate chip scone from the counter and tore off a piece, tossing it to Res.

I stared at him. "Scones? Scones are not part of a crow's diet!"

"We ran out of chicken," Caylus said simply, as if that explained why he was now feeding Res sugar and flour. "He wanted breakfast," he added.

"All he ever wants is breakfast," I replied with a groan. "And lunch and dinner and a thousand snacks in between. You'd think all that energy would make for *some nice lightning.*"

In response, Res ruffled his tail feathers and snatched another piece of scone from Caylus's hand. His beak was almost as large as Caylus's palm now, but he moved with a delicate grace that left me unconcerned for the safety of Caylus's fingers.

I released an overdramatic sigh and handed Caylus the package of fresh chicken. "My sister said a friend of ours thinks he needs a push."

"What sort of push?" he asked, returning the scones to a box along with the chicken.

I shrugged, glancing at Res, who was eyeing the box. Taking a deep breath, I focused on the cord between us. Pulses of contentment slid down from Res, intermixed with excitement and craving. Lady Kerova had said to use the bond between us to push Res into using his magic.

I sent a nudge down the cord. Res paused, silver gaze switching from the scones to me, but nothing more. No spark, no gust of wind. I looked helplessly at Caylus.

"Maybe you just didn't push hard enough?" he suggested.

I focused on the link again. It hummed, pulling at the spot just below my rib cage, and I imagined myself traveling down it. I thought of reaching into Res, of finding the magic lying coiled deep inside him, and—

The floor rocked violently. The connection between us shuddered, and I stumbled back, gasping for breath. The room rocked again, and I nearly lost my footing when Caylus seized my arm, steadying me.

"What's happening?" I asked. But even as I asked, I saw.

Out the window, the once cloudless sky had turned darker than dusk as heavy clouds materialized from thin air. A powerful gust of wind rattled the windowpanes, screaming as it whirled down the street. Thunder boomed, echoing like the march of an army.

And before me, Resyries crackled with lightning.

Res stood in the center of the room, his wings lifted, the tips pointed down. I gaped at him, unable to think, unable to move. The wind howled louder, coming alive in the room. It lifted plates and food and utensils off the island, swirling them about the room in a massive whirlwind. Outside, lightning crackled across the sky.

My hair ripped free from my braid, buffeting my face with sharp, tiny lashes. I couldn't tear my eyes away.

A warm hand found mine, and I felt Caylus beside me a

moment later. "The opposite!" he yelled, and my shocked mind struggled to understand. "Do the opposite!"

The opposite of what I'd just done. I nodded, reaching out for the cord, and recoiled with a cry. The link vibrated viciously, the feel of it sharp and hot as the lightning erupting around Res's body.

Despite the way the thought made my stomach turn, I seized the cord through the pain and *pulled*. Res let out a cry, sharp as the snap of bone, and the link shuddered.

A burst of energy barreled through me, throwing me backward. Caylus caught me as my vision blurred, then cleared. Res stood before me, the lightning gone, his silver eyes back to their usual stormy gray, wings lowered to his sides as things came crashing to the floor.

My lips parted as I took in the chaos. Shattered pieces of plates and bowls littered the floor, scones and cakes torn apart and scattered. A bread knife had been driven into the wall right where Caylus had been standing. Outside, broken branches hung at awkward angles on trees along the street, leaves scattered like flower petals.

What in the Saints' name had just happened? The ground had shaken. Thunder alone couldn't do that. It was like— .

"Caylus?" A voice called from outside the door. "Caylus, what's going on in there?"

We both spun for the door. The locks were undone. Caylus had forgotten them in his excitement to see me. I shot forward, but it was too late.

The door opened.

TWENTY-SIX

The new girl from the bakery stepped inside.

I froze, my mind racing as she surveyed the room. She couldn't see. She couldn't know.

"What happened here?" she asked, her face growing slack as she took in the damage, her eyes sliding across the island, to me…and right over where Res was standing.

She looked at Caylus expectantly.

My breath shuddered, and I locked it in my throat. Had she not noticed Res? I glanced at Caylus, carefully sculpting my expression into something calmer.

Caylus blinked at her, startled. At least she wouldn't find his behavior strange; he was always a little strange.

"The storm," he said, and that was it.

The girl's brow furrowed. "The shaking did all this?"

"Yes," I said too quickly. But half my mind was on trying to understand how she hadn't noticed the three-foot-tall crow behind me.

Her gaze fell on the knife sticking out of Caylus's wall. She placed her hands on her hips. "You were doing another one of your experiments, weren't you?"

"That too," I said. "The shaking messed it up. It exploded."

Her expression grew hesitant. "This'll come out of your pay, Caylus."

He nodded, but his face had gone empty. His mind was somewhere else, likely wondering the same thing as me: why in Saints' name didn't she care about Res?

Giving the room a final sweep, the girl let out a sigh of resignation and stepped back out onto the landing, closing the door behind her.

For a moment, the room was utterly still. Then I bolted for the door and turned lock after lock so fast, I scraped my knuckles. Slumping back against the door, I faced the room.

Res was gone.

My heart stopped. I blinked, thinking it a trick of my vision, but he wasn't there. Yet I could feel the cord pulsing between us.

"I swear he didn't move," Caylus muttered, brow furrowed.

"Res?" I called hesitantly.

In the corner, the shadows looked strange, like a distorted reflection in a rippling lake. A spot behind my temple began to pound, and I pressed my fingers to it, blinking to clear my vision.

Then the shadows moved. They shifted like ebbing fog, growing and stretching until a piece pulled apart from the rest, coalescing first into wings and then a body and tail and head and—

"What—?" I gaped at Res as he finished detaching himself from the shadows.

Caylus's eyes widened, his head tilting in consideration. "I didn't think storm crows could bend shadows."

"They *can't*." My voice strained on the word. None of this made any sense. Was that why the earth had shaken? Had Res somehow used earth crow magic too? But that was absurd.

"Interesting," Caylus muttered to himself. His fingers tapped along his leg in thought.

I took an unsteady step toward the island and dropped onto the nearest stool. Res let out a low caw as I buried my head in my hands, trying to parse this impossibility. Surely, the shaking had just been a result of Res's magic releasing after being pent up for so many days. But that didn't explain how he'd *disappeared*.

"We're not stopping, are we?" Caylus's voice drew me from my thoughts. I blinked at him, and he nodded at Res, who looked completely unfazed by the sudden rush of magic. In fact, he looked stronger, his posture straighter, his feathers darker, as if not using his abilities had been hurting him somehow.

I felt cautiously along the cord between us, questioning gently. Was he okay? Res let out a low coo and lifted his wings, stretching them wide as if insulted by the question.

A grin slid across my lips. "I need a pen and paper."

Caylus retrieved them for me, and I began scribbling out a plan at the kitchen island. "There are different programs for different crow types," I told him, knowing he'd want every detail. "We have basic sets of maneuvers for them to start out with, to get a feel for their power and help strengthen the bond between them and the rider."

His green eyes glimmered with curiosity. "What's first?"

Facing Res, I focused on the connection between us. "A spark." As I spoke, I sent a thought down the cord too, imagining Res producing a small spark of lightning. It was one of the most basic storm crow maneuvers, a simple show of energy that many newborns produced on reflex.

Res cocked his head.

"Focus on the source of power inside you," I said, repeating words I'd heard Estrel whisper to hatchlings first discovering their magic. "Imagine it as an extension of yourself."

Res swayed, sending groan-like sounds along the cord, before spreading his wings and falling flat onto his back.

I blinked. He lifted his head gently, as if checking that I was looking, then let it flop back down.

"Is he okay?" Caylus asked.

A low rumble in Res's throat mirrored the vibration of feeling he sent down the cord between us. Something that translated loosely to *food food food*.

I groaned, dragging my hands down my face. "You've got to be kidding me." I crossed my arms. "You're not getting anything until you make some more lightning, you overgrown chicken."

Another cooing noise reverberated in Res's throat.

Caylus turned, withdrawing the box he'd tucked the chicken into. The moment the air caught the scent, Res snapped upright, flaring his wings to flip himself over in a show of agility that left me staring. Caylus tossed him a chicken slice, and he caught it, swallowing in one gulp.

"Sucker," I muttered.

"More after you're done," Caylus told him.

Res straightened, and like a dam releasing a river, lightning erupted around his body, singeing the air in a crackle of sparks and jagged cracks. Caylus leapt back, but I grinned wildly as the yellow-white energy surrounded Res like a spiderweb. Then as quickly as it came, it vanished.

I expected Caylus to be afraid, but he was staring at the crow with a mix of bewilderment and utter fascination. Leave it to him to be curious about something that could fry him alive.

Res clicked his beak, cawing softly, and I turned back in time to see Caylus break from the trance he so often lost himself to. He tossed Res another chicken piece, and the crow gobbled it greedily.

Caylus went to toss Res a third piece, but I stepped between them. "Hold up! I said a spark, not a ball of lightning. You have to be able to control it." Erupting into a flurry of searing energy hardly seemed conducive to crow riding.

Res huffed but did as I said. Or tried to. Every time he made to coalesce the lightning, it sputtered wildly. More than once, Caylus and I had to duck behind the island to avoid getting shocked. It took several more tries before Res managed to maintain the energy in a spark at the tip of his beak before releasing it in a snap of sizzling air. Caylus gave him the next chicken slice, and around we went. We worked on the spark of lightning several more times before doing a few wing exercises to help strengthen his muscles.

It would take a while for Res to truly master the basics of his powers, but we wouldn't be able to try anything more advanced until we were away from Illucia.

That storm had been too close a call.

I helped Caylus clean the kitchen before returning to the castle. Apparently, everyone just thought the weather a freak storm, despite the sky being almost clear of clouds. With sunlight streaming down to illuminate the dark stone streets and deep green foliage, Sordell almost looked peaceful.

Even its buildings wore masks.

Despite the sunny day outside, the castle corridors still prickled with cold. A breeze brushed my skin. I looked up for the source, slowing as I approached Kiva and my chambers. Tension crept up my shoulders. Something was wrong. The door hung open at an awkward angle, and I glimpsed an overturned chair.

I shot forward, silently cursing myself for not carrying my bow and arrows.

The room was empty, and it was a mess. Chairs overturned, plants knocked askew, slices deep into the couches. One window had been broken, letting in the cool breeze.

"Kiva!" I moved deeper into the room, checking her room,

then mine. Nothing. I sprinted back into the hallway and almost ran straight into a servant. "Have you seen my friend?" I demanded.

The girl stiffened. "She was escorted to see Her Majesty this afternoon."

My heart stopped as I sprang past her, darting out into the hallway and down to the great hall. Razel wasn't there. She wasn't in her rooms either. By the time I reached the throne room, my throat was raw.

The two guards outside the doors didn't stop me from bolting through. Razel stood on the dais, arguing in heated whispers with Ericen. Shearen stood at the foot of the dais, smirking. He had a growing bruise around his eye, and his left forearm had been bandaged. Beside him stood Auma, her face impassive as ever, head bowed. Bruises peeked out from the edges of her clothing and darkened her face.

My footsteps echoed like thunder in the high-ceilinged room, and all four sets of eyes snapped to me.

"Where's Kiva?" I halted at the base of the dais, ignoring Shearen's growing grin.

Ericen started to answer, but Razel cut across him, her eyes flashing. "This again, Thia dear? I thought we understood each other. Propriety would have you wait to be announced and to bow before addressing me."

"What did you do to her?"

Razel raised a single golden eyebrow, expectant. Her lips pulled into a thin smile. She waited.

Who knew what she'd done to Kiva, what she was doing to

her right now? I didn't want to give her the satisfaction, but I had no choice. My nails dug into the palms of my clenched fists, and against every fiber of my being, I bowed.

Shearen snickered quietly. I drew a short breath and straightened, meeting the queen's cold gaze.

"Kiva," I repeated through clenched teeth.

Razel stepped back and dropped gracefully into her throne, lounging like a satisfied jungle cat. "Your friend is in the castle dungeons—"

"Why—"

"Don't interrupt me." Razel's eyes narrowed dangerously. She turned and, in a voice smooth as Ambriellan whiskey, said, "Bring the girl."

Shearen bowed and struck out for a door in the far corner. My eyes followed his steps with growing anxiety. He was limping.

"If you've hurt her—"

"I'd advise you not to threaten me either." Razel's tone changed, sounding almost bored. She leaned back, peering down at me like a goddess passing judgment. Her hair glowed from the firelight, but her eyes were as icy as ever.

The silence stretched. In it, my gaze switched from Razel to Ericen, who looked ready to jump out of his skin, then to Auma, whose impassive mask had started to crack. She kept casting split-second glances in the direction Shearen had gone. My mind raced my heart. Was this about the storm? Did they know about Resyries?

I checked the link between us. It hummed stronger than

ever, layered with contentment. At my frantic touch, he tugged questioningly, but I pulled back.

The sharp sound of sliding metal shot through the room. Everyone except for Razel flinched, all eyes falling on her as she twirled an unsheathed moonblade around one finger. Then a door opened. I whipped around to find Shearen leading Kiva by her chain-bound hands. She had a bruised jaw, but otherwise, looked unharmed. I let out a breath. That explained Shearen's state—he'd gotten more than he bargained for with Kiva. He'd probably needed help.

"Are you okay?" I asked.

"She's fine," Razel answered before Kiva could speak. I caught Kiva's eye, and she nodded before her gaze sought Auma. She took in the bruises, the scratches, the fresh blood at Auma's shoulder, and a dangerous stillness settled over her. By the time she faced Razel, a silent, deadly promise prowled behind her eyes.

The queen rose fluidly to her feet, the moonblade clasped in one hand. I focused on keeping my feet rooted to the spot, afraid if I moved an inch, I'd charge Razel. "Are you going to explain what this is about now?"

Razel paused at the base of the dais as Shearen and Kiva arrived beside me. "That, Thia dear, is what this is about. You see, I thought you and I had come to an agreement, but it seems you are intent on pushing your limits with me."

"What are you talking—"

Quick as a wingbeat, Razel had the moonblade at Kiva's throat. My cry of surprise came out silent as the air evaporated from my lungs. Kiva stiffened, eyes dropping to the blade. Razel smiled, and seemingly content she had my attention, lowered the blade. Behind her, Auma had taken a step forward.

"It seems you only respond to shows of force," Razel said. "Not surprising. I've come to realize power, control, and violence are most of what your people understand."

You're one to talk. I managed to keep the words inside my head, but I couldn't stop my face from contorting with fury.

Razel tilted her head, considering me like a lamb for slaughter. "You think I'm the monster, don't you? Yet you're the ones who sent soldiers to decimate entire families, to tear them apart in front of the ones they love."

"Those soldiers weren't under orders—"

"Is that what your mother told you? That she didn't know Lord Turren was planning to kill not only my family but countless Illucian innocents? Innocents like Shearen's mother?"

Shearen paled, swallowing hard.

"Of course she didn't," I said.

Razel laughed. "Poor dear. You've been lied to. Your mother knew full well what Lord Turren was doing. She gave the order."

My stomach flipped, and the ground tilted, even as my mind screamed she was lying.

"Enough." Ericen's voice was quiet but strong. I clung to it, reassuring myself Razel was only trying to get inside my head.

She rounded on him. "You're right, Eri. That's not why we're here." She twirled the moonblade, eyes roving over Kiva. "We're here because my servant refuses to tell me what she's done with the letter she took from my room."

My eyes flickered to Auma, who to my surprise had shed her meek exterior entirely. She stood straight, hands clasped so tight, the knuckles had turned white, as if her hands couldn't be trusted not to wrap themselves around the queen's throat. Razel had clearly tried to beat the information out of her to no avail.

"What letter?" I asked.

Razel smiled dangerously. "I was hoping you'd make this difficult."

She glided over to one of the two hearths housing a strong fire and pulled a key out of her pocket, tossing it into the flames. Tension crept up my shoulders and into the back of my neck.

"I can take your friend away whenever I want. I can take your kingdom whenever I want." She stalked toward me. "I can make you do whatever I want, whenever I want, because if you don't listen, if you continue to defy me, I will take everything from you."

My throat closed.

Razel twirled her moonblade and smiled that vicious, shark-like smile. "Retrieve the key."

"What?"

Razel stepped past me, holding the edge of the moonblade to Kiva's chest. "The key is to your friend's shackles. Get it, or I start carving her pretty snow-white skin."

My mind refused to process Razel's words. I stared first at her, then Ericen, whose face had gone pale, before settling at last on the flames. They snapped like liquid orange teeth, waiting to tear me apart.

I have to get the key.

The words slowly sank in. Panic rose in my chest, my heart thundering in my ears. The tether between Res and me roared to life, and he pulled for my attention.

"I'm fine, Thia. Don't—" Kiva's words dissolved into a hiss. Razel had dug the moonblade's grip spike into Kiva's skin below the collarbone.

"What is it they call children like you in Korovi?" the queen asked sweetly. "*Okorn?* Perhaps I'll carve it here."

"Stop." My voice was barely more than a whisper, and I hated myself for it. Hated myself for being so afraid, for letting her win, for waiting long enough for her to send a bead of blood trailing down Kiva's chest. I swallowed hard, gathering my voice and strength. "I'll give you the letter."

"I know you will." Razel lifted the blade to Kiva's neck. "Now get the key."

"Thia—"

Kiva fell silent as I caught her gaze. I held it a moment longer, then faced the hearth and stepped toward it.

The key sat at the base of the hearth. It hadn't been in the flames long enough to glow, but I'd have to reach through the fire to touch it. My mind drifted, remembering the acrid smell of burning skin and singed hair, the sharp, white-hot pain like thousands of needles digging into my skin.

The flames swirled and snapped, as if daring me to try and get past them. My nails dug into my palms, sweat building on my skin. *I can do this.* The fire crackled, making me break out into a cold sweat. Res's call along the line was distant.

Calm down. You have to do this. The key is iron; it won't be that hot yet. One of Caylus's experiments had taught me that. Some metals heated faster than others. Iron fell somewhere in the middle. *The longer you wait, the hotter it gets.*

But no amount of science could change what else I knew: the fire was too hot. If I reached in, I'd never use my hand again.

A low hiss broke my concentration, and I whirled around. Razel had drawn a sharp circle in Kiva's skin, and blood ran in little rivulets from the wound. Kiva gritted her teeth and caught my gaze. In it, I found the strength to face the fire again.

Before I could talk myself out of it, I crouched and snatched the key out of the flames with my scarred hand, the fire so hot, it felt cold. The feeling barely had time to register before I'd pulled my arm free, the key clutched in my palm. Then my mind caught up to my body. I screamed.

My hand sprung open of its own accord, but the key didn't fall; it'd been seared into my palm. I shook my hand wildly without thinking. The key clattered to the ground, taking the first layer of my skin with it and leaving behind a key-shaped burst of angry red and white over the scar tissue of my palm.

Somewhere in the back of my mind, I was distantly aware of Kiva screaming and Ericen yelling, of someone laughing and my own sanity slowly slipping, and behind that, something else. Something I couldn't process.

Suddenly, Kiva was beside me, and I wondered when I'd fallen to my knees. My right hand clutched the forearm of my left, my eyes pinned on the key-shaped design, my breath refusing to come. Pain ripped through my hand and wrist like a thousand shards of glass tearing through my veins.

I stared at the burns, distantly registering that Kiva's hands were free, that Razel must have unlocked her shackles, that the key I'd pulled from the flames hadn't been for her restraints at all.

A shadow fell over me, and from far, far away, Razel's voice reached me. "Next time I see you, wear your gloves."

Then something shifted inside me. My vision blurred, then went black.

TWENTY-SEVEN

I woke in the healer's quarters, the room heavy with the sweet scent of the murkwood root used in pain tonics.

At first, I didn't move, didn't even open my eyes. Something was wrong. For some time, I lay there, letting my mind slowly remind me what it was.

I'd been burned. Badly.

The memory came back gradually at first, then all at once. Razel's laughter, Kiva's screams, the fire, the key, my hand—I squeezed my eyes shut tighter, desperate to block out the image of the key clinging to my seared skin.

I gave myself another moment and then forced my eyes open.

My hand had a loose bandage on it from my fingers to my wrist. It'd been propped on a pillow, and there were several jars of herbs and ointments on the table beside me. I recognized the murkwood vial, which explained the thick and heavy feel of my head.

Asleep in a chair on the other side, her mouth open and emitting snores, sat Kiva. The mark below her collarbone had stopped bleeding.

The bed I lay in was small but comfortable and warm, a single sona lamp burning dimly. No one else was around.

I looked again at my hand, and panic rose inside me, as white-hot and raw as the burns themselves. I gasped, hot tears threatening at my eyes. Kiva bolted upright at the sound, blinking rapidly, then sprang to her feet. "Thia!"

"I'm okay," I whispered, but my voice broke, and suddenly, I was crying. Kiva dropped onto the bed and pulled me into her arms. I melted into her and cried until my throat turned raw and my nose began to run.

When I was able to breathe normally again, I slowly sat back and wiped my tears with my good hand. Kiva gave me a cloth to blow my nose and a glass of water. I drank it all, then set the cup aside.

"How long was I out?" I asked.

"Just a few hours. The healer said your hand will be fine. The burns..." She trailed off, eyes narrowing. I remembered looking at my hand and not understanding.

"They're not as bad as they should be," I finished for her.

She nodded. At least I hadn't imagined that, as little sense as it made. Still, I didn't want to see yet.

"What happened to Auma?"

Kiva bit her lip. "I don't know. She vanished in the commotion, and I haven't seen her since."

"Vanished? With three Vykryn right there and two more at the door?"

Kiva's dark expression told me she'd had the same thought and had already followed it to its inevitable conclusion: Auma was not who we thought she was. I'd nearly forgotten what she'd said about the Jin princess, but before I could tell Kiva, the door opened.

A nearly full moon illuminated Ericen in the door frame. He stopped when he saw me awake, the color draining from his face. He was a ragged mess, his hair nearly as chaotic as Caylus's and his clothes unchanged.

Kiva stiffened. "What do you want?"

"To check on her," he said quietly.

"Great. You can go now."

Ericen ignored her and stepped deeper in the room, eyes on me. "Can we talk?"

Kiva started to protest, but I cut her off. "Yes."

She looked down at me, frowning, but grudgingly climbed off the bed and made for the door. As she passed Ericen, she leveled him with a glare fit to kill before stepping outside. The door slammed shut.

Ericen took her seat. "How are you?"

I wished my eyes weren't red and puffy. "Fine. What do you want?"

"To apologize."

"It's not your fault your mother's a monster."

He winced. "I'm sorry, Thia. Part of the reason she did that was because of me. I—" His jaw tightened. "I said something that made her angry. This was her way of showing me she was still in control. She did it to hurt me."

I let his words sink in. *She did it to hurt me.* Because my pain hurt him. Because he cared, more than I wanted to admit. Afraid of where my thoughts were leading, I said quietly, "And to hurt me."

"You're not breaking like she expected," he said. "In Illucia, subordinates obey, and those who don't are punished. She's treated the other kingdoms the same. It's all a power play. That's even why she has those moonblades. They belonged to the queen of Jindae. They're trophies."

"And she thinks Rhodairens are cruel?" I asked. "She makes soldiers out of children and workhorses of their parents. How can she say she's never torn a family apart?"

Ericen snorted softly. "She thinks it's an honor for them. They all get to serve the great Illucian Empire, to serve Rhett. Especially the children. They get the greatest honor of all, serving in our army. She even thinks it's a better life for them. Jindae was racked with civil war between the guilds before we took over—"

"The king and queen were making progress on that. Before them, Jindae's rulers were horrible people. But they were changing things!"

"I know, Thia. I'm not supporting it. I'm just...telling you how she sees it." His voice dropped, as if he didn't quite understand himself why he'd said the words. "My mother's always been a volatile person, but she's been getting worse."

"And you?" I asked. "What's her excuse for the way she treats you?"

He stiffened, edges turning sharp as a blade. For a moment, I thought I'd gone too far. Then he said, "She hates me."

I lifted my gaze to his face, but he wouldn't look at me.

The words came pouring out of him. "She says every time she sees me, all she can think about is what those soldiers did to her family. She says I look exactly like my father, that I'm just a reminder of him. She sent me away to Darkward as soon as she could, breaking years of tradition of training the royal children in the castle. She seemed to think if she treated me terribly enough, I'd disappear, and so would her memories."

"That's horrible." My hands trembled. "Is that why you're going along with this marriage? You think it'll change the way she treats you?"

"At first." He smiled faintly. "But despite your best efforts, my feelings toward you changed while I was in Rhodaire. I tried to make you feel powerless, but you stayed strong. You didn't care what I thought. You said what you wanted, and you didn't back down." He leaned closer, eyes falling to my lips.

My face grew hot, and I looked away. I didn't know what I felt toward Ericen anymore, but it wasn't what his eyes implied he felt. His words made my chest ache. This wasn't how I'd been expecting this all to go when I'd come to the home of my enemy.

When I didn't respond, Ericen stood to go. My throat tightened as I tried to school my expression into something that didn't betray every emotion hurtling through me.

"Why does your mother want us to marry so badly?" I asked. "It won't give Illucia control of Rhodaire. Are you going to hold me hostage to convince Caliza to hand the kingdom over? Because she won't do it."

His eyes glowed silver in the moonlight trickling in through the high windows. "I don't know why she's so determined to have it done. Maybe she just wants to establish a connection." His tone was short, curt, like a person who'd made himself vulnerable and felt uncomfortable about it.

I should have said something back.

"I don't think your mother ever intends for you to rule Illucia." There was only one way establishing this connection between our kingdoms would do her any good: if Illucia conquered Rhodaire, deposed Kuren and Caliza, and appointed Ericen and me in her place. Then Rhodaire would be under her control, but it'd have a Rhodairen queen. A smooth way to handle a hostile takeover, but it also meant Ericen would be king of Rhodaire, not Illucia.

Ericen's jaw tightened as he saw where my mind had taken me, deep scarlet flushing his pale skin. Without a word, he stalked for the exit.

"Ericen!" I called, and he paused, turning in the doorway. A question I didn't want to ask but knew I had to burned in my throat. Finally, I forced the words out. "Did my mother order that attack?"

His eyes narrowed. "Don't listen to her. She's trying to justify what she's doing."

"You don't know then," I said quietly.

He hesitated, then shook his head.

I dropped my gaze to the foot of my bed, stomach turning. "Thia?" I looked up at his voice. "I'm sorry I didn't stop her."

He didn't wait for my reply before exchanging places with Kiva, and I was thankful. I didn't know what to say. *Didn't* stop her. Not *couldn't*. He hadn't done this to me, but he hadn't prevented it either, and that was the problem. He kept following Razel's orders.

How could I compete with a control rooted that deep?

Kiva refused my attempts to get her to sleep in her bed. Even awkwardly splayed in the chair, she was out before me. I stared at the ceiling for some time, trying to imagine the mother I thought I knew ordering Lord Turren to kill Razel's family, my mind running rampant with thoughts of crows tearing people apart.

Had it been revenge for my father's death, another turn in this endless cycle?

I tried counting crows, but it was no use. Despite the murkwood-induced grogginess, my mind wouldn't rest. Not with my hand aching despite the pain tonic, not with so many unanswered questions rebounding in my head, and not when my fate and the fate of my kingdom would be decided in the next couple of days.

Then there was Ericen. I didn't know what to make of him. He was a product of his mother's neglect and cruelty, but he could change. I'd meant what I had said to Kiva: Illucia needed a ruler like him.

And he likes me.

Guilt rattled my chest. Using Ericen's feelings for me to manipulate him into joining me was something Razel would do. No, I hadn't given Ericen any reason to think I thought of him as anything more than a friend. Besides, manipulation required subtlety. Not my greatest skill. But maybe that was okay. If he didn't immediately refuse to ally with me, it might mean he was interested and willing to listen.

I groaned and pressed the fingers of my uninjured hand to my temples, the beginnings of a headache threatening. This was too much to think about at midnight after a long day, but sleep still proved elusive.

Carefully, I slid out of bed. My dress had been replaced with a thick nightgown and a long pair of socks, which I covered with my boots. A cloak hung in the corner, and I secured it over my shoulders before slipping outside.

The sona lamps scattered throughout the training grounds were dim, the moonlight mostly obscured by clouds. The cool air soothed my stress and the heat of my burns. I took a deep breath, then froze.

I wasn't alone.

I turned but saw no one. A presence in the shadows pulled at me. Familiar, quiet, comforting. I followed it. The feeling grew stronger as I entered the lounge beside the training grounds, then followed the hallway past the kitchens and servant quarters. I was about to round another corner when voices echoed down the corridor.

"Is everything ready?"

Shearen. I stopped, pressing my back to the wall.

"Yes, my lord. The queen has requested your presence," responded a female voice.

"Fine. Leave."

I slipped into a nearby alcove, trying to make myself as small as possible as an older servant bearing a torch walked past. Once she was out of sight, I crept to the edge of the hallway and peered around in time to see Shearen disappearing around another corner.

Keeping my steps light, I followed, staying a good distance behind as he took turn after turn deeper into the belly of the castle. The humming grew stronger, dancing through my veins and settling in my stomach, drawing me closer.

Shearen halted outside a padlocked iron door, withdrawing a key. I dared a look around the corner. He unlocked the door and pulled it open, and as the door slowly closed behind him, a humming blasted me with an echo so strong, it shuddered through my chest.

Magic.

TWENTY-EIGHT

K iva! Kiva!" I shook her vigorously with one hand, though her eyes flashed open at my touch. Moonlight illuminated her disgruntled face, and she swatted at me lazily.

"I'm awake!" she grumbled, sitting forward in her chair. "Why are you?" She blinked, then coming fully awake, sprang to her feet. "Are you okay?"

"Yes. Fine. Shearen was in the halls, and I followed him. The door he went through, it's locked, but when he opened it, I felt magic!"

She stared at me like I'd lost my mind. I replayed my rambling in my head. Taking a deep breath, I relayed it all again, taking pains to explain carefully what I'd seen.

"Humming?" she asked. "Like you felt with the egg?"

I nodded, and she folded her arms.

"You think Razel has some type of magic stored in there?"

"I don't know, but we need to find out. It doesn't seem likely, but strange things have been happening." She listened as I explained about Res using shadow crow magic to conceal himself and the possibility that he'd used earth crow powers too.

Kiva rubbed her face. "That's not possible."

"Neither is this." I held up my injured hand, which wasn't quite so injured as it should have been. "We have to see what's inside that room. If Razel has magic, we may not be prepared to fight Illucia after all, alliance or not."

Kiva sighed. "You want to break in, don't you?"

I grinned, and she rolled her eyes.

"How do you plan on getting past the padlock? Did you become a picklock when I wasn't looking?"

"No, but I do know a few common infirmary ingredients that make for a nice acidic solution."

"Saints. You've spent too much time with Caylus."

I smirked. "Lord Rynthene's ship will be in Port Maranock in two days. That means we need to figure out a way to escape by then."

"It won't be easy." Kiva rocked onto the back legs of her chair. "We'll have to leave at night, and we'll need horses. If we're lucky, we won't be discovered until morning. But if Razel learns we've left before we reach the port…"

I nodded, not wanting to imagine what would happen. We didn't have a choice.

We searched the quarters for the ingredients we would need to mix the acid. The healer might miss them, but she wouldn't come accusing the Rhodairen princess. Kiva tucked them away in her pockets, and I climbed back into bed.

I slept all morning and into early afternoon. When I woke, joy washed over me like sea spray, prickling with frantic energy. It took me a moment to realize it was Res, the link between us strong enough that his emotions flowed almost seamlessly into me.

I'm okay. I sent reassuring waves along the cord, guilt twisting in my stomach. Had he felt my pain last night? My fear? From how frantic his energy was, it seemed so. But why hadn't I sensed him when I woke last night? I eyed the murkwood vial on my bedside table. Had the drug numbed more than my pain?

When the healer changed the bandages on my hand, it took a good minute for me to convince myself to look.

The worst spots were swollen and blistered, the best merely an angry shade of red. The shape of the key was still discernable on my palm, and the skin was sensitive and stung all over, but I kept silent. Along my forearm, the old scars gleamed.

I stared at the burns, confused and a little unsettled. They'd healed considerably already. I wasn't complaining, but what in the Saints' name had happened? Maybe the fire hadn't been as hot as I'd expected. Maybe I'd grabbed the key fast enough to prevent the worst. I turned my hand over, inspecting every inch.

If I didn't know better, I would have said it looked like the work of a sun crow. But that was impossible. Still, I couldn't shake the quiet voice that whispered this wasn't normal. It was magic, magic I didn't understand.

A servant had brought me a change of clothes, and once the healer finished applying new bandages, I changed, and she granted me leave without asking questions, despite her confused expression.

Kiva followed me out, and I sucked in a lungful of fresh air as we stepped outside. Mist clung to the air, obscuring some of the moving figures in the training grounds. We skirted the edge, ignoring curious gazes, and returned to our room.

Someone had done their best to rearrange it. It looked nearly spotless, as if nothing had happened. Only the whistle of wind through the cloth-patched window remained to mark the incident.

Exhausted from keeping vigil at my bedside, Kiva collapsed onto a couch and promptly started snoring. I could tell she was worried about Auma but trying hard not to show it, and we were both on edge. Tonight, we would break into the room I'd discovered. Tomorrow night, we would run for our lives.

A flash of color at the edge of my vision made me pause. A vase of bright-red roses sat on the dining table beside a small box with a note attached.

Tension crept into my neck as I crossed the room and opened the card.

Thia dear,

In case you've lost your other ones.

Razel

A hollow pit opened in my stomach as I pulled the lid off the box. I knew what was inside before I looked, but at the sight of the blue silk gloves nestled inside atop a bed of rose-colored paper, I had to repress a scream of fury. Seizing the box, I hurled it across the room, sending the gloves and fancy paper skittering across the floor. I turned, ready to strike the vase of flowers, and stopped.

I was angry because Razel had made me feel powerless, and that was exactly what she wanted. The bright-red flowers, the gloves, the way they'd been given as a present—it was all posturing, a power play meant to make me feel weak.

But I wasn't weak.

Strength comes in many forms, Auma had said. She was right.

Strength was Caliza taking on the weight of a kingdom without a single complaint. Strength was Kiva's willingness to give up everything she'd ever known to protect someone she loved. Strength was Caylus's curious mind, Auma's unwavering determination, and Ericen's struggle to remain honorable in a kingdom that had forgotten the meaning.

Every day, they fought, and every day, they were strong. And I could do the same.

I'd worn gloves out of fear and shame, but I never should have. There had been nothing shameful about my pain, nothing I'd needed to hide or hide from. I'd been afraid to face what the pain had meant, that my life as I'd known it was over, that I had to choose a new path.

Kiva had done everything she could to help me see that, and I'd thought after everything, I'd finally understood. But I hadn't shaken my past. I'd still let my fear control me. I had let fire send my heart racing and small setbacks crush my hope.

No more. I refused to let Razel control me, to let her make me feel powerless. I wasn't powerless. I had survived Ronoch, and I had survived the loss and the depression thick as mud that came after it, and I would keep surviving them.

Don't let her silence the storm inside you.

I clenched my fists, thinking of the way Caylus had depicted me in his drawing. Proud. Strong. A force of steel and arrows, a crow at my back.

I would not let her break me.

I am more than my emotions, more than my depression and fear.

Fire and I would never be friends, but I wouldn't let it or the horrible memories it represented hold power over me any longer.

"I am more," I promised myself.

Reluctantly, I gathered up the gloves. As much as I'd have liked to drop them out the window, I would wear them. Not only to placate Razel but also to show her that I could.

Someone knocked, and I answered the door. A servant stood in the hall, a box in his hands. "From Prince Ericen, Your Highness." He handed me the box, bowed reluctantly, and left. How many presents was I to get today?

Retreating inside, I closed the door and opened the box. A pair of brand-new, fingerless leather gloves rested inside. Beside them sat a note saying he'd be at the training grounds today if I wanted to spar.

Grinning, I set Razel's gloves aside and slid on the leather ones. They were smooth and incredibly well made, and my satisfaction at subverting Razel's order was all the warmth I needed as I dressed in my flying leathers and set out for the training grounds in the chilly air.

As it was just after lunch, the grounds were busy, but I easily spotted Ericen in one of the grappling rings, sparring with a stocky soldier. In the time it took me to cross to the ring, Ericen had struck him in the ribs, gut, and face, dropping him to the floor.

The Centerian was days away, and Ericen looked more than ready.

The soldier was back on his feet by the time I arrived, wiping blood from his lip with the back of his hand. He clasped hands grudgingly with Ericen and climbed out of the ring. The prince noticed me a moment later. I waved as he came to sit on the edge of the ring, his earnest expression dissolving into a smile that reflected none of last night's despair.

"Did you get my present?" he asked.

I held up my gloved hands. "Not bad. And here I'd have expected something gaudy and gilded."

"If you're implying Illucians have a thing for gold, then you are entirely correct."

Smirking, I jerked my head toward the far side of the grounds. "Do you have a second to talk? Privately."

His smile faded, but he slipped from the ring, leading me over to the edge of the courtyard and into the healer's quarters. The healer leapt up.

"Your Highnesses." She bowed her head to us both. "Is something wrong with your hand?"

"No, thank you," I replied. "Can you please give us the room?"

She nodded and gathered a few pieces of paperwork before exiting through the door we'd entered.

"I wanted to talk to you about last night," I began. His expression darkened, and I hesitated but pressed on. "You seemed upset, and I kept thinking about it, and I...well, do you ever think about leaving? Abandoning it all and going?" More direct than I'd meant, but either Ericen was willing to hear me out or he wasn't. And if he wasn't... I shoved the thought away. He wouldn't tell Razel, would he?

"Now that you mention it, I could use a vacation," he replied. "If you were me, would you risk the freezing ice lands of Korovi or the sea serpents off the Trendell coast? My options are rather limited. Not very popular, you see."

I smacked the back of his head lightly, earning myself a grin. "Serious answers."

Leaning back against one of the supply tables, he crossed his arms. The grin faded as he let his gaze wander along the room, looking everywhere but at me. "Sometimes," he said hesitantly, then as if regretting it, added, "But it would be disgraceful."

Him and his stupid honor. Why did one of his most redeeming qualities have to be one that kept getting in my way?

"My mother would send the Vykryn after me," he continued. "Sometimes I swear she's waiting for a reason to. Hells, Shearen would volunteer in a heartbeat. He seems to have it in his head if I'm out of the way, she'll make him Valix instead."

Even as he said it, the heat faded from his words, and I

wondered if he hated Shearen as much as he seemed to. Whatever burned between them, it seemed incapable of completely destroying the bond they'd once had.

I leaned against the table beside him. "How could you serve someone like that?" I asked. "Someone who would willingly send people to hunt down and kill her own son?"

I was pushing against some invisible boundary, and any minute, it might shatter and send me careening off an edge. But I needed to do this, not just because Ericen would be an asset but also because if my plan worked, I'd be leaving him behind.

I'd never have thought that would matter to me.

Ericen laughed mirthlessly. "What else would I do? Where would I go? She'd hunt me clear into the Eastern Wastelands."

"You could come to Rhodaire. With me." Even as I said the words, I marveled at them. How had we gotten here? "We could protect you."

Doubt flickered across his face, drawing forth a spurt of indignation into my chest, though I understood. He didn't know what I did about Res or the alliances being formed against his kingdom.

He didn't respond. I could see his indecision, see him thinking maybe I'd said those things because I felt the same way he did. I felt something for him, something that made me want to get him out of here for his own sake as much as mine, but it wasn't the same thing I had experienced with Caylus.

"I've worked my entire life to become a Vykryn," he said.

"Your people don't give you the respect you deserve."

"They see the way my mother dismisses me, and they do

the same. If I win the Centerian, I can earn her respect." His hands tightened on the table edge. "I shouldn't even react to it. I shouldn't care. It's half the reason people look at me the way they do."

I pushed off the table, stepping in front him. "You don't deserve it. You can make another choice."

He met my gaze, holding it like a drowning man clinging to driftwood. His eyes searched mine, looking for something that wasn't there. He looked away.

Shouting echoed in from the courtyard. Ericen's eyes snapped to a spot above my head, and he pushed off the table, hurrying to open the door. I darted to his side in time to see Shearen at the front of a small formation of soldiers.

"Kiran, Seina, Raelynn." Shearen eyed each soldier as he named them.

"What's going on?" I asked.

"He's forming a team for something." Ericen stepped into the courtyard, and I followed.

"Marin," Shearen continued. Then his head jerked up, eyes falling on us. A cruel smile spread across his lips. "Ericen."

Ericen stiffened, and I almost screamed. He'd been listening. He'd been about to say yes!

"Her Majesty has informed me a servant by the name of Auma is actually a rebel spy," Shearen said. "We've been tasked with retrieving her. Any questions?"

"No, sir!" the soldiers said in unison, save for Ericen.

"Then move out."

My mouth had gone dry, my throat rough as sand. That was

why Auma had stolen the letter for me—she was a rebel, working against Razel for years. Had she run because Razel found her out?

I found Ericen's eyes. "Don't go."

He hesitated, his expression fraught. This was the end of our conversation. This was his decision.

"I have to." He didn't look back as he joined the group of selected soldiers gathering beside Shearen.

I watched the team leave the training grounds, the rest of the soldiers dispersing. I didn't move. A weight slowly settled on my chest. Then everyone was gone.

TWENTY-NINE

Y ou're going to wear a hole in the rug," Kiva warned half-heartedly from the couch in our room. Razel had canceled dinner, and the riders still hadn't returned with news of Auma. Food had been brought to us, and the remains of it sat on the table by the fire. We'd barely touched it. "Do something useful and mix the acid."

"I can't. Not right now." I was too anxious, too overwrought to keep my hands steady, and this was one mixture I didn't want to spill. Was this what it was like for Caylus? Unable to do the thing he loved because his body wouldn't comply? Except I didn't love what I was about to do. I was making liquid fire to burn off a lock so we could sneak into a secret room full of magic.

I looked at my hands, clad in the gloves Ericen had given

me, then out toward the open window. Our room faced the front castle yard, the rain pelting stone and glass the only sound. I hoped I'd hear the thunder of hooves at any moment.

"It's been over two hours, and they're not back yet," Kiva said. "That's a good sign, especially considering they took dogs with them. If they haven't found her by now, they probably never will."

I'd told myself the same thing several times, but the words fell flat. Until the team returned empty-handed—until Ericen returned empty-handed—I wouldn't be able to relax. I doubted Kiva even believed her words, but I didn't challenge her. This was how she handled things. She stayed calm. Logical. Freaking out was my job.

Another hour passed, during which Kiva convinced me to sit. I complied only because I knew my anxiety made hers worse. I might have been the one pacing, but Kiva's hands were clenched in fists so tight, the knuckles were white. As we waited, I focused on the thrum of the cord with Res as he slept, letting it center me.

Suddenly, I sat up. I thought I'd heard—there! I leapt from the couch and rushed to the window, the sound of dogs barking mixing with the clatter of hooves and the bellowing of soldiers' voices. The dim lantern light barely illuminated the procession as it rode into the courtyard in front of the castle. Was that a limp form across the back of that horse or a saddlebag? I leaned closer, but it was no good. I couldn't see.

"I'm going downstairs."

Kiva bolted upright. "Sure. And why don't you just announce

to the entire castle how concerned you are with Auma successfully escaping? I'm sure they won't wonder if you had something to do with it at all."

I glowered at her and resumed my pacing. She was right, but the knot of nervous energy in my chest was close to bursting. Just when I couldn't take it anymore, someone knocked. Kiva sprang to her feet, flying across the room to wrench the door open. A rain-drenched and earnest-faced Ericen stood outside.

"We couldn't find her." His eyes lifted over Kiva's shoulder to me. "I thought you'd want to know."

My jaw tightened, but I said nothing as he turned on his heel and marched down the hall. Kiva closed the door and leaned back against it, letting out a breath.

"I'm going to mix the acid." I crossed to the dining table where we'd set out our supplies. Kiva had had the foresight to swipe a pair of leather gloves from the training grounds, and though they made my fingers a little stiffer overlaid on my fingerless gloves, they were at least a barrier between my skin and the acid.

Kiva moved to the chair beside me to watch while I carefully measured out ingredients and mixed them together. Minutes later, I poured a muddy green liquid hissing into a glass vial.

"Hopefully, it's strong enough to eat through iron," I said.

"Oh good. I always love it when plans rest on *hopefullys*."

I gave her a flat look. "Fine. Do you have anything iron we can test it on?"

Kiva pulled out one of her earrings and offered it to me. I grabbed one of our glass dinner bowls and dropped the earring inside.

Uncorking the vial, I carefully let a single drop out and shoved the cork back in. The liquid struck the iron and sizzled, and we watched as the earring slowly dissolved into nothing.

"It takes a little bit," Kiva observed.

"I'll pour more on the padlock, but we'll have to make sure no one comes around for a few seconds." I set the bowl aside. "The real problem is there's no way to cover up someone's been there. We have to make sure Razel doesn't suspect us."

Kiva's face lit up, and she dashed into her bedroom, returning a moment later with Auma's scarf. I resisted asking what Auma had been doing in her bedroom.

"She knows this belongs to Auma," Kiva said. "They'll be suspicious if they find it near the door, and if they're still looking for her, this will make them think she's still here and give her more time to get out of Illucia."

"Perfect." I took the scarf and wrapped the vial in it, then tucked them both in the pouch on my belt. I'd be wearing my flying leathers tonight. The plan relied on not running into anyone, but I wanted to be prepared if we did.

Later that evening, I went looking for Ericen, intent on finishing our conversation from earlier, but he wasn't in the training grounds or his room. Finally, I found a servant who'd seen the prince near the northernmost tower. I followed her directions to a flight of spiraling stairs.

The air grew colder the higher I rose, a light mist filtering down the staircase, which opened to a small circular platform overlooking the city. Wind buffeted me the moment I stepped out, fluttering loose strands of hair around my face.

Ericen stood across from the door, leaning against the damp guardrail. Fog floated below, thin enough for me to see the glowing lights of the Colorfalls over the River Ren. Beside him stood Shearen, muttering in a low voice. Whatever he was saying had turned Ericen to stone.

When I stepped onto the platform, Shearen fell silent, glancing at me. He smirked, said something quietly to Ericen, and then brushed past me with a sneer. I glared after him before approaching the prince.

Ericen didn't look up as I leaned against the wall beside him. His hands were clasped over the edge, his jaw clenched tight.

"Did you have to pick the coldest spot in the castle to hide in?" I wrapped my arms around myself. He didn't smile, and my own faded. "I brought you something." I pulled a small orange cake wrapped in a napkin out of my pocket and set it on the wall beside his hands. "Lyren said you had him make them."

His eyes flickered to the cake, then back to the city below. "Why are you going through with this?"

I knew what he meant. Why had I accepted the marriage proposal? Why had I come to Illucia to marry the son of my kingdom's greatest enemy?

"I didn't have much of a choice."

Ericen finally faced me, the intensity of his stare making me flush. "No one makes you do anything. So why did you?"

I let out a breath, and it blended into the wind. "I'd turned my back on my kingdom long enough. It was time I did something to protect it."

"And now?"

The question caught me off guard. This time, I wasn't sure what he meant. Did he think my reason for coming here, for staying, had changed? I found his eyes, searching their blue depths for an answer I wasn't sure I wanted.

"I'm doing what I have to, Ericen. I—"

He kissed me, a hard, demanding urgency behind the soft warmth of his lips. I went rigid, my heart jolting. Before I could even process what was happening, I'd pulled away. The look on his face made my stomach turn. He stepped back, the realization of his mistake spreading like wildfire across his face.

"I'm sorry," I breathed. "I—"

"Still? After everything?"

"I—"

"Why did you ask me to come with you to Rhodaire? Why did you listen to me, talk to me, spend time with me? Because you had to?"

My lips parted, an icy bead rising up from my stomach to my throat. Words rose and died, and I lashed out a hand, seizing the wall for support. My fingers struck the orange cake, sending it tumbling off the edge. "No, that's not...that's not why—" I shook my head, taking a deep breath. Ericen's eyes were like a blizzard, boring into me in floods of icy wind.

"Were you just using me to get to my mother? Did you think I'd turn on her and help you instead?"

"Yes!" My heart jolted. "No. No. I wanted your help, yes,

but I wasn't using you. Is it so hard for you to believe I care about you? That I want to help you? You're my friend!"

"But you don't love me."

"No."

The wind carried the word away. Ericen didn't say anything, just turned and left through the open tower door. I stared at the spot he'd been standing in, the chill of the evening digging into my bones.

I didn't tell Kiva what had happened. I was still processing it myself. There'd been moments since coming to Illucia where I'd wondered if Ericen cared about me more than I wanted to admit. But I'd never thought it would reach this point. Or perhaps I'd only been afraid it would.

By the time midnight came, I'd become a jumble of nerves. We stepped quietly out of the room into the empty hall.

The vial of solution felt like it was burning a hole through my hand as we walked. I held it gingerly as I led the way down the corridors, retracing my steps from the other night, afraid every corner we turned would look unfamiliar. Yet I knew we were heading the right way. The humming called me closer.

Kiva kept a hand on Sinvarra while my free one remained on the string of the bow slung across my chest, ready to pull it free.

The dim glow of the sona lamps melded with the light of a full moon. We moved slowly, checking every corner before we turned, listening intently for any sound. Once or twice, we had to leap into the alcove of a doorway or hurry down a hall to avoid a servant, but otherwise, the corridors stayed quiet.

Adrenaline scurried through my veins like fleeing spiders, slicking my palms with sweat. It grew worse the closer we got, until we rounded the final corner and faced the padlocked door. Even through the iron, magic hummed.

Kiva took up her post at the corner as I approached the door, uncorking the vial. The first drop missed, hissing when it made contact with the stone ground. The next one landed on the metal and began eating through. I added another couple of drops then stepped back, thankful for my gloves as the metal sizzled away.

The bubbling slowed, and I added the last couple of drops to finish the job before corking the vial and tucking it in my pocket. The lock groaned quietly as it split apart, and I caught the pieces in Auma's scarf before they could fall. Setting them aside, I beckoned for Kiva to join me.

"I take back everything I ever said about Caylus," she whispered.

I grinned and pulled open the door.

The humming crashed into me like a strong wind, then settled into a steady flow that reverberated in my chest. It was oddly comforting, like a lullaby without sound. Kiva watched our backs as we crept slowly down a narrow set of stairs toward a dim light. The staircase was short, the room surprisingly warm as we reached the bottom.

Shadows flickered on the wall in the light of a single torch, sparking familiarity. The room buzzed with magic so thick, it was nearly tangible. As I turned the final corner and my eyes adjusted to the faded light, I froze.

The room was full of crow eggs.

THIRTY

Eggs of every kind were scattered across the floor on a bed of hay, illuminated by the soft glow of a lamp. My eyes couldn't move fast enough, taking in the shiny red shells of fire crow eggs next to the pure black of shadow crows, which blended almost seamlessly into the sparkling night sky of the storm crows.

Razel hadn't destroyed the eggs on Ronoch; she'd stolen them.

My throat burned. I gulped down a mouthful of air and looked at Kiva, who stared openmouthed.

I blinked. Then blinked again. When the scene didn't dissolve, I dropped to my knees beside the vibrant forest-green shell of the egg of an earth crow and laid a hand over it. The same hum I'd felt from Res's egg rushed through me, softer but clearly magic.

I touched another and another, the same reverberation emitting from all of them. Laughter choked my throat, soft and tentative as the truth of what I was seeing began to settle.

Resyries wasn't the last crow.

Rhodaire, our way of life, everything, could be *rebuilt*.

My heart had become a drumbeat in my chest. "We can't leave these here." I turned to Kiva. "We have to—"

The words froze in my throat, blocking the warning I tried to cry. Kiva recognized it an instant too late, stopping halfway in her turn as a sword point appeared at her ribs.

Shearen stood behind her, a dangerous smile darkening his face. Even his eyes seemed full of shadows. "You weren't supposed to see these yet."

I rose unsteadily to my feet, mind racing.

His smile widened. "Imagine my surprise when I went to your rooms to get you and found you gone. I've no idea how you found this room, but it seemed like the natural place for you to come. Her Majesty says you're drawn to the magic."

"Just run, Th—ah!" Kiva cried out as Shearen's sword dug into her side.

I stepped forward, but Shearen raised his eyebrows as if begging me to give him a reason to push the sword in.

I backed off, barely keeping my voice even. "Don't hurt her. We'll come willingly."

He laughed. "I'm sure. You first then, little Crow Queen. Throw away your quiver and friend's sword, then shut the door once we're out."

I locked eyes with Kiva, and she nodded. Slowly, I removed

Sinvarra and tossed it aside. Her eyes followed the sword mournfully, and I flung my quiver beside it. Shearen moved back to let me pass, and I slid around them and climbed the stairs. Shearen marched us down the hall and back the way we'd come to the main corridor.

Forcing myself to take slow breaths and stay calm, I worked through our options. Shearen wouldn't kill me. If I could get him away from Kiva, we might have a chance. I slowed, my gaze sliding toward them. There was no way. Shearen would cut her before I could act.

"What did you mean we weren't supposed to see the eggs yet?" I asked. A small stain of blood had bloomed on Kiva's right side. Fury twisted through me.

Shearen smirked. "We know you hatched a crow."

My heart stumbled, and me nearly along with it. They knew about Res. Frantically, I reached for the cord between us.

It was quiet.

My breath caught, panic rising to fill my throat. How had they found out? Had someone seen the storm and investigated? Panic rose like a wave, my breathing turning shallow. Why couldn't I feel him? Why—

"Thia," Kiva hissed.

I jerked back from the edge of my spiral, sucking down a sharp breath of cold air. Losing myself to fear wouldn't help. But Res... And if they knew about him, then—

My stomach dropped. Caylus. Razel might not hurt the crow, but she had no reason to spare Caylus.

"Thinking about your inventor friend?" Shearen asked,

directing us down the hall toward the throne room with a sharp prod into Kiva's back.

I snarled. "If you've hurt—"

Shearen laughed. "You're in love with him, aren't you? Does Eri know that?"

Eri. There was something in his voice when he said the nickname. A familiarity Ericen and I didn't have. What had Shearen said to him out on the tower? They'd almost looked like friends.

"He won't like what you're doing right now." I tried to manage the panic threatening to overtake my voice.

I tugged along the cord again, praying the silence had been a fluke. There was no answer, but the cord hadn't broken. It felt like it did when Res was asleep but without the gentle contentment, as if I were linked to a stone wall. I pulled harder, trying to wake him, but got only fuzzy humming in return.

"Last I heard, you two weren't on talking terms," Shearen said.

"Lovers' quarrel," Kiva interjected. "I'm sure he'll have your head on a stick by morning."

"Or maybe the queen will have promoted me to second in command of the Vykryn. I like my odds."

I forced myself to breathe, to think. I had to rescue Res and Caylus and escape, but to where? Lord Rynthene's ship wouldn't arrive for another day.

The throne room doors stood open, dual hearths flooding the room with light. Shearen forced us inside, but the room was empty save for a servant nervously clutching a torch. She bowed to Shearen.

"Tell the queen I've found them," Shearen instructed, and the servant hurried off.

Minutes passed. I became aware of my breathing, of Kiva's growing labored. The torches played tricks of light, making the walls grow taller and reach over me, encroaching. I could feel the humming of the eggs. It pushed into my mind like roots into soil.

The shadows shifted, pulling my gaze. Something gold flashed in the darkness along the wall. Then voices.

Razel entered the throne room, flanked by the servant with the torch. Ericen followed, his eyes widening at the sight of me.

I barely noticed him past that, because there was something in Razel's arms. Something dark and feathered. My vision narrowed, the room tilting.

Resyries.

I went still. Then his sides expanded. Air rushed from my lungs, and I drew another ragged breath, my entire body wilting with relief. He must have been drugged.

"Get your hands off him!" I was halfway across the room before Ericen sprung forward. He caught me by the shoulders, pushing me back. I shoved at his chest, but he didn't give. Over his shoulder, Razel smiled.

Three guards entered, Caylus held between two of them, his hands bound before him. He had a bruise around one eye, and his lip was split and bloodied, but he otherwise looked okay. He struggled with his captors, and a female Vykryn drove a foot into the back of his legs, forcing him to his knees.

She looked familiar.

My lips parted—it was the girl from the bakery. The new one who'd started after I'd begun visiting.

Caylus spat blood, then lifted his head, spotting me for the first time. "Thia." His eyes hardened. "Thia, are you all right?"

"I'm fine," I whispered. "I'm fine!" I slammed my hands into Ericen's chest, and this time, he stumbled back, looking alarmed. "Did you know about this?" Was that what he and Shearen had been talking about in the tower?

"Thia—"

"I swear to the Saints, if you knew—"

"Do you think he should have told you? He's loyal to Illucia. To me." Razel swept forward, the servant staying close by. The queen cradled Res in one arm like a mother might her child, using her free hand to pull a crumpled paper from her pocket.

Caylus's drawing. She must have taken it from my room when it was searched.

Razel held it up. "I was just going to take the crow, but with your feelings for the boy, I thought he might be useful for motivating you to do as I say."

She tossed the paper into the flames. I lurched, watching as glowing embers ate away at the edges of the drawing until nothing but ash remained.

Out of the corner of my eye, I vaguely registered Ericen's shocked then hurt expression.

Razel pounced on it. "Oh, Eri dear, didn't you know? I thought she would have told you."

I didn't know what to say to him. I didn't even know if I *should* say something to him. My heart cracked open, releasing a storm inside my chest. Everything was happening too fast, and it was all out of my control.

Razel smiled. "This is the problem with having people you care about—they can be used against you."

"What do you want?" I snarled.

"The secret, of course."

To hatching.

Slowly, things fell into place. By marrying me to Ericen, Razel would not only gain control of Rhodaire if something happened to Kuren and Caliza, she'd also gain control of the crows. She could hatch as many as she needed year after year, because she would have me, and my blood, and my experience.

She'd have an army perfectly suited for taking control not only of Rhodaire but the entire continent.

I swallowed hard. That was what Ericen had been looking for in the library in Aris: information on crows.

Razel approached me, and I tensed. "I intended to wear you down, to break you until you did as you should and obeyed me. Come the winter solstice, I'd have an army. Imagine my surprise when I learned I didn't have to wait so very long."

The girl holding Caylus smirked. She must have known what had happened when Res had lost control of his powers and gone straight to her queen.

Razel stopped a step away. My fingers twitched, desperate to snatch Res from her hold. "Now, Thia dear, you will hatch me my army."

"No."

She smiled and then nodded to the female guard beside

Caylus. There was a cry, and I spun as she knocked Caylus to the ground. She kicked him again, driving her foot into his ribs, his legs, his back. He curled into a ball, trying to protect his stomach.

"Stop it!" I yelled.

Razel raised a hand. The guard froze midkick and lowered her leg.

"The secret," she said.

"Don't!" Caylus rasped. "Don't do it, Thia."

I stared at him, paralyzed. Razel would kill him if I didn't, but I couldn't give her what she wanted. She would destroy everything.

"Is this really necessary?" Ericen demanded.

I whirled around to face him.

He stared imploringly at his mother, his hands clenched. "You're forcing her to make a difficult choice. Give her time."

"She doesn't have a choice." The amusement in Razel's voice had vanished, her tone dropping low and predatory. She eyed her son, as if daring him to contradict her again.

He didn't. He drew back beneath her sharp gaze, averting his own.

Razel nodded to the guard, and she seized the collar of Caylus's shirt, driving her fist into his jaw. Caylus struck the ground, and the guard kicked him in the stomach.

I stayed rooted to the spot, my nails digging so harshly into my palms, I drew blood. The sound of each punch landing made my skin crawl and my stomach turn. But I didn't move. I couldn't give Razel what she wanted. I couldn't.

The guard paused, looking up at Razel. The queen watched me, waiting like a jungle cat ready to pounce.

Still, I said nothing.

Razel faced Shearen. He seized a dagger from his hip and drove it into Kiva's shoulder.

I screamed as Kiva screamed, dropping to her knees as Shearen ripped the dagger free and put it to her throat. I stumbled toward her, legs weak, voice breaking. "I'll show you! Just let her go!"

"Thia, no!" Kiva cried.

Shearen pushed the blade closer to her neck, drawing a thin line of blood.

"I said I'll show you!" I yelled, looking desperately to Razel. "Take me to the eggs. I'll show you. Just call him off. Please."

Shearen pulled the knife away from Kiva's throat, then drove his foot into the back of her injured shoulder. Kiva cried out, crumpling to the ground.

I surged forward, but Razel stepped into my path. "Wrong way, Thia dear."

Breathing heavily, I turned toward the door. Something tugged inside me. My heart fluttered as a humming threaded along my skin. In Razel's arms, Resyries shifted. I felt the cord between us pulse. Then again.

In the midst of everything, with Caylus and Kiva injured, with Ericen standing idly by, Shearen smiling and Razel staring me down with the judgment of a goddess, simply feeling that pulse centered me.

Now. I shoved the word down the line.

Res's body crackled with lightning.

Razel screamed, releasing him. His wings flared as he tried to catch himself, but the drug was still in his system, and he hit the ground hard. At the same time, a guard yelled and crumpled to the floor, revealing Auma's small form several feet behind, her arm still outstretched from throwing the knife.

And she wasn't alone.

THIRTY-ONE

At Auma's back stood five masked Trendellan monks in black robes. Kuren had told me about them once; they were a special part of Trendell's small army so well trained in stealth, they could even fool a shadow crow. And now they stood here, at the back of a girl who had vanished in the world's most heavily guarded city and, with the single throw of a knife, had downed a Vykryn.

The other guard charged one of the monks, but Auma intercepted him. She was so light on her feet, so quick. She slit his throat in an instant.

There was another cry, and I whirled back the other way. Kiva had driven her foot into Shearen's knee, then stumbled to her feet. Razel yelled for more guards as Shearen regained himself and launched at Kiva, dagger raised.

I seized the torch from the servant and slammed it into Shearen's chest, throwing him back. His uniform caught fire, and he screamed.

The Trendellan monks broke into action. One surged toward Shearen, who frantically tried to put out the flames on his chest, and another toward Ericen, who stood frozen with shock and indecision. As the monk bore down on him, he broke free of his trance and threw up a block in time to avoid getting hit.

Another monk went for Razel, and she whipped her moon-blades from her back. As the shouts of approaching guards echoed from the hall, the other two monks went to meet them.

Auma appeared at my side. I flinched, my mouth opening and closing, everything from words to the simple act of breathing failing me. Then I realized I was holding a flaming column of fire and chucked it across the room. The torch bounced, sending up a shower of sparks before settling against the wall.

"You have to go," Auma said.

Behind her, Kiva was charging toward us. To my right, Caylus had regained his feet unsteadily. Someone had cut his bonds.

Crouching down, I scooped the disoriented Res into my arms, Auma guarding my back.

"There are horses outside the stables," she said. "Follow the road west toward the nearest port. Find a ship to take you to the Ambriels. Lie low. Someone will find you." Nothing of the demure servant was present.

"Who are you?" I asked before I could stop myself.

"There's no time!"

Kiva and Caylus both reached us. I could tell Caylus was in pain, but he barely grimaced. *The tolerance of a fighter.* Then I noticed his hands. They weren't shaking.

Kiva's eyes went to Auma. They stared at each other for the briefest second, thoughts and questions and flashes of emotion whirring across Kiva's face, and then Auma shot past her with a brush of her fingers along Kiva's hand.

"Can everyone move?" I clutched Res tight to my chest. They nodded, and we bolted for the exit, Kiva casting one last backward glance as we fled.

I led the way down the corridor to the front of the castle, avoiding the two monks holding off a trio of Vykryn. We sped out onto the grounds and around to the stables. Rain fell in sheets, the chill in the air sharp as a sword. I held Res tighter.

Three massive Illucian warhorses waited for us, but as we grew closer, Kiva stumbled. Caylus caught her before she struck the ground and heaved her to her feet. "You're losing too much blood."

"Comforting."

"I'm just saying that—"

"I'm fine," she hissed, trying to push off him and move on her own. But she swayed, and he quickly ducked under her arm to support her. Shifting Res to one arm, I doubled back to slide under her other side, and together, we helped her onto the nearest horse.

"Ride with her," I told Caylus. "Make sure she doesn't fall."

He swung onto the horse behind her, and I handed him Res, who gave a weak caw, then undid Caylus's horse's reins and those of the one beside it. Once I'd mounted, he handed Res back, and I clutched him to my body with one arm. Then I drove my heels into my horse's sides.

The amount of power that exploded out of the beast felt like a crow taking off. It sped down the road in a whirl of hooves and wind. I glanced back only once to make sure Caylus and Kiva were with me. As we curved around the bend to the front of the castle, I caught a glimpse of blue and snapped my head to the side.

Ericen stood in the castle doorway, his chest heaving, blood smearing his neck. For half a second, I panicked it might be his, then guilt swallowed me. He'd made his choice, but I still didn't want to leave him.

We locked eyes, that brief second stretching into eternity, and then we'd passed him, and he was out of sight.

Rain barreled into my face, blurring my vision and testing my hold on Res. I could feel the cord between us strengthening as the drug wore off. Gripping the horse harder with my knees, I pressed my legs into its sides, urging it faster. It complied, producing new bursts of speed each time I thought we couldn't possibly go any quicker.

The road shot through the city and down toward the river. We crossed through the Colorfalls, over the bridge and through the colored lights reflecting off the fog like moonlight on water. We raced to the countryside, past quiet houses illuminated by the bright glow of a full moon.

We left Sordell far behind, speeding toward the Verian Hills and the ocean beyond. The horses lasted much longer than normal ones, and even as my muscles tired and the rain slowed, then stopped, we galloped. Two miles, three miles, four, five, and we finally hit the base of the hills and slowed the horses to a fast trot.

Everyone was breathing hard, the horses most of all, and as they began the climb up the hills, we slowed them to a walk.

The first thing I did was check on Kiva. I brought my horse closer to theirs, and she lifted her head, offering me a reassuring smile. But her already pale skin had turned nearly white, and crimson stained her shoulder. I couldn't tell how much blood she'd lost.

"The monks would have kept them busy," Caylus said between heavy breaths. "We should have a head start. Unless the prince called for help..." He trailed off, glancing back the way we'd come.

"Do you know how far the port is?" I asked.

"Just another mile once we're over these hills."

"Good." I eyed Kiva. "Whether they're close on our trail or not, we need to hurry."

When we neared the top of the summit, I glanced back. A wall of fog and heavy clouds rendered Sordell invisible. If someone pursued us, they were far enough behind that we couldn't see them. Ericen had been right there; he'd seen us escaping. If he'd called any nearby soldiers, they'd be close.

I saw no one.

As we crested the summit, the dark, shapeless mass of the ocean stretched before us. Even from here, the rush of waves was audible. The salty smell of the sea lingered in the air, mixing with the clean scent of rain. Spots of lantern light dotted the land, and we nudged our horses toward them.

At the bottom, I urged mine into a canter, and Caylus followed. Kiva's head started to loll. There was too much blood on her shoulder. We'd have to find a healer before we found a ship, no matter how much time it cost us.

"Faster!" I called to Caylus, kicking my horse into a gallop again. Its heavy breathing filled the air alongside the thunder of hooves. Guilt pulled at me, but I pushed my mount harder. The wind tore at my hair, pulling it loose from the braid to whip at my face. A few minutes later, Port Maranock came into view.

It was a small town, filled with the smell of the ocean. Mist danced against my burning skin, and our breath fogged in the cold air. We raced down the nearest street, the smack of our horses' hooves causing more than one lantern to be lit. My eyes darted from building to building, looking for the sign of a healer or a shop that might have supplies.

We'd reached the docks by the time Caylus shouted, "There!" and pointed at a small house with a low-burning candle and a sign with a healer's symbol.

I leapt off my horse, Res bundled in my arms, and pounded on the door. "Help! Open the door!"

Light filled the window as someone lit another candle, and a half-asleep older man pulled open the door. He took one look at our Illucian warhorses and our anything-but-Illucian faces and slammed the door shut.

"Hey!" I screamed, pounding as hard as I could.

"Thia?"

"Open the damn door, you bastard!" My throat tore with every word, my voice turning hoarse.

"Thia!"

"What?" I shrieked, rounding on Caylus.

He blinked, head tilted, then lifted his gaze to a spot over my head where a line of ships was secured to the docks. He pointed at one with orange and green flags depicting a stag's antlers. "I know those flags. We have to get to that ship."

"She needs a healer." Kiva had slumped over despite the fact that Caylus had torn off a piece of his shirt and pressed it firmly against the wound.

"There will be one on board. Trust me!"

With a final kick to the door that sent one of the hinges clattering to the ground, I gave Res to Caylus before leaping onto my horse. Once I had him back, we took off along the docks to the ship. Moonlight bathed the deck and quarters, but it was otherwise dark, and the only way up meant scaling a mooring rope.

"There's no one here," I hissed.

Caylus rode past me to the water's edge. "Talon!" he shouted at what looked like an empty lookout perch. "Talon!"

For half a second, nothing happened. Then a shaggy mop of red hair appeared slowly over the edge of the lookout, followed by the rest of the yawning young man. He put a hand to his forehead as if to shade his eyes from some invisible sun. "Who's there?" he called.

"Damn you to Duren, Talon! I know you can see me."

I blinked. I'd never heard Caylus use that tone, let alone

curse. Though I was about to do a whole lot more if Talon didn't hurry up.

The redhead waved. "Hiya, Caylus. Have a nice time in Illucia, did ya?"

I stared at Caylus. "Is he serious?"

"Talon, get Samra. Now."

Something about the other person's name sent the redhead into action. He scurried down from the lookout like a rodent, landed on the deck, and disappeared inside the ship. I eyed Caylus. He'd sounded confident, in control. So different under pressure.

"I need your vest," I told him.

He looked at me, brow furrowing, but did as I said, unbuttoning the vest he wore over his long-sleeved tunic and handing it to me. I wrapped Res in it, careful to leave part of his beak exposed so he could breathe.

You'll be okay, I promised him. Faint pulses of indistinct emotion came back down the cord.

A moment later, Talon reemerged beside another figure, each holding a torch. The firelight illuminated a dark-haired woman with a scar across one eye. I gaped. It was the woman from the ball. Her lips pressed into a thin line as her eyes fell on Kiva, scanning her wound, before she faced Talon.

"Lower the gangplank," she said. "I'll wake Luan." They both vanished over the edge of the ship.

"What's happening, Caylus?" I asked. "Who are these people?"

"Later. Help me," Caylus began, already sliding from his

seat. He kept both hands on Kiva as he went, and I leapt down to help him lower her from the horse with my free arm. We each slid under one of her arms, but she barely supported any of her own weight, and she was muttering incoherently.

"Kiva," I said. "Kiva, stay awake. Stay with me."

She groaned.

Caylus and I moved as quickly as we could to where Talon had lowered the gangplank. He practically skipped down the wooden board and slid his arms under Kiva's legs.

When we reached the top, Samra had returned with a wisp of a redheaded woman who resembled Talon almost identically save for the length of her plaited hair. She took one look at Kiva and said in a low voice, "This way," before turning back into the cabin of the ship. We followed, taking the first turn into the now-lighted hallways and then a left into the open door of a small infirmary.

"Lay her down on the bed," Luan ordered. "Then get out."

"I'm not le—" I started, but Caylus was already dragging me out of the room. "Let go of me!" He reached over my head to shut the door once Talon was through.

"Best to let her work," Talon said with a nod.

I glared murderously at Caylus and shook off his hand. Clutching Res to my chest, I stalked back the way we'd come to the deck of the ship. Voices reached me a second before I stepped out. I reflexively shrank back into the shadows and then stuck out my arm when Caylus started to go by me. I pressed a finger to my lips.

"They went farther down the docks," Samra was saying.

"They abandoned the horses here as a distraction and fled on foot. You're at least ten minutes behind them." Another voice I couldn't make out answered, then Samra said, "Search the ship if you don't believe me, but do it quickly. I've already wasted enough sleep yelling at those damn fools for all the racket they were making." She moved toward the gangplank.

Tension coiled my muscles, and I started looking around for something to use as a weapon before remembering the bow strapped across my chest. Then Caylus grabbed me, jammed his fingers into the wall, and shoved me toward it. Except the wall had vanished, and I stumbled into a dark space. He joined me, then slid the false wall closed, enveloping us in cool air and the scent of oak.

Footsteps thudded, dulled voices not reaching through the thick wood. Seconds stretched into minutes as I fought to keep my breath silent, my senses blind to everything save for the hard press of Caylus's body against mine and the traitorous thundering of my heart. Then everything faded.

The false wall slid open. "They're gone," Samra said.

I let out a breath. "Thank you."

She ignored me, her eyes locked on Caylus. "What in Duren's name do you think you're doing bringing Illucian soldiers to my ship? I ought to toss you into the sea."

Caylus's wide-eyed look made me think she'd do just that. "It's a long story. Is there any way you can ship off a little early? Before dawn?"

"Those soldiers may come back if they don't find us where you sent them," I added.

"I've thought of that, thank you," Samra snapped. I scowled, but she was already looking at Caylus again. "What are you doing here?"

Caylus stepped aside, putting me squarely in Samra's line of sight. "She's holding the only chance the Ambriels has of ridding themselves of Illucian control once and for all."

I waved best I could with an armful of crow.

THIRTY-TWO

S amra woke the rest of her crew quietly. Everything was
done quietly. The ropes and anchor were pulled up, the
mast adjusted, the sails set. A half hour later, a favorable wind
carried the ship out to sea, and Caylus and I sat in Samra's quarters with her. As I took the chair across from her, Res in my lap,
I nearly bolted back up.

Curled on the desk, a paw tucked over his nose, lay Gio.
I blinked, the sight of the little white kitten from the bakery
throwing me off completely. It was miles from Sordell to this
port. How had he gotten here? I shook my head. That question
didn't even begin to cover how strange this was.

Samra's gaze followed mine down to the sleeping kitten.
"Aroch. He's been keeping an eye on you for me."

"How—" I stopped. I had enough unanswered questions.

Samra's gaze dropped to the bundle in my lap. "Why is your vest breathing?"

Slowly, I unwrapped the cloth to reveal the half-asleep crow. Samra's eyes flared wide, and she leaned carefully over the desk for a better look.

"How is this possible?" she asked.

"I found a surviving egg in one of our rookeries," I explained.

She lifted a hand as if to reach across and touch him but lowered it, her fingers curling into a fist. "You intend to use it to fight Illucia?"

I nodded.

Samra considered us in silence, her face expressionless. Then she rose, stepping around the desk. "I'll prepare rooms for you," she said before slipping outside.

I watched her go, marveling at how controlled she was. It was as though I'd showed her a flower, not a magical creature meant to be extinct.

That was the kind of poise I had to learn if I was ever going to be a leader.

Suddenly left with nothing to do and afraid to let my mind wander to Kiva, my eyes snagged on Gio again. Or Aroch, apparently. It made no sense how the kitten had managed to travel back and forth between Port Maranock and Sordell, unless—

I cast a sidelong look at Caylus, who rubbed his eyes with his palms. "Samra was at the ball," I told him. "Who is she?"

He looked up, distant gaze focusing. "She's the smuggler friend I told you about. The one that got me out of Seahalla when…" He trailed off, shrugging as if it would complete his story.

"Oh."

"She's an Ambriellan noble," he continued. "Her father was the leader of the high council. He's one of the few who kept his power. Samra pretends to be loyal, but her family runs a whiskey-trading business, and she uses it as a front to smuggle for the rebels."

That explained both her presence at the ball and the disgust with which she'd treated me. She'd likely been staying somewhere in Sordell, then brought Aroch back with her when she left. "Samra's a Trendellan name," I said.

"Her mother was Trendellan."

Was. Had Samra lost her to Illucia? Was that why she played this dangerous game?

Caylus hesitated, then added, "Samra is Diah."

I stiffened, everything falling into place: what she'd said to me at the ball about not being sure if I was a friend or an enemy. The dullness of the left side of Diah's mask, where the wood covered her blind eye. She was a rebel leader.

My eyes wandered across the bruises darkening Caylus's face and the part of his ribs visible from where he'd torn his shirt to stop Kiva's bleeding. It took everything I had to sit patiently in my seat and not burst into Luan's room and demand to know what was happening to my best friend. I'd even wrapped my feet around the legs of the chair to keep myself rooted.

"Are you all right?" I took his hand.

His fingers curled around mine, and he tried to smile. It didn't work. "I'll be fine. I've had worse." He meant to make me feel better, but it made me feel sick.

"I'm sorry," I blurted suddenly. He stared blankly at me, and I continued, "I couldn't do it. I couldn't give Razel the crows. But then when Shearen was going to kill Kiva, I just—" I couldn't lose both of them, couldn't lose everything. Not again.

He squeezed my hand. "I wasn't telling you not to for show. I didn't want…" He shook his head. "Not for me."

I made my own attempt at a smile, but it failed as miserably as his. "I know. Thank you."

Samra returned to escort us to our rooms. We'd barely stepped into the hallway when Luan emerged from the surgeon's room. Her sleeves were stained with blood, her face set in a grim expression that wiped away every ounce of happiness that had welled up inside me.

I lurched forward. "What happened? Is Kiva all right?"

Luan paused. "Your friend is alive, and I'm mostly certain she'll stay that way." When I started forward, she held up a hand. "What she needs now is rest. Give her a few hours before you barge in."

Anxiety twisted in my stomach, but I relented. Samra showed us to our rooms. The one I would share with Kiva was right beside the kitchen, and Res knew it too. He cooed softly, the cord between us humming stronger as the last of the drug faded away.

"Oh, now you're fine because there's food nearby," I said, and he nudged my cheek with his beak. The room was small, with two bunks and a small washstand. The walls had hooks for clothes that I hung my bow on and a small circular window filled with endless ocean blue.

I sat on the bunk, Res bundled in my lap. My eyelids felt

heavy, and sleep pulled at me. I fought it, wanting to be awake the moment I was allowed to see Kiva, but in the end, I succumbed.

Gentle hands roused me all too soon. Caylus stood over me. "Kiva's awake."

I nearly sprang to my feet before remembering Res in my lap. I prodded him, and he complained but rose with a ruffle of his feathers. The link felt back to normal, and he looked it too as he leapt to the ground and nipped at the feathers beneath his wing. He followed behind me as I slipped past Caylus and down the hallway to the infirmary.

Luan met me at the door. Her gaze dropped to Res, her lips parting, but she said nothing except "Five minutes" before striding out.

I stepped inside to find Kiva lying propped on a thin bed. She was snow-white and bare to the waist save for a band of cloth around her chest and the bandages encasing her shoulder. Her eyes were closed, but they opened as I sat down beside her.

"I was dreaming of punching Shearen in the face," she murmured, licking her dry lips.

I picked up a glass of water from the bedside table and helped her drink from it. "You need to have better dreams. Try stabbing him next time."

Kiva laughed, then winced, and I resolved not to make any more jokes.

"How are you feeling?" I asked.

"Weak," she replied. Her eyes dropped to her bandaged shoulder, and my stomach roiled.

"You can…move it, can't you?" It was her sword arm.

Her jaw clenched, her voice coming in a whisper. "Barely." She leaned her head back, staring up at the roof and blinking rapidly. "What if I can't? I won't be able to protect you. To help you. Even if I do recover, I'll be useless the next few weeks. A liability. You and Caylus should just—"

I flicked her in the forehead. She blinked, startled, and I smirked.

"I don't care if I have to carry you, Kiva. I'm not leaving you behind. I need you."

She held my gaze a moment, then swallowed hard. "You definitely can't carry me."

"Caylus can."

She laughed weakly, but the threat of tears in her eyes receded, and she relaxed.

I leaned forward. "I have someone for you to meet."

Her eyes widened. I grinned and leaned aside. Res cocked his head, emitting a low caw.

Kiva's head dropped back onto the pillow as she let out a laugh. "Thank the Saints. He's beautiful, Thia."

I sat back in my chair. "It's barely two days' sail to Seahalla, you know. You'd better heal quick."

"What's our plan once we're there?"

A good question. With everything that had happened the last several hours, I hadn't had the time or foresight to think about it. I doubted Razel's plans had changed—she would still want me to marry Ericen and to place us on Rhodaire's throne.

"We'll have to find somewhere safe to lie low for a few days while you recover," I said. "Razel can't hatch those eggs without me, which means she'll have people looking for us."

"She might attack Rhodaire to draw you out."

An image of the army sitting on Rhodaire's doorstep rose. "Which is why we need to get a letter to Caliza. She needs to be prepared. Once you're healthy enough, we need to get Res to the meeting in Trendell. Otherwise, they won't believe we've hatched him." Then we had to recover the remaining eggs.

"Maybe Razel won't attack," Kiva said. "She'd lose the chance for a peaceful takeover, and she'd have to pull troops out of Jindae and the Ambriels to manage it."

"I hope you're right." If Razel did attack, how long could Rhodaire hold out?

"Well, at least you don't have to marry Ericen," Kiva said.

I sighed, leaning back in my chair and looking at my leather gloves. "He saw us, Kiva. In the courtyard. He could have called the guards, but he didn't. He let us go."

And I'd left him behind.

She frowned. "He made his choice."

I nodded slowly but without conviction. I'd been honest with Ericen when I said I didn't have feelings for him, but somehow, he'd become my friend, even if that wasn't what he wanted. I'd told myself he was too consumed by his desire to prove himself, that he couldn't extricate himself from the web of pride, loneliness, and need he'd woven around himself.

But in the end, he'd chosen me.

"At least he wasn't secretly a knife-wielding assassin." Kiva's tone was flippant, but she didn't look at me, and I could hear the truth behind it.

"Auma had to keep her cover."

Kiva shrugged. "I always knew I didn't really have any idea who she was. Saints, I liked the mystery. I just..." She trailed off, and we sat in silence for a minute before she asked quietly, "Do you think she made it out?"

"Yes." If I'd learned anything about Auma, it was not to underestimate her.

Kiva nodded. She thought so too, but the hard press of her lips betrayed her worry.

The door opened, and Luan entered, ushering me out so Kiva could rest. I hugged Kiva gently, then stepped out into the hallway and traced my way back to the top deck with Res on my heel, thinking about everything we needed to accomplish.

Illucia was after us, Kiva was recovering from a serious wound, I had a hatchling to raise, and Caliza didn't know any of it. Not to mention in a few weeks, I'd have to convince the world's leaders to go to war.

I expected to be overwhelmed by everything, to want to crawl under the covers of a warm bed and hide from the world. I didn't.

Instead, as I stepped out into the morning sun with Res at my side, I felt a familiar lightness, like a forgotten friend. It was the feeling I used to get when I'd fly, as if I'd become the air itself.

Light. In control.

Free.

That heavy feeling might never fully leave me, but I could live with it. I'd survived, and I would continue to survive.

I stepped up to the ship's edge, one hand on Res's head as I faced the rising sun, my skin glowing in the light.

I had a lot to do, but I was ready.

THE WORLD OF THE
STORM CROW

WINGS OF ARIS

THE THEREAL WING

SAINT: Edair Thereal
CROW: wind crow
EGG: creamy white
HEAD OF HOUSE: Lady Dovelin Thereal
INDUSTRY: entertainment, such as theater, music, and artwork. Wind crows protected crops from storms, helped facilitate flight paths throughout Aris for other crows, provided favorable winds for sailors, and helped with city maintenance, such as sweeping up feathers.

THE KEROVA WING

SAINT: Harla Kerova
CROW: shadow crow
SHELL COLOR: matte black
HEAD OF HOUSE: Lady Kumia Kerova

INDUSTRY: highly involved in the military, with a focus on espionage. Shadow crows helped conceal spies from both sight and sound, and also made up a large percentage of the military crows.

THE TURREN WING

SAINT: Royceir Turren
CROW: battle crow
SHELL COLOR: dark metallic gray
HEAD OF HOUSE: Lady Ryna Turren (previous head, Lord Zeir Turren, banished for treason)
INDUSTRY: weapons production, most famously black gold weapons, made from the feathers of a battle crow. Aside from producing feathers for black gold, battle crows also made up the bulk of the military crows, helping with patrols, and also with transportation of heavy materials with their increased strength.

THE RYNTHENE WING

SAINT: Selka Rynthene
CROW: water crow
SHELL COLOR: deep ocean blue
HEAD OF HOUSE: Lord Relel Rynthene

INDUSTRY: highly involved in the navy, as well as trade and transport of goods, with a focus on production of ship and fishing supplies. Crows helped purify water, water crops, and manipulate the ocean for easy sailing and fishing.

THE BRYNTH WING

SAINT: Shaldra Brynth
CROW: earth crow
SHELL COLOR: forest green
HEAD OF HOUSE: Lord Culveir Brynth
INDUSTRY: architecture and city infrastructure, as well as the heart of Rhodairen knowledge pursuit. Known for crafting stone and woodworks. Crows helped with construction of new buildings and manipulation of farmland and tended to city landscaping.

THE GARIEN WING

SAINT: Azrel Garien
CROW: storm crow
SHELL COLOR: shiny black with specks of color
HEAD OF HOUSE: Lady Idrel Garien
INDUSTRY: produced the majority of crow provisions, from

riding leathers to saddles. Storm crows helped with weather control, particularly for agriculture, and also marked time for important events through thunder.

THE CYRO WING

SAINT: Ciaran Cyro
CROW: fire crow
SHELL COLOR: bright red
HEAD OF HOUSE: Lord Ressen Cyro
INDUSTRY: food production and distribution, from restaurants to shops. Fire crows maintained the central forge, used by Turren smiths and Brynth crafters alike.

THE CARAVEL WING

SAINT: Adeliza Caravel
CROW: sun crow
SHELL COLOR: pale gold
HEAD OF HOUSE: Lady Rasara Caravel
INDUSTRY: healers, production of herbs, tonics, and poultices. Sun crows worked with healers, healing the sick and injured.

KINGDOMS

RHODAIRE

CAPITAL: Aris

RULED BY:

Queen Caliza Cerralté

King Kuren Rebane

Crown Princess Anthia Cerralté

Queen Alandra Cerralté—deceased (killed on Ronoch)

King Caros Cerralté—deceased (killed during the Last Crow War)

ENVIRONMENT

Located in the Southwest

Hot, humid weather with frequent storms and high rainfall

Dense foliage in tropical landscape

RELIGION

Rhodairens pray to the Saints, eight legendary crow riders said to have established Aris with the help of the Sellas, but religion isn't highly ingrained in society

ECONOMY

Once centered around the crows

Large exporter of raw materials, grains, fruit, and other foods

Known for their black gold, a steel-like material made from battle crow feathers

Leaders in architectural and agricultural studies

CULTURE

Very open, straightforward, and trusting

Family-focused with an emphasis on sharing

ILLUCIA

CAPITAL: Sordell

RULED BY:

Queen Razel Rulcet

Crown Prince Ericen Rulcet

King Gavilan Rulcet—deceased (killed in the Last Crow War)

Queen Ranielle Rulcet—deceased (killed in the Last Crow War)

Princess Kashel Rulcet—deceased (killed in the Last Crow War)

Prince Consort Celin Inastra—deceased (killed in the Last Crow War)

ENVIRONMENT

Located in the West

Cold, cloudy weather, with winter snowfall and frequent rain

Vast green grasslands and rolling hills with numerous lakes and small rivers

RELIGION

Illucians pray to Rhett, a god they worship through bloodshed and war, which is heavily ingrained into society

Many willingly give their blood during prayer as a sacrifice to Rhett

ECONOMY

Supported by conquered nations (Jindae and the Ambriels) which provide food and raw materials and are highly taxed

Once exported weapons, armor, fine horses, wool products, and meat, but no longer trades with other kingdoms

CULTURE

Conniving, manipulative, and power-hungry

Very militaristic and focused on honor, status, and strength

|THE AMBRIEL ISLANDS| —

CAPITAL: Seahalla

RULED BY:

Illucia

Previously ruled by the high council, which consisted of representatives elected from the noble houses

The leader of the council, Kovan Castair, remains a figurehead

Part of Seahalla is also under the influence of the Drexel crime family

ENVIRONMENT

Located off the western Illucian and Rhodairen coasts

Mild weather with frequent fog and occasional high winds

Surrounded by dormant sea volcanoes

RELIGION

Ambriellans pray to Duren, the god who rules the sea by day, attending temple whenever they choose, often to pray for safe travels on the sea for themselves or family

They also believe in Duren's sister, the goddess known as Diah, the Night Captain, who rules the sea at night

More superstitious than religious when it comes to daily practice, for example carrying rope tied in different knots for luck, or happiness, or safety

ECONOMY

Exports large amounts of seafood, ships, products made from the coral surrounding the islands, whiskey, oil, and sona lamps

CULTURE

Very giving, with a focus on community and sharing food and belongings

Easygoing and peaceful

KOROVI

CAPITAL: Vashka

RULED BY:

An elected government of only noblewomen, led by Vokana Mirkova

ENVIRONMENT

Located in the North

Covered in snow almost year-round, save for the thaw during the summer months

Lots of mountains and thick pine forests

RELIGION

The Korovi pray to the goddess Lokane, who is served by her priestesses, which are made up of the noblewomen, believed to be daughters of the goddess

The right to lead the Korovi government is considered goddess-granted

ECONOMY

Korovi trades very little with other kingdoms

Occasionally exports animal products, work animals, and is rumored to have recently discovered oil in their mountains

CULTURE

Extremely isolationist

Straightforward, unforgiving, and orderly

JINDAE

CAPITAL: Shalron

RULED BY:

Illucia

King Kycyra Kura—deceased (killed when Illucia invaded)

Queen Seyfyer Kura—deceased (killed when Illucia invaded)

Crown Princess Elkona Kura—rumored to have survived assassination

Heavily influenced by the leaders of each Guild prior to Illucian invasion

ENVIRONMENT

Located east of the Ardrahan Sea

Vast golden grasslands and forested valleys

Four distinct seasons, tending toward dry and warm

RELIGION

The Jin believe art and religion are one; they worship creation of new, beautiful, and creative things

ECONOMY

Divided into several guilds, such as artist, gem, hunter, agriculture

Large exporter of precious stones, jewelry, metal, wood, and glass, as well as seafood and grain

CULTURE

Extremely resilient, hardworking, people who are very good at dedicating themselves to something and mastering it

TRENDELL

CAPITAL: Eselin

RULED BY:

King Calren Rebane

Queen Luhara Rebane

Crown Prince Seren Rebane

Prince Kuren Rebane

Princess Kashna Rebane

ENVIRONMENT

Located in the Southeast

Hot, dry, with golden hills and scattered woods

RELIGION

While the Trendellans have a vast array of myths, including many lost legends regarding the Sellas, religion plays little role in their day-to-day lives, with their focus on science and knowledge

ECONOMY

Large exporter of wine, chocolate, and new technology, as well as rare spices, ingredients, and historical information

CULTURE

Very intelligent, wise, and learned

Peaceful, curious, kind

ACKNOWLEDGMENTS

This book wouldn't exist without the help of so many amazing people.

To my mom and dad, for all the love, support, and opportunities you've given me. Thank you for always believing in me.

To my Guillotine Queens: Alyssa Coleman, Sam Farkas, Jessica James, Tracy Badua, Jessica Cooper, Brittney Singleton, Kat Enright, Jenn Gruenke, Amy Stewart, and Ashley Northup. I couldn't have made it through this process without all your wisdom, love, and beautiful stories inspiring me every day. Here's to the beginning of the Guillotine Court—I know you'll all be here soon.

Thank you to my amazing editor, Annie Berger, for all her hard work and dedication, and for answering my constant emails and questions. Her vision for *The Storm Crow* took this book to the next level.

My agent, Carrie Pestritto, is a superhero for walking me through so many rounds of edits and helping me through this entire process. Thank you so much for everything you've done.

Thanks to the entire Sourcebooks Fire team, Sabrina Baskey, Sarah Kasman, Cassie Gutman, Travis Hasenour, and everyone else who helped make *The Storm Crow* a reality. A special thank-you to Nicole Hower and Tran Nguyen for my beautiful cover. You captured the heart of my story with your work.

Kyra Nelson and Elizabeth Buege, your editing early on helped shape this story. And to Amber Duell and Alexandra Overy, all your constant feedback and support through multiple drafts has been so incredibly helpful. Thank you also to my many CPs and readers, and to all of the P2P ladies whose presence has been a constant anchor.

Lastly, thank you to my family and friends for your love and support, and to my roommates for understanding when I just need to hide in my room for a bit.

I love you all.

Read on for the thrilling conclusion
to the Storm Crow duology in

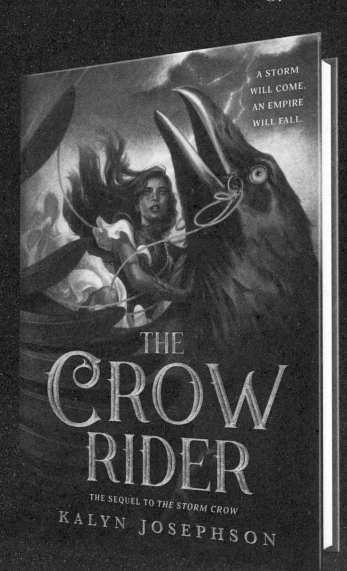

A STORM
WILL COME.
AN EMPIRE
WILL FALL.

THE
CROW
RIDER

THE SEQUEL TO *THE STORM CROW*

KALYN JOSEPHSON

ONE

The ocean had always reminded me of the sky.

Both were vast, ancient domains that we could never hope to control, and each time we entered them, we placed our lives in the hands of something that could crush us.

Something about that thrilled me.

I stood at the bow of the *Aizel* dressed in my flying leathers and a thick green cloak the ship's captain, Samra, had reluctantly lent me. Salt air nipped at my face, the wind running long fingers through my curls and lifting them to dance like ribbons.

A shadow rippled across the water ahead of the ship. I lifted a hand, feeling the brush of feathers a moment before Resyries landed on the railing before me. Wings outstretched against the wind, the crow balanced effortlessly, the gossamer shine of his dark feathers blending into the blue predawn light.

The connection between us thrummed with quiet contentment, something neither of us had had much of in recent days.

After our flight from Illucia, we'd headed to the Ambriel Islands but had decided to skirt around them rather than make land, since the islands were likely full of Illucian soldiers searching for us. Their queen was not going to let me escape so easily. Not when I was the only one who could hatch the crow eggs she'd stolen from Rhodaire. Not to mention I was technically still betrothed to her son.

I winced at the thought of Ericen. Unexpectedly, we'd become friends during my time in Illucia. The fingerless leather gloves I wore each day had been a present from him, a symbol of strength when I'd needed it most. But the prince was loyal to his kingdom. Loyal to his mother.

"I have to let him go, Res," I said into the wind. So why couldn't I?

Res trilled softly, sensing my melancholy mood. Nearly a month old now, he was almost big enough to ride, a thought that both thrilled and terrified me. I was days away from reaching a goal I'd been working toward my entire life, but I couldn't separate it from what else it meant: war was coming, and we were ill-prepared.

I crossed my arms against the chill wind. "This is all such a mess. Caliza doesn't even know about the eggs Razel took, let alone that we've escaped and are heading for Trendell. She's probably worried sick." I had a letter prepared for her but hadn't yet been able to send it.

It pained me to think of her worrying, though she'd never

let her distress show. It'd always been that way. Her the sturdy land, me the wild air, our mother the ever-changing sea.

What would she think of her daughters now?

Res turned, leaning his head toward me. I placed a hand on his beak, and for a moment, there was only us. A girl, a crow, and the vastness of the empty sea. I gathered that feeling of serenity and tucked it away inside myself. Whatever came next, I wanted to remember this moment of peace.

A thin line of sunlight cut a red slash across the horizon, softening quickly into the warm orange of a candle flame. It illuminated a distant coastline like the spine of a slumbering beast.

Rhodaire.

Our route had taken us far out to sea in a broad arch, consuming two weeks and most of our supplies but hopefully throwing Razel off our trail. All that mattered was that we still had enough time to reach Trendell before Belin's Day, when the other kingdoms had agreed to meet and hear out my pleas for an alliance against Illucia.

In a couple of weeks, we would either stand united against the empire or fall divided beneath their blades.

The deck creaked, and Caylus appeared at my side. Every inch of him was pulled tight, from the rigidity of his broad shoulders to the steel in his green eyes. Words had never been his strength, but our proximity to the Ambriels had only made him more withdrawn.

The sea breeze caught my hair again, lifting and tossing my dark curls as a slow, heavy unease curled in my chest, thick with guilt. It was my fault Caylus had been torn from yet another home. My fault Kiva lay injured in bed, her sword arm now useless. My fault everyone on this ship was now a target for a cruel queen.

I wanted to be a leader, to be the sort of person people wanted to follow. So far, I'd only made things worse.

I slipped my hand into his. "What are you thinking about?" I asked. It was one of his favorite questions. He might be shier than a spring flower in winter, but he did like to talk to me, and I liked to listen.

"Crows," he said with a hint of a smile. "Magic." The smile faded. "War."

I squeezed his hand. "I know I said it before, but I understand if you don't want to do this. It isn't your fight." Though the idea of doing this without Caylus at my side hurt more than I wanted to admit. He was a steady rock, a comforting reflection. We understood each other, and in a way, we'd help rebuild each other.

But that didn't make this his war.

He bit his lip, but before he could respond, footsteps made us both turn. Samra stood in the center of the deck, her unruly black curls pulled up in a tight bun, her good eye sharp as freshly cut glass. "We need to talk."

In the warmth of Samra's small office, Caylus and I sat in two handcrafted chairs opposite the captain's own. Loathed to be left out of anything, Res had crowded in behind, though he was as tall as Caylus and twice as big around. He dropped his head onto my shoulder as if it might make him smaller.

I was keenly aware of Kiva's absence. Her shoulder had healed quite a bit in the last couple of weeks, but the pain tonic the ship's healer, Luan, had her on made her sleepy. She often wasn't up until late in the afternoon.

A pot of tea steamed in the center of the great oak desk, a matching set of carved antlers supporting the tabletop. The office was simple, almost bare, save for a narrow shelf lined with trinkets and books. A worn flag bearing the ship's namesake, an aizel—a snow-white, horned cat—sat beside tiny wooden ships painted pure black, colorful bits of rope tied in complicated knots, and small sandstone figurines of seahorses and miniature krakens.

Two weeks on her ship had done little to warm Samra to me, though I was starting to doubt "warm" could ever describe her. The captain was gruffer than a jagged cliff. If she weren't the leader of the Ambriellan rebels and didn't share my goal, I'd have expected her to throw us overboard by now, if only because Res's talons had left more than one scratch on her ship, not to mention the wind, rain, and lightning.

His control over his magic had grown considerably, though he still had far to go. Not for the first time I wished Estrel was here. She'd taught me everything I knew. I felt like a pale imitation trying to do the same for Res, but I had to try. His mastery over basic winds and rain could only take us so far. We needed lightning and thunder, powerful gales and torrential downpours.

We needed a storm.

Samra didn't sit as she poured light golden tea into handle-less mugs smaller than my palm. The steam carried the flowery scent of chamomile as she passed each of us a cup with the solemnity of an Ambriellan priestess handing out prayer candles.

"We're approaching the Rhodairen port of Cardail," she began, long brown fingers curling around her mug. "We'll stop there to resupply and then strike out for Trendell. It should take us just over a week, which will put us in Eselin several days before Belin's Day."

A quiet excitement swelled inside me. Cardail wasn't Aris, but it was still Rhodaire, and not too long ago, I'd thought I'd never see it again. Res let out a low trill as my emotions seeped down the bond.

"You're going to love it," I told him. "We have the best bakeries."

I shot a glance at Caylus, expecting him to protest, but his distant gaze was set on the small round window at Samra's back overlooking the sea. I'd hoped some distance between us and the islands would return the curious, absentminded boy I knew, but he hadn't even shown much interest in Res's training the last few days.

"The point of this stop isn't to indulge the crow's sugar addiction," Samra growled, ignoring Res's squawk of disagreement. "We get in, get what we need, and get out. Cardail is too close to the Illucian-occupied area of Rhodaire to risk staying for long."

Illucian-occupied area of Rhodaire. How could five words turn my blood to ice so easily? My hand tightened around the warmth of the mug. Surrounded by endless water, it was easy to feel disconnected from the truth waiting for us on land: an army sat on Rhodaire's doorstep, and it was poised to attack.

I started to object, but Samra talked over me.

"On that note, any of you making the trip onto land will do so cloaked and hooded." She downed the last of her tea as if it were a shot of Ambriellan whiskey. "I don't want word getting back about my connection to you."

Samra might head the Ambriellan rebellion, but she was also the daughter of the kingdom's council leader, and that council was pledged to Illucia. It was her pretense as a loyal servant of the empire that made her such an effective rebel, and being seen harboring fugitives wouldn't just mean the end of her façade but potentially her family's lives, something she'd made quite clear when she agreed to take us to Trendell.

"That also means no crow," she said.

Res lifted his head with a snap of his beak, a spark of lightning buzzing at the tip. The captain stared flatly back at him.

"You do draw a bit of attention," I said reluctantly. He straightened, rolling back his shoulders as if to say "as I should." It lasted all of a second before he perked up, head tilted as if listening.

A moment later, the door burst open, and Kiva appeared in the doorway, pale, sweating, and clutching her injured shoulder.

"Come quick. Something's wrong."

ABOUT THE AUTHOR

© Alex Hayashi

Kalyn Josephson is a fantasy writer living in the California Bay Area. She loves books, cats, books with cats, and making up other worlds to live in for a while. *The Storm Crow* is her debut novel. Visit her at kalynjosephson.com.

FIREreads

#getbooklit

Your hub for the hottest young adult books!

Visit us online and sign up for our
newsletter at FIREreads.com

 @sourcebooksfire

 sourcebooksfire

 firereads.tumblr.com